CATALYST

Copyright © 2018 Leon Soma Creations

Catalyst

Published by Leon Soma Creations

ISBN: 978-1-7753210-4-0

CATALYST

LEON SOMA

PROLOGUE

10822 BCE

Predating recorded history and archaeologically lost to the weathering of time, a technocratic civilization once spanned the globe. What would seem like mysticism to foreign eyes, was derived from science; not magic or faith. Their temples were shamanic institutions, focused on expanding consciousness and discovery, instead of pushing any lone agenda or philosophy. Schools were open access forums of shared information, with knowledge being both a point of pride and symbol of social and political standing. An artificial Intelligence governed the robotic workforce, leaving people to their own devices, while arts and sciences flourished. On the cusp of long-range space travel, with mining colonies and terraforming experiments operating throughout the solar system, interplanetary expansion was becoming interstellar.

This would-be utopia was tarnished, however, by cold wars between rival cultures and brutal hostility off-world, away from prying eyes. Each faction, fighting to claim territory and resources, so that *their* people could branch outward, instead of facing the global population restrictions on Earth. This conflict bred paranoia, which fed the fires of a war machine that churned out weapons capable of astonishing destruction. As enlightened as they may have considered themselves, their primal instinct for dominance remained a deep-seated, driving force behind their progress, as was and will forever be human nature. Peace was kept, only by the fear of an open conflict that promised Armageddon.

Ancient humanity was contacted by an intelligence, far more sophisticated than their own. A muse, communicating through elaborate inspiration, gave them the blueprint to their ascension, and a grave warning of why they'd need it. Death was coming.

Though great power was promised, many were unwilling to proceed without contingencies. Earth's leaders came together, unified by a greater threat. They appointed the top minds from across the globe and began work on what they called, Exodus.

Never before, or since, had humanity been so equipped to handle whatever the universe had to throw at them. The world's governments organized mandatory genetic screenings, followed by skills training for those deemed worthy. Those found to be unsuitable were put to work with

the robots, building the factories that would construct great space-faring arks. Every aspect of the operation was compartmentalized for security so that even those in charge never had the full picture. Once a factory was complete, it was sealed off and activated. A hive of machines built more machines that worked in perfect, tireless harmony, driven by each ship's own artificial intelligence. Its sole purpose was to ensure humanities salvation, and the construction of the arkships was a part of that.

Three hundred men and women, between the ages of fifteen and thirty-five, would be assigned to each ship and given the responsibility of protecting and propagating the species. Each ark contained a vault, housing genetic material from every known organism on Earth, and was uploaded with a digital cumulation of human knowledge, spread across a ship wide-intranet and maintained by the same AI that built it. Those selected were taught everything, from basic farming to molecular engineering. Even though the ships were heavily automated, once they arrived on a suitable world, they'd need to be able to function autonomously and colonize their new homeworld. The chosen would board the automated escape ships, and enter a cryogenically sustained hibernation that would preserve them as they travelled in search of their new homes. Each arkship had a designated course plotted to a different Earth-like planet in the Goldilocks zone of distant solar systems that had been deemed suitable for colonization with minimal terraforming required. They would jettison from the Earth and spread out into the stars, like dandelion seeds on the wind.

Thanks to the forewarning of the benign visitor, they knew where to look. They saw them coming through a vast network of long-range, broad-spectrum scanning satellites outfitted with an imposing arsenal, designed to take out potentially dangerous near-Earth objects, and repurposed them as the first line of defence from this new impending threat.

When the alien armada suddenly disappeared from their scanners, nobody knew what to do, or how to react. There was a collective moment of panic among those monitoring it, when the invasion force reappeared several seconds later, having closed the gap between them. They weren't ready. All of their planning and preparation for the arrival was still days away from reaching completion. It would have all been for nothing if they couldn't launch the ships. They knew that their time had run out, but it was now, or never, and for the sake of humanity they had to try.

The defence satellites simultaneously and unexpectedly powered down as the alien ships passed by unharmed and descended into the atmosphere. Dispersal freighters broke off from the flotilla leader and spread

out over major population centres. Each freighter was essentially a cluster bomb, launching thousands of pods that slammed into the ground, like bus-sized bullets. Along with an electromagnetic pulse, each spire emitted a frequency into the ground, triggering earthquakes and collapsing subterranean pockets, creating sinkholes and tenderizing the foundations of what their cities were built on.

The air hummed as flocks of military UAVs moved in on the spires. People below scattered for cover in the crumbling remnants of what were once great cities. An EMF pulsed outward and the sentry drones fell from the sky, with their armaments exploding in the crashes. On the ground, there was chaos. Streets and buildings cracked and trembled, while those that weren't tending to the wounded fled for shelter and hoped for rescue. Some tried to help those that had already taken action, but many were too shaken by the devastation to be of any real use, and unwittingly harmed more than they helped.

While the powerless masses outside suffered and died, each arkship facility went on high alert, and the emergency launch sequence began to countdown. The crews boarded like they had been drilled on so many times in their training, and the first wave of Exodus began.

Dozens of arks were rocketing skyward around the world. As the second wave's countdown finished, their launch bay doors retracted, revealing bursts of blinding light in the sky, and the fiery debris of the first wave raining back down. The satellites had somehow been reactivated and were targeting them as they attempted to escape.

With the satellite network depleted, the second wave launched. Almost none of the arks had completed preparations, resulting in a myriad of problems. Many of the launch facilities had been hit directly by the pods as if they had been specifically targeted, even though they were designed to be visually inconspicuous from an aerial perspective. Destabilized power cores detonated before some ships could even take off, decimating the landscape for miles around and vaporizing anything in the vicinity.

Many ships would escape and embark upon their long voyage, but without a fully functioning AI to pilot and automate life support systems, they would have to hibernate in shifts, exhausting their resources before they'd have a chance at reaching a new world. Others had perfectly working systems but lacked the resources needed for sustained life support and would inevitably die in cryo-sleep.

Only a small amount of pristine arks had remained. One of which had been commandeered by a posse of disgruntled workers that had been

leaked information by mutineers inside the facility. The whistleblowers had been subsequently caught and executed for treason, but not before divulging the critical information needed to breach the facility and take the ship. They'd planned an insurrection and took it by force when the alien crafts appeared in the sky. Upon boarding the ark, the ship's AI warned them that their numbers were too little and lacking in diversity for a genetically viable population. They had recognized that form of defeat but also saw an opportunity for retribution. Awash with emotion, they were forced to accept their fate. They all knew what had to be done. After they had said their goodbyes, they got to work disabling the ships fail-safes; overriding the life support systems and rerouting the power to the gravity drives and plasma thrusters. Disengaging the navigation systems allowed them to crudely maneuver the ship manually from the bridge, and overloading the power core would give them the extra punch they needed. The launch bay doors lurched open, struggling under the rubble that was falling through and crashing onto the ark as it clumsily ascended. Careening off of walls and grinding the hull all the way through, they figured out the makeshift controls as they went. Grace was of no concern, as this was to be a very short, one-way flight.

Steam burst through fissures in the scorched obsidian shell of the alien spire. A dense fog billowed out and churned inside the crater as the pod began to bloat and crack. Viscous slime seeped out, and an internal membrane ruptured, spewing forth a translucent fluid that hissed and boiled as it ran down the smouldering exterior. The rocky husk exploded open, as the creatures inside leapt into the surrounding mist. Deep rumbling breaths emanated from the dense, swirling gas and a trumpeting roar tore through the air as more could be heard, like war horns in the distance.

The alien's imposing silhouette appeared at the edge of the fog, joined by two more, with air blasting from their nostrils as they huffed at the mixing atmospheres. Their heads on a slow, focused swivel, scanning the area for movement. One turned and crept quietly along the perimeter, before disappearing down an alley. Another, darted back into the mist, headed in the direction of a noise on the other side of the crater. The big one, stood stone-still, eyes locked on his quarry.

A young child clutching a tattered doll wandered through the destruction, bawling obliviously for her parents.

The sole survivor from a partially collapsed ark facility near the crater's edge regained consciousness and dragged himself in the direction of the helpless orphaned girl. She stood in the open, rubbing her eyes with a

balled fist, trying to wipe away the endless flow of tears running down her soot-stained face, as the fog crept around her ankles. The man saw her now, and the looming shadow in the mist, backlit by columns of light pouring in through the structural beams of pulverized buildings. He watched in terror as it stalked the shambling girl from the fog, trying to call out to her, but only choked on the blood and grit filling his throat. As the creature slowly emerged, his vision grew dark, and he lost consciousness.

When his eyes opened again, he was on his back, being dragged through what was left of the hangar, inside of the facility that he had just pulled himself from. Looking up, he saw the severely damaged robotic face of one of the ark's medical droids, staring back as it loaded him onto the ship. He struggled to free himself from the harness that it put him in, but he couldn't move. His legs were limp and numb, his arms weak and throbbing. He could barely lift his head to see the crumbling hangar wall burst inward as the beast from the mist clawed its way through. The android operated the controls by the ship's cargo door. The monster broke through the wall and launched itself at the closing hatch, as the wall came crashing down behind it. It grasped the open seal, pressing against the hull trying to pry it open, but the hydraulics were too strong. Another set of taloned claws reached in through the closing gap and knocked the droid from the panel. As the door sealed, he could hear the howling agony and rage of the creature outside as it clawed ravenously at the hatch. Its severed limb laid next to the controls, twitching and spasming before it went still and drained thick, dark blood onto the floor.

A prerecorded voice came over the loudspeaker, giving a detailed, but garbled exposition on the situation and the mission ahead. It stuttered and crackled while the quasi-functioning droid worked on another panel. The man noticed a raggedy bit of red stained cloth, with a sewn on smile dangling from the dismembered appendage and knew that the little girl was gone. Lights dimmed, and the voice went quiet as he fell into a deep sleep as the weakened structure of the facility gave out and crumbled under its own weight, burying the ship in the ruins of the fallen city.

Above the glacial expanse of North America, a commandeered arkship slammed into the alien flotilla leader's stern, tearing through its hull and destabilizing the rigged core. The detonation ripped through the alien vessel, sending the fiery remains plunging into the frozen tundras. The fallout would sweep much of the globe as debris continually rained down from low orbit for years. Ice sheets melted, swallowing and burying coastal cities. The devastation was such that it changed the climate and the course of

evolution on Earth. Human civilization was all but lost; genetically bottlenecked and knocked back to the stone age, but this time, under the protection of those empowered by the catalyst.

Without leadership, the aliens became feral. Driven by instinct, they continued to hunt the humans and other megafauna to near extinction. Significantly depopulated by the cataclysm, their shallow gene pool caused wild mutations from inbreeding, and their numbers dwindled over the centuries until the last of their kind died off.

Conversely, humanity continued to rise up. Backed by the power of the first gods, those that were left fought back against what remained of the demons from the stars. Elaborate legends were passed down through generations, which became mythical tales and bedtime stories of courageous knights battling fearsome dragons. Historical fact devolved into glorious fiction and the world moved on.

PROLOGUE RETURNS

1982 – 2023 CE/Zero-Day ACE

One of the few arks that escaped had remained within the Solar System, juxtaposed with the Earth; hidden behind the Sun. Their cryo-stasis system was mostly inoperable, making the long journey to any other star system suicide, or even genocide for all they knew. Instead, they remained hidden, and used the ark as a base to build on. The ship would grow into a space station and function as their own artificial world.

Elders would tell stories of how their ancestors lost the Earth to the aliens. Because they feared being discovered, return was strictly forbidden; even discussing the idea was a punishable offence. They'd managed to maintain their utopian ideals for hundreds of years, but with every new generation, the ruling council of elders had become more corrupt and politically motivated to stay in power, instead of focusing their efforts on improving the deteriorating quality of life of their people.

They'd continued to advance through the generations, adapting their lives to the artificial ecosystem. Fibre optic solar lighting provided a measured exposure to ultraviolet rays from the sun and artificial gravity provided a representation of Earth-like conditions. Materials between satellite strip mining operations on wrangled asteroids provided a richer abundance of minerals than alternative terrestrial sources. Most of this was done autonomously but required a physical co-pilot after a solar flare caused a system glitch that would later be exploited. The virtual intelligence, which was primitive compared to any AI, disconnected, sending its transport into one of the docking bays at speed, which resulted in the loss of both lives and vital resources.

Decades ago, a young man named Vonn, who had been a flight engineer and payload specialist on one of the crews responsible for the external expansion of the arkstation, stumbled upon something that would change the course of history, for all of mankind.

Vonn was alone, prepping his ship when he was startled by a commotion in a hidden away warehouse section of the port. Going to investigate, armed with a long wrench, he discovered the bodies of two men and a strange device on the ground between them. Though he'd never met them personally, he knew who they were. Through the burn holes of their inconspicuous outerwear, he could see their uniforms. Both men were high-

ranking members of rival factions, who'd killed each other in a trade gone wrong. Bad news, not just for them, but for anyone unlucky enough to get tied up in it. He knew better than to get involved, but he also knew that his presence alone would implicate him, making him a target for at least two-thirds of the population. There was no way to make the situation any better for himself, so out of compulsion and reparation for his life being derailed in an instant, he took what they'd killed each other over, and left.

With the die cast, his only chance was to run and hide, far, far away. He'd modified his ship so that he could override the VI and take full manual control by simulating a navigational glitch and masking the error report as diagnostic maintenance. He'd altered the manifest to avoid raising suspicions when he loaded his transport with supplies, instead of clearing it out to make room for the pickup that he was supposed to make. He took his ship and set off like any other day, but cut his comms and departed from his scheduled trajectory before coming within visual range of any other vessels in the area.

It would be a long journey around the sun, but he was ready for it. The ship's power core would be more than enough to get him there and back if necessary. It was charged by solar radiation through hyper-efficient materials on the surface of the hull and held a tremendous capacity for its size. He set a new course and hoped that he'd gotten out of range before anyone noticed that he'd stolen the ship and fled with their supplies.

After weeks in space, Vonn couldn't believe what he'd found when he finally arrived on Earth. He discovered that despite what he'd been told growing up, the aliens had been gone for a *very* long time. Humanity was thriving once again as the dominant species. The humans of Earth had their problems with pollution and unsustainable resource depletion, but with the ark dweller's advanced tech, they could help them to move into a new age and recreate their terrestrial utopia. This, he thought, would be enough to buy his life back. He could return to the ship and be hailed as a hero when he told the elders what he had found. It was time for their homecoming, but he didn't dare return empty-handed, with nothing but his word to back his claim. For a time, he would stay, integrate into their culture and learn what he could, to better educate his people.

More than a year later, Vonn prepared his ship with items that he'd collected to bring back as proof of their civilization. In the short time he'd been on Earth, he had picked up several of their languages. He adopted their styles and mannerisms and developed a taste for their lavish foods; things that were sorely lacking aboard the arkstation. He had fallen in love with this

world, and with Felicia; the woman that he was bringing back with him. She had brilliant cerulean eyes, with smooth milky skin that contrasted the darkness of his own. On the day that they were to leave, she told him that she was pregnant with his child. The love and hope for the future that he felt that day were almost too much to bear.

With their preparations complete, they sealed the ship and began booting up the drive core. Vonn went through his checklists over and over so that everything should have been perfect. He activated the final sequence, and the ship went dead; the navigational computer and it's VI, wiped clean.

A holographic recording of the arkstation's elder council played out in front of them, and though Felicia wasn't yet fluent in their common tongue, she was able to understand the basics of the message. They told Vonn that because of his egregious transgressions against members of their royal families, he'd been banned from returning and exiled to death on the wastes of Earth.

His heart sank, but not all was lost. He had a new home, which was a veritable paradise compared to what it was thought to be, and a new family on the way.

The ship couldn't remain cloaked forever and would eventually be discovered, which would be disastrous. In the undeveloped wilderness of California, they were far enough removed from any city or anyone that would bring too much notice the excavation, or construction when they buried the ship and built on top of it.

To fund their lives and projects, he'd drip fed bits and pieces of advanced technology to private buyers, through proxies, from wealthy countries around the world. They were very careful about their secrecy to ensure that no one grew suspicious of what they were hiding.

When the baby was born, Vonn finally felt like this was his home. They'd built a ranch and expanded the homestead to accommodate their growing family. Their daughter; Emilia, would grow up homeschooled, learning about the technology that her father had brought and applied that knowledge to her own inventions. Eventually, she'd leave to travel the world and spend much of her time helping to bring new water purification and agricultural techniques to developing nations, often finding herself in the middle of conflicts beyond her ability to affect.

Years later, Emilia would return home with a like-minded group of people that she'd worked with and come to trust. Her vision was to get them involved in developing upon what her parents had started, as far as creating an entirely off-grid, self-sustaining community; a green think tank for a

better tomorrow. They'd start at home and apply their R&D successes to future projects. The now old man; Vonn, couldn't turn them away, after being banished himself. Their ideals seemed to match what he believed his people needed to get back to. Vonn and Felicia kept their secrets closely guarded, but with their daughter vouching for them, they welcomed the others in, continuing to build and expand what was quickly becoming a small town. That wasn't the only surprise she had for her parents. Emilia was pregnant. She'd met the father, Hudson, while on one of the few vacations she ever took. He was a field medic, turned wilderness guide, who happened to have a cottage on the same lake as the one she was staying. They met one sunny day after he noticed her paddling by in an old canoe and invited her over for a fish fry and drinks later that night. The two had been inseparable ever since.

Over the years, Vonn's obsession with the strange device only intensified. He kept it locked away and his research private, as it was his greatest and most dangerous secret. A secret that was discovered by one of Emilia's newcomers, who'd come to Vonn with the notes he'd found and his own interpretations of their details. It almost seemed like he knew more about it than Vonn himself, with next to nothing to go on. Impressed and intrigued by his unusual aptitude, he took him on as an apprentice of sorts. Through cloak-and-dagger meetings, they made great leaps and bounds in their studies, until together they were able to unlock the hidden power of what they called, the *Catalyst*.

One day, the apprentice came to Vonn with the truth. He was not who he'd claimed to be. He was a wolf in sheep's clothing that had decided in the middle of the hunt, that he preferred the sheep to the wolves. He revealed that he was sent from the arkstation with a team to take the catalyst back, but like Vonn, he'd been seduced by what this new life had to offer and suggested that he too may soon have familial ties to this world. He laid it all out and presented an idea as a peace offering that would benefit them both. He would use the catalyst on himself and gain the power to make sure that Vonn and their community had nothing to fear from the arkstation or anyone else, ever again.

A month before Emilia was due, the old man sat on his porch, waiting for news of his collaborator, who'd yet to return, and witnessed something that he never thought he'd see. Massive rocky ships appeared in the sky and began launching dark javelins into distant cities. He knew the stories from old nursery rhymes that he was told in his youth. He'd passed those stories down to his daughter and hoped to one day share them with

his grandchildren, but he'd never imagined that they were anything more than myths.

Vonn hurried to gather everyone but his missing apprentice and the woman he'd sent after him. He brought everyone together, and took them down into the enduring ship under his house for the first time. It would act as an impromptu fallout shelter for the small community and give them plenty to talk about while they were down there.

THE NEVER-ENDING PROLOGUE

Invaded

Year 1 ACE

Within a few days of the shelter being sealed, tensions began to rise, due to the relatively confined space that they all had to share, the shock of discovery, and the stress of their world as they knew it coming to an end. An alien invasion was not the ideal time to tell a scared and confined group of people that you're not really from Earth and this is your spaceship.

A week later, the subject of limited food and water came up, and panic started to take hold. It was true that they would run out *eventually*, but in the depths of cabin fever, no one was willing to listen to Vonn's explanation on how long, or why he wasn't worried about that particular issue. After a heated, one-sided argument, a few of the men volunteered to go out and quickly scout the area, but didn't return.

Hudson had to feed his family, and that wasn't going to happen if everyone turned on each other. Though Emilia protested, Hudson was never one to shy away from duty when things needed to get done. He went out that night, alone. He could stay hidden and move quietly that way. When he stepped out of the house, he couldn't believe his eyes. Smoke billowed on the glowing horizon, and their little hamlet had been ransacked.

Moving cautiously between what was left of the small buildings, he headed toward the pump house. Something big was shuffling around the corner ahead of him, so he cut through the backyard and picked up his pace. Having made it inside, Hudson manually pumped water from the well, through the filtration system, and into jugs as quietly as he could. Occasionally he'd stop to peek through the shutters but couldn't see much from where he was. Once the containers were full, he tied them together on a rope bandoleer carried over his shoulder, then took one last look to make sure it was all clear and snuck out, trying not to let the bottles rattle together as he went.

Hudson nearly had a heart attack when one of the dairy cows from the barn was grazing in front of the house he had cut around and mooed loudly before he saw it. It scared him witless for just a second, but this gave him some relief, knowing that it was just a loose cow. He chuckled to

himself as he walked down the middle of the road, back toward the shelter. Passing his house, he wanted to stop and pick up a few things but decided that he'd make a food run later after they had the water. Especially with the babies, he didn't want to worry Emilia any more than he had to.

The cow's head perked up, and its ears darted around. Hudson knew what that meant and dove under the porch, dropping the jugs behind him. The cow became spooked at the sound and started to run, but was taken out before its first hoof was planted.

A reptilian monster lunged through the air and slammed into the cow, taking it off of its feet. Holding the crying animal with its upper arms, the alien eviscerated its body with a smaller, sharper set of talons below its sternum. It lifted the carcass over its head and pulled it apart, showering in the blood. The monster's tongue slithered out of its toothy jaws, under the exposed rib cage and pulled out the still-beating beef heart, then ate it and tossed away the body, like unwanted leftovers. This was for sport, not nourishment.

Frozen in terror under the porch, Hudson could see the whole thing. Out of the corner of his eye, he noticed movement coming from the house next door. Two of the men that had left as scouts were hiding inside, waving him over and signalling to him to stay low and quiet. With his scent masked by the stench of the slaughtered cattle, he waited for the monster to move off, and crawled out, taking cover where he could along the way. He joined them inside, hidden from the windows to the street, behind an overturned table where they had huddled together in the grip of the most profound fear any of them had ever known.

They explained that they went to the barn first to get tools to defend themselves, but that it didn't matter. The men that they'd left with didn't make it. The others had been ripped to shreds, and these two snuck away in the frenzy. Armed to the teeth with scythes, chains, pitchforks and anything else that could be used as a weapon, they thought that they were prepared for trouble, but there was no amount of preparation that could have made them ready for what found them. What they couldn't have known, was that they were being hunted by predators so savage and singularly purposed, that even access to a military armoury would have provided an insignificant increase to their odds.

The description they gave matched what Hudson had seen outside: quadrupedal theropods with as many arms as legs, and according to them, there were two more out there.

Obviously in shock, the two men forgot their volume, bickering over conspiracy theories, whether or not the aliens were actually dinosaurs from an alternate Earth that was never hit by an asteroid, or if they served the same purpose in space, as sharks in the ocean. Before any logical conclusion was made, they were hushed by the sound of the back door creaking open.

One of the aliens was in the street, looking for movement inside, through the shattered bay window. Loud huffs and snorts could be heard coming from the kitchen, as well as scratching on the roof.

They knew that they were inside.

There was nowhere to run when it entered the room, hunched over to fit. It toyed with them, pulling each in, one by one and batting them around, then letting go and starting over when they tried to get up, like a bored cat playing with wounded baby mice.

A chipped claw slashed Hudson across his chest when he tried to help, knocking him through the table, flipping it upside down and breaking off the wooden legs. The alien grabbed the other two and slammed them together over and over again, like an angry child with action figures, breaking more bones with every connection. It dropped one on the ground, and he folded up like a rag doll, as it sunk its teeth into the other's head, and a stomach-churning crunch brought an end to his screams.

The blood speckled alien moved toward Hudson, who had propped himself up using one of the table legs as a cane and held another like a club, but the cuts through the musculature of his torso limited his range of movement, rendering him weak and lethargic. Just as it was about to finish him off, it stopped when its eyes were drawn to a commotion in the street. It hissed with rage, then knocked him aside and smashed out of the broken window into the front yard. Hudson wiped the broken glass from the sill and pulled himself up to see what had happened.

The largest of the trio was trying to *mount* the smaller female in the middle of the road, and the third flew into a fit of jealous rage, attacking the other male, mid-coitus. They rolled in the dirt, tearing flesh and snapping at each other's throats. The female screeched and shrieked, circling the fight and presenting itself to them in an antagonistic mating display.

Hudson snuck away, out the back of the house, holding a bloody towel to his chest that he'd grabbed from the counter. Taking the long way around, he wanted to be sure that they wouldn't be lead back to the shelter. Roars of agony and blood-curdling shrieks echoed behind him the whole way there. The noise was oddly reassuring. As long as he could hear them, he knew where they were. Thankfully, they were still battling it out and had

lost interest for the time being. He would make it back to the bunker, worse for wear and empty-handed, but still alive.

Hudson snuck back into Vonn's dark house and felt his way down to the fallout shelter through the basement, and pounded on the door to let them know that he was back. After waiting and getting no response, he slammed on the door again, harder and louder than before. Nothing. He beat on the door with a shovel that was hanging on the wall but froze when he heard a crash from upstairs.

The door leading back up to the main level was ripped off of its hinges and Hudson's ears stung from the roar that blasted through the cellar. He took the shovel in both hands and held it like a spear. If he was going to die, he'd go down fighting.

In the dark, he could hear its heavy footsteps, coming down the stairs. The creaking of the boards, strained by its weight and the clicking of its talons on the risers made the hair on Hudsons arms stand on end as his skin began to bead up with cold sweat. As it took its first step onto the basement floor, the airlock opened, and an arm reached out, grabbing the back of his jacket and pulling him in.

Hudson tripped over the transition, landing hard on his back as the hatch slammed shut and the wind was knocked out of him. Emilia rushed over and laid on his chest, hugging him as tightly as she could and weeping. He sat up and squeezed her back as much as he could bear to with his wounds, then wiped the tears from her cheeks while he caught his breath.

"It's okay. I'm okay. I'm back. I told you I'd come back." He said, trying to calm her down, holding her close again. They rocked back a forth for a moment before Hudson realized that he didn't hear anyone else in the shelter with them. He looked into her tear-glazed eyes and knew that something had happened.

"Th- They…They…" Emilia whispered, "They're all dead. All of them. Everyone is dead. Everyone is de-" Her voice was drowned out by ferocious clawing and pounding at the door. The alien wanted in.

"It's okay. It'll never get through that door." Hudson assured her, stroking her hair. "Slow it down. Who's dead? What happened?" He asked, never looking away.

"My mom and dad. With the others missing and you out looking, there was no one here to stop it. They were arguing, and mom tried to calm them down and they-"

Her head was buried into his shoulder as she wept and he looked behind her into the bunker for what she wasn't telling him. A pile of

withered corpses laid in a semi-circle in the corner. Felicia was slumped against the wall with a gunshot wound, just below her collarbone and Vonn was on the floor in front of her with his skull caved in. A small calibre revolver sat next to a bloody pipe between them and the group in the corner. The withered bodies were so decayed that he could only tell who was who by their ratty clothing.

It was a horror show in there.

With the crime scene in front of him and what little she said, Hudson was able to make a few inferences. He didn't know what happened to set it all off, but one of them had to have pulled the revolver on Felicia when she tried to mediate, and shot her in the chest. There was no telling if it was an accident, other than where she was hit. Vonn must have gone for the gun, which was when they hit him on the head with the pipe. That left Emilia, who huddled herself in the corner protecting the babies.

"The babies!" he cried, putting his hand on her stomach, "Emilia! Are the babies okay? Did they hurt you? Did they hurt the babies?!"

"I…I think the babies *saved* me." She told him, confused by her own words.

"What?"

"They murdered my parents, and then they tried to-…My stomach tingled and…I watched them rot. Like, the life was being sucked out of their bodies." She whispered sheepishly, knowing how ridiculous that must have sounded at the time. She sat back and stared off blankly, rubbing her stomach over and over. "…Dad's treatments…"

The sound of snapping bolts and tearing metal rang out through the bunker as the top of the exterior door peeled open. Hot breath blasted in through the opening that stunk of putrid meat. The light from over their heads glinted off of its teeth as it tried to fit through, reaching in and swiping blindly with sickle claws. Hudson helped Emilia move back, out of its reach and picked up the revolver off of the floor. He checked the cylinder, cocked the hammer and waited for the alien to show its face again. As soon as it pulled its arm back to look in, Hudson marched up and put four rounds between its eyes. The monster recoiled and shrieked, then pulled the door open wider and stuck its head all the way through, crown and all. The bullets only left shallow gouges in the bone of its snout. He lowered his gun, and the alien mimicked a human laugh as it pulled itself further through the top of the door. With no way to escape, Hudson brought Emilia to the back of the shelter, and they held each other tight as it clawed its way in.

Hudson felt something strange, and Emilia's look was acknowledgment enough that it wasn't just him. The alien sensed it too. It stopped and stared at them, tilting its head from side to side, trying to figure out what they were up to. As it sniffed at a change in the air, a spot on its nose began to sizzle and decay. It frantically tried to wipe away whatever was causing it, but its hand began to do the same. It was mad with panic, as bones in its face were starting to show. Its lips and gums receded, and flesh sloughed away from its arm. Unable to fight what was hurting it, the alien retreated from the basement and smashed its way out of the house, leaving bits of itself behind as it went.

"Is that what you meant? Is that what happened before?" he asked, remembering to breathe.

"Ya. It is. They *protected* me. They protected *us*. Whatever my dad did, it just saved our lives." Emilia told him as she stopped crying and had him help her up. She headed for the door with a new confidence that she'd never felt prior. "I'm thirsty."

"Wait. You can't go out there. If they come back, you won't be able to run. Let me go. I dropped some water jugs, they're just down the road. I'll grab them and be right back."

They could hear the monsters stirring outside of Vonn's house now.

"I'm not going to die down here; *we* aren't going to die down here." She told him adamantly, holding her stomach and looking back at her parent's bodies. She pushed Hudson to the side and grabbed a folding chair to stand on when she climbed through the gap in the door.

"…Okay. Just let me go first so I can make sure it's clear on the other side, then I'll help you through. Okay?" he said, realizing how traumatizing it must have been for her to stay down there any longer.

Emilia nodded, and he used to chair to climb through and dropped down to the other side, where he saw the damage the alien had done. The metal around the door was gouged with claw marks, and the concrete floor had been pulverized and torn up during its tantrum. The stairs were caved in at the bottom, and the door frame was blown out. He saw the broken shovel, buried in the rubble and shook his head at the futility of his efforts.

"Help me through." she told him, standing on the chair and holding her arms out.

He quietly brought over a bench and carefully pulled her through, then gently dragged it back over to the broken stairs. They waited, listening for anything outside, and once Hudson was satisfied that there was no immediate danger, he boosted Emilia up the stairs, into the kitchen and

climbed up after her. The exterior wall was gone. The alien had run right through it and weakened the creaking structure. They huddled together and walked out into the road, where everything seemed calm and safe; eerily so.

They made their way to the water jugs that Hudson had dropped earlier. He took a sip from one of the bottles and gave another to Emilia, then shouldered the rest and winced when the strap rubbed across the wound on his chest.

"You're bleeding!" Emilia whispered when she noticed, nearly making a fuss, but stopping herself before she gave away their position.

He gave an Oscar-worthy performance, pretending that the pain was gone as he shrugged it off and raised a finger to his lips, then gestured to the rooftops behind them. The aliens crept along after them, observing, but keeping their distance.

Emilia suddenly stopped walking and turned to face them.

"What are you doing? We need to go!" Hudson pleaded, but she wouldn't listen.

"What are you waiting for, you cowards!?" she screamed.

Hudson wondered if monsters like these had ever known fear themselves. He'd also wondered if Emilia had completely lost her mind. The largest of the three; with the dead hand and half a face, leapt down onto the road and began to strut toward them, limping slightly as it tried to keep weight off of its front leg. The disfigured alpha kept its pace, slowly moving closer and testing its range. Leery from their previous encounter, it still didn't understand what had happened. Sniffing at the air and reaching out with its good arm, it was feeling for something that it couldn't see but knew was there. As it got closer, it became more and more skittish, but the fact that nothing had happened to it yet, grew its confidence to keep moving forward. The alien could smell the blood from Hudson's chest and hear the rapid beating of their hearts. It could sense their fear.

The monster bluff charged, stopping only a few metres away from Hudson and Emilia, who held their ground. Emilia's forced confidence began to waver when still, nothing happened. Her heart rate increased, tipping the alien off that something wasn't right. It huffed and stomped around, pacing in front of them, trying to make up its mind, while the other two crept up behind the alpha, waiting to follow its lead.

Lowering its head down to their level, the alien sniffed Emilia's stomach as tears ran down her face. Turning to Hudson, a long, prehensile tongue slithered out of its mouth, slowly licking the blood from his chest. Barbed like a cat's, it snagged on bits of skin, reopening the freshly clotted

wounds. His chest felt like it was on fire and head was spinning, but all of his pain faded into the background when the alien's attention went to his wife.

The stench from the alien's rancid breath and rotting face made Emilia gag and heave. She took a stutter step back and nearly fainted, but Hudson had her hand and kept her up. The alpha swung its head over to her and let out a roar that it blew her hair back and sprayed her face with saliva. Her ears rang, and everything else got the volume turned down. Her hair was dripping wet, and Hudson couldn't tell her tears from its spit. It was nose to nose with her, and the other two seemed to be losing their apprehensions about proximity. Hudson was the first to notice when the drool oozing down Emilia's stomach began to sizzle away, like drops of water on a hot stove.

Necrosis spread slowly through what was left of the alpha's face. Its eyes widened when it realized that it was happening again, then went milky and withered into its skull, like raisins in an oven. It tried to roar, but the skin and some of the cartilage had come away from its throat, and the tendons around its jaws let go. The hiss came out as a wheeze, and its lower mandible swung free, causing its tongue to hang down, like a meaty necktie. Its atrophied front legs buckled as it tried to back away, bringing its weight down on weakened bones.

The two behind it were sniffing at the air, then became agitated and started making chirping and clicking noises to each other. They backed off slightly but continued to watch the alpha die, as the bigger of the two excitedly licked the drool from its lips.

Emilia fell to her knees, and Hudson dropped down next to her, trying to take some of her weight.

"They're coming!" she told him, breathing heavily with a look of horror in her eyes. His head spun around to two remaining aliens, still standing in the street. They weren't advancing. In fact, they seemed startled and backed off a bit when he looked in their direction. Emilia grabbed him by his collar and shouted, "The babies! The babies are coming!"

Her water had already broken, and she was having contractions, just minutes apart. With the houses falling in on themselves and the aliens between them and the bunker, there was nowhere safe to give birth to the twins.

The road became spotted by the first drops of rain as thunder echoed in the distance and storm clouds kept the sky darker than it should have been just before dawn.

Hudson helped Emilia off of the road, into the barn near the pump house and boarded the door, even though he knew it wouldn't stop them. Up in the loft, he helped her undress, then laid her down on an old blanket in a bed made from loose straw bails.

Rain pounded the roof and dripped through the rafters, but they'd found a dry place in one of the stalls. Hudson found a propane torch and lit some sawdust and scrap lumber in a metal trough to give them light and heat.

He'd never delivered a baby before; his medical experience was on the battlefield, not in pediatrics. Luckily, Emilia had plenty of experience from the clinics she'd worked in. She'd have to guide him through the whole thing.

Emilia was taking panting breaths and gently pushing with each contraction, while Hudson crouched nervously between her legs, holding his jacket out like a blanket.

"Hhhh-hhh-ahh hhnnnnnnn! When you see the baby's head you need to place your hand on it to guide it out, but don't -hhhrrnnnhhh, don't pull." Emilia instructed him, starting to push harder.

Outside, the aliens feasted on the alpha's rotting corpse. One had been lashing the flayed bones to its body as it finished the tough meat off of them, while the other gorged on the softer flesh at the base of its tail. Even though one of their own had died, this was beneficial for both of them. The carcass would provide an abundant food source for the future brood mother and meant a promotion by default for the beta.

"Hhhhhnnnaaaaa!! N-now stroke hhha-hhhhhaa-hhuunh stroke down on the baby's nose to clear the fluid" she panted, reaching for it as it was born. She held their new little girl against her bare chest with tears of both pain and joy streaming down her face as her husband got ready to do it again.

"You're doing so good! We can do this! One more!" he cheered, squeezing her free hand and getting ready for another round. She was too exhausted to walk him through it again, but he knew what to do. She pushed and the second baby's head began to emerge. Hudson did exactly what he'd learned delivering the first, but something was different this time.

"No. No. Please, no." he muttered, as he cradled their stillborn baby boy in his hands.

The umbilical cord had wrapped around his neck, and his skin was a pale blue. Hudson broke down in tears as he untangled it and gave the baby to his wife. He kissed all three of them on their foreheads as they wept

together. Their little girl wailed with strong, healthy lungs and reached for her brother. Her touch flushed his skin with colour, and he whimpered back to life. Hudson and Emilia were awestruck when they heard both of the babies crying in their arms, in what would have seemed like a miracle, but they knew better.

As the sun rose, the clouds broke, and warm light poured through the gable door in the loft. Hudson tied the water jugs to the front of a farm wagon and padded the inside so that Emilia could recover with the twins while they travelled. They couldn't take any of the vehicles because they all stopped working when the power went out. He took a sealable can and filled it with dry sawdust for tinder. Some folded tarps, a digging spade, a hacksaw with a handful of blades, and a coil of nylon rope in a shallow stainless steel bucket went into the undercarriage. He also brought his old double bit logging axe, but carried that up front with him, just in case.

They were as ready as they could be to depart on their journey. Emilia was in the back of the wagon, nursing the twins with an A-frame tarp over them to block the sun and protect them from the elements. Hudson climbed back up into the loft to find a decent heading and make sure that they had a clear path out. He could see the female alien outside of Vonn's place, rummaging through debris from the fallen houses and gathering it all back down in the basement. The other seemed to be patrolling the area around the bunker, wearing a sort of headdress, made from the alpha's hollowed out skull. A gust of wind made the gable door bang against the outside of the barn, alerting the grotesquely adorned monster to his location. They locked eyes with each other, and it immediately bolted for cover, screeching and chirping at its mate as they scurried away, down into the basement together. They were behaving more like prey than predators toward him now, and that gave him the confidence he needed to leave of the barn, towing his family in the covered wagon behind him as they set off to make a new life together at the end of the world.

█

RILEY'S ORDEAL

2023 CE – 8 ACE

A tech-head with an itch for adventure had driven across the country with a few old highschool friends that he'd reconnected with after college. Riley had scouted the location online before the trip, doing his homework so he'd have a few surprises to impress them with. Following a wild night in the desert with a few cases of cheap beer, a bag of shrooms and some cute, local Cali girls, they set up camp and slept under the stars.

The next day, they worked through the hangovers, getting their gear ready to do a little reconnaissance for what was next on their agenda. They planned to take the last guided cave tour, just so that they weren't going in completely blind, and as a tease for what was to come. That night, after the tours had shut down and everyone had left, Riley and his friends snuck back in. They'd spelunk into the restricted areas and see what that the normal public couldn't. That was the plan, anyway.

After dark, they avoided the few security cameras that they'd spotted earlier and passed the superficial gate. Riley was in no way an expert but was by far the most experienced of the group and after a little hair of the dog, acted as their overly confident, amateur guide, volunteering to take the lead. The group had made it fairly deep into the uncharted section of the cave when one of the girls felt a vibration in the rock as she squeezed through. It was dismissed as nerves at first until the vibrations became loud, rumbling tremors and the group began to panic. Crumbling stones came loose and pelted them like hail from all directions, ricocheting off of the uneven walls. Everybody had heard of '*the big one*' and were all sure that this was it.

The rock split between Riley and the others and the gap in the walls closed as the ceiling collapsed in on his friends. Before he could comprehend what had happened, his ropes were sheered by the shifting rock, dropping him blindly into a pitch black cavern.

Having survived the fall, he was pretty badly beaten up, but able to walk. The lamp on his helmet was still working, even though it took a hit on

the way down, which was the only reason he was still alive. He'd fashioned a sling out of his torn t-shirt and held himself up with his good arm against the cold, wet rock. Shuffling carefully along the cavern wall, he looked around the chamber for a way back out to the surface, but all he found was more darkness. Riley was exhausted after calling out for what seemed like hours, and hearing only distorted echoes in return. Considering his location, the severity of the quake, and the fact that nobody had any reason to come looking for him, he had all but given up hope.

Something moved horizontally just beyond the cone of light, and Riley's heart skipped a beat. He swung his head in that direction, cracking it off of a rock jutting out from the wall and killing the light. More movement could be heard coming from where he'd seen it last, but with the headlamp dead, he was effectively blinded. If it were one of his friends, they'd have spoken, and the way it hid from sight, flooded his mind with visions of creeping ghouls and chattering molemen. His heart was pounding so hard he could hear it.

An odd sound grew ahead of him, like the mechanisms inside of a bank vault door. Another small tremor shook the cavern, raining down stalactites in the black. Stone slid against metal, and there were a few seconds of relative silence as it fell. The impact of the slab sounded like a distant explosion. The cavern had become unstable, and he could feel the ground beneath his feet tremble as it began to give way. Riley clung to the wall as tightly as he could to avoid the falling debris, but he could feel the air whoosh by as larger rocks fell dangerously close.

A light pierced through the darkness, accompanied by the sound of heavy hydraulics and hissing gas. He let go of the cave wall and hobbled as quickly as he could toward the only thing he could see. It was a huge mechanical door, partially opened; blocked by displaced boulders. He looked up at the bright light pouring out and reached toward it, trying to find hand and foot holds to pull himself up with. Halfway there, a falling rock about the size of a football caught him in the back of his leg and he let out a howl of agony that echoed through the chamber. Riley lost his grip on the smooth metal as his stomach tensed and his eyes widened, teetering backward on one foot. Just as he was about to topple back, he felt hot breath on the back of his neck and cold metal clamped down around his forearm. Being pulled up in one quick, jerking motion nearly dislocated his shoulder, and when he flopped onto the hard floor, his full weight came down on the injured arm. The pain made him sick to his stomach and his vision blurred

in the brightness; he felt like he was going to blackout. Something sharp jabbed him in the leg, and the pain receded.

Riley pulled himself over to a wall beside the door and used it to prop himself back up. He glanced down at himself and saw the blood running from his arm and pooling in the sling; the bone was badly broken and sticking out of the skin, just above his elbow. His shin was at a slight angle where the rock hit him, and a sprained ankle from the initial fall made his foot look like an eggplant with toes.

He unstrapped and tossed away his now useless climbing helmet. The shell was cracked, and the bulb had gone out with the lens. His eyes slowly adjusted to the bright interior lights as he watched the busted helmet skip across the floor and slide into the feet of a metallic, androgynous humanoid. Riley couldn't believe what he was seeing and hoped that this wasn't a result of head trauma.

The android's eyes flickered as it observed him. The door sealed itself shut, muting the cave in. Riley flinched as it approached, and pulled away, but it was pointless; there was nowhere he could go and nothing he could do. He struggled briefly against the android's grasp when it pulled him to his feet, but he lost his balance and put weight on the wrong foot. Even with the pain dulled, he felt his leg throb when he the fracture gave. Pins and needles shot up his spine when he heard the snap, like fresh celery and saw his broken leg fold under him.

The android carried Riley into a room lined with strange machines and empty chambers. All but one. A frail body full of tubes, suspended in a translucent fluid, with clouds of metallic particles that moved like schools of fish churning around it. Riley saw an ancient face, whose sunken, milky eyes followed him as they passed and a small crease formed by the corner of the old man's mouth. The android loaded Riley into the next empty chamber, sealed him inside, and began interfacing with a console between the units.

The chamber began to flood with a transparent liquid that dissolved his clothes, hair, and nails on contact and washed away the dirt and blood that was caked on him. Riley held a deep breath as the fluid rose above his head and the air was displaced from the chamber. He pounded on the curved glass and pried in vain at any seam he could find. His chest ached and his body spasmed before an involuntarily gasp for air filled his lungs with liquid. After a few panicked moments, he'd realized that he wasn't drowning.

The metallic cloud filtered in, entering his body through his wounds and Riley watched as the nanomachines reset his broken bones and repaired

his torn flesh. They provided a scaffolding for stems cells to grow new tissue, but they were doing more than just fixing him. He could feel them under his skin. His bones itched, his brain hummed and his muscles burned. The tiny workers were adding on; building beneath the surface.

Riley pressed his hands and face up against the glass, trying to see through the semi-transparent fluid, which had a pink tint to it now, diffused with the blood that had escaped from his now sealed wounds. The nanite clouds were no longer swarming in the liquid around him and the strange sensations seemingly washed away with any pain. The bloodstained liquid became clear again, and Riley was filled with an odd tranquility.

Colours appeared more vivid, and their fringes trailed in motion. It felt as though ants were crawling around inside of Riley's skull; a dull, electric tingle, swept throughout his body in pulsating waves. Ever-shifting, complex geometric patterns faintly glimmered through the veil that separates the unconscious mind from waking reality.

He closed his eyes and seemed to be transported to another plane of existence. Drifting through endless nebulae, wisps of light danced in elegant unison around his ethereal body. Then, everything fell away, leaving him alone in a vast cold nothingness. But he *wasn't* alone. An orb appeared, with a focal lens that glowed blue with a strange intensity. The wisps returned in droves from beyond the fog of darkness, moving with dauntless purpose, engulfing the orb, like white blood cells, swarming a parasite. Arcs of indigo lightning clawed their way out and webbed across the dense mass of swirling illumination, filling the cloud with inky scars that twisted and infused with the light. The orb broke free and put itself between Riley and the weakened cloud, waiting defensively while it faded away. The orb dissolved into a swarm of nanobots, which first took the rough shape of a human brain. A cloud of dark metal he didn't recognize sparked with glowing blue circuitry, gradually constructing a duplicate synthetic version of him as the machines intricately reconstituted. His doppelganger's eyes began to shine bright like the sun, though it didn't hurt him. He could look right into it and it into him. It was inviting; difficult to look away, so he didn't. The darkness behind him disappeared, as its nurturing warmth washed over him and he was engulfed by the light. The blue shifted to a deep red, and in that instant, he was torn apart from all directions. Total obliteration.

Riley opened his eyes, and the old man was now staring at him, floating almost motionless, from across the aisle, with only a slight disturbance in his long silken hair to indicate that he'd moved at all. A voice spoke to Riley from inside his own mind. He didn't recognize the words, but

he knew what it was saying, with a bizarre, connected understanding. It told the tale of the aliens and the arkships and the cataclysm that followed. It explained how the facility that housed this ark collapsed, killing all but one of its crew. Its damaged AI was residing in a single android unit and rescued the sole survivor after he had somehow escaped the ruined building. It explained that they returned to the buried ship and the man was put into cryostasis, remaining in that state for over 10,000 years. For the next few millennia, he was kept alive inside one of the regeneration chambers, but the damaged arkship was nearly depleted of resources. They had believed that the aliens had won and that the Earth had been decimated, until Riley came along and unwittingly shared his knowledge of the modern world. The voice explained that it was dying. It told him that even if the ship were fully operational, the ravages of time were too much for this mortal body and mind to endure any longer. The voice became whisper quiet, trailing off as the old man's eyes slowly closed.

The arkship trembled as the Earth around it quaked. Lights flickered and dimmed. The glass in Riley's tank cracked and the pressure inside caused it to spider web. He pressed his feet to the rear wall and tucked his body, like a tightly coiled spring. Covering his head with his arms, he launched himself at the weakest point. He slammed into it with all of his might, but the glass was thicker than he'd imagined. Another tremor rocked the ship, and its structure moaned like a submarine that's gone too deep, as metal twisted and crumpled under the incredible pressure on the hull. The far wall bent in, and the ceiling partially collapsed, dropping a heavy panel on top of the row of tanks, causing them to buckle and blow out.

The liquid from Riley's chamber gushed out, carrying him with it as he was washed across the floor with the broken glass. The old man's tank was dark and still, with the android nowhere to be seen. Riley struggled to find his footing on the slippery floor and stumbled from the room, down a long corridor, toward the hatch where he had entered the ship.

Everything shook and shifted, and he tumbled down the hallway at a steep angle, catching himself on a dividing wall. The end of the corridor fell away as the ark sheered in half. He didn't hear it land over the roar of crashing waves and wailing wind. Riley clawed at the floor as he slid toward the bright abyss and a familiar metal hand reached out, grasping his wrist as he slipped over the edge. He dangled by one arm as he looked down into a massive crevasse devouring the landscape and flooding the gap with murky water. Riley used the metal arm that grabbed him to pull himself back up into the ship and broke free of its weakened grip, pinned under heavy

equipment and badly damaged. A compartment opened in the side of the robot's head and it reached in with jerky, stuttering movements as sparks flew out from its joints. The android removed an ornate metallic orb, with a shifting light that seemed to subtly shine through the opaque, figured metal. It laboured to extend its arm, handing the sphere to Riley, as its eyes dimmed and hydraulics lost pressure.

Riley scaled the slanted hallway, scouring several partially intact rooms for salvage. The regeneration chambers were gone, and the room had been pressed flat under the mountain. What was left of the structure hung precariously from the face of the cliff and shifted as he moved, making it difficult to traverse with any real finesse. Inside the second room, there was a stockpile of what seemed like wetsuits, similar to what the old man wore, and were somehow completely undegraded. He put one on and fashioned a pack for the mysterious orb, tying together the arms and legs, and using them as shoulder straps. Riley pulled himself through a gap in the hull and out onto a broad stone ledge where he could survey the area from, in relative safety.

The coast had fallen into the ocean, and there was an upheaval in the land.

He began his free climbing ascent up the jagged rock wall and grabbed at a buttress that dislodged a loose section of stone that crumbled away, raining down onto the remaining section of the ship. Riley swung away with one arm and watched as the wreckage tore from the wall and fell into the water, hundreds of feet below. Being much more careful picking his holds, he continued on, and after an exhausting climb, he pulled himself up and over the edge, rolling away and taking a moment to rest. He laid on his back with his eyes closed, basking in the sun and gripping the pack tightly at his side.

A terrible roar echoed in the distance, waking Riley several hours after succumbing to exhaustion. The sun had been set for a while, and the sky was clear. He'd never seen so many stars in his entire life and stared up in wonder until another roar broke the silence. This time it was louder; closer than before. He jumped to his feet and reached down to scoop up his pack, but instead, grabbed a handful of dirt. His pack was gone, and the orb with it. He felt around in the dark, like someone who had dropped their glasses. Nothing.

Looking up, Riley saw the outline of a small person standing in the clearing before the woods, holding something that glowed faintly in its hand. He got up and moved forward slowly, trying not to startle the child,

but before he got more than a few steps, it let out a hideous cackle and darted into the tree line. Disturbed by the awful noise that it made, he decided to stay put and wait for daylight, instead of diving blindly into a deeper mess. Unfortunately, Riley wouldn't get any more sleep that night. He felt eyes on him the entire time. Occasionally, the unnerving laughter would break out around him, but disappear when he turned toward it. Screams and howls came from deep in the woods that he didn't think a living thing could make. He sharpened the end of a long stick to a point against a flat rock and kept his back to the cliff so that nothing could sneak up from behind, and waited for them to come. With the morning light peeking over the horizon and illuminating the treeline, the whooping and hollering quieted, and Riley feared that he'd lost the orb.

As the sun rose over the clifftop, the glint of two eyes in the bushes was like the sound of a starting pistol to a sprinter. He tore through the bushes and hopped over fallen trees, like pommel horses. The kid was ahead of him, dragging his pack and moving through the woods with inhuman agility, until the rumble of a waterfall up ahead made him slow his pace. He crouched down behind a thick fern and watched as the kid scurried up and down trees, trying to find a way around as if it were nothing but a simple obstacle course. Riley stayed low and snuck up, reaching for his pack while it was distracted. Just as he thought he had it, the child spun around and screeched loudly. It wasn't a child at all.

The creature was covered in dark, matted fur, and constantly chuckled, like a clown with a nervous tic. Its body was lean and muscular but built like no animal he'd seen before. It was hunched over and obviously deformed but moved swiftly and without hindrance. Its lips curled, baring pointed teeth and elongated canines. Its posture changed and it tossed the pack, lunging forward. He ducked out of the way as it flew past, and the creature turned to rush him again. Riley shouted aggressively and threatened it with his spear. It bluff charged, over and over again, screeching and chattering back. When it stepped in too close, he plunged the tip of his spear into the meat of its ribs, glancing off of bone and tearing out the other side. It yelped and leapt backward, hissing at him as it scurried away, plucking splinters from the tip.

Riley used the spear as a walking stick and caught his breath, making his way to the pack that was snagged in a tree over the river's edge. The water was white with strong rapids, dropping off nearby into a ravine. He held onto to a branch that could take his weight and leaned out over the river, trying to snag the pack with the spear. The strap slipped on the first

try, nearly losing it in the torrent. On his second attempt, he almost went in himself. They say the third time's the charm, but just as he began to reach out, the creature returned from behind him. Even over the noise of the crashing water, he could hear it trying to stifle its sinister giggle. He readied the spear, but lost it when his feet slipped in the muck as he turned, and he swung out over the rapids.

The creature was frothing at the mouth, flipping rocks and tearing up plants in a fit, as the pain in its side only enraged it further. Pacing by the shore, it only stopped to shake the branch that Riley was hanging on, unaware that its tantrum was beginning to attract the attention of other wildlife in the area.

Something big crashed through the trees like it was running through tall grass. The furry little monster finally shut up and ran, but to Riley's surprise, it turned and jumped for the pack, knocking it off of the branch and into the water. Clawing its way back up and hanging similarly to Riley, it spat the water that it had in its mouth at him, then erupted into uncontrollable, maniacal laughter, nearly causing itself to fall in again.

The great beast in the woods charged out into the river, locked onto the noise, and snapped up the evil little creature in its jaws. It stood in the middle of the white water and thrashed its head back and forth, flailing the corpse around before chomping it down. Riley watched in terror as it took the tiny morsel down like an hors-d'oeuvre, then raised its head from the river and turned to him.

Riley immediately let go of the branch and dropped into the water. The current pulled him under, and he crashed over and over again into the rocks at the bottom, before being spat back out again for another round. In a blur of stones and froth, Riley caught a glimpse of his lost spear, wedged between boulders, and only avoided it thanks to the violent current whipping him across the river. Each time he surfaced, the falls got closer, and each time he surfaced, so did the beast chasing him. The only reason that he escaped it was the straight drop over the edge, into the lagoon at the bottom of the falls, where he tumbled in the plunge basin, pinned underwater.

QUARTET

6 – 8 ACE

Gaia; a young girl, no more than 6 years old, gathered berries with her twin brother Rayn, not far from their family's camp. Her curly blond locks, dark bronze skin, and piercing heterochromatic blue-green eyes mirrored her brother's. Wherever they went there always seemed to be an abundance. Their father was the most experienced outdoorsman of the group and taught his skills to the others. He'd taken a small band of the older boys on their first boarffalo hunt, earlier that day. It was a dangerous task, especially with improvised weapons, but it was a necessary skill for survival these days. Their mother had disappeared not long after their birth, and the community did their best to fill her role in raising them. Even with the support of their extended family, the twins always got anxious when their father was away for long. The children began to worry when the sun fell low on the horizon. They'd brought back what they had collected, and helped to build a fire in preparation for the feast, staying busy to keep from thinking too much about when he'd return.

Gaia looked to her brother when she heard him drop the bundle he was carrying. His bottom lip quivered, and his eyes overflowed with tears. A scream came from the edge of the camp and a large figure approached from the darkness. She could barely make it out in the dim light cast by the torches that ran along the perimeter of their temporary settlement. As the figure grew closer, she saw the face of her father. His severed head dangled from a rope, threaded through his bottom jaw and worn ornamentally around the neck of the towering fiend. A draconid centaur carried a dismembered torso in its claws and hurled it into the fire, sending burning logs and glowing embers flying. Pine bow huts were engulfed in flames, and everybody scrambled to save what they could, while Gaia rushed to find her brother, who she'd lost sight of in the commotion.

Rayn held a burning spear, three times too big for him, with both hands, and charged bravely at the monster from its flank. Despite his best

30

effort, the sharpened tip glanced off of its tough, leathery skin, and the spear fell pathetically to the ground. It looked down at the annoyance and swatted him, like a mosquito into the dirt, where he laid motionless. The brute snarled, wrapping its clawed foot around Rayn's head and pressed it into the ground, as Gaia watched helplessly.

Two more entered the camp and began tearing through villagers, playing with them as they died.

Gaia's eyes rolled back into her head. The stress and trauma set off a grand mal seizure, and she went into a convulsive fit. The whites of her eyes turned jet black and the air distorted around her. The distortion reached out, in an expanding bubble that spread instant decay and quick death to anything it touched.

The next morning, everything was gone, and she was alone. She laid there in the fetal position at the centre of a large circular depression strewn with ash. She stayed there, without food or water; feeding off of the ambient life energy in the area for years.

Seven seasons later, a man travelling alone entered the barren ring. He was unkempt, even for the times, though it was clear that he was comfortable in the hostile wilderness. A thick beard covered his grimy, weather-beaten face, and a loosely stitched leather hood was pulled low over his brow. He approached her with caution, bordering on hypervigilance, knowing that this was a place no one else dared to come.

This wasn't the monster he'd come to slay.

Weak and malnourished when he found her, she barely reacted when he scooped her up in his arms and wrapped her in his heavy pelt jacket. Before long, she stopped shivering, and he brought her to a stream and fed her as much water as she'd take. Once she was stable enough to travel, he carried her through the forest, toward the mountains along the coast. They travelled throughout the day and made up a camp just before the sun went down. He was confident, but not stupid. This was a dangerous place, especially in the dark, and he had more to consider than himself this time. He stayed awake and watched over her as she slept by the fire until morning, taking note of the odd silence in the woods that night. They set off early and made good time. Another half day of trekking and they'd arrive at the place he called home.

Though he still bore the mental and physical scars of many battles, Connor had little to no working memory of his past. He lived a fairly hermitic life now, keeping to himself for the most part, but travelling to barter with other groups and using his special talents to fill a vital niche in

the new world as a freelance exterminator, though he prefered to think of himself as more of a part-time monster hunter, considering that he was the only one up to the task.

His home was secluded at the foot of the coastal mountains, surrounded by intermingling tropical and temperate rain forests. He'd built his sanctuary into an alcove, tucked away inside of a ravine that opened up onto the ocean. It was incorporated into the rock, on the shore of a large pool that was fed by a tall, narrow waterfall. There was a constant supply of fresh water, local game, and resources. The lagoon would light up with a golden glow in the mornings when the sun would hit the mist from the falls. It would bake the rocks and sand during the day, and they would hold their heat into the evenings. It was an idyll refuge, hidden within a savage wilderness.

He'd built no defences. He didn't need any.

His companion; Fen, like everything else in the region, was a hybrid. A hulking black mass of fur, claws, and teeth, in the shape of a giant, stocky wolf. His coat so dark, that it was practically a silhouette, contrasted by bolts of white fur that shot up his chest and behind his amber eyes. He moved swiftly and stealthily, on constant patrol, as his prey drive compelled him. Fen was a highly intelligent, powerful hunter, but also possessed an equal capacity for love. Fen had imprinted on Connor when he was just a pup. His biological father was killed by his mother when he'd begun cannibalizing their offspring. She died shortly after from her wounds, leaving the newborns vulnerable to predation. A swarm of piranha-rats had devoured the rest of his littermates and had gone to work on the carcasses of his parents when Connor discovered the scene and cleared them out. When the vermin were charred, and the danger was gone, the last of the pack emerged from hiding. The cute little fluff ball was the only one left of his kind. Orphaned and unable to fend for himself, Connor took him in as his own. Seeing Fen fully grown, in all his majesty, it would be hard to imagine him as a tiny pup, curled up in his arms while he carried him home. From then on, their bond was unbreakable.

When Connor and Gaia arrived, Fen was standing over Riley, who was soaking wet and lying unconscious on the rocks. He had pulled him from the lagoon, shook the water from his fur, and dragged him to a sunny spot to dry out, presenting his body like a dog would proudly bring a mauled rabbit to its master.

Connor's first priority was to the girl. He took her inside and gave her his bed. Only once he was satisfied that he'd done all that he could to

make her comfortable, did he head back outside to see what kind of trouble Fen had delivered.

Riley was still breathing, and aside from some cuts and scrapes around the fringes of his prosthetics, appeared to be otherwise without injury. Connor set up a cot for him to use while he recovered and had Fen help get him into it. Without knowing if he was dangerous or not, he wouldn't take any risks with the girl around. He'd have to stay outside for now.

Hours later, Riley woke up to the loud crack of splitting wood, as Connor built a large bonfire nearby. He shot up off the cot in startled confusion, and scuttled himself into a corner when he spotted Fen, who hadn't taken his eyes off of him the entire time. Connor stopped what he was doing and rushed over when he noticed Fen creeping away from the fire toward the empty bedding.

"Fen! Back!" he shouted, running over to them. "Easy boy, eeeeaaasy…we're all friends here," he told the furry goliath, patting his chest to calm him down. "Isn't that right *friend*?" he said, looking at Riley with an expression that suggested he should agree.

"Y-yeah! T-that's a good boy." Riley said nervously.

"Hmm…Stay right here. *Don't* move." Connor ordered, and disappeared into the cabin for a moment, mentioning nothing of who or what was inside.

Riley stepped toward the outer wall, trying to peer through the gaps where light leaked out, but he was stopped when Fen picked him up by the back of his wetsuit, and held him dangling there until his master returned. Connor chuckled on the way back out and gave the signal to let him down. Fen obediently dropped Riley and walked off in a huff, finding a spot to lay by the water. Connor reached out, offering Riley his hand to help him up, but he had already hopped to his feet and was grumbling under his breath as he brushed himself off. Fen was watching him distrustfully, having heard every bit, and let out a rumbling growl which shut Riley up fast.

Connor shook his head and reached out again, this time offering a glass. He had one for each of them and a dusty old bottle of scotch in his other hand. Riley took the glass and Connor filled it before they each sat down on the log bench by the fire pit. Riley held the glass up to his nose and took a whiff of the strong drink, waiting for Connor to take a sip of his before he tried it. After a deep inhale of its aroma, Connor took a swig, and Riley cordially followed suit. The rich, peaty flavour was something that he hadn't realized that he'd missed so much. He took a bigger gulp and

coughed from the burn in his throat, but it helped him to relax. Connor slugged his back and refilled their glasses.

"Found this in a swamp that used to be an old golf resort. The clubhouse was barricaded and pretty much untouched by the shit going on outside. The place looked like it could've been open for business if the lights still worked, but not a single survivor. Just one body, dressed to the nines in the cigar lounge, sitting in a big leather chair, like an old king on his throne, surrounded by hoarded treasures…So, I tossed the body and moved in there for a while. Brought a few boxes of what were once nice cigars, and a case of this ridiculously high-end scotch. It's older than I am, and just keeps on getting better. So, kid…" Connor said, trying to break the ice with his nose rarely leaving the glass, "You're obviously a long way from home. Tell me a story."

Riley looked up from his drink and said with a doubtful look on his face "This is going to sound crazy-"

Connor let out a laugh and cut in with, "Look around you and then tell me about crazy" prompting Riley to continue.

He explained what had happened in detail, from his ruined vacation to losing the orb in the river and falling in to escape the monster. Connor listened intently, allowing Riley to ramble and get it all out. The sun had set, and they were halfway through the bottle by the time he was all caught up. He swirled his drink around in the bottom of his glass, mulling over what Riley had told him.

"Congratulations, kid. That *is* some crazy shit." he laughed, validating his story.

The moonlight was reflecting off of the water, and Riley noticed something caught in the rocks behind the falls. He stood up and staggered over toward it, to get a better look. Connor followed him, and Fen shifted around where he was lying so that he could see what they were doing. Riley perked up and dashed clumsily down the path that ran along the edge of the lagoon, behind the waterfall. He'd recognized the tattered material that had washed up from the river as the pack he'd made from the ship. Riley's buzz didn't help his balance, and he slipped on the smooth, wet stones, falling hard on his ass and into the dark water. He was nearly scared to death when Fen rose up from beneath the surface, lifting him out and back onto the trail. Connor rolled around, holding his stomach and howling with laughter, while Riley grabbed the pack and carefully made his way to the fire to dry off and warm back up, his teeth chattering all the way. They'd emptied the

remainder of the bottle into their cups, and he dug through the bag for the orb, but his arm poked out through a large hole in the bottom.

The next morning, Riley woke up to a dry mouth and splitting headache. Groaning as he crawled out from under the bench where he'd slept, he slithered down to the pond to rehydrate. Connor was already up and around, having checked in on Gaia and set up a drying rack for the fish he planned on catching that day. Gaia was still resting, only partially waking up when he would feed her water and a paste he'd made from mashed fruits and vegetables. She hadn't opened her eyes yet, but he could see that she was beginning to recognize his voice when he spoke.

Riley hung over the edge of the rocks and splashed water onto his face when the sun reflected off of the bottom of the pool, and he noticed a glint of light coming from under the falls. Always watching, Fen saw it too and went in before Riley had a chance. He dove in with a pin-drop splash and moved effortlessly through the water, reemerging with the orb pinched between conical incisors. Riley couldn't believe it. His curiosity had overridden his fear, and he ran straight up to Fen, who wagged his tail playfully, then took off down the beach and into the woods. Riley was too hungover to bother with chasing him down and let him be, as if catching him was an option to begin with.

Connor left the cabin carrying a pronged wooden spear and a rolled up towel under his arm as he walked up on Riley, who was cursing belligerently and kicking at the sand.

"Ya! You tell that bastard!" He cheered on, mockingly. "Hungry?"

"Ugh, I'm starving." Riley blurted out, holding his gurgling stomach.

"Good!" Connor said, tossing the bundle to him and slapping his back as he passed. "Let's go get breakfast. You look a little dehydrated, a quick dip'll do you good."

"Huh? Ya, I guess…So, I still don't know anything about you, other than the fact that you keep strange company…I think it's your turn to talk for a while." he said between burps, trudging along behind Connor as they followed the stream through the woods.

"Not much to tell. One day, I woke up with no clue who I was, or where I came from. My memories of the old world are slippery, like trying to remember a dream. I get bits and pieces, but nothing solid… and then the aliens came and that world ended, so what does it matter?. I don't really remember, so I don't really miss it. You know, I don't even *really* know my own name. The tag sewn into the sweater I was wearing said 'Connor' so,

I'm Connor." he explained. "I've just been out here, living off the land; thriving, really. I found this little haven and settled in. I love it out here."

"Amnesia."

"Sure."

"What's up with the wildlife? That shit's not normal."

"I know, right? I'm not sure *why* they are the way they are, but it's not just the animals. The plants are the same way. The forest gets *really* dense around the base of the mountain." Connor said, pointing back the way they came.

"That's where *I* came from. If we go back there, I can show you-"

Riley stopped talking when Connor interjected.

"*Pass.* That place is crawling with nightmare fuel...Doesn't help that you've got an empty bag and no pockets."

"...Where are we going anyways?" Riley asked.

"I've got a boat tied up on the beach. Beauty little catamaran I pieced together. We'll untie her and head to the reef. *You'll* take that spear there, and dive. Stick it in anything that looks delicious, and bring it back up. Easy."

"ME?!"

"Ya, you bet. Gotta work of your tab."

"I suppose that's fair...There's no *jaguar-sharks* or anything that I have to worry about, is there?"

"Don't be ridiculous...It's the mantis-squid that you need to stay away from, but they're pretty shy, and their colours make them easy to spot when they get agitated...and then there's the candiru-urchins, but they're not around much this time of year."

"Oh good. Can't wait to get in there."

"Ah, don't be such a pussy. You slept outside last night. You don't even want to know the kinds of things that live around here."

"Ar-Are we in danger right now?" Riley asked, suddenly much more aware of their surroundings.

"Nah. They probably smell Fen on us. They know to keep their distance."

"Probably?" Riley asked, but Connor either didn't hear, or wasn't listening.

They found the boat, anchored in the surf and tied off to a tree by the path. It was well built; impressive for something that had been patched together from washed up wreckage. Connor pulled it into shore so that they

could load up, and Riley helped him push off into the water when they were ready to go. He was even more impressed when it stayed afloat.

Looking back to the land as they paddled out, they could see the mountain and the sheer cliff from where it had broken away. So much had changed, from the wildlife to the environment, there was no point in dwelling on the past. Anything left of the old world had been irreparably lost.

"Here we are!" Connor said, tossing his oar onto the netting and leaning over the side.

"What are you-"

"All clear." He reported, squeezing the saltwater from his hair after dunking his head in to take a look around. Handing Riley the spear and nudging him toward the edge, he teased, "…Are you waiting for that to change?"

Riley dove into the crystal clear water and resurfaced a few seconds later, spitting water and shouting "There's a city down there!"

"Been down there as long as *I* can remember." Connor told him, " They say '*the big one*' finally hit when the aliens showed up. Sorry if I'm a little foggy on the details. All I've got to go off of is second-hand information from strangers. C'mon, let's get what we came for and hustle back."

Watching the horizon as if he was expecting to see something, Connor seemed slightly on edge but said nothing of it. Riley brushed it off as safe practice and swam back down toward a large bloom of coral, covered in the descendants of mollusks and shellfish. It grew over everything, like underwater ivy and had overtaken what was likely an eroded apartment complex. Sea life was strange enough as it was, but the hybrids were flourishing out there as well. Their oddity was matched by the beauty they brought, making the ocean he remembered seem practically devoid of life by comparison.

The water grew warmer when Connor suddenly appeared behind Riley and grabbed his arm, spinning him around. He made panicked signals with his free hand, pointing to his eyes, then out toward the deep water and up, as he pulled Riley with him to the surface. He climbed onto the pontoon first and helped Riley up after him.

A ravenous fever of lamprey-rays came into view, and Riley started kicking his feet as hard as he could, trying to get back onto the boat as a wall of toothy death cut through the waves.

"Shit! Hold on to something and keep your head down!" Connor ordered with authority after hauling him up.

"What? Why?! How is that going to-" Riley clamoured, before Connor grabbed the back of his neck and forced him down.

He dropped to the netting and laced his fingers behind his head. The craft began to vibrate, and the water around it boiled. There was a sudden burst of momentum and the thunderous crashing of waves as the boat rocketed back, toward the shore. With only the sandbar to slow them, they were bucked clear as the catamaran washed up, high above the tide line and was mangled by the trees.

He rolled over in the sand that broke his fall and watched the parted water crashing back together behind them. Riley kicked up sand as he sprinted to save his unconscious fishing partner from being washed back out to sea with a wave that would sweep the shoreline. As he dragged Connor's dead weight up the beach, the water came in around them, carrying the boiled bodies of a thousand hybrids. Their ever-gaping mouths were packed full of hooked teeth, surrounding a beaked throat. Their long tails and wing-like fins were thick with muscle. A quick fillet notwithstanding, their lunch was cooked and delivered.

BONDING

Riley's stomach whined at him cartoonishly as he dragged Connor up the trail to the lagoon. He was heavy enough on his own, so the extra weight of his soaked clothes and the seafood piled on top wasn't helping. Tired, dehydrated and hungry, he felt like he was hallucinating when they reached the lagoon.

From the falls, down the beach, over the rocks and into the woods, the whole place was overgrown with flowering vines and lush moss. It was a far cry from the way they left it. Fen was in the middle of it all, rolled over on his back with Gaia laying on his chest, scratching his armpits with a big smile on her face.

"There you are!" She called out gleefully, then awkwardly slid off of Fen and skipped over to meet them.

Riley was at a loss for words.

The bright-eyed little girl smiled at him and reached for Connor's hand, unphased by his appearance. After a few seconds, he woke up and the scrape on his forehead disappeared.

"Hello, sleepy head. I'm Gaia! She told me all about you. " she told Connor, who was starting to come to and was clearly confused.

"Uhh, hey. I'm Connor."

"Uh, I *know*. She already told me, *remember*? You're weird. But, she said you're friendly, so it's cool."

"Who's '*she*'? Who are you talking about?"

"Oh! I have a present for you!" she told Riley, yelling over her shoulder as she ran back to Fen.

He was laying down on the big rock with something shiny between his paws. Gaia grabbed the bauble, absent-minded of the potential danger, but Fen just huffed and let her take it. Riley felt it in his bones as she brought it closer. It was the orb. Fen had brought it back while they were gone and something had caused it to activate.

The ornate patterns in the metal were constantly reconfiguring with complex clockwork mechanisms beneath the shifting lattice. Light from its core passed through the metal unimpeded, and Riley felt subtle feedback

when he touched it. A faint current ran through his fingertips and up his arms, into his chest and throughout his body. He began to hear a voice, speaking to him inside of his mind; a secondary internal monologue. The light now came from his pupils, and the orb levitated out of his hands. Riley stood there, entranced by it, and Connor took Gaia's hand to move her behind him.

"It's okay…It's just trying to help." She assured him.

"What do you mean? What is that thing?" Connor asked, looking on in perplexed curiosity, as it silently interacted with Riley.

"It needs to talk to him…It's got a super important job to do, but it wouldn't tell me 'cause I don't got the… Ay-jee-us? Eejits? Ages? I don't know what it is, but Riley's got it, so I helped. I'm a good helper." Gaia rambled vaguely, without context, like Connor knew what she meant. He didn't.

"What do I do?"

"Nothin'. This might take a while. Come see what I did!" she grabbed either side of Connor's hand and led him over to the cabin. She'd drawn a mural on the rock wall, using charcoal from the fire pit. It was surprisingly well done for a kid her age. "See? See? That's you, and that's me, and that's the big puppy, and that's Riley, and that's the lady, but they're not here yet, and *that's*-" she trailed off when she noticed Connors expression. "…You don't like it?"

As she pouted, the foliage where she stood began to lose colour.

"No, no, it's not that at all. This is actually amazing. You're obviously a very talented kid." he reassured her.

Her smile returned, and a flower blossomed between her toes, with new growth sprouting all around.

"It's just- How did you know Riley's name? …How'd you know *mine*? Why are you so comfortable with us? Who're the others in your picture? How long were we gone? When did you wake up? Where did all of this come from? The plants? That weird ball? Can you tell me anything? This is all so-" He collected himself and continued, "…I need you to help me understand what's going on". Gaia stared back at him like he was a crazy person, and he realized that he was asking too much all at once. "Sorry, I'm not used to this…I'm not very good at talking to kids." He explained.

"That's okay!" she said, shrugging her shoulders "I've never talked to a caveman before."

"Oh, I see how it is." he laughed back, "So how about we just talk to each other like regular people then, huh?"

Gaia nodded in agreement with a grin on her face.

"Riley can explain this stuff better than I can though. It showed me things, but it said I'm not 'conpaddleable' and it needs the 'agees' to 'func-'...to work." Gaia tried to explain as best she could.

"Hmm...what about the plants? Where'd all of this come from?" Connor asked, taking another opportunity to look around.

"Oh! I waked up and-"

"You *woke* up." he corrected her. "...Sorry, keep going."

"Oops! Ya, I *woked* up and you weren't here n' this is how it was already, so I went outside to look for you and the big puppy wanted to play, so I threw his shiny ball for him, and when I picked it up, it talked to me in my head and showed me a bunch of stuff." She explained, "It said it knew Riley and needed to 'innerface' with his 'ayjays'...whatever that means."

"Fen didn't scare you? He can be a little intimidating..." he asked, brushing off the rest as he waded through the nonsense. "I just need you to be more careful, okay? You can't just approach strange animals like that. What if he was dangerous?"

Gaia didn't have a reply and looked like she thought that she might be getting in trouble. Fen came over and nuzzled her arm with his head, then sat behind her with a regal posture.

"Well, I guess that's *one* you don't have to worry about." He told her.

"Wow! Did *you* do that? Who's the off-brand C-3PO?" Riley asked as he walked over to join them. The orb floated over his shoulder and now had a glowing lens on the front of its solid shell.

"Yep! The *what?* That one's you!" she told him, beaming with pride and pointing at what looked like a cartoon robot on the mural.

"That's a uhh...an interesting vision. Very creative."

"That's really good, Gaia. But listen, I need to talk to Riley about this now. So, is there something you can do in the meantime?"

"Ummm, sure! Like, what?" She asked.

"You tell me. What can you do to help out?"

"Oh! I know what plants are safe to eat...and I can get the best sticks for starting the fire to cook 'em up!" she bragged.

"Awesome! Take Fen and get us something good to go with lunch, okay? Don't wander too far off. Fen'll be with you, but these woods can be dangerous." Connor instructed.

She seemed excited to help and took off down the path toward the wooded area, and Fen was right behind her, acting as her own personal bodyguard.

"So?" Connor asked Riley, "What can you tell me?"

"Have you got any more of that scotch?" Riley said, half-jokingly. "I just absorbed more information in the last few minutes than I have in my entire life. What I learned wasn't exactly easy to stomach. My brain feels like scrambled eggs…and we still haven't eaten yet."

"Ha! Hold on." Connor said, pulling the knife from his belt. He cleared the vines from the cabin door and went inside. He had collected several melon-sized eggs from a nest lower in the valley a few days prior and kept them in a hollow at the back of the alcove. He brought them outside with a large skillet and a jar of rendered fat.

"What do we need those for? I hauled like, thirty pounds of those damn fish back from the beach."

"I don't eat those. They're as tasty as they are friendly, and I fry a hell of an egg."

Riley shook his head and started building a fire, but had no kindling yet, since Gaia had just left to get it. He looked off in the direction that she had gone and saw the trees shake, then their leaves dried up and fell off.

"What the hell was that?"

Fen ran out of the bush with his tail tucked between his legs, which made Connor very nervous. He had never been one to back down from anything before, let alone run from it. The two men set down what they were doing. They had no interest in finding out what in the world could have scared Fen, but they needed to make sure that Gaia was safe. Before they could take a step in that direction though, she emerged from the tree line with a bundle of twigs and small, dry branches that she'd collected for the fire.

"What happened?! Are you okay???" Connor asked, rushing over and noticing the ashy footprints that she was leaving behind.

"I'm fine…But I lost the berries" she told him, disappointed in herself.

"Don't worry about the berries. You're sure that you're okay? You've got to tell me what happened."

"Well…Ummm…This thing tried to sneak up on me, but Fen saw it first and then I saw it…But then it ran away…Look, I got some good sticks for the fire though!" she said, holding out the bundle and avoiding the topic of what had just gone down in the woods. Connor was still leery about whatever was out there, but Fen had settled down, which made him a little more at ease. He took the kindling from her, tussled her hair and sent her to go sit with Riley while he got the fire going.

Once the wood had burned down and the coals were ready, he tossed one full egg to Fen, then cracked the remaining egg into the pan with the melted fat. The smell wafted around and filled the area. Riley's mouth watered. Connor scooped the fried eggs with their deep orange yolks into carved wooden bowls and handed them out with matching spoons. The three of them buried their faces in their bowls and practically inhaled the delicious meal. As they were finishing up, a roar came from the path through the valley.

"Where did you get these eggs?" Riley asked with a hint of worry.

Connor looked back at him and tipped his head toward where Gaia had been foraging, as Fen got up and took off down the path toward it. There was a loud yelp, then silence. Moments later, Fen returned with the withered hindquarters of some feathered beast in his jaws. He strolled back up to the fire and laid down, like nothing had happened, chomping away on the sinewy carrion.

Everyone finished eating and scraped their bowls, letting the big pup lick them clean when they were done. Riley threw some wood on the embers and got the fire going again, while Connor tucked Gaia into bed. He came back with a bottle and tossed it to Riley, giving him a look that made it clear, he wanted answers. Riley yanked the cork and took a swig straight from the bottle.

"Ahh. I've got to warn you…" he said, passing the bottle.

"Let me guess, it's going to sound crazy?" he retorted, taking the bottle and smelling the smoky liquid before pouring it into glasses and setting them down beside him. He lowered his voice so that Gaia wouldn't overhear him, "Aliens have taken over the Earth. I'm pretty sure that my dog is part killer whale. And, that little girl in there grew an entire goddamn ecosystem in the time it took us to go fishing, and I don't think I need to remind you how that turned out. Oh, and I found her in a fucking crater. So please, spare me the warnings and just give it to me straight." He handed Riley a glass and waited for him to speak.

"Okay, let's see…Think of the orb like an emergency backup of the arkship's artificial intelligence. It needs a powerful CPU to function properly. Its onboard processor is insufficient and restricts it to the most rudimentary functions. While I was in that tank on the ship, they grafted something onto my skeleton called an AEGIS. The process was interrupted before it could be completed, and the AI was never fully integrated. Now it wants to do so, but without the nanomachines from the ship to print and install the remaining hardware, the software could overwrite my

consciousness... I'm not really into that sort of thing at this stage in my life, you know? Anyways, it turns out that the ark wasn't *completely* destroyed like I thought. The orb has detected its energy signature, coming from deeper within the mountain. That means, whatever is causing the signal is still functioning. It's probably the genetics lab, considering the changes to the surrounding environment. If it is, then it's almost certain that I'll find a cache of nanomachines there." Riley explained.

"The only problem?" Connor asked, sarcastically.

"I believe you referred to it as '*nightmare fuel*'? Also, the simple fact that I have no idea what it'll do to me. The AI is being somewhat vague with the details. Honestly, I don't know if it'd be wiser to just leave it alone and stick to something with a little more safety and certainty, like *fishing*." he joked.

With the mere suggestion of abandoning the mission, the orb took action. It quickly moved down his arm from his shoulder, opened up, then closed itself around his wrist, forming a locked gauntlet. Illuminated symbols around the glowing lens implied a countdown. It spoke to Riley again, confirming his suspicions and gave him an ultimatum. He was to complete the process and fulfill its mission, or forfeit control of his body and have his mind erased; upgrade or die.

It showed him that the AEGIS was designed to work symbiotically with the host. However, in dire situations, the AI could override this by spiking the brain with electricity and putting its host into a trauma-induced vegetative state. It would take rudimentary control over motor functions and have access to sensory input, but it would be more like a puppeteer than a pilot. The body's autonomic nervous system must then be controlled, just like any other part of the body. Too much strain on the AI would lead to potential system errors and catastrophic failure, killing the physical vessel. Death of the host was not ideal, but in situations that would justify an over-write, the AI would need to take into account many environmental factors, such as decomposition rates and range; as long as the muscles and tendons were intact, the body could move.

With access to the ark's nanomachines, the AI could not only maintain the body, but restructure the brain for smoother, more efficient operation. Given enough time, the AI would replace the dead organics with enhanced prosthetics and convert the cybernetic components to a fully robotic android form. The AI made this information very clear in Riley's mind, but it also emphasized the importance of symbiosis to the AEGIS's

design. It needed two halves to function as a whole. It was giving him the equivalent choice of the easy way, or the hard way.

PERVERSIONS OF NATURE

Leaving Gaia back at the lagoon with Fen, she'd have all of the protection she needed, while Connor took Riley to find what *he* needed to save his life. After a long journey upriver, they came to a compound built into the mountain where a spring fed a small lake. The vegetation around the water's edge was unnaturally thick with mangroves and mossy oaks, like a tropical jungle was trying to grow through a temperate forest.

Riley found a familiar door, but it was sealed tight. Connor pounded on it and tried to wedge it open with his knife, but it wouldn't budge. As soon as Riley laid his hand on it, the gauntlet lit up and the door opened, granting them entry.

"Think this is it?" Connor said, sarcastically.

Inside the building, a long hallway echoed with riotous hoots and howls and roars and screams. Riley recognized the internal architecture; they were definitely in another part of the ark. The walls were lined with sealed portholes that let them see into adjoining enclosures. They'd both stopped at different windows and peered through, trying to see what, if anything was inside.

Each window had a small inscribed plaque. The first one that Connor noticed read 'Sepia Ophiophagus'. He couldn't see anything in the partially aquatic habitat until the creature inside approached the viewing port and made itself visible. Its serpentine body shifted in colour, and its neck fanned out, revealing a hypnotic display of kaleidoscopic iridescence. It was beautiful, like nothing he'd ever seen. He leaned in, mesmerized and put his hand to the glass, trying to interact with it. The creatures head separated into eight tentacles with dripping syringe-like teeth that hooked back, toward its beaked throat.

He jumped back and bumped into Riley, who was staring through the port across from him into an empty habitat.

"What the hell are these things? What's in there?" Connor asked.

"Well, these plaques are a combination of Latin genera. *'Ursus Chelydra'* here, means Bear-Snapping turtle."

"Oh, I know him. Ornery bastard. Fen has to chase him off on occasion when he gets bold."

"Top of the falls? We've met."

"And, your colourful new buddy there's name means, Cuttlefish-King cobra. Probably don't take him out of his cage to pet him."

"They're hybrids."

"Ya, but...who made them? This ship was designed to terraform and populate a new world. Gene splicing was never really part of the program. That, and this ark predates Latin by a few thousand years. This wasn't a glitch. Somebody did this."

"Well, let's see if they're in."

Riley translated as they continued down the hall, passing by all manner of oddities. "*Isurus Mellivora*. Ugh, that's a Mako shark/Honey badger. *Harpia Mandrillus*; that's a Harpy eagle/Mandrill. *Piranha Rattus*; Piranha/rat. That's disgusting."

"I met *those* pricks when I found Fen. They're worse than they sound."

"Damn, *Smilodon Desmodontinae*...That's a sabre-toothed tiger/Vampire bat... and *Casuarius Dendrobates*, of course, is a cassowary-poison dart frog. Fuck me."

They made their way to the lone door at the end of the hall, and it slid open for them as they approached, then closed behind them when they entered the large, bright, circular arena. Identical doors lined the rounded walls, leading to more hallways and habitats. Above them, was an unlit viewing gallery, separated by a clear dome.

The intercom boomed, making them both jump.

"Gentlemen! Come in! Come closer, so I can see your faces." The boisterous voice said, through a heavy vocal fry.

"Who are you? What are you doing here?" Riley asked defensively.

"NO!! This is MY house! You will answer to ME!" the voice bellowed, flipping from hospitable to hostile and back again, sending distortion and feedback through the speakers. "Ahem. Forgive me, friends. It's just been so long since I've had...guests. I seem to have misplaced my manners" He said, collecting himself. His voice gained a false warmth, "Please, after you."

Connor and Riley looked at each other skeptically and remained silent, hoping that he would volunteer more information. They'd spotted a figure in the shadows above them, looking down from the gallery.

"Very well, then." The man said, coldly, as one of the doors opened to their left. "If you won't talk to *me*, then maybe you'd be more comfortable sharing with one of my children." He gloated, with a sinister tone. "Oh, what a lovely treat! I never get to show off like this. What an honour for you." He said with bipolar glee, as another door could be heard opening down that same hallway. "It is with great pride that I bring you…'*Theraphosa Cubozoa*' Isn't she beautiful?"

"Goliath bird-eater tarantula/Box jellyfish." Riley sighed, translating for Connor.

Bioluminescent hairs covered the arachnid's body, and it left a trail of silky tendrils from spinnerets on its pulsating, basketball-sized abdomen. It circled the room, again and again, covering the walls and floor around them with webbing. Connor and Riley were forced to the raised centre ring of the arena, and the main lights went out as a spotlight lit them up from above. They could see it scurrying around in the dark by the glowing hairs on its back and legs. Suddenly, it disappeared as the hairs went dark, but they could still hear the eerie patter of its feet.

There was a hiss and a thud, and the glowing hairs lit back up as they shot out from the darkness. Riley used the gauntlet to block most of them, but dozens made it past and stuck into of his arm, neck, and part of his face, like porcupine quills. He erupted in pain as the barbed hairs burrowed into his skin, releasing immobilizing toxins. As he fell to the ground, it rushed on top of him, frantically spinning a cocoon around his paralyzed body.

Connor punted the spider-thing as hard as he could, crippling three of its legs and sending it tumbling away. He pulled the strong webs off of his boots and realized his mistake immediately. The thick strands were laced with nematocysts that carried the same venom as its hairs. His hand felt like it was on fire and he couldn't move his arm.

Another door began to open.

"ENOUGH!" Connor roared, "That's enough…What do you want?" he panted as his breathing became laboured from the spreading toxins.

"Hmmph, yes, I would imagine so," Morrow said condescendingly.

Both doors closed and the floor around them electrified, burning the creature and its webs away, while the fumes were cycled out through filtered vents above the doors. Riley wasn't moving. The flesh around the embedded hairs had sizzled away and shed them to the ground. A fog poured out of the ventilation system and flooded the area, neutralizing the toxins.

"My name is *Doctor* Nathaniel Josef Morrow. This is *my* kingdom, and in my kingdom, *I am god*." His voice resonated throughout the arena, "I am creator and destroyer. I see all, and I know all. You live, because *I* will it!"

"Rrrriiight," Connor said under his breath.

"Lucky for you, I'm in need of a proxy. There is work to be done here, and I require a new specimen. You owe me a replacement."

A robotic foot-long millipede materialized from a slot in the floor. It climbed up Connor's leg, over his shoulder, and down his infected arm, attaching itself end to end, interlocking its sharp needly legs into its body and forming a tight band around his wrist. He felt a pinch and the bangle lit up with the same symbols as Riley's gauntlet, counting down in synchronicity.

"What *is* this?!" he shouted, clawing at it.

"Added insurance. I wouldn't tamper with it if I were you…Now then. I've been monitoring a nest, North East of here. Half a day, if you keep a good pace." He explained, "You will go there and collect a sample for me. In return, I'll make sure that your friend here gets what he needs. If you have not returned with it by the time the countdown finishes, he will die, and you will have to learn to wipe with the other hand."

"A sample of what? What am I going to find?"

"The brood mother will have rejoined her pack by now, but the hatchlings should be emerging soon." Morrow explained with deliberate ambiguity, "I need a tissue sample…If you can bring me an intact egg, I just may sweeten the pot. Now go!"

The door slid open behind Connor, as did the exit at the end of the hall. He looked back at Riley, lying wounded on the ground, then ran out of the building and the door sealed behind him as he left.

Morrow exited the viewing gallery and the lights came up as the door opened and he entered the lower arena. He hobbled in with a heavy limp and used a cane to walk, the result of a wound that hadn't healed properly and kept him from leaving unassisted.

Years ago, he was mauled by one of the first generation hybrids, narrowly escaping into a cave in the mountain, where he discovered the source of the extreme overgrowth in the region. A technician's headset connected his conscious thoughts to the ship and gave him control over many of the lab's remaining functioning systems. His brain waves were human, and his knowledge of science and medicine met the basic

requirements to operate it. With access to the systems, he took over control and made it his own.

The genetics facilities included a variety of isolated programmable habitats. They allowed cloned animals to grow to sexual maturity, increasing their rates of survival once they were released onto a newly terraformed world. The ark was not a small ship.

With the ship's AI absent, the nanomachines were dormant, and without them, the regeneration chambers could not rebuild his damaged organic tissue. He was trapped inside, too debilitated to escape anything that might come after him if he left. He'd sustained himself on the nutrient slurry that was fed into each habitat, and passed the time by experimenting with what the facility was capable of. He'd splice together different species, pitting his creations against each other in the arena, for his amusement. As time wore on, his grasp on reality became tenuous, and his sanity slipped away, leaving him in a very dark place.

Riley's face and arm were severely damaged by the corrosive toxins in the spider's barbed hairs. The skin in the affected area was completely dissolved, through the fatty tissue and into the muscle, in the worse parts, revealing the endoskeleton grafted to his bones. If the toxins had gone unchecked for any longer, it would have spread to his internal organs and killed him.

He woke up to the crippled man talking to himself and digging around in the open wounds with his hands, trying to expose more of the AEGIS.

"G-Get off of me!" Riley screamed in disgust.

"Oh! I was just admiring your enhancements. It's amazing what this technology is capable of…when it works." Dr. Morrow mumbled, shuffling back and wiping his hand on his tattered lab coat.

"Who are you?! Where's Connor?! What happened to me?!" Riley shouted frantically while his mind struggled to catch up. "Wait. That voice. It was you…You did this…you-"

"Shhhh, you must rest now." Morrow told him in a tone meant to be soothing, right before he cracked Riley in the head with his cane, knocking him out again.

Meanwhile, Connor walked back home through the night, where Gaia and Fen awaited his return. He didn't know what he was about to go up against and wasn't going to take any chances by facing it alone, besides, with Fen to carry him, he could make it there and back in a fraction of the time that it would've taken him to make it one way on foot.

Fen was in the lagoon, tossing a log into the falls and chasing it downstream when it popped back up, essentially playing fetch with himself. He could smell Connor, long before he could see him. He shook his wet fur off and ran up the beach to sit with Gaia while they waited for him to come around the bend. She was excited for them to return and had a look of confusion on her face when Connor showed up by himself. She ran over and jumped up, and he caught her in a tight hug, before setting her back down and calling Fen. He whispered into his ear and Fen went to go dig around in the supply cache by the cabin. Connor then took a knee and wiped the hair and dirt from Gaia's face.

"Hey sweetie, listen. I've got to go somewhere that isn't safe for little girls…and I've got to take the pup with me, okay?" Connor tried to explain, "But I-"

"…Where's Riley?" she asked as if she knew something was wrong.

"Riley's back at the mountain. I need to go get something so that I can bring him back. Everything will be okay, I promise you, but I need to hurr-" he said before she cut him off again.

"Riley's in trouble?! We have to help him!" She exclaimed, packing up her charcoal drawing sticks and some fruit into a bindle. "C'mon! He needs us!"

She put two fingers in her mouth and let out a sputtering attempt at a whistle. Fen dug around in a pile by the cabin, then hurried over, wearing a loose harness with saddle bags. Connor tightened the straps around Fen's chest and stared down at the brave little girl struggling to contain herself. He knew that he couldn't leave her here alone. With Fen gone, she'd be helpless if anything came sniffing around. She'd have to come along.

He brought her into the house and outfitted her the best he could with what he had available. She looked silly in the oversized riot gear, but it would help protect her if anything happened. He took down a blanket and cut a hole in the centre for her to wear as a poncho, and she flung her arm around so that the front of the blanket went over her shoulder and hung like a cape. She put her hands on her hips looked toward the mountain with confidence and determination. Connor couldn't help laughing but stifled himself when he realized that she was serious.

Once Gaia was ready, he sent her outside to make sure that Fen was ready too. Connor moved his bed and dug through the hard-packed dirt until he came to a large flat rock, a few inches below the surface. He heaved the stone out of the hole and set it down beside him, then reached in and pulled out what appeared to be a gun of sorts, though it had no ammunition

or moving parts. The body was built like a fifty-pound sledge and shaped like a drop point knife. Its surface had a texture like Damascus steel, scarred with Lichtenberg figures. His touch brought it to life and the ornate weapon resonated with power. The pistol grip was moulded to his hand, and he picked it up as if it were weightless, like a natural extension of himself. Memories of his past flickered at the fringe of his thoughts but faded before he could make anything of them. He could already feel its pull.

Outside, Fen trotted up and down the beach, like a show horse with his most regal posture, while Gaia rode in the sling saddle attached to the harness. The elation on her face gave Connor pause, knowing the danger that he was about to put her in. He was aware that if she were to be hurt in any way, it was solely on him and he couldn't let that happen. Connor donned an old pair of aviator goggles and strapped a large holster to his thigh.

"I need you to listen to me very carefully. It won't take us long to get where we need to go, and when we get there, I need you to stay *completely* quiet and out of sight. Otherwise, I might not be able to protect you…Do you understand?" Connor said, holding Gaia's hand and staring up at her in the saddle.

She nodded her head and gave him a little smile instead of saying anything, to show him that she understood.

He put his boot in one of the saddle straps and climbed up onto the big dog's back. Lowering the goggles over his eyes, and looping the short reins around his wrist, he patted Fen twice on the neck, and they were off.

Fen leapt up the rocks and over the edge of the falls with ease. He bounded over the rapids and crossed the river onto a game trail, where he could really let loose. As they gained speed, Gaia felt herself being forced back into the saddle sling. The wind whipped around her, and she held onto Connor's waist as tightly as she could. Fen's muscles rippled with every launching step he took. He was a blur, hurtling through the forest. Connor stayed low, like a jockey, to cut wind resistance and keep his grip. He'd been thrown before, and been caught by his fair share of low hanging branches, having since learned from his mistakes.

It was dark again by the time they reached the nesting site, but the nearly full moon made it easier for their eyes to adjust. They stayed downwind and found a vantage point on the high ground to survey the area before moving in. Boulders on the ridge provided cover and a safe place for Gaia to hide while Connor went looking for the nest itself.

"This town seems empty. Either we're too late, and they're already gone, or they haven't hatched yet, which would mean that momma could still be around." He looked at the band around his wrist and actually hoped for the latter.

Connor unloaded Gaia from the saddle and left her with Fen, then crept down to search the houses. Most were inaccessible, because of the extensive damage. Falsetto snarls and screeching sounds drew him to a demolished building that hid a partially excavated bunker. He approached cautiously and discovered a nest inside of the pit, up against the wall of the shelter. A hatch behind the nest had been breached and pried open at the top, but the fortified door remained mostly intact. Large egg shells littered the hollow, with indentations in the soil where others had been. The eggs were about the shape and twice the size of a rugby ball, with a texture like an oyster shell.

"Imagine passing that." He chuckled to himself, wincing at the thought, but quieted down when he noticed that some of the eggs were cracked open from the outside in, and realized that he may not be alone.

After a moment of waiting in near silence, he was sure that there was something else down there with him. Muffled sloshing and scrapping noises came from further into the nest but stopped as soon as he began to approach. In the back, He found two intact eggs among several half-eaten bodies of the nestlings. He squatted down and needed to use both hands to pick up just one. It was heavy and shifted its weight around inside when it was moved. He carried it out of the hole and started hiking back up toward the ridge, when Fen quickly stood on alert, looking in his direction. He stopped and turned on the spot when he heard the shriek from behind him.

"Shit."

This young alien was bigger than the other hatchlings; about the size of a Great Dane, and was covered in their blood. It must have been the offspring from a previous generation that had returned for an easy meal. It postured up and hissed, baring its needly teeth, then dove forward, charging at Connor. He stumbled back and dropped the egg as he reached for his weapon. It hit the ground with a damp crunch. The alien juked and snatched it up, tumbling over and scrambling to defend it. Connor drew and charged his weapon as he trained it on the alien. It swiped and snarled at him while fumbling with the egg, flipping it around and trying to find the weak spot. It peeled away the rough outer layer and plunged its clawed hand though, tearing out and devouring chunks of dripping meat.

Connor took the shot. A beam of tightly focused plasma ripped through the alien's torso, disintegrating part of its rib cage and knocking it back, like it'd been hit by a truck. Because most of its vital organs are protected in the centre mass of its lower body, the blast was not *immediately* lethal. Though the wound had been cauterized, the alien struggled to its feet and tried frantically to pack dirt into the gaping hole. Two younger hatchlings smelled the seared flesh and emerged from under some rubble nearby. They circled around the injured alien, testing its reach and mobility before pouncing on its back to finish the job and cannibalize its remains. Their teamwork quickly broke down over the small amount of meat left on its bones, but the squabble ended when their attention was drawn back to Connor, who'd snuck back down into the nest to retrieve the second egg.

The young aliens moved quietly, practically slithering over to the entrance. Once he had the other egg in his arms, he hurried back out, right into their ambush. While still concealed, one of them slashed his calf. He stumbled forward with his weight on one leg, as the other jumped down onto his back from above, sending him crashing into the dirt. The egg wobbled and rolled under the partially collapsed porch. Connor brought himself up onto one knee and reached over his head, grabbing the small alien by its upper arms and throwing it hard onto the road. He turned to the second alien that was poised to attack, when Fen rushed to his aid, slamming his jaws shut around it. He shook the flailing corpse back and forth until parts began to separate and blood spatter painted the dirt.

"NO." Connor gasped when he realized that the other alien was no longer laying in the road.

He looked up to the ridge and watched helplessly as it scurried up and over the rocks, where Gaia was hiding by herself. As it disappeared, she let out a bone-chilling scream. Fen sprinted back to the rocks and Connor grabbed the harness as he passed, pulling himself up into the saddle and nearly dislocating his arm in the process. Fen was there within seconds, ready to tear the thing to shreds. Connor jumped off and rushed over to Gaia who was rocking back and forth, holding her knees and sobbing.

It looked as if the alien's shadow had been scorched into the rock and the only thing left of it blew away in the breeze.

"W-why didn't you shoot them?" she asked, trembling, "I saw you shoot the other one with your gun…and you just let the other one go…and I *had* to-" she said before going quiet.

"I didn't *let* it go. I hesitated, then it got away while I was distracted. That's not the point. I told you that this would be dangerous...but it seems that you can hold your own."

"You made me do it!" She cried. "It was gonna eat me! It's not my fault!"

"You're right it's not. I'm sorry that I hesitated...I shouldn't have brought you...I was afraid." he admitted.

"Afraid of what?!" She snapped back at him.

"Losing you. Losing control. Just losing." He told her, "...and it's not a *gun.*"

"*Whatever.*" She huffed.

"If one of those got you, I'd be beside myself...But if *I* ever lost control and hurt you in *any* way, I wouldn't be able to live with myself." He said, holstering his weapon as he turned back toward town.

Connor limped down the hill and pulled the egg from under the porch. Fen trotted down and joined him with Gaia, saddled up on his back. He packed the egg into one of the saddlebags and went back into the nest to find a counterbalance. Grabbing a cinder block from the rubble, he loaded it into the other bag to even out the load.

"Okay. I'm all ready to go. You good Fen?" he asked his beastly companion, who just wiggled his stout tail at him. "Gaia? We good?" he asked, looking back over his shoulder, but got no response from her as she pouted to herself with her arms crossed.

"...hmph."

"...Okay then. Off we go."

There was no way that he could take her with him this time. When they arrived at the base of the mountain, he tossed away the block from the saddlebag and took the egg with him, before he sent Gaia back home with Fen. She looked back at him with tears in her eyes as she rode away. They'd gotten off to a rocky start, but he knew that beating himself up over it wouldn't help the situation, so he switched his focus to the one that truly deserved the blame.

Connor didn't bother waiting for the door to open. His eyes blazed as he charged the weapon and did it himself. The door gave like wet tissue and the walls smouldered from the blast. He stormed down the hallway and began charging his weapon again when the door at the end opened for him.

"Whoa! Whoa! Whoa! Let's settle it down. There is no need for this. Those were *perfectly* good, until y- err... We have a deal!" Morrow shouted

over the loudspeaker, trying to reason with him from the lit up viewing gallery as he entered the arena. "I see you've brought me an egg! Good boy!"

A vein throbbed in Connor's forehead, and he took a shot at the doctor, but the blast was inconceivably nullified by the dome. He began to sweat and grind his teeth as the weapon charged again. Morrow raised his arm and tapped his wrist. Connor looked down at the metal wristband and the charge that had built up in the conduit dissipated as he slowed his breath and struggled to collect himself.

"We had a deal, and I am a man of my word. You've *graciously* brought me what I'd asked for, and for that, you have my *sincerest*…recognition. As for the bonus we discussed, I'll overlook the surprise renovations on your way in. I can give you what you want, as soon as I know that you won't attack me…again. Now we're even, yes?" Morrow appealed.

Connor holstered his weapon and shoved the egg with his boot, rolling it to the door at the other side of the arena.

"Take it. Get this thing off of me and let us go." he demanded.

"How do I know that you won't just come back and kill me, once you have what you need?"

Connor's teeth ground together, and the muscles in his jaws flared out before he gathered his words."Like you said, we have a deal. I too am a man of my word. You'll never see us again once this is over." He said, undoing his belt and placing the holster on the ground to show his willingness for a peaceful resolution.

"An impressive show of civility for a Neanderthal." Morrow jabbed, flaunting the upper hand.

The door below the viewing gallery opened, and Riley stepped out. The wounds from the hybrid's toxins were gone, but everything that had been damaged was replaced with cybernetic prosthetics. His eyes were vacant, and his movements were cumbersome when he walked out to retrieve Morrow's prize.

"What'd you *do* to him?!" Connor bellowed as Riley left the arena with the egg.

"I don't see what you're so upset about. I administered the nanomachines, and they've bonded with the AEGIS, *beautifully*." The doctor said flippantly, "I've simply partitioned his consciousness so that the AI is in control of his motor functions. Less talk, more… *obedience*." Morrow said, grinning mischievously. "Now you'll have someone to watch that little girl of yours, while you're out collecting specimens for me. It was *very* irresponsible

of you to put her in danger like you did. Tsk, tsk, tsk. You may have figured it out by now, but that wristband isn't coming off *quite* yet. I still have need of your unique talents. You can start by bringing me that wonderful '*Lupus Orcinus*' of yours. You can keep the saddle, we won't be needing it."

Connor went wild with rage and reached for the holster on the ground. He drew the weapon and it flared wildly as he infused it with a massive charge. His pupils glowed with a golden light and electricity arced up his arms. His power surged and overloaded the band around his wrist, unintentionally triggering it. Its scorched metal legs began to rotate and revolve, faster and faster, like alternating teeth on a chainsaw. The bangle closed in on itself, shredding flesh and sawing through bone. His vision blurred and his ears rang as he let out a horrible wail. He dropped to his knees and gripped his forearm as tightly as he could, to keep from bleeding out.

"Perhaps not." Morrow sighed, as the lights in the viewing gallery dimmed, and he disappeared.

Every door, aside from the exit and the one Riley had come from, opened, and Connor could hear what was coming to finish him off. Growls, shrieks, and roars echoed down the hallways when the gates opened to the arena in a cacophony of death.

Every hair on Connor's body stood on end and there was a flash.

He was immune to the damage of the intense outburst, but not the seductive nature of its power. He'd charged his weapon with enough energy to punch a hole in the ship, only reserving enough to ensure that he'd be able to make it out afterward.

His weapon; the conduit, channelled his power. To varying degrees, it would insulate and direct the energy that he created, as he needed it. Without it, he was unable to cap his output, and to use it unfiltered, came with arduous consequences. His power was like a drug; the more he used, the more he wanted to, and the harder it was to stop. To unleash that power unchecked was its own kind of overdose. Without the conduit, there was nothing to taper his output. He could unleash a blast powerful enough to shatter mountains, but it was always too much output for his body to handle. Each time he'd gone too far, his memories were wiped, and he spent the next few days in a coma, pummelled by the force. This time, he'd have to inhibit his urges if he was going to make it back home.

Flesh charred and metal began to glow in the half second before the white flash. Burnt trees lined a scar in the earth that reached out to the horizon from where he stood. Lake water poured into the cavity, and the air

billowed with steam as the trench floor rapidly cooled. Connor's adrenaline redlined and he pressed his bloody, stumped arm into the searing hot metal in an attempt to cauterize it, then charged into the mist, through the bath warm flood water and out into the wilderness.

His restraint granted him the conscious wherewithal to separate himself from the conduit to block out temptation, and he hurled it into the half drained lake. Energy arced back like it was reaching out to him before it plunged into the dark water and sank to the bottom. As soon as it was out of sight, he felt a bit of relief, but not so much that he didn't have to fight with himself to not dive in after it.

He ran like it was chasing after him, through the thick bush, with steam rolling off of his tattered clothes and melted boots. He ran until his legs cramped up, and his sides were in stitches when he hit the ground completely winded. Sweat soaked through his charred clothes and the spit running down his chin was frothy. His heart felt like it was going to jump out of his chest if he laid still for another second, so he got up and pushed through the pain that tangoed with euphoria, as he was flooded with endorphins.

"Move." Connor grunted to himself to push through the pain.

When he'd nearly made it home, he collapsed in a shallow part of the river. Physically incapable of continuing, he nodded off and woke up choking on the water splashing over his face. Connor felt a strange sensation from his submerged stump and held it up to see the engorged parasites that covered it. He grabbed one by its sausage-sized, tadpole tail body and pulled, but its head was embedded like a tick. The harder he pulled, the deeper the legs clawed in. They were getting heavy with his blood, and it took all of his remaining strength, just to keep his head above the rising water.

Fen caught his scent, even from the heavily diluted blood running down the river and over the falls. He found him floundering in the rising swift water and bounded up through the rapids to save him. Connor was battling exhaustion and going on fumes when Fen appeared over him, casting a broad shadow over his sunburnt face. He held onto the fur around his neck as he helped him up, out of the water by taking his weight with his muzzle. Fen shrugged, and Connor flopped over onto his back, where he stayed for the short ride home.

The adrenaline had worn off, and he was woozy from blood loss. Tick-leeches on his arm dangled off of him, like water balloons, but he couldn't cut them away or they'd become spigots. Gaia was down by the beach collecting shells and paid no attention to his return. Connor went to

the cabin, opened his footlocker and ripped the lid off of the whiskey crate inside, then grabbed a bottle and his flip lighter. Outside, he poured the bottle over the leeches and lit the alcohol. Their soft flesh thrashed and blistered as they pushed desperately to retract from his flesh, tearing themselves apart trying escape. The dead parasites dropped into the sand and oozed like used condoms as he relentlessly stomped their bodies. When the rush faded, the dizziness that came over him was reminder enough that there was no time for messing around; if he didn't take care of his wounds quickly, he was going to die.

5

SLAVE

Riley stood at attention, like a good soldier awaiting orders, while Morrow clamoured over his trophy. He was a slave now, and a prisoner in his own body; seeing and hearing everything that was happening, but with no way to affect it. They could both hear the carnage in the arena, even through the thick walls of the clean room. He wanted, so badly, to grab *any* of the surgical tools from off of the table in front of him and murder the bastard that did this to them, but all he could do was observe and obey.

Robotic arms held the egg in place, inside of a refrigerated incubation chamber which slowed the alien's metabolism, keeping it from hatching on its own. A third of the shell was cut away and removed, revealing the sedated infant, curled up inside. Morrow looked on with his face pressed up against the glass, glancing back and forth between the baby and the control screen he was fiddling with.

Riley watched on beside him, dead calm, on the outside. He thought that nothing could shock him anymore, but this was the first time he'd seen a real alien. He was both scared and fascinated by it, forgetting his situation, just for a moment.

The alien shifted inside of a slimy translucent membrane that retracted like cooled elastic when another arm delicately cut it open. It lazily blinked its oversized eyes and tried to move, but the cold kept it sluggish and weak. The alien's plates and spines were still soft nubs growing out of delicate skin. It yawned, displaying rows of needle teeth and slowly stretched out its eight sinewy limbs, with unworn, razor-sharp talons.

"Are you enjoying this? Does this interest you?" Morrow asked Riley, "Well?…" Riley stared at him silently with no physical response. "Bah!" Morrow grumbled, accessing the implant on the back of Riley's head.

The implant wasn't part of the AEGIS, but a device installed by Morrow to bypass the AI and compartmentalize Riley's consciousness. It was the same thing that he used to control his hybrids. They all had one, including the doctor himself; the master that controlled the slaves. Morrow adjusted the settings in the implant, unlocking the partition and returning possession of some of his faculties. Riley felt his mind flood out and

reconnect with his body. He examined his new augmentations and stretched his tense muscles, then with a surprise move, spun around a grabbed Morrow by his throat.

"I'll kill you!" he screamed, standing over him and wrapping his other hand around too. He wanted to wring his neck until his eyes burst and his head popped off of his shoulders like a cork from a champagne bottle. He wanted to so badly, but he couldn't. Every fibre of his being was screaming "*DO IT!*" but his body wasn't responding.

"Oh! What's the matter, boy? Can't bring yourself to do it?" Morrow said, taunting him.

"Wh-wh" Riley muttered to himself with tears welling up in his remaining organic eye. His hands were where they needed to be, but no matter how hard he tried to squeeze, he couldn't muster more than a gentle touch.

"You're pathetic. The implant has fail-safes that prevent you from doing any harm to me. Now, help me up." Morrow demanded, and Riley did so, without hesitation, or of his own free will.

"Asimov's first law of robotics. A robot may not injure a human being or, through inaction, allow a human being to come to harm." Morrow lectured, even though he knew that it was bullshit. The man was certainly impressed by the sound of his own voice.

"I'm not a robot!" Riley protested.

"Well, technically, you're a cyborg...But for all intents and purposes, you're my little helper bot." The doctor told Riley, knowing that it would infuriate him. "Now, go clean up the arena, robot. My children can be messy eaters." He ordered, "and once you've got them all put away in their habitats, I want you to bring me that joy buzzer your dead friend brought. Now get out of my sight, robot. *I've* got important work to do."

The slave implant compelled Riley to let him go and leave the room, even though every bit of him willed against it. The doctor cackled as Riley obediently exited the lab. He fought against the urges the implant imposed upon him as it marched him down the hallway, but with the AEGIS's prime directive bypassed, he was helpless against it.

The AI's access to the ship was limited by the implant but allowed Riley to enter the arena since it pertained to Morrow's orders. Several security doors slid open before the main gate, which he was surprised to find, was welded shut. He took the elevator up to the viewing gallery and felt some relief and a bit of hope when the doors opened, and he saw daylight.

Water leaked in from the lake outside and mixed in with the ruptured aquatic habitats as they flooded into the arena and washed out with the burnt blood and bones that littered it. The protective dome was warped and dripping with condensation from the steam off of the recently solidified, dripping metal gates and walls. Scorch marks were etched deep, through both the arena and out the base of the mountain.

Riley noticed a smeared hand and footprints in the ashy muck leading from the base of the conical dugout and disappearing into the water. He knew that Connor was still alive, but then it dawned on him that there'd be no keeping it a secret from Morrow. He returned to the lab to give his report. The doctor stood up from the incubation chamber and cracked his neck and back, then hobbled over to Riley and looked up at him expectedly.

"Did you get lost?!" he chirped, sarcastically. "What are you doing back here already?"

"The arena is inaccessible. The damage is extensive and beyond repair. The hybrids are gone and so is the weapon." Riley told him, giving the information requested, and by force of will, volunteering nothing more.

"…Gone…" The doctor muttered as his eye twitched and the muscles in his clenched jaw bulged. A throbbing vein grew in his forehead, and his face took on a red hue. "GONE!?!" He shouted through his teeth, punching something into his control pad. Riley's arms dropped to his side, and he was frozen in place again. Morrow raised his cane over his head, winding up to strike. "You did this! You brought this on yourself!" he snarled as he swung, aiming for his shoulder, but gleaning off and cracking Riley on the side of his face. His cheek turned purple, and his eye swelled shut. He felt every bit, but couldn't so much as flinch. If Morrow felt any bit of remorse for the accident, he didn't show it.

A notification chimed from the control panel, and Morrow's rage suddenly left him. He turned from Riley and shuffled excitedly over to the incubator. A monitor indicated that the temperature had risen to 100°F. He was allowing it to wake up. The DNA extraction and analysis of the sample was complete, and the system was ready to accept it for genetic recombination.

There was no need to thaw out the infant for the process to finish any faster, but the doctor's arrogance and curiosity had gotten the better of him. With no available habitats, the incubator would serve as its cage until they were rebuilt. A cramped cage was fine by the doctor, but the hatching was already trying desperately to get out.

"Ugh. There's a light blade in the maintenance locker. Use it on the door." Morrow ordered, releasing Riley from the lockout and handing him a cartridge with three metal pucks, each about the size of a pocket watch. "Implants. The same as yours. Don't worry, there is no brain surgery required. Just press it to the back of their head and the device implants itself." He explained, then gestured to the incubator "If you fail me again, I'll feed what's left of you to this little sweetie. Then I'll have myself a proper assistant, I think."

Riley took the implants and left. He cut through the gate into the arena and waded into the murky water that had risen considerably since he'd seen it last. The footprints had washed away, but he knew where he was going. He marched through a storm in the middle of the night to get back. The cold rain's numbing sting had him losing concentration and allowing the AI to autopilot. His cybernetic eye could see a much broader spectrum, higher frame rate and resolution than he could naturally, allowing him to move through the forest at night without the hinderance of the dark. Riley traced his path back down river, through the woods, to the plateau above Connor's lagoon. Light shined out through cracks in the cabin walls, and he could hear Connor and Gaia inside, even over the rain and falls. The AEGIS had built him a new ear along with the eye, which actively filtered and amplified their voices when he focused on them. He climbed down the slick rock face, using his augmentations to anchor himself as he went, and waited under the overhang, in the shadows and out of the rain, listening in.

Inside, Connor sat by the fire, getting ready to perform surgery on himself to prevent infection and save the rest of the arm. After rushing Gaia into the next room to draw, he then tied off his arm with a rubber hose below the elbow. Sanitizing his knives with fire and alcohol, he took a swig from the bottle, then bit down on a chunk of leather and injected what would pass for anesthetic into his forearm.

With his scalpel-sharp fillet knife, he carved away as much of the dead tissue as he could, trying not to cut too deeply into living flesh. He pulled bone fragments out of his muscle and sopped up the blood with boiled rags, heated in a pot over the fire. When there wasn't enough skin to cover the stump, he had to clip and cauterize the ends of exposed bone with red-hot pruning shears. The crunch jolted his bones, and he felt the ache all the way up into his shoulder. Connor's eyes fluttered, and he threw up on the ground between his feet, then wiped his face with his sleeve and tried to thread the needle to sew himself up. His hand was trembling, and he tried,

over and over, but couldn't line up the eye with the tip of the thread sticking out of his mouth. He needed help.

"Gaia? Can you come in here for a minute, I need a hand with something really quick." Connor hollered but got no answer. "Gaia, please, I need your help."

Nothing.

He shot more anesthetic into his arm then draped a clean rag over it and stood up. As soon as Connor was on his feet, the room began to spin. He lost his balance and slipped in the vomit, then stumbled forward and crashed through the door. The rag pulled away from his arm, and he fell onto the ground in front of the bed where Gaia sat, polishing up some shells that she'd found earlier.

Riley heard the scream from outside.

She knew that he was hurt, but she didn't know until then, how badly. He'd startled her when he fell in, but it was the bloody stump that made her scream. The petals dropped from the flower in the bottle by her bed, and she backed away, not out of fear for herself, but for him. The colour ran out of Connor's face, and his once dark hair became streaked with silvery white, as he felt his life-force being wrenched from his body. He scrambled to his feet and ran out of the room, putting his shoulder to the door as he charged through it into the rain.

"Calm yourself. To control your power, you need to control your emotions." A soothing, ethereal voice told Gaia. " Your negativity will sap the life from everything around you. Channel that energy and use it to heal. The well of energy is not infinite and must be replenished. You need to work hard to find the balance, to save those around you, but also yourself." the sage-like voice said before trailing off, like an echo in her mind.

Connor smashed out the door and plowed through Riley, who was sneaking up on the cabin. The cartridge of slave implants went flying, and Connor rolled on the ground, holding his arm. His momentum knocked Riley back, and he hit his head hard off of the rocky ground. A spark shot from his implant, then two more, and he could feel static in his head from the rain entering the cracked casing. Riley stood up under his own free will and reached to the back of his skull. He dug his fingertips in, under the edges of the tiny puck and pulled. He felt his skin tear away, like peeling off a scab, and a strange sensation of pulling roots, then everything went black. He collapsed in the rain with the implant in his hand and blood running out of a small hole in the back of his head.

Gaia ran outside after Connor to convince him that it was okay now. She ran over to him, and he flinched when she came near. She held her arms out and offered her hand to show him that the danger was over and he hesitantly took it. He felt a warm energy flowing into him, from her hand, through his body, to his amputated forearm. The hand he'd lost was growing back. He thought for sure he'd overdone it on the anesthesia. Tendons formed and anchored fresh muscles to new bones that grew from the stump. Nerves and veins webbed their way through, as baby-soft skin covered his new hand. He'd need to build the calluses back up, but aside from that, it was perfect. Everything that had been taken from him was returned, better than before.

"I...I...Holy shit. I had no idea you could do that." he panted, overcome by it.

"Umm, ya. YA."

Gaia's self-worth grew, and she began to feel like she might have a purpose. Connor saw it too, and the fear washed away, like his tears of joy in the pouring rain. He laid on his back with his new hand in front of his face, blocking his eyes from the downpour and admiring what would have otherwise been regarded as a miracle.

Riley slid down the wet rock and came to rest, partially submerged in the lagoon. Connor snapped to and hurried over, pulling Gaia with him. Neither of them expected to see him there, and it was another test of Gaia's self-control when she saw what had happened to him. Connor pulled him from the water and into the cabin, out of the rain. He put him on the bed and grabbed the leftover clean rags from the other room. Gaia stood beside the bed holding Riley's hand, trying to heal him like she did moments ago. Connor came back, then sat Riley up and leaned him forward when he saw the red stained hair at the back of his head.

"I tried to fix him. I tried, but-" Gaia told him, worried and confused.

"Hey, this isn't your fault. Not even a little bit. Okay?" Connor assured her, and she nodded, wiping her cheeks dry.

He parted Riley's hair to examine the source of the blood. Where he should have found a wound, there was more of the AEGIS's cybernetics. Gaia couldn't heal him because the AEGIS had already replaced the damage to his scalp, skull, and brain like it did with his injuries from the arena. Riley's eye fluttered, and his optic sensor blinked on as he sat straight up, wide awake and startled. He looked around and saw Gaia's surprised smile and Connor's concerned frown.

"Restrain me! I'm being controlled!" He warned them.

Gaia stepped back toward the door and looked to Connor for direction. He brought her out of the room and sat her down by the fire, then grabbed some rope and the fire poker and went back in. Riley was out of the bed and standing in front of the tarnished mirror on the wall, staring at himself with his back to Connor. He turned when he saw him come in behind him and raised his hands in surrender when he saw the fire poker held against Connor's leg.

"Wait. You don't need that. I'm back in control now." Riley told him.

"That was quick." Connor said sarcastically, "I think I'll just hold on to it for now. That okay with you?"

Riley nodded, and Connor held up the rope then looked over at the chair beside the bed. Riley knew what he was getting at. He pulled out the chair and sat down.

"Here, this should help explain things," Riley said, setting down the implant that he'd pulled from his own head. Its metallic tendrils dangled over the edge of the nightstand, sticky with blood and still wriggling, like a bundle of horsehair worms.

"What *is* that?!" Connor shouted, cocking back the poker, ready to smash it.

"Slave implant. Morrow put that thing in my head after you left. He made me his minion; he made me a prisoner in my own body. He maimed and tortured me…And then he sent me after you and Gaia."

"I'll kill him." Connor snarled.

"No." Riley shot back, "*I* will."

"Isn't *that* proof that he's not in control? I mean, this 'slave implant' isn't exactly implanted anymore and you're sitting here, plotting to kill the guy that you think is controlling you." Connor reasoned.

"You don't know what it's like to lose your free will."

"I know better than you'd think," he replied, admiring his new hand, while considering how lucky he'd been that his disfigurement wasn't permanent, and that Riley would have to live with the consequences of his for the rest of his life. He looked over the cybernetics that covered nearly a third of Riley's body, then back to his perfectly regenerated hand. When Connor lost control, it was still a part of himself that would take over, but to lose control and have someone else running the show, while you helplessly watch, was incomparable.

"Are you high?" Riley asked manically. "You're supposed to be interrogating a cyborg sent to kidnap you, and you're just staring your hand

like it's the craziest thing you've ever seen. What am I missing here? If there was ever a time to Bogart a joint, this isn't it."

"I'm sorry for what happened to you," Connor said, tossing the rope aside.

"What are you doing?" Riley looked at him like he'd lost his mind. "You have to tie me up so that I can't hurt you or Gaia."

"No, you're not going to hurt us." Connor said, laying the fire poker across Riley's lap. Riley was flabbergasted and almost wanted to pick it up just to teach him a lesson. Connor turned his back to him and dug around in the footlocker at the end of the bed, while Riley quietly got up and left the room, shaking his head.

"Riley?" Connor called out when he turned around to see an empty chair. For a moment, he questioned his judgement in trusting him. "Where'd you go, bud?" He walked apprehensively to the door and pulled open the divider. Riley sat in front of the fire, holding Gaia in his arms, rocking back and forth, humming some lullaby with a strange electric tone behind his voice.

Connor stepped into the room, holding the fire poker in a tight fist and walked up behind them. He let out an exasperated sigh of relief when Gaia opened her eyes a crack and smiled at him, then went back to sleep. He set the poker back in its holder by the fire and took a seat beside them.

"Guess you were right." Riley said, staring into the flames.

"Glad to hear it." Connor said, unwrapping the protective cloth from around a couple of whiskey tumblers and setting them down on the table with a fresh bottle.

"No." Riley stopped him, "Not yet." he said with the reflection of the fire in his eyes. "There's something I- we need to do first. None of us are safe while he's out there." he proclaimed, stroking Gaia's hair. "We're going back."

"Here we go. What's your plan?" Connor asked, clapping his hands and rubbing them together excitedly.

"When the rain stops, we are going to find the other implants and gut them. We'll take the shells and make it appear that I've captured you and that everything went as Morrow intended." Riley explained, "I've already duplicated the signal that the implants transmit. Once we find and deactivate the others, I can broadcast those as well, and when he sees that I have you, his arrogance will allow us to get close enough that I can take him out. He's completely blinded by his own ego. He'll never see it coming."

WHEN STRENGTH IS A WEAKNESS

Several hours prior

Dark storm clouds rolled in as the sun sat low in the sky. Cool rain spat down, and Fen watched on as Connor hurried Gaia inside. Worried about his human, he began to grow restless with them indoors, but then something else caught his attention. Two distinct scents cut through the petrichor, not far down the path toward the coast. With Connor back, Fen left Gaia with him and disappeared into the woods after the trespassers.

He stuck to his game trails to follow the scents that he'd picked up, and found a small, well-hidden camp near the wrecked catamaran. The camp was empty, but he could sense that they were close. Fen circled the camp over and over; he knew they were there, but he just couldn't find them. He tossed the lean-to shelter and searched the trees for movement, sniffing the air. The smell was right in front of him, but nothing was there. Fen was getting frustrated. Even the rain wasn't falling the way it should.

A twig snapped and the illusion faded. A young woman was standing in front of him, backing away slowly, until she realized that Fen had finally seen her, and she bolted. The chase ended as quickly as it started when the source of the second scent showed itself. A hideous giant, made of callus and muscle, grabbed Fen around his chest, then lifted and slammed him into the ground on the other side of the camp. He had never felt such strength and didn't know what to make of it. He'd always been at the top of the food chain, but this new challenger made for a worthy contest.

Fen rolled through the landing and launched back with incredible agility. He sunk his teeth into the large man's forearm and shook his head violently, pulling him off balance and whipping him to the ground. He stood over him, snarling with terrifying ferocity as the man sat in the fetal position, covering his arm and audibly sobbing. Fen approached him carefully, maintaining a low rumbling growl, warning him to yield.

"Stop." A calm, confident, ethereal voice commanded. "We are not your enemies."

The voice in Fen's mind spooked him, and his senses went on high alert, trying to find the source. While he was distracted, the hulking mound of muscle stood and swung a heavy back fist, connecting with Fen's side as he let out a yelp. He got up more slowly this time, limping forward and whimpering. When he man assumed the fight was over and relaxed his guard, Fen didn't waste a second of his bluff, as he leapt around, out of his reach and raced toward the woman, who strangely hadn't fled.

"Clever boy!" she said, praising him and waving off her bodyguard.

Her soothing presence made him feel at ease. He didn't know why, but it didn't seem to matter. He bowed his giant head down to hers, and she pressed her forehead into his, where she disappeared into the small blind spot between his eyes. She reached up and scratched behind his ears like she was hugging the hood of a car and Fen let out a low, rumbly, contented moan as he nuzzled into her.

"Take me to them." She whispered, holding the harness and looking up at him.

He bowed down, and she climbed into the sling. They turned away from the wrecked camp and headed upstream toward the lagoon, as the lumbering hulk stomped through the mud, trying to keep pace.

The rain was tapering off, and it was light enough that Riley was outside, trying to find the cartridge he'd lost earlier that morning. He heard them coming. Connor heard it too and joined him out on the rocks, staring into the dark misty woods.

When they came up the trail, Fen ran up the beach and excitedly presented the young woman to Connor like a gift, but under her influence, he was just as much presenting Connor to her. She looked down on them, paying particular attention to the AEGIS and smirking. They smiled back, entranced by her bewitching looks, hidden under the grime of the road.

"Would one of you get me a towel? I'm soaking wet." She said, pushing the hair out of her face and over her ear.

"I've got it!" Riley said, turning to the cabin, oddly overeager to please.

"No, I'll do it! You don't know where anything is." Connor countered, grabbing Riley's shoulder hard and holding him in place.

Riley saw the fight in Connor's eyes and felt a familiar urge himself, which tipped him off to at least part of what was going on. He backed off and let Connor go for the towels. Riley used the AEGIS to scan his mind for intruders, but detected no current foreign agents, though he felt that something was teasing at the fringes.

He'd been building defences against another remote hijacking since he ripped out Morrow's implant, but this was different. This was alive. It was her in his head, and she was strong. Riley would've stood no chance on his own, so he could hardly blame Connor. The AEGIS' AI was now integrated with his mind, and they were able to learn from the telepathic prodding. The partition that was once Riley's prison would now act as a trap for any uninvited presence that would defile the sanctity of his mind again.

The rain had stopped, and Connor returned with a stack of soft pelts from off of the bed. Fen laid down, letting her off, and she took one of the large furs to wrap around herself. Rubbing her arms and subtly pouting, she shot Connor a look that sent him over to start a bonfire to warm up by, as Riley watched on with a disapproving scowl. The young woman walked past him with a sly grin and gestured come hither with her finger.

Through sheer determination, Connor got a fire going in the wet conditions and plumes of thick white smoke rose up over the falls as the golden glow of the morning sun reflected off of it. The three of them sat down with the pelts draped over the wet benches. The large man hung back out of the way, and neither Connor nor Riley paid much attention to anything else with this enchantress in front of them.

"You two look famished." She said, closing her eyes for a moment before introducing herself, "Jessica Satori…and you are?"

"I'm Connor." He blurted out while preparing the grill rack over the flames.

"Connor? Just Connor?" she asked playfully, as if already knowing the answer.

"As far as I know." He said, smiling bashfully.

"And you?" She asked, turning to Riley.

"…Riley." He responded with suspicion in his eyes.

"Oh, come on. 'Riley' what? I don't need to, but I'm asking politely." she goaded, "Look, breakfast has finally arrived!" She exclaimed as a potbellied creature crawled up through the fire and onto the hot grill. "Remember bacon?" she said rhetorically, "well this is almost as good!…a little gamy, but good!"

Riley looked on in horror as the thing in the fire seemed to casually lay down to rest, while the flames charred its skin and cooked the meat on its bones. He looked to Connor and saw nothing but the dumb-love look of infatuation on his face.

"Mmmm mmm! Smell that!" she said, sniffing the cooked meat from the air as Connor pulled it off of the grill and began carving it up. She

looked at Riley as if she were measuring him up, and then to Connor and asked: "Don't you think Gaia's hungry too?"

"Of course! She must be getting sick of jerky by now. We went fishing the other day, but-" Connor stopped abruptly, and his eyes went blank for a second before he went to the cabin to fetch her.

"Try that shit with me, bitch, I fucking dare you." Riley growled when Connor was out of earshot.

"Oh sweetie, do I make you nervous?" she said patronizingly, "I'm just having a little fun." She walked over to Riley slowly, and reached out, caressing the soft side of his face. "Don't you want to have fun with me?"

He could feel the presence at the edge of his mind grow and seep into his consciousness. He started to lose himself to her power, and all apprehensiveness toward her began to fade. The crease in his brow smoothed to an expression of tranquil nothingness. Suddenly, his mind was his own again, and he caught her as she collapsed into his arms. The trap had been sprung.

"You want inside my head? Fine. You'll see what I've been through. You'll feel it. All of it." Riley projected his voice into the mental cage where he held her. Silent screams of indignant protest did nothing to help as he forced her to relive the torture that he'd been put through. While she underwent her re-education, he scanned and mapped her mind, learning what he could of her and her powers.

As soon as her knees buckled, everyone held by her influence was released. At the same time, her companion came running to her aid, looking distraught through his ghoulish features. Riley gently laid her down on the bench and backed away, so that he'd have some room to maneuver if this guy was coming after him. Luckily for Riley, he slowed to a stop by the fire and crouched by Jessica's side, nudging and trying to shake her awake, but to no avail.

"That's not going to work." Riley said, trying to mask his nervousness with a deep, confident voice that he dropped as soon as he looked up at him, sniffling and growling. "She's not dead! She didn't die big guy! She's...sleeping!" Riley backpedalled hard, "No need to get upset...she just needs to rest for a bit. Everything is okay. Okay?"

"RRRrrrrraaaaaaaaaggggrrggrghhhhhhlllllraaahhhhh!!!" the colossus rebutted. He stepped over Jessica and lurched toward Riley with grave intentions.

"Shit. Connor?!...Fen?!" Riley screamed effeminately, backing away and looking for an exit route.

Connor locked Gaia in the cabin and ran to the fire, where he grabbed a branch sticking out from the embers, and rushed to stop the attack. Before he could get to them, Fen seized his opportunity to get retribution for what happened in the woods, and T-boned him over the edge of the rocks and down into the lagoon, where he'd have the advantage.

Fen moved with the same power and finesse underwater as he did on land. He pushed him to the deeper water and beneath the falls, where Riley had nearly died. Huge, rough hands clawed at Fen's fur and flailed around helplessly as the man tried to swim to the surface for air. Every time he'd kick off of the bottom, Fen would swoop in and push him back down, then swim circles, waiting for him to finally stop fighting it. Slits on the man's neck flared opened along with his eyes. When the supposed corpse restarted the battle, Fen pushed him away and returned to the shore. The now amphibious ogre chased him up the bank and past the cabin, where he picked up a scent that stopped him dead in his tracks.

While this was going on, Riley was negotiating with Jessica to settle the raging beast and promise not to use her powers on anyone in the group, in exchange for her freedom. She agreed to help them, and it seemed to him at least, that she genuinely wanted to. He touched her head with the tips of his fingers, and a mild current passed through cybernetic electrodes into her brain, reverting the data representing her brain wave patterns back into biological consciousness. She woke, and sat up to see what could only be her companion, tearing the door off of the cabin, and hearing Gaia's terrified screams as he did.

Jessica reached out to calm him, but whatever he was focused on had his sole interest and attention. Gaia was the reason that Jessica had travelled so far to be there and she wasn't about to lose her before they'd even met in person. She overloaded his mind with a psionic blast that would have been the end for just about anyone else, and he dropped on the spot.

Connor was the first through the door, with Jessica and Riley close behind. Gaia knelt on the floor with the hideous mass laying in front of her. She was sad and confused but maintained her collectedness. She reached out to the man on the floor and pressed her tiny hand to his callused flesh. No one stopped her, as they were all too caught up by the drastic transformation taking place.

Her regenerative touch caused a strange reaction with his adaptive abilities, and she pulled her hand away. He began secreting a syrupy fluid from his pores that built up, covering his entire body and hardened over in layers, like a chrysalis. It was the about size of a pair of refrigerators and the

slime that covered it was reaching out and affixing itself to the floor and wall.

"It knew my name." she told Connor.

"He spoke? Gaia, he spoke to you?!" Jessica asked, in excited disbelief.

"He's never spoken to you before?" Riley asked, looking like he had about a million questions queued up behind that one.

"*He*?! How does *he* know *my* name? How do *you* know my name? Who *are* you?!" Gaia shouted at Jessica, holding her arms out wide and leering, prompting an explanation.

Jessica looked to Riley for permission, and he nodded after a brief pause of deliberation.

"Hello Gaia, It's me." The ethereal voice spoke inside of Gaia's mind again, soothing her. "It's me." Jessica said in her normal voice, offering her hand to help Gaia hop over the cocoon.

"Oh…hi!" she said in a dreamy haze.

"Gaia, show her your drawings, they're really good. " Connor told her.

"Okay!" she said excitedly, making her way into the other room and forgetting her argument.

Riley looked sternly at Jessica and waited for her to speak. Connor's gaze shifted between her and the chrysalis. She didn't have to read their minds to know they wanted answers.

"I'm the reason that she was comfortable with you, right off the bat. I've been with her, telepathically, since before you found her. I could tell you what you want to know, but it'd be better if I just showed you." she told them, waiting for their acknowledgment. She took their hands in hers and closed her eyes.

7

SHARING THE PAST

A torrent of sights and sounds bombarded their minds. Her memories poured in without context, like a whirlwind of unintelligible emotion. Suddenly, Connor, Riley, and Jessica found themselves standing among the cacti and rock formations in the arid Joshua Tree campgrounds.

"Holy shit, did we just time-travel?!" Connor asked.

"No. This is her memory." Riley told him. "An oddly *familiar* memory."

Another younger version of Jessica stood nearby, and Connor waved his hand in front of this young Jessica's face with no response. She walked forward, passing through him like a ghost, to join her friends by the fire. They were invisible to her and everyone else around.

There were a few tents set up with lawn chairs encircling the fire pit. A smug young hipster sat with an acoustic guitar, over singing every note and taking himself way too seriously. Two girls danced in front of the fire with earbuds in, passing a joint back and forth, and the rest of their group laid on the rocks, staring up at the stars in the clear night sky, blasted on psychedelics.

They followed young Jess around the camp, noticing that whatever she wasn't paying attention to went out of focus and became difficult to look at. They were in her memory and were only experiencing what she did. Soon after, they began feeling euphoric, insightful, and full of wonderment. Vibrant chromatic aberrations trailed whatever moved and hugged everything that didn't in an aura of energetic oneness. Luminescent fiddleheads began spouting from the barren rocks and sandy dirt, swaying with her breath and humming symphonically. Doubles of the stars seemed to float down from the sky, like snow, as rich auroras flowed in and churned around them.

"Trippy." Riley muttered with a wide grin looking around and trying to find himself. "This reminds me of th-"

An apparition revealed itself to young Jess as a negative space in the array of lights and colours that spoke in a language none of them knew but somehow understood. It conveyed its message on a higher plane of

consciousness, and she'd assumed that she had tapped into it through the psychoactive effects of the once sacred experience. The truth was that it was the awakening of her power. Connor and Riley felt every emotion as she originally had, on top of their own, which was a taxing but enlightening experience for all of them. They felt the change when Jessica was imbued with her power, but it felt more like something had been unlocked rather than granted. Her full abilities hadn't awakened yet, but the seed had sprouted.

Her memories rolled on like a montage, showing them glimpses of her past, slowing down for what she felt was important and glossing over the rest. Connor recognized a town that she'd frequently visited and the house he'd retrieved the egg from, though she remembered it being in much better shape than he did. Riley had never seen the town, but he noticed something as well. He saw a beardless and wrinkle-free *Connor*, speaking with an old man. Riley wouldn't have seen him if Jess hadn't been paying so much attention in the first place. This wasn't even what she wanted to show them, and they would have been completely derailed if they had free range of the situation. Instead, they went inside, where she met with a very pregnant young woman.

"This is Emilia...Gaia's mother." she explained

"Wow! Must've been a big baby. She looks like she's going to pop!" Riley exclaimed.

"Normal-sized baby...babies; twins." she corrected him.

"Looks like *you* had a little something going on there, yourself." He pointed out, making an innocent observation that struck a nerve.

"There are some things that I'm not willing to talk about. Not yet." She told him, struggling to keep her mind from wandering and taking them along for the ride.

"Sorry, I should have thought first. Won't happen again. Probably. Hopefully."

"You still with us? There's nothing we can do about that right now, this is only a memory." she told Connor, who was staring out the window at Vonn's house.

"Huh? Ya. Go on, I'm listening." he said, bringing himself back into the moment.

"She invited us in, to live and work in their little village when it was still an off-grid think tank. I've got a background in neurosciences, and I was developing a way for people with disabilities that prevent them from being able to speak, to communicate without the limitations or learning curve of

sign language. We all had our own specialties. The old man's work was so advanced and influential to the group that for a while at least, they revered him like the Catholics did with their pope. I left when some of the others they'd invited started behaving more like a cult than a commune...You'd expect better from a group of pacifist intellectuals. The kinds of things Vonn was coming out with, were so far beyond what was available at the time, to them it must have seemed like they'd come from a higher power. This was the night I left."

"Did you at least get matching jumpsuits and running shoes? What flavour was the kool-aid?" Riley joked without putting any thought toward how serious it may have been.

"It's not funny. People died." she shot back at him with a scornful look on her face that faded as she realized that he couldn't have known.

"Damn, sorry again. You're right. I shouldn't have- Umm...What is that?" Riley said, staring at the wrapped satchel that Emilia had taken out of a hidden compartment, behind a tall baseboard at the back of the closet. She checked out the front window to make sure no one was coming, before inconspicuously handing it to Jessica and whispering in her ear.

"What did she say? I couldn't hear." Riley asked, brimming with curiosity.

"She told me that I needed to keep it a secret." she reflexively teased.

"Then what's the point of all of this? What did she say?" Connor demanded with authority, stepping back in and taking a stern tone with her. She stood there silently, looking at him warily, while the memory faded away and another replaced it.

"She told me what it was." Jess said, smirking mischievously through a facade of guilt.

"Hrrmph." Connor grumbled and patronizingly gestured to continue.

"The device in the satchel is just a *component* of something called the 'Catalyst'. Emilia's husband, Hudson had stolen it after finding out what Vonn had been working on in secret." She quickly explained, looking at Connor, "Without this piece, Vonn wouldn't be able to continue using what we thought was a WMD after discovering how much power it really had. It wasn't. Not in the traditional sense, anyway."

"What do you mean?" Connor asked.

"The way I understood at the time, it was developed to help themselves adapt to the challenges of living in space. It would bond with its host and force a massive leap in evolution, compressed down to a matter of

minutes. Vonn took that technology and used it without considering why nobody else had. He was right about *what* it was, but not what it was capable of." she said, trying to simplify things as much as she could. "Once he found out, things snowballed in a hurry. It was and is, too much power for any single person to control. We had to take it away. Separated, neither piece posed a threat. Despite it all, Emilia wouldn't leave her family, and I would have to take it myself."

"We all had so much conviction back then. Looking back on it now, after everything that's happened since…I'm not sure that we were right."

"So he wasn't just some mad scientist?" Connor asked.

"That's not what I said. Better the devil you know, than the devil you don't…which is exactly what we got. If we hadn't taken it from him and the aliens never came, who knows what would have come of his vision. But they did, and maybe he could have used it to stop all of this."

"Maybe, but that's in the past now. Unless you've got a time machine or-"

"Umm…*Do* you have a time machine?" Riley chimed in.

"No." She told him bluntly.

"Great. Moving on then…So, where are we now?" Riley asked, examining their changing surroundings. It was like an immersive time lapse, with the near total destruction of everything man had built, and nature's shockingly aggressive repossession of it all.

"This was a few years after the last of the pods dropped. I'd made my way north and went into hiding, like the rest of the survivors. I travelled from camp to camp, searching for others with abilities like me. Most of them were just delaying the inevitable. I used my power to give them hope…but I know that it wasn't enough. There was nothing more I could do for them without help, so I kept searching." Jess told them. She paused for a moment, and they felt her pain and guilt for leaving them behind. "I knew they were out there. I could feel them. I just had to find them. Help them understand their powers, so that they could help me to help everyone else."

"How is it that there were others out there with powers?" Connor asked.

"I believe that these cases were all essentially trial runs for something bigger. Vonn wanted to save humanity by creating a living god that he could control, but not everything works out the way that you want it to." She said, looking at him with a slightly furrowed brow, "*Someone* was working with Vonn to distribute them."

"You mean...You think it was me? You think I was a terrorist?" he asked.

To answer, she showed him her many memories of seeing him going down into the basement, where no one else was allowed to go, for his secretive collusion with Vonn. When he still saw her visions as speculation, she showed him glimpses of the intimate moments that she'd shared with him.

"We-..."

"That was in the past. Leave it there."

"But, I-" he began to say, but something came over him, and the thought left his mind. "You're right. Forget it."

"Okay, so..." Riley said, breaking the awkward silence between them.

"Not a terrorist, but a fundamentalist, helping to create the new religion....You did the things that Vonn couldn't bring himself to do. You did things that you knew were wrong, to achieve what you believed was right." She said as she turned away, again directing their attention to the memories playing out around them.

After the invasion, she had found and recruited a group of powered individuals and banded them together as a team. They understood their goal and worked together to learn about and hone their abilities. They'd been together for months and wielded their powers masterfully. Her eye's welled up. Connor and Riley could feel both her pride and foreboding as they watched her students' chance encounter with the very thing they'd been training for.

"They thought they were ready. *I* thought they were ready. But we were wrong...How could you ever be ready for a thing like that?" she sobbed.

"We don't have to..." Connor said, putting his hand on her shoulder.

"Yes, we do." Riley insisted.

"He's right." Jessica responded, shrugging his hand off of her shoulder and continued through the memory.

Her team was scavenging an old mall complex when it found them. Jess spotted it after she felt one of her teammate's consciousness go out like a candle. She couldn't sense its mind at all, but there it was, never the less, standing over one of Legion; the multiplier's duplicates. Its claws sunk into her back, pulling her apart at the hips and chomping into the meat of her thigh like a bear with a salmon.

"What in the absolute fuck is that!?" Riley asked, reacting to his first full-grown glimpse of the planet's new top predator.

"That's what we're up against…That's what we've *been* up against for almost a decade now. What, have you been living under a rock?" Jess responded.

"Kind of."

The young Jess blasted an all points bulletin out to the rest of the team, telling them to regroup as she laid out their plan of attack and began giving orders. They rallied in the parking lot and prepared to take it down.

The weakened Legion prime paired up with the one they called Chimera. She used her power of fusion to temporarily meld with the minds and bodies of other powered beings, into a single vessel that was greater than the sum of its parts. They joined with Blare; the screamer, whose ability allowed her to generate concussive directional sonic waves with her voice. Once they were combined, they'd created enough duplicates to encircle the alien and pummel it from all sides in a converging assault on the centre of their ring. Graviton flew overhead, focusing on the ground beneath the alien's body and created a gravity well that increased its weight, tenfold. The asphalt cracked and collapsed under the crushing pressure and spears of hardlight produced by Photon, grew upward into the underbelly of the alien as it was being forced down and impaled. They strained themselves and pushed their abilities further than they ever had before, until eventually the alien stopped fighting and went limp under the barrage of attacks. They'd toppled the giant.

The team rejoiced and congratulated each other on their victory. Chimera, Legion and Blare separated and fell back into the long, thick grass on the berm where Jess and Photon were waiting. Graviton floated down to join the rest of the team, already reclined, with his legs up, eyes closed and fingers laced behind his head, well prepared for some much deserved R&R.

Connor's eyes began darting around, looking for the others. Riley had never encountered them in the wild before, so he thought the behaviour was suspicious. Jessica had noticed as well and surmised that he'd faced off against the aliens himself at some point in the past.

"What are you looking for?" Riley asked.

"The others."

"Who? I don't se- OH! Oh no…" Riley said with dismay, finally seeing what Connor had been looking for.

"I've never seen them hunt alone."

Jessica closed her eyes and turned away as the female alien snuck up on the team from the other side of the small hill that they were resting on, and the other male came around the corner of the building in front of them,

dragging its claws across the brick wall to draw their attention. The team hopped to their feet and readied themselves for a second battle.

"NO!!!" Graviton bellowed as he turned to see the female coming over the berm, like a horse over a hurdle. Young Jess was standing directly in its path, and he reached out to her as she fell toward him, out of the way.

Photon put up a shield over the team, but he was a split second too late. The female had gotten an arm through before the shield had solidified. Her claws were buried into Blare's chest with a talon digging around in each lung. She tried to scream, but no sound came out, other than the gurgling of blood in her throat. Blare's lifeless body fell to the ground with the alien's twitchy severed limb still embedded in her. Photon's anguish gave him a burst of strength that launched the alien back over the hill, buying them a few more seconds on that front, but also depleting the shield around them.

The male alien rushed in as soon as the shield went down and eviscerated Chimera, Legion and Graviton, mid-transformation as they attempted to fuse, leaving a twisted mess of entangled bodies. Photon ducked its swing and drove his fist into its torso, creating a hardlight blade over his arm and piercing the tough hide. It swiped down, separating Photon from the blade, and the hardlight construct disappeared. His balled fist fell from the bleeding hole between the alien's forelimbs, along with a steady flow of its blood. It wound up and knocked Photon over the hill, where the female caught him in the air, then pinned him hard to the ground and silenced his cries.

Jessica discovered a new way to use her abilities that day. While she couldn't sense, or command the aliens, she found that she still had a subtle influence. She made herself disappear. Connor and Riley could still see her, but her power made it so that the alien's mind wouldn't process any of the sensory input they'd received from her. She was still there, and still very much in danger, but to them, she simply wasn't. She'd been curled up in a ball, trembling with fear until she realized what she was doing and made a break for it. She'd gotten halfway across the parking lot before the effect wore off and they were after her again, but as soon as they got close, her influence kicked in, and she was gone.

The memory was over, and the three of them stood huddled, supporting each other through the dark emotions that weighed on them after reliving the loss of her team, like they were their own. The way they'd shared her memory made Connor and Riley feel like they'd known them themselves. She wiped the tears from her eyes and insisted that they keep going.

"Hey, maybe we should take a break. Besides, I want to check on Gaia." Connor suggested.

"This isn't real-time. To her, only seconds will have passed." Jessica responded, brushing him off and continuing to the next memory.

"Hold on, I've got a quick question." Riley interjected,

"You're not paying attention, are you? Everything will be answered wh-" Jessica replied, losing her patience before being cut off.

"Listen! You just said that we were moving on, but I've still got a question about the last part. I know reliving this is hard for you. We're experiencing it too, but there's no need to be such a hard ass about some simple questions, when the whole point is to have them answered. Now, you can answer a very simple question and be civil about it, or you can go back in the box..." Riley told her, sternly delivering his ultimatum, then pausing long enough to allow her to process his point and the proposed consequences of not cooperating. "Here it is. Nice and easy. What's with the code names? It's not like you had secret identities to protect, right?" he asked with a subtly jovial tone, trying to add some levity to the moment.

"Ugh. Fine. They were more like nicknames. In training, Graham became Graviton, because Pam, who became Legion, thought she was hearing her name whenever somebody needed his gravity manipulation abilities. Then, Photon sounded cooler than Farzan, and Mya... It wasn't conducive to our progress to use our real names and have to stop every fifteen minutes because of an argument. Besides, it was fun for them. Why bother with 'why', when 'why not' is just as applicable?" She explained to them as if it should have been obvious.

"Hold on. Now *I* have a question. What did you mean when you said 'back in the box?'" Connor inquired, looking to Riley for the answer.

"When she got here, she tried to use her telepathy to sway us. She got you...I know you felt like you just wanted to help, but that was her not letting you decide for yourself. I saw it. She tried the same thing with me, but wasn't expecting the AEGIS to get involved. So, we had a little time out." Riley said, shooting her a look.

Connor looked at her with disapproval, but said nothing and waited for her to finish her story. They were both getting frustrated with her disingenuity.

PROTEAN RAYN

"I did what Emilia told me. I took it, and hid it away, where only she and I would know to find it." Jess explained. "But after I lost my team…with the world only getting worse, it was being wasted, and someone needed to step up."

The trio stood under the stars at the ruins of the Los Angeles Public Library, before it sank, and watched as a much more familiar looking Jessica climbed the front steps with an empty duffel bag and a large pry bar. The last time she was there, she'd chained and locked the doors, hence the tool, but to her surprise, the locks were broken on the ground in a pile of snapped chains. That's when the tool became a weapon, held up and ready to strike. She slowly pulled the door open as quietly as possible, in case whoever had forced their way in was hostile. She stepped inside and waited for her eyes to adjust, listening for anything stirring that she might not be able to sense with her mind. It was still relatively bright inside with the moon shining through the large windows, and after a few minutes of searching in the dark, she found the floor plan. Brushing the dust off, she refamiliarized herself with the layout and headed straight for the stairs.

Looking down into the darkness, with the wind whistling in through the collapsed atrium, she was having second thoughts about being there at all. Jess broke the leg off of a chair and tightly wrapped the charred pages that covered the floor with some tattered cloth around it. She pulled a bag of assorted lighters and a small bottle of isopropyl from the worn satchel that Emilia had given her so long ago. With the torch soaked in alcohol, she lit it and packed everything away while the blue flame burnt through and lit the material she'd bound it with.

With enough light to see at least a few feet in front of her face, she descended into the lower levels of the library. It was eerily quiet and pitch black without the torch to light her path. If it went out, she might not have been able to find her way back up. As she went further down, a tiny voice grew louder in her mind. She wasn't alone down there. The voice was almost unintelligible, but the cadence of its inner monologue suggested that

whoever it was, was reading. It was puzzling for the lack of light, but promising, in that it denoted intellect, rather than some mindless aggressor.

The presence Jessica felt was so close now, but there was no other light than hers. Suddenly, the reading stopped, and there was a thunderous crash, just ahead, as a series of bookcases toppled over like dominoes and heavy footsteps ran in the opposite direction. She felt their intense fear and reached out with her mind to calm them. It seemed to work, and it let her in. *It* was a *he*, and he was afraid.

He'd been alone for so long, that he almost forgotten how to speak aloud. The books were the only thing that kept him relatively sane, living vicariously through the characters in the stories and learning about the world that came before. He studied science, the arts, history, philosophy, everything; anything he could learn about, he did. It was all theory; nothing he'd applied, but reading helped him to escape and forget the pain he'd suffered in the past, that brought him here to be by himself. The intellectual was only a part of his psyche though, and a feral creature of instinct also resided within him. It was the part that Jessica had calmed, but was already beginning to wake.

"You don't have to be afraid of me. I'm not here to hurt you. It's okay...you can trust me." She told him, while Connor and Riley watched, rolling their eyes. "It's so dark down here...how can you see? Where are you?" she asked, while gently manipulating his thoughts so that he'd feel safe with her.

"I'm here." A deep, gravelly voice said, skirting around the edge of the light. She saw eye shine, and could hear him move whenever she'd get closer with the torch.

"Why are you hiding? It's not fair that you can see me, but I can't see you, is it? You have me at a disadvantage." she said, trying to entice him into showing himself. She felt their connection fading like she was gradually being shut out.

"Because, I'm a monster." he responded, with his rumbly voice full of self-pity.

"No, you're not. I've felt inside your mind and believe me when I tell you that you are anything but a monster. You're beautiful." She told him, waiting for a verbal response since she could no longer read his thoughts with the same clarity as before.

She could still sense his presence, and felt him circle around behind to approach her. She turned around to see him coming and raised the torch up to get better light coverage, but her quick movement startled him, and

the fire was knocked out of her hand. It rolled under the toppled stacks, igniting bone-dry paper in the mess of books lying all around.

In the flickering light of the quickly spreading fire burning around her, she could see what looked and moved like a hairless, albino gorilla, stomping around and smashing at the fire with his fists, incessantly yelling "NO! NO! NO!" while trying futilely to put out the flames. She could smell his flesh cooking as he dove on the books, again and again, trying to save them.

Thick black smoke filled the area, and Jess lifted her shirt up over her nose as she hurried back to the stairs. It was absolute darkness on the level above the fire, and she was choking on the smoke that had risen up with her. She was feeling around helplessly in the warming darkness and trying to remember the way she came, while listening to the roar of the inferno below her. Screams of pain and anguish echoed out from the blaze and went quiet as the oxygen was consumed by the fire. She was getting lightheaded herself and couldn't stop coughing from the smoke that she couldn't see she was breathing. There was a loud crash and seconds later she lost consciousness.

"...What happened?" Riley asked eagerly, and Connor nudged him with his elbow while shaking his head with a smirk on his face.

"Well, we'll just have to wait and see, won't we?" Jess said, also shaking her head, but lacking the smirk.

When she came to, the sun was just peeking through the buildings of the city. They were outside of the library, near a pool of stagnant water and rows of tall trees, watching flames lick out of the upper windows. He knelt beside her with his enormous, ghostly white frame, cloaked in torn curtains and hiding his eyes. The fabric had slipped off of his forearm, revealing the darkly charred calluses that had already healed over from where he was burnt.

She couldn't read his thoughts anymore.

Jess got up and brushed herself off, before cautiously approaching her rescuer to see if he was okay. She lifted the ragged material from his arm, careful not to agitate anything sustained in the fire, but to her surprise, he seemed to have no visibly recent injuries. He had completely healed, but it wasn't pretty. From what she could see, his thick, callused skin was completely covered with prominent pits and gouges from healed over slash and stab wounds, not just scars from the fire. He let her continue the examination until she lifted the cloak away from his face.

The shock at the sight of him made her reflexively gasp. He recoiled, and they both felt shame and disgust, not toward one another, but about

themselves. He hated himself for how he looked, and she couldn't believe that she could be so insensitive. Even if it wasn't her intent, she could see that she'd hurt him, and pleaded with him to forgive her. Seeing the sincerity of her regret and that she wasn't running away, he faced his learned fear of rejection and persecution. He pulled the cloak back like a hood, unveiling the monster for her to see.

Before anything else, she saw the sadness in his eyes. They were large, and jet black, set back deep in their sockets, and glossy with welled up tears. His dilated pupils shined with the reflected light from the fire. There was almost no evidence of any other facial features; his ears were cauliflowered and healed over, flush to his head, same as his nose, which was barely a pair of slits above his pursed lips, trying self consciously to conceal the gnarled teeth jutting out of his overdeveloped, hyperdontic jaw.

"I'm sorry, I admit I was startled, but...You don't have to hide from me. You don't have to be ashamed of the way you look." She assured him, taking his giant, deformed hand and looking into his eyes to convey her sincerity "You saved my life, big guy. Thank you..."

"You aren't like me; you're fragile." He told her, "Your mind is strong, but your body is weak."

"Oh, well ya, I guess you're right about that. Maybe we can help eachother...So...What do I call you? 'Big guy' is cute and all, but how about a name?"

"Rrr-...I-I have none." He said sorrowfully.

"Oh...Well, I think that means you get to pick one!" She said, trying to turn his mood around and lift his spirits, even if just a little. "What do you think?"

"Like what?" he asked, stopping to ponder the idea she'd presented.

"Anything you want! Maybe your favourite character in a story, or maybe just one that you like the sound of. My friends had their own *superhero* names. You saved me, so you could do something like that if you wanted to. The possibilities are only limited by your imagination." She encouraged him.

"Let me think about it?" He said as if he were asking her permission.

"Sure thing, big guy!" Jess said cheerfully, as she dug through her pack and he continued wandering through the court, still wrapped up tight in his oversized security blanket.

Over the roar of the fire, they heard movement coming their way from the bank across the street. She tried to discern who, or what it was, but their minds were shrouded in void, like a pronounced nothingness. The 'big

guy' couldn't see them yet, but he was sniffing at the air, becoming panicky and agitated at their familiar scent as they grew closer. She took his hand and pulled him along, guiding him away, through the overgrown gardens and into the street to put distance between them and whoever was coming.

His lumbering steps slowed the pair down until the group came around the corner. They were dressed in what looked like cyberpunk riot gear and started firing some sort of energy rounds from metallic stone blades, held like mock pistols.

"What?" Connor asked, portraying his innocence when Riley and Jess both looked at him with condemning stares.

Bolts of lightning exploded the ground at their feet and blew pieces off of the buildings around them, sending chunks of dirt and burnt concrete flying as they ran. Muscles in the pale giant's legs contorted and realigned as he threw off the cloak, scooped Jessica up into his arms, and began to sprint faster and faster. Holes burnt through the curtain as it floated back down, temporarily blocking the gunmen's line of sight and then blinding them with the rising sun, as it fell to the ground. By the time their eyes adjusted, the pair was gone.

Jessica looked up at her saviour and watched as the morning sun burnt his peeling, muted skin and caused his big, black, dilated pupils to cloud over and contract as he squinted against it, trying to see what was ahead of them. His skin went from white to pink, to blistering red, before it healed over with a dark bronze. His eyes were more human now, but with a tinted membrane that worked as an extra set of eyelids. She heard bits of shrapnel dropping to the ground as they were displaced and fell from hemorrhaged boils on his back, that calloused over once the foreign objects had been expelled. All the while, he hadn't said a word, just clenched his jaw and bore through it.

Running toward the sun, they were ducking through alleys to change streets, trying to throw the group off of their trail, if they'd been followed. They came upon a dilapidated stadium that *looked* like a good place to hide out. Approaching the entrance, they were stopped by a chorus of roars that shook what glass remained in the building and sent the pair on hastily on their way.

They crossed a highway, filled with vehicles that hadn't run in years, most of which had been picked over by scavengers and marked. Continuing past the automotive graveyard, there was a building that caught the big guy's attention. It was in decent shape and appeared to be vacant, so they went in.

She sensed no other presence, but called out anyway, just to be sure. Her powers *had* betrayed her before.

They were alone.

It wasn't exactly well hidden, but she knew why he'd chosen it. The natural history museum was built like a fortress, but he was more interested in what was inside. He set her down, and she locked the doors behind them, while he wandered in, like a kid in a candy store. She'd never seen wonder like that before, in anyone.

Jess was alone with the skeletons of two dinosaurs, posed as if they were locked in battle. She had a few MREs left and headed back to the gift shop to look for any glass bottled water since anything in a plastic container would have been undrinkable by now. She wasn't expecting much, if anything, but they'd hit the jackpot with an unopened case. A set of souvenir mugs and dishes just needed to be wiped off and they would be all ready for breakfast, whenever he got back from his self-guided tour.

While they had lost their tail back at the burning library, they had picked up a new one outside of the stadium, and a few more out in the open, while crossing the highway. They were being stalked from a distance, mostly on the scent, but when Jess raised her voice to call out, she had drawn them to the museum, where they prowled around out of sight, searching for another way in. She was caught up in her find and only noticed the occasional movement out of the corner of her eye, but there were a lot of things in there that could play tricks with the light, and she was past jumping at shadows. She'd figured that if anyone had followed her, she would be able to sense them and hide before they could even see her. She kept on setting up, even though she should have known better. Despite what her senses told her, they had company.

The big guy came running when he heard the crash. He slid fast around the corner and launched off against the base of the display in the lobby. Changing directions, he leapt over Jessica, who was crouched behind one of the counters in the shop. There, he faced off against one adolescent, and three juvenile aliens that had come in through the gardens at the rear of the building. The largest of the young aliens blocked the exit and screeched at the smaller three, who were disorganized and clamouring to attack.

Two of the juveniles scurried around the clutter in the store and took his flanks, while the third threatened to attack head-on. This was a distraction tactic that they'd often used while hunting, and this time was no different. One pounced from the side, but was spotted and blocked with a broad forearm. The other leapt onto his shoulders, digging in with its claws

and trying to get its lion-sized jaws around his gorilla-sized neck. The third rushed in, attacking his legs, trying to immobilize him. They piled on in a frenzy, and he dropped to the ground.

The larger adolescent watched from the doorway, barking orders at the trio in a primitive sounding language of snarls, clicks, and hisses. All the while, it was keeping an eye out for Jessica, but couldn't focus and got distracted whenever it became curious about the area on the other side of the store, where she was hiding.

Jess unbuckled a small padded camera bag from her pack and lobbed a capped pipe, wrapped with duct tape, deck screws, and roofing nails at the adolescent, who caught it like a dog playing fetch. The alien chomped down aggressively, trying to chew through the metal, and gulped it back like a pill. Throwing its arms back, the alien let out a triumphant roar, before it was jolted by a sudden expansion in its abdomen. The roar turned into yelps and squeals as it clawed at its stomach, trying to remove the source of its pain. Stretch marks ripped the skin over its shattered ribs and bits of metal shrapnel poked through the bruised and bloated flesh. Blood began leaking out from its rear end, and up from its nose and throat as the creature's eyes rolled over in its head. The dying alien stumbled forward and collapsed on the floor, next to the feeding frenzy taking place in the middle of the shop.

Jessica's hulking companion laid on the ground, gurgling in a pool of his own blood, pinned down by the three juveniles, who were tearing off chunks of meat and gorging themselves on his constantly regenerating muscle tissue. She was crushed at the apparent loss of another teammate, but just as she was about to use the distraction to escape, she noticed his hands begin to ball up, and his veins bulge. The aliens were tearing away less and less meat each time they went back for more, as the muscle was becoming denser and the skin was healing over, faster and tougher with every wound they inflicted. Eventually, they were unable to penetrate the hardened scars that covered his body and began breaking teeth and talons off in their efforts to continue feeding. He'd reached up and grabbed the first one that he could get his hands on. His muscles twitched with renewed vigour as he squeezed his grip ever tighter around its head and shoulders. It flailed around desperately trying to escape, as its shoulders met, its bones crunched with a sloppy squish, and its eyes popped out from their sockets.

"Did you hear that?" Connor asked

"Ugh, yes! It was like-" Riley said, thinking of how to mimic the gory sounds with his voice before Connor cut him off.

"Not that, listen…" He said, hushing him, and waiting for the sound he'd heard again, but there was nothing.

The alien remains oozed through the gaps of the brute's fingers, and he shook off the other two as he stood back up. Using the carcass like a mace, he swung it hard overhead and down onto one of them, audibly breaking its back. Even though it was hard to tell with their inhuman features, the last of the juveniles had a genuine look of surprise on its face. Its eyes darted back and forth, between the rage-filled, ogreish man staring at it, and the other dead aliens that littered the area. For just a second, it looked as if the last juvenile was going to try and take him on, but one step forward was enough to make it flinch, then run for its life.

"*Waaaaakkkeee uuuuuupppppp*" a voice whispered like a recording played in slow motion with the volume turned way down.

"There!" Connor declared, looking at Riley and Jess for affirmation, "That's what I heard! You heard that right?".

They both seemed confused, shaking their heads. He felt like he was going crazy, hearing things, but he was also actively experiencing someone else's memories, so he assumed that it was some sort of side effect and brushed it off as his imagination playing tricks on him.

Jessica waited a moment for the big guy to calm down before getting too close. She didn't want to catch him off guard, just in case the adrenaline made him do something that he didn't mean. With his size and strength, even the slightest lapse of control could break her. He took a few deep breaths and turned to her, looking down at the bits of bone, suspended in the dark, sticky blood that covered his trembling hands.

"Are…are you okay?…At this rate, I'm going to need to start a list, just to keep track of the times you've saved me."

His mouth moved like he was trying to respond, but no sound came out. He touched his throat and tried to speak, but his eyes welled up with tears of helplessness as he began to understand why he couldn't. When the aliens eviscerated his skin, it grew back tougher, so that they couldn't cut it. When they shredded his muscles, they grew back denser, and consequently, stronger, so that they couldn't overpower him. The gurgling sound he'd made during the attack was from his lacerated throat. They'd ruptured the carotid artery and breached his esophagus. His throat healed, just like the rest of his body, making it harder, tougher and stronger, including the vocal cords in his larynx. He'd been made mute.

"Oh no…" she said, making the connection herself.

He put his back up against the wall and slid down into a squat, crossing his arms over his knees and sombrely burying his head in them. She picked up the MREs that had been scattered around, and offered it to him with a bottle of water that seemed cartoonishly small compared his gargantuan hands. He raised the bottle to his lips, and it shattered like he was changing a light bulb with a pair of vise grips. The unwieldy size and strength that he'd developed fighting the aliens would take some getting used to.

"Hey, don't worry about it, big guy. We've got a whole case here." She said, pouring a few of the bottles into a sturdy bowl.

He needed to be able to get a drink without having to worry about breaking anything else and without having to be fed like an invalid. He looked at Jessica when he heard her calling him '*big guy*' again and mouthed part of a word, but stopped at the reminder of his disability. He leaned over to the pool of blood on the ground and smeared it around with his hand. Using it like finger paint, he wrote on a clean patch of the floor in front of him with big clumsy letters, "PROTEUS". He looked back to her and pointed at himself, doing his best to communicate that he'd chosen his name. She smiled and nodded, validating his choice.

"Proteus?" Connor asked, looking for some reasoning behind the name he'd chosen.

Before either Jessica, or Riley could tell him what it meant, he heard the voice again.

"*WWWAAAKKKEEE UUUUUUPPP!!!*" The voice echoed through their minds. This time they all heard it, loud and clear. Jess looked worried, and the two men both looked to her, assuming that she knew what it was.

"Ya, I heard *that*. Hold on, I'm ending this…" She said without him having the chance to ask.

They closed their eyes, and when they opened them again, they'd come back to reality. Back in Connor's cabin with Gaia pulling on their clothes and shouting at them to wake up.

9

DIVIDED WE FALL

"What were you doing? Why weren't you talking to me?" Gaia asked, in a worried and wavering voice. "I thought something happened to you! Something's outside. I got the bar across the door, so it can't get in, but it keeps trying."

"What do you mean? What is it? …How long were we out for?" Connor asked, looking back and forth between Gaia and Jess for an explanation. Gaia shrugged, and Jess looked just as confused as he was. The fire was going was out now, and the embers were cooling, which tipped him off to the amount of time that had actually passed. "What happened to this only taking a few *seconds* in real time?" He spoke calmly for Gaia's benefit, but shot an accusing glower at Jessica, assuming some kind of attempted deception.

"I-I don't know! That's how it's always worked before…Do you feel that?" Jessica responded, looking like she was about to faint.

"Feel wha- Whoa! Ya, I'm am feeling a little…Gaia? Are you doing…Are…Are you-" Connor muttered before falling back onto the bench along the wall and passing out.

"It wasn't me! I didn't do that! I'm not doing this! I-" Gaia desperately refuted before falling unconscious herself, but Riley was there to catch her.

As he was setting her down, Jessica fell too. There wasn't time to catch her, but luckily she'd been standing beside Connor, and he'd broken her fall when she toppled over and landed in his lap. Riley felt dizzy for a brief moment but was otherwise unaffected by whatever it was that caused their affliction.

The AEGIS alerted him to the presence outside of the cabin that Gaia had warned them about. It'd stopped actively trying to enter, but he could hear it out there, breathing and pacing on the rocks. The lack of windows made the only exposed wall secure from break-ins, and the sturdy logs that it'd been made from kept anything from getting through, but the lone point of egress had them trapped. He couldn't unbar the door without knowing what it was he was dealing with, but the AEGIS had that covered. Riley's

bionic eye layered over filters into his field of vision allowing him to see beyond the normal visible spectrum, displaying a large thermal signature on the other side of the wall. In conjunction with the thermal image, the system overlaid sonar based readings of the area using an ultrasonic ping to survey and map his surroundings, both inside and out. This gave him a detailed view of what was out there, without a direct line of sight. He saw the waterfall and the sound echoing off of the rocks in the lagoon, but there was no immediately apparent threat. Fen was out there, but he was definitely alone.

Riley quietly unbarred the door and cracked it open to get a clear view. He wanted to see for himself and validate the readings that the AEGIS had given. Fen was standing about twenty feet from the door with his eyes locked on Riley as he peeked out. The usual intensity in Fen's eyes was gone, and they were glazed over with a dead emptiness to them, like a shark. Something was very wrong. Riley felt an unsettlingly familiar static feedback coming from him, and then he noticed the glint of metal from above Fenrir's twitching eye. It was one of the slave implants that had been lost earlier, now embedded into his temple. Fen sniffed at the air, turning his head slightly and revealing the other two that had also burrowed in like ticks behind his ear.

They had taken too long, and now, not only did Morrow have a new puppet, but Riley could only assume that his plan was shot, since he must have known by then that his implant had been disabled. Thinking quickly, he hurried into the bedroom, past the dried out cocoon to retrieve the defunct implant that he'd previously extracted from himself to see if he could get the transmitter module working again. His implant was no different than the three on Fen. Thanks to the computer that had integrated itself with him, Riley was able to assume administrative control over the other implants that were intended for the rest of the group. If he could assimilate that tech, then there was a chance that he could control Fen and eliminate the threat. He closed his hand, and it disappeared into his palm.

Heavy logs shook as Fen rammed the wall with his broad head. An uncharacteristically crude tactic for the normally cunning predator. Riley moved Gaia and Jess to the back of the room, away from anything that could fall on them while they were unable to protect themselves. Connor's solid frame made moving him much more challenging, and he had to be ungracefully dragged by his feet across the dirt floor. Proteus's hardened scaly chrysalis was affixed to the ground and partially up the wall, so he'd

have to stay where he was, though from what Riley had seen of him, he was sure that he'd be okay if anything did happen.

The tech from the slave controller had been integrated into the AEGIS now, and Riley would be able to overwrite any of the programming that Morrow had been using. Fen's siege had ended for the time being, but there was no doubt that he'd be back. Riley reached out and connected with the implants, attempting shut them down, or failing that, to at least reset them. With the controller boosted by the AEGIS, Riley had no trouble tapping into their systems, killing the uplink, and giving Fen back control of his own body and actions.

Everything should have gone back to normal, but Fen's erratic behaviour continued. He'd hoped against it, but Riley knew that it was possible for the implants to have been made with a failsafe, separate from the main system to prevent remote tampering. He was going to have to get hands-on with it, and interface with each unit directly in order to cease their control over Fen.

Riley checked on the others, trying to make them as comfortable as possible with what was laying around until he could figure out what had happened to them. Since he hadn't been affected by whatever it was that put them out, he'd deduced that it was related to their powers and that he'd be on his own for now. The data feed from the implants was dead, but he could still access their onboard memory caches and see if there was anything that could clue him into what was going on.

Fen was racking his head against the outside wall, and Riley was worried that he might be doing harm to himself, trying to dislodge the implants. This appeared to be what he was doing now, more so than trying to breach the wall itself; he was begging for help, not trying to attack. Riley had a feeling that if Fen really wanted to hurt them, a few logs wouldn't stop him. With the implants highlighted on Riley's internal HUD, he could see that their tendrils had barely made it through Fen's tough hide, and hadn't breached his thick skull before being shut down. It would have been impossible for him to be under their control, which meant that he was lashing out, solely from the severe discomfort. Riley needed to get them out before Fen hurt himself, or damage to the cabin, putting the others at risk.

Searching Connor's gear, Riley borrowed the large hunting knife that he kept strapped to him, and gathered his courage before venturing outside. Fen was halfway seated, trying to scratch off the metal protruding from his head with his hind paw, up near the fire pit. As soon as he caught sight of Riley sneaking out of the cabin, Fen bolted toward him, startling him into a

panicked sprint in the opposite direction. When he ran, Fen's instincts drove him to chase. Before Riley could get ten feet from the door, Fen was on his back and had him pinned to the ground. He turned him over effortlessly, and leaned in so that they were nose to nose. Riley thought that he'd made his last mistake, but instead, Fen eased off and whimpered, turning his head and pawing at his ear. He let Riley get back to his feet and sniffed at the knife that he was holding. Riley didn't need a translator to understand what Fen was trying to communicate.

"Hey buddy. I'm going to help you, but I need you to let me." Riley told him, petting his shoulder and gesturing for him to lay down.

He knelt closely beside him to examine the pucks. Even though they hadn't fully attached themselves, the barbed tendrils were causing great pain as they burrowed a little deeper with every attempt to remove them. He could cut them out, but without anything to numb the area, he was afraid that Fen might fight back. That would have to be his last resort. For now, while he was compliant, he'd try jacking into the implants to see what else he could learn.

"It's going to be okay." Riley told him as he moved closer, connecting to their transmitters while scratching around the big dog's ear to ease his stress.

He'd been right about the secondary system. There was an offline failsafe built in and shielded alongside a backup battery, separate from the control module. Shutting down the units remotely had triggered the fail safes and deleted the self-extraction code, which would have told the implant to retract its barbs and pull out, cleanly. If the metal tendrils had entered his skull, they would've discharged their power source when it was triggered and cooked his brain. Luckily, they were shallow enough that it wasn't going to be fatal, but they were shocking him as they shorted out, making his face twitch with spastic contractions and causing his lip to curl, which made Riley very uneasy. He was able to stop the current, and access the rest of the unit, but he wasn't going to be able to remove the tendrils without cutting him.

"Alright, buddy...I'm just trying to help. This is going to hurt. Please, please, please, don't eat me." he whispered to Fen in an effort to calm the both of them before the minor surgery that he was about to perform.

Taking hold of the implant with one hand, and shaking with nervousness, he readied the blade with his steadier prosthetic. The synthetics felt none of his anxiety. Fen cowered down, squeezing his eyes shut. Riley took a deep breath, and as he touched the blade to the entry

point, his cybernetics autonomously went to work. He dropped the knife and watched as the AEGIS interacted with the first implant. With select functionality restored, it retracted smoothly with the barbs folded back flush, causing no additional damage. He held the extracted puck in his mechanical palm, and the tendrils recoiled into the body of the device, like slurped up spaghetti noodles. His metal hand opened up and closed back down around the repacked implant, dismantling and absorbing the components into itself. Without having to touch the other two, they extracted themselves in the same way and used their robotic strands as legs to walk across Fen's head and climb up onto Riley's arm, then stack into his palm to be taken in as well.

Distracted by the discovery of this new ability, he was taken by surprise when Fen rose up and once again pinned him down with a massive paw. His hot, slobbery tongue lapped over Riley's face, over and over again, drenching him in excitedly thankful monster kisses.

"Sorry to break you love birds up, but there's something you should see." Connor chirped in a groggy voice.

"Ugh! Get off me Fen!" Riley shouted, pushing his head and sitting up as Fen backed off, wagging his tail.

"Proteus's cocoon just cracked open and uhh...Just come see." Connor said, waving him over.

Riley hurried into the cabin to see Jessica holding a fair-haired young boy with dark skin. The cocoon had taken the monster that they believed to be a man, and with her help, returned him to his purest form; he was reborn.

"Proteus? Can you hear me? Proteus? Come on, heal up for me big guy" Jessica said, cradling the small boy in her arms.

"That's not his name..." Gaia said quietly, sounding like she was about to cry. "Tha- That's my brother...*Rayn*. But he- This can't be him...He died! I saw it-!"

"Gaia?" the meek boy whispered, raising his head in the direction of her voice and struggling to open his new eyes as they adjusted to the light for the first time.

"Rayn?!" she shouted, diving in and wrapping her arms around him, squeezing tight. "I thought you were dead!"

"Gaia let go!" Jessica pleaded, trying to pull her off of him.

"No! He's my brother! It *is* him! I'm never letting him go, ever again!" she protested, hugging him even tighter.

"Gaia! Stop!" Connor shouted, grabbing her arm and pulling her back off of the boy.

He let go of her arm when he felt a searing pain where he'd touched her skin, and stepped back in fear of the little girl losing control. Her eyes went black, and her temper flared as she looked at them, angry and confused as to why they were spoiling her reunion.

"Please Gaia, you have to stop! Look at him! Look at what you're doing!" Riley begged her.

"Wha-? …N-no! " she whimpered.

Rayn reached back to her and as their hands got closer, his fingers crusted over and the chrysalis reformed around his shoulders where she hugged him. Riley stepped in for Connor, pulling her hand away with his prosthetics so that he didn't get burnt as well, and reluctantly, she went with him. Once she was far enough away, the chrysalis shrunk and came off like an old scab, again leaving fresh, new skin. Jessica calmed the boy, who had crawled back up into her arms after being knocked over, then flung his arms around her and cried.

Outside, Gaia pushed herself away from Riley and ran as fast as her feet would carry her, down the path to the beach, yelling at him to stay away. She moved through the fresh, overgrown vegetation, leaving withered rot in her wake. Riley let her go for a moment, not wanting to end up like the plants, but picked up the chase, after she had disappeared from sight. Fen got up to go after her, but Riley signalled for him to stay and he hesitantly obeyed.

She ran and ran as the path widened before her and rotted trees fell behind, closing the trail off. She ran until she was too tired to go any further, stopping just short of the beach. Her face was wet with sweat and tears, and she threw her head back, wailing at the top of her lungs as a ring of death blasted out around her, radiating through the forest.

Riley, who was traversing the fallen logs, stopped when he heard her piercing scream ripping through the woods and turned to retreat when he saw the wall of grey coming toward him that accompanied it. There was no way that he could outrun the wave, so he did the only thing he could. Duck and cover.

Hot air rushed over his head, pelting him with crumbled bits of charred wood and covering him in a thick layer of ash. When he got back up and turned around, there was an open clearing where the forest had been, blanketed in what looked like dark snow, as the soot continued to fall. He trudged on forward, taking knee-high steps through the deep snowy ash, searching for the confused and distraught little girl.

Connor came hurtling down the path atop Fen, chasing after them and caught up to Riley in the lifeless field. The dead zone reached almost all the way back to the lagoon, a far greater radius than where Connor had found her. She was getting stronger. From his raised vantage point, he spotted a depression in the middle of the powdered desolation and rode hard to get to her before she was buried by it.

Fen gently nuzzled her and dusted off much of the accumulation, but she didn't have the energy to stand on her own. Riley hurried over to join them and lifted her up so that they could take her back. They'd been in a rush to get there, and Connor hadn't had the time to spread the saddle; he'd ridden over bareback and would have to take it slow for their return trip over the rough terrain of petrified logs that hadn't yet crumbled.

"Hey…are you uhh- are you feeling okay?" Connor asked Riley, looking down at him as he walked alongside of them.

"Ya, I feel pretty good actually, why?" He answered optimistically, but grew suspicious as to why he'd have asked the way that he did.

"You were pretty close when it happened. I mean look around. *Everything* else is dead." He told him, implying heavily that something seemed off.

"I'm telling you, I feel fine! Better than fine." Riley reassured him

"I'll take your word for it." he replied.

As they walked, Riley kept catching Connor staring at him, and a troubled look on his face raised his suspicions ever further about his concerns.

"Alright, what is it?" Riley demanded, stopping Fen and waiting for an answer.

"I know you *say* that you feel good…But you *look* like shit." Connor told him, bluntly.

"Aww, you're going to make me blush"

"It'd be an improvement. Really. You should see yourself."

"Okay, now you're just being a dick." Riley said, letting his criticisms slide off of his back and changing the subject. "Looks like Fen's feeling better."

Fen's coat gleamed in contrast to their surroundings and the glimmer had returned to his eyes. Gaia's hands moved slowly back and forth, petting him as she rested on his back. Her eyes were still closed with a subtle, content smile on her face as her worries drifted away in the company of her colossal companion. Fens wounds had already healed with her touch.

When they returned, Jess and Rayn were busy packing away supplies onto the gurney and lashing together another sled, so that they could make their next journey in a single trip.

"Hey! That's my stuff! What are you doing?!" Connor shouted as they rode up.

He lowered Gaia down to Riley and hopped off of Fen's back, then ran over to confront them about their apparent thievery.

"We're taking it. We can't stay here. Don't worry, you're coming too." Jess told him.

"You didn't think to run it past me first? Explain yourself." He barked, storming up the path.

"STOP." Rayn told him, stepping between them and puffing out his chest.

"Don't get tough with me. You're not 'Proteus' anymore. You're just a kid...Go play somewhere. The grown-ups are talking." Connor said, easily moving him aside.

Rayn seemed surprised that he could do so, still used to the strength of his old form. Jessica did not look pleased with the way he was treating him but knew that starting a fight wouldn't help anything.

"We can't all stay here. It's time we found someplace that'll hold all of us. This quaint little cabin of yours is great and all, but it's gotten kind of cramped, don't you think? Besides, our local resources just dropped right off. We need to think about the future. I know a place."

FAILED EXPERIMENT

After sending the enslaved Riley out to acquire the rest of his group, Morrow redirected his attention to his new specimen. The alien hatchling was undergoing an alarming rate of growth. Just a few hours after its eyes first opened, there was more than a noticeable change in size and appearance. Its soft skin was beginning to harden into leathery scales, and what looked like feathery down quills were compressing into each other. Thorny reptilian spikes ran along its jaw line, over its head, down its back, and to its tail.

The large incubation unit that he'd kept it in was no longer suitable for the alien, and wouldn't be able to contain it for much longer. The doctor gathered his equipment from that section of the lab and activated the bio-hazard lockdown protocols, sealing off a large area around the chamber. A thick wall of wire inlaid safety glass moved into place, sealing off that part of the room just in time, as the incubator's seals failed under the hatchling's relentless attempts to escape.

Curled up inside of the cramped chamber, it was hard for Morrow to gauge the aliens growing proportions, but now that it was out and free to move around, it was really something to behold. The length of its bony, whip-like tail alone was unnerving enough to have the doctor double-checking the locks and making sure that the system was functioning properly, with *no* chance of failure. Once he was satisfied that all of the safety conditions had been met, he started at the controls that would install the slave implant, and give him the absolute control over the creature that his ego demanded.

It stretched out its limbs, then ran full tilt at the doctor as soon as it saw him. It slammed into the glass barrier, not knowing what it was, or that it was even there at first. The impact rattled the walls and made Morrow reflexively jump back and check its stats, but the clear shielding remained intact. It took another run at him before figuring out that there was something in its way. The alien clawed at the glass, feeling around to the edges of the walls like it had with the incubator, but there was no opening

for it to pass through. It watched the old man and every movement that he made. They were studying each other now.

Scanners on Morrow's side of the lab tracked his hand gestures, which translated the motion commands to a pair of articulated, robotic arms on the other side; a scaled up version of those he'd used to hatch the egg in the chamber. One of the arms came overhead with the sound of whirring servos and clamped down around the alien's back, holding it firmly in place despite its struggles. The second arm moved in, around to the back of its head and injected the implant, which took over from there, penetrating between its toughening scales and into the still vulnerable underlayer. There was a soft crunch as it entered in through its skull and fastened down the outer body of the device to the back of its head. With the implant branching out inside and making new neural connections, the alien was flailing around spastically, twitching and receiving a disorienting flood of false sensory information in the process.

Once the installation was complete, Morrow released the clamps that held it, and waited for the young savage to regain its bearings. He was not a patient man and lacked any empathy for the creature, so when it took longer than he was satisfied with to recuperate from the forced surgery, he sent a command to the implant to correct its behaviour. When the command wasn't followed, because it was still physically unable to do so, an electric current surged through the hatchling's head and down its spine, seizing up its muscles and throwing it into convulsions. When he grew bored with that form of torture, Morrow moved onto the next phase.

Gene-splicing had been his forte and was something that he'd been dying to try with an alien specimen ever since he first became aware of their existence. Samples were taken to determine its genetic makeup. Usually, his work would be done with embryos stored on the ship, but he had been successful in the past with mutating fully-developed organisms. The process was gruelling. Less so for him, than the poor suffering creatures that he was experimenting on, <u>but he</u> had absolutely no qualms about hurting them to achieve his goals. He relished it. Nathaniel Morrow was a true sadist.

Though he'd found that certain species were easier to merge than others, he was a fan of challenge and enjoyed discovering how far he could push the limits of their diversity. Some of his favourites were from lines that he'd never imagined would work together, but the ones that didn't work, and they frequently didn't, generally ended up a steamy pile of biological waste, as their DNA unravelled during the transformation. He carefully studied the alien's genes, so that the alterations he made would undoubtedly

succeed. He cherished this project more than any before it, not because he valued its life, but because it was the only one he had access to. He was fickle with his attachments and held no regard for the sanctity of life, save his own.

"Well, isn't that something..." he muttered, staring at the readout of its genetic analysis and then over to the snarling savage, as it backed itself into the corner, taking a defensive posture after the metal arms retracted. "You aren't quite as alien as it would seem, are you?"

While most of its DNA was unique and appeared very alien, certain things stood out to him that were very familiar. There was evidence of reptilian and bird genetics that he would expect to find in theropods but also traces of simian ancestry among the strange findings. He looked at the hatchling in a whole new light now, pondering what it could mean.

"I have competition." He said to himself, balanced between spiteful and curious. This was an exceptional creation, but he was going to have to take it a step further to leave his mark. He was compelled to do better.

Going through the ark's available catalogue, Morrow chose several samples that he would use to alter and enhance what he believed to be weaknesses in the alien's physiology. After selecting the ingredients and inputting them into the system, the lab's computers took over and mixed the cocktail. The mechanical arms moved in once again, pulling the cowering alien from the corner and holding it in place. Syringe tipped hoses emerged from the base of the clamps and guided themselves into the hatchling's main arteries, pulsating like hornet stingers as the mutagen was pumped in. Once the full dosage of serum was deposited, the needles fell out, and the hoses recoiled along with their metal arms back into the ceiling.

First, came inflammation and tenderness in the alien's flesh, followed by aching bones and joints as the mutagen began to work, preparing its body for the violent restructuring that was to come. Its scales were durable, but the gaps between them were vulnerable if an enemy knew where to strike. Splicing in select pangolin genes made its scales grow out, like hard, thick overlapping spades, from its brow to the tip of its tail and reaching down the outside of its arms and legs. Exoskeletal armour-like plates formed over its chest and abdomen, limiting its already few vulnerabilities. Its limbs became temporarily palsied while segments of vertebrae reconfigured, allowing for further range of motion and running new nerves, tendons, and musculature to give it prehensile control of its tail, which had become like a bladed whip.

As cunning as the aliens may have been, they were still just savages, seemingly incapable of higher thought. Morrow wasn't satisfied with that

limitation for his masterpiece and increased the simian gene ratio, adding human DNA to the mix. He would have used his own, but certain hereditary disorders would have produced less than ideal results. Luckily for him, Riley had been purified by his time in the ark's rejuvenation chamber, and Morrow had helped himself to a large tissue sample while he was administering the nanomachines and enslaving him.

The alien gripped its head and screamed through the excruciating ordeal, while the bones of its skull made sickening cracks and crunches as they expanded then reformed, making room for the growing grey matter inside. A process that would have made a migraine feel like a relaxing massage.

The ark's proximity sensors had picked up movement outside. Two figures were approaching the entrance, so Morrow sealed the remaining airlocks between it and the lab, locking them out. He would not be interrupted before his new masterpiece had completed its transformation and was ready to be tested.

He couldn't have been bothered with them, until the airlocks started opening one by one, as they came toward the lab. Pulling up the video feed on one of his monitors, Morrow watched Riley coming down the hallway. He had a woman with him, but there was no sign of Connor, the little girl, or the tamed hybrid that he'd sent him to retrieve.

"Where are the others, robot?!" Morrow shouted over the intercom, "I told you what would happen if you failed me again." He attempted to access Riley's implant to disable the autonomy that he'd granted him, but the unit was unresponsive. Another door opened as they grew closer and the doctor was struggling with the idea that he may have made an error in letting him go. "I don't know how you've broken free from my control, robot, but I made you a promise and I intend to deliver on it. Come on then. I have something for you." He taunted.

"Oh, I'm coming, you son of a bitch." Riley snarled back, then disabled the cameras and comms.

As the alien completed the first stage of metamorphosis, its potential expanded with its growth. As it continued to mutate and evolve, the hatchling began looking itself over and re-examining its surroundings, like it was seeing it all for the very first time, all over again. Heaving and exhausted from the transformative growth spurt, it was obvious that the baby was hungry. The massive caloric expenditure left it gaunt and ravenous, trying again to get through the glass.

"No! I am your *master!*" Morrow scolded, shocking it through the implant, which had become ingrown between the plate scales. "You do *not* eat your master!"

The alien stopped what it was doing and stood upright, staring at Morrow intently and tilting its head, like it was trying to understand something. It let out an almost human sound, "*EEEEEaaaaaaa MMMMaaaaa*" then reverted back to its clicking growls and hisses, pacing and twitching its tail.

Moving to the far end, the doctor activated another of the containment dividers, locking himself in with the controls and disengaging the locks, which retracted the glass on the other side. The mutated hatchling pried at the gap as soon as there was an opening and forced its way through into the main section of the lab.

The final airlock was still closed, but Morrow spotted Riley through the porthole when he arrived, whose eyes were fixated on the alien in the middle of the room. The door began to open, but Riley quickly overrode it to keep the creature isolated. It turned to the door at the sound of it opening and stared at Riley through the glass, tilting its head in the same way it had just looked at the doctor.

"What in the hell is that thing?" Jessica asked.

"I think it's the alien from the egg he hatched, last time I was here." Riley replied.

"No, I can feel its mind. Kind of. It's strange. I can't do that with the aliens, remember?"

"Well, this one's clearly not normal. I mean, *look* at it."

"Come in! Come in! Bring that tasty little morsel you've brought with you, too." Morrow shouted through the barriers, licking his lips and making pruned kissing faces at Jessica. "By the way, *robot*, when's the last time you looked in a mirror? You look like you're coming apart at the seams. Need a good doctor to patch you up, Frankenbot?"

"Ohhh, I want to shut him up so badly" Jess grumbled, "save some for me?"

"Well, it doesn't look like I'm going to get my hands on him from here. Not with that thing in our way. So, go ahead. I insist." Riley told her, smirking.

"Here's one for both of us." she said, closing her eyes and concentrating. A look of disgust came over her face, and Morrow's pants became saturated when she shut off his bladder control. "Ugh, I don't want to see in his head ever again. That man is seriously twisted."

"Ha! You made him piss himself?!" Riley laughed

"That's not the only thing he's stewing in." she told him, shivering again at the thought of what she'd seen in his mind. She pinched her nose and grinned at Riley, then looked through the porthole and stuck her middle finger up at the doctor, who looked oddly relaxed, then horrified by what'd just happened.

"Y-You bitch! You fucking bitch!" Morrow screamed at her with his voice trembling.

Incontinence had become an occasional issue for him in the recent years, and the soft spot stood out to her, like a painted target.

"Old man, you know what I can do. Don't make me, make you, open that divider." She replied aloud but also pushed the thought into his head to be certain that she'd gotten her point across.

The alien hadn't taken its eyes off of Riley since he got there, but turned to growl at Morrow when he yelled. When it did, Jess noticed the metal sticking out from the horned ridges on the back of its head and quietly pointed it out to Riley.

"You can communicate with those implants, right?" she said rhetorically.

"Yes, I can. Good eye...Oh! That's-"

"What is it?"

"The implant isn't responding normally. It's receiving, but it seems to be taking commands more like suggestions. It...knows me. Or, it recognizes me, but there's something more..." He tried to explain, but couldn't find the words.

"Well, can you shut it down?"

"Honestly, I don't know if that's the best way to handle this." He told her, "Hear me out. I don't think it wants to hurt me."

"What?!" she squawked, looking at Riley like he was a crazy as he sounded.

"I think that it thinks-...I think it may have imprinted on me. Back when it hatched. I think, it thinks that I'm its-"

"Don't you say it..."

"MMMAAAAaaaaaa" The alien tried to vocalize with gravelly chirps, reaching up and slapping the airlock window, startling them both.

"Riley, no...*Riley*?" Jess said, watching him step closer and pressing his hand up to the other side of the glass. "It's a trick. It's got to be. Morrow's demented. This has got to be one of his tricks." She pleaded with him as she heard the locks in the door slide back, "Stop! If you open that

104

door it'll kill you and then it'll kill me. I don't want to die here, Riley! Please!"

He stopped, looked her in the eye and said, with all sincerity, "Trust me."

The door slid open.

She stepped back, wanting to run, but was frozen in place as it opened, concentrating as hard as she could on blocking herself from the alien's perception. Morrow was looking on, practically drooling and completely ignoring the shit dripping down his inner thigh.

"Oh, ho, ho! You're done now, Robot! I haven't fed it yet." Morrow taunted and then punched himself twice in the face, as Jessica scowled at him.

The alien stepped to Riley and sniffed him over, grabbing and pulling him around; inspecting the differences between them. It felt around to the back of its head where the implant was located, and then the Aegis at the back of Riley's. Beads of sweat formed on Riley's brow and the alien's tongue snaked out of its mouth, lapping it up and leaving behind a coating of saliva that dripped down his face. It smacked its lips, tasting the salty liquid and Riley started to get nervous about his decision.

"This is it!" Morrow cheered, like a giddy schoolgirl, then ran headfirst into the glass.

"You just don't learn do you?" Jess asked him, as he held his bleeding nose.

Shifting its focus to the noise from the divider, the alien's attention returned to the doctor. Remaining concealed, Jessica watched in astonishment as it left Riley unharmed. It dove, slamming into the glass, then righted itself and looked back. The alien stopped momentarily and pointed into its open mouth, then continued to pound on the glass.

"You're right old man, he does look hungry. Why don't you come on out of there and feed this poor, starving baby?" Riley heckled.

Morrow was aghast, tapping away at his controls and trying to figure out why the implant wasn't working. All diagnostics came back with zero errors and reported no hardware malfunctions. He snarled back at the alien and cranked up the voltage, hoping to drive it into a frenzy. It screeched and reared back, clutching its head, with its tail lashing around wildly. Riley moved out of the path of destruction as broken equipment was hurdled around like a tornado had manifested in the room with them.

"What are you doing?! Stop!" Riley shouted over Morrow's maniacal laughter, "Morrow, you sack of shit! I promise you right now that you're not walking out of here!"

Lights flickered within Riley's eye, while he remotely intercepted and disrupted the signal as quickly as he could, then cut off power to the controller that Morrow was using. The doctor was locked out of the system now, and locked in, behind the contamination divider with no way to override it, and no way to access any life support functions. Morrow could have waited them out before, but with Riley in full control, he only had two options. He could cooperate and *hope* that they let him live, or eventually die of dehydration, trapped in quarantine. There was always the chance that they'd just open the divider and let the hatchling have him, but at this point, that could happen either way.

"Wait! Wait! Wait!... I'm ...sorry?" Morrow said, coyly, like he wasn't sure if he was using the right word. "You've disarmed me. I can do no harm. I'm at your mercy! Please...I-I can help you! Surely you can see the benefit of having a *doctor* around." He pleaded.

"You're pathetic." Riley responded, then walked over to the exhausted hatchling, comforting it with limited success. "Jess? He's all yours. I can't look at him."

"My pleasure." She told him, stepping out of the illusion like it was a shadowy corner of the room.

"No! I can help him. I-I can help!"

"Riley?" She sighed, "I read his mind, and he really does believe that he can help you. He's a psycho, but he's a brilliant psycho."

Morrow smiled, then hit himself.

"Help me with what?" Riley asked, dubiously.

"Have you really not seen yourself? You look...sick." she told him, pointing to the mirror on the wall over the scrub station.

Riley looked at her with confusion and some worry over the sincerity in her tone. He didn't feel any different and hadn't thought about it since Connor had brought it up. Looking down at his hand that was stroking the scales of the hatchling's forehead, what should have been a healthy pink with a slight tan, was instead a lifeless grey, pruned and fissured in the creases. He rushed over to the mirror and looked at himself for the first time since he was bonded with the AEGIS. Jessica shot a look at Morrow, expecting some kind of snide remark, but at this point, he'd learned his lesson enough to know that it was in his best interest to keep his mouth shut.

"Jess…You go ahead. Give the others a heads up. We'll be out shortly." Riley told her sombrely. "And see if you can get them to make up another sled, or even just some rope to drag him, I don't care. He won't be walking on his own."

"Riley…are you going to be okay?"

"No. We'll be out shortly." He responded.

The coldness in his voice almost made her feel pity for the old man. She nodded and left, out the way that they came. Jogging down the hallway, she could hear the locks of the glass wall disengage and the mechanical arms coming out of the ceiling. She focused her mind away from whatever was about to happen back there and pressed forward. Outside, she found Gaia and Fen, with Connor's clothes and gear piled up nearby.

"Where's Scruffy?" she asked.

"Takin' a bath." Gaia said, sleepily.

She pointed over the water, but the surface was flat with no sign of him anywhere, until a flurry of bubbles erupted from the shallow lake, and the water around it churned up. A light flashed from the bottom of the dark pool, and the body of a large, serpentine creature floated to the surface with a hole burnt through its mouth and out its spine.

"Whew! Did you see that?!" Connor shouted, popping up out of the water in front of where they were watching, startling Jess and making Fen's tail wag. "Look what I found." He said proudly, holding up the weapon that he'd thrown away when he escaped. He tossed it up on shore, and it landed, point first with a dull thud as it stuck into the soft ground. Pulling himself from the water, he covered up for Gaia but displayed himself more freely from Jessica's point of view, not overtly flaunting, but pausing briefly, so that she could take it all in.

"Congratulations, you got your dick back," Jess said sharply, gesturing to the conduit, embarrassed that he'd caught her looking. "Now holster it. We're going to have some unusual company. Even for this group."

With his consent, she pushed the information into their minds, but without their knowledge, helped them to understand the situation and remain calm about it.

"Well, if he really can help him, then I guess we don't have much of a choice. But, for the record? I don't like it, and if he blinks in a way that I find disagreeable, I'll do him, like it did that…snake…thing." He said, holding up and admiring the conduit as he got dressed.

"Then we're in agreement."

"You're sure about the hatchling? The *alien* hatchling?"

"Of course not. I'm half expecting it to come out of there by itself, but Riley was pretty adamant about trusting him that it'd be okay. They do seem to have a connection, but I'm actually a lot more comfortable with the whole situation now that you've got that thing back." She told him earnestly. "Here they come. Fen? Settle."

Riley came out of the darkened arena first, his face blank with a thousand yard stare. He led the way for the hatchling, whose scales were standing up, as it cautiously exited the hole in the ship.

"You 'explained' everything?" Riley asked, and Jess nodded. "Good. He's still inside, I just wanted to make sure the kids wouldn't see him. Do we have anything that we can carry him with? We're bringing him with us. If he really can fix…*this*, he's under my protection. Got it?" he said, looking at Connor who'd had his own retribution in mind.

"Ya, bud. I'm all up to speed. Whatever you want to do." he told him, nodding.

"Thank you. Now help me carry him out. We'll tie him on with the supplies."

While they were gone, Jess sat pensively with Fen, between the kids resting in the saddle. They were staring at the alien hatchling, who seemed to be avoiding them and behaving very strangely for its species. It was being submissive, but less like an animal than a shy child that'd been left alone in a public place.

"It's different than the others." Rayn said, leaning over and resting his head on Jess's shoulder.

"I think you might be right." She said back, doubtful of her own words and hesitant to say them out loud. "But we can't be too careful."

"Jess, grab some rope and make room on the sled." Riley called out, holding Morrow up, under one of his arms, with Connor on the other side, doing the same.

The old man was unconscious when they strapped him down to the back. There was barely any room, even after repacking it, and Morrow's legs would have been dragging behind, over the edge, if they were still a part of his body.

Fen led the way, carrying Gaia and pulling the sled, with Jess and Rayn walking beside them. Riley stayed back with the hatchling, keeping an eye on Morrow, while Connor followed behind them. He kept the conduit holstered but ready, constantly on edge, watching the alien. The group travelled like this in awkward silence, all the way to Vonn's compound.

KEYS TO THE CASTLE

The compound was in ruins, just as they'd left it. The carcasses of the other hatchlings that they'd encountered had been picked clean, leaving only bits of sun-bleached bones behind. After making sure that the buildings were vacant and the area was cleared, they unpacked the sled and set up a temporary camp that backed onto the door to the well house. Jessica stayed with Rayn, watching over Gaia at the camp, while Connor took Fen on patrol.

Riley could feel the ship buried below the house on the hill and went to investigate with the mutated hatchling that he'd taken to calling 'Bas'. It followed him around like a lost puppy, which would have been cute, if not for its demonic appearance. He lowered himself into the basement, careful not to step on any of the nails sticking up in the pile of broken steps on the ground. Bas leapt over him like a cat, landing near the breached door and sniffed at the musty air inside, then crawled in through the gap. Riley switched to infrared and followed after him, running scans on the derelict ship as he went.

He was amazed at the sophistication of the technology on board, even in comparison to that of the arkship. Its core was almost entirely powered down but seemed to be in working condition. There was a single rejuvenation tank that looked like it had never been used, similar to the one aboard the ark, but with some major upgrades and a nearly untouched stockpile of nanomachines. The cockpit, however, was locked. He'd need to get in there to gain access to the ship's CPU and change the admin privileges. Without authorized systems access, all he'd have is a cosmetically dazzling bunker with a broken door, but at least it would be more secure than the open-air buffet they'd set up outside.

Bas was rummaging through a pile of bones in the corner, chomping through them for the marrow, but they were all dry, brittle and hollow. He was hungry again, and getting antsy. Because of his rapid alien metabolism, he was growing quickly and needing to feed frequently. Noise by the door triggered an instinctive action, and Bas aggressively rushed toward whatever had just dropped through.

The lights came on, and the ship's systems started up when Rayn landed inside. He stood at the door, defiantly facing his attacker, who had the agility to stop himself when he'd realized that he was threatening one of the group. Though no harm had been done, Bas bowed down in submission and acceptance, expecting a punishment that wasn't coming.

"How'd you do that?" Riley asked Rayn, while trying to soothe Bas.

"How'd I do what?"

"The lights. Everything. They all turned on when you came in. I couldn't do it. What's the trick?"

"I didn'do anything. I just got bored n' came to see what you were doin' down here. I wanted to see…the *alien*." He whispered, covering his mouth. "It's different than the others. Bas, right? As in Basilisk?"

"Smart." Riley praised. "So you're into mythology?"

"How'd you guess?"

"Smartass…So you're bored, huh? Looking for something to do?" Riley asked, looking around the interior of the lit up ship.

Rayn lit up with equally with excitement, "You want my help?"

"Sure do! You seem to be the key to the castle here, and I need to figure out why." Riley told him, pleased with his eagerness.

"What *is* this place?" Rayn asked, stepping over the skeletons like they were just another exhibit.

"Well, it's very similar to the giant spaceship buried under the mountain, where I got all this." He told him, pointing to his cybernetic eye with his robotic arm. "I wouldn't call the hill that the house is sitting on a mountain by any means but-"

"Wait, why's it buried under a mountain if it's a spaceship?" Rayn asked before Riley could finish his sentence.

"It was built there a long, long time ago, but there was a cataclysm and time rolled on without it." He explained.

"So…Is this a spaceship too?"

"I don't know. It's a lot newer than anything I've seen so far, and I can't connect with its systems. But apparently *you* can." Riley said, showing him to the sealed door at the far end. "Think you can get this open for me, so we can find out?"

"I'll try, but I'm usually a lot stronger."

"I don't think you'll need your muscles for this." Riley told him, Placing his hand on the door and motioning for Rayn to do the same. Bas ran up to the door and pressed his hand to it, just like Riley, and looked up to him for approval. "Your turn, Rayn" He chuckled.

"It's a good thing I know not to judge a book by its cover." Rayn joked, looking at the door and focusing on the metal showing through Riley's knuckles with the scaly clawed hand pressed up beside his.

"Hilarious." Riley said back, "See that tank over there? It can heal me. If we can get this door open, I'm hoping that I can get access to the system and use it to give me back my devilish good looks…Well, back to normal anyway. If that's the case, Connor and Bas will have to fight over Ol' stumpy out there."

Rayn touched his hand to the door, and it opened up, just like Riley predicted. Inside, was another room, about a quarter of the size of the other. A pair of seats were surrounded by control panels and facing out toward an oblong, half-dome windshield of what was clearly the cockpit.

"Given the airlock in the back, and my assumption that it's not some crazy submarine, I'm going to say that's a confirmation on your spaceship theory." he told Rayn, who'd hopped into one of the seats, barely restraining himself from playing with everything within reach.

Riley took the seat beside him and tried to interface with the controls, but they remained unresponsive. When Rayn leaned in, he saw them lighting up beneath his hands as they hovered over the panels, which got them both excited, and gave Riley an idea.

"Hmm, I think we're going to need Jess to help us out here. In the meantime, let's see if we can get the airlock opened properly, so we don't have to crawl through every time to get in and out. We'll get this place cleaned out and see if we can do something about those stairs before we get them down here. Sound good partner?" He said, already knowing the answer by the look on his face.

Suddenly, the ship rumbled, and Riley had to call Bas and Rayn back, who had both started headlong toward the surface. Once the rumbling was over, he brought them out to see what had happened. The block and mortar walls were heavily cracked from the tremors and would need to be reinforced if they were going to be using that passage to move back and forth between the ship and their camp. Rayn, who was accustomed to being much larger, looked up at the collapsed steps that he'd climbed down and realized that he should have at least dropped a rope on the way in. Riley stood at the bottom and laced his fingers together, offering to give him a boost back up, but the boy was caught by surprise when strong, clawed hands suddenly grabbed him by the shoulders and a smaller pair wrapped around his waist. Before he could react, he was safely on the landing at the top of the stairs, and Bas released his careful grip on him. Riley was starting

his ascent when he was pulled up and placed next to Rayn just as quickly. Bas was still small in comparison to what he would be fully grown, but he was growing quickly and getting stronger by the hour. Once they were out of the basement, they had to hurry out of the house, which was ready to come down around them due to the intensity of the quakes.

Outside, Connor was getting reacquainted with the conduit. Riding atop Fen, he was blasting a trench around the perimeter of the compound, which breached the water table and partially filled as he went. It was as deep as it was wide, with steep walls that would ideally keep anything from crossing over and be unable to get back out without assistance. It was the first step in building their defences.

"What the hell is he doing?!" Riley shouted to Jess as they jogged over to meet her at the camp.

"He was really itching to use that thing, I guess. Came back from his patrol, going off about how vulnerable we are here, then left again in a huff, and started doing what he's doing." She explained as best she could, also fairly confused about it.

"Call him in." Riley told her, nodding to convey permission.

She closed her eyes and entered Connor's erratic mind. He was agitated and growing more so, but with that, she could also feel the pleasure he got from using his power. She was only supposed to deliver the message, but he wasn't listening; he was entirely focused on the conduit. Fen's mind, however, was clear. Other than being a little disappointed that he had to stop, Fen slowed down, leaving the C-shaped canyon and returning to camp. Connor stopped firing when they broke away, and was about to fly off the handle, but Jess thought fast and gently sedated him.

"What was that all about!?" Riley shouted at Connor, who was now looking like he had just woken up.

"Moat." He yawned. "We're out in the open. We know that this is a nesting ground. We've got no walls, and even if we did, what's to say that they'd be strong enough, or tall enough."

"Oh." Riley said, recognizing the logic. "Well, that's actually good idea. But you couldn't have said something first? By the way…Sounds like you were getting pretty rambunctious for a bit there. What's up?"

"It's nothing, just got a little carried away is all." He said, looking down at the conduit and reabsorbing the energy that was surging through it.

"Ya lets keep that holstered for now." Riley insisted, "I need to borrow Jess for a bit. Gaia's up now. Why don't you take her and Fen and find us something for dinner."

"You giving the orders now?"

"What? No, I- Sorry. We're all getting hungry. You're the best suited for the task. Please?" Riley rephrased himself.

Connor backed down and nodded, then reached out offering his hand to Gaia, who'd wandered over to climb up into the saddle with him. As she took it, Bas's stomach let out a tortuous growl, and he took off into the woods after something that'd had his attention since they got outside.

"I guess I'll take Bas too." Connor groaned through his teeth, "Don't worry. We'll be back in a little while. Hopefully. This is fine."

"Thanks. Good luck." Riley told him before they took off in the direction that Bas had left in.

Gathering up the bound and gagged doctor, Riley and Jess headed back down to the ship, leaving him in the basement, outside of the busted airlock. There was no way that he'd be able to climb back out without the stairs, and the door was curled open at the top; too high to reach from the ground. It was a perfect little dungeon for him to stay while they were busy.

Inside, Jess saw the clothes on the skeletons, and her eyes welled up when she recognized who she was looking at. She pulled Riley aside, while Rayn went into the cockpit ahead of them.

"Those two...I knew they'd be down here, but I wasn't ready to see them." She said, looking at the clothed bones. "That's Vonn and Felicia; their grandparents...Does Rayn know?"

"I don't think he's put it together. Not yet anyway, but I'm sure he'll figure it out eventually." Riley told her, handing over part of a torn photograph that he'd found of everyone that'd lived there, which was dated back before the invasion. "Pretty sure he'd recognize his mom and dad if he saw this. They got their eyes from grandma. Heh...and Connor looks like a baby without his beard."

"Should we tell him?" she asked, staring wistfully at the photo.

"Connor? I dare you. Rayn? Not yet." Riley said, bringing her into the cockpit. "I need your help first. Both of you."

"What is it?"

"Our boy Rayn here seems to have access to the systems, but doesn't know how the ship works. I can operate the systems, but I don't have access. See where I'm going with this?" Riley said, setting Jessica's hand on top of Rayn's head, then sitting down in the other chair beside him.

She understood.

"Rayn, you know what we're going to try?"

"Yep." he responded, nodding impatiently.

"Okay, let's give this a shot."

They both pressed their hands to the console, and she stepped between them, cradling the back of their heads in her hands and creating a bridge between their minds. Once the connection was made, Riley's eyes lit up and his enhancements had the work done in seconds. It now identified *him* as the systems administrator and the AEGIS, by association, became the new onboard AI. The ship sprung to life like it was stretching out after a long nap.

"Are you doing that?" Jess asked, taking her hands away and stepping back to look at the holographic displays popping up all around them.

"All me. This thing is incredible!" Riley said, boastfully.

"Great, now can we get back to this?" She said, putting the photo back in his hand, face down.

"Huh?…Listen, don't you think that it'd be better just coming from you?" he said distantly, with his eyes darting around at all of the projections.

"What's that?" Rayn asked, catching the photo as it fell out of Riley's suddenly apathetic grasp.

"Come on." Jess said, taking his hand before he could look it over, "Riley's *busy*. I need to talk to you about something."

MORROW'S SORROWS

Morrow woke up to throbbing pain in his thighs, as the anesthetic wore off from the surgery. His mouth was stuffed with an old dirty sock, and his hands had been bound together with coarse rope around a support post in the gloomy basement, filled with nesting materials and broken egg shells. Light was shining out from the top of a bent hatch, and dim, natural light was coming in from an elevated open doorway, but with no steps to reach it. The muffled voices of a woman and child came from inside the bunker, but he couldn't quite make out what they were saying. He was alone, for now.

Still drowsy from the sedatives, Morrow clumsily tried to free himself. The floor jack was smooth for the most part, save the weld spatter along the seems. He'd create friction by scraping up and down on the post, gradually weakening the fibres of his bindings, and causing them to fray enough that he would be able to break free. Until then, he'd have to work diligently, careful to not tip them off to what he was doing, but quickly enough to get it done before anybody came around and noticed.

Voices on the other side of the hatch stopped, and he heard the clunky, grinding mechanisms in the door struggling to operate. It sounded like the airlocks in his lab, but rusty and disjointed. The whining of the metal ceased when the final bolt retracted, and the door unlocked but failed to open. The heavy door held itself in place by the twisted metal and warped hinges, which would need to be cut away or pulled loose by heavy equipment to open.

When the last strand of the dried out rope snapped, he sat up against the post, holding his hands behind his back to give the appearance that he was still tied up. Not a second later, a child popped its head up and peeked through the top of the bent hatch, looking back and forth between Morrow and the ground, then dropped back down again. There was a thump against the door, and an audible one-sided battle as the child futilely tried to force it open.

The pain below his waste was excruciating now, and Morrow grabbed for his legs, but felt the dry dirt on the floor instead, and watched it pour out from his trembling fists as he raised them. He began to

hyperventilate. He could still feel his legs tingling like they'd only fallen asleep; hot and cold at the same time, but they just weren't there.

The last thing that he remembered was the dark silhouette looming closer, and the face of a robot wearing a human mask, with surgical equipment on mechanical arms behind him, like his automated minions. The hatchling paced at the other side of the lab, watching and waiting, restrained by the robot's will alone, as the contamination barrier was retracted. There was a quick jab and his vision blurred as the anesthesia took hold.

Sounds of rending metal tore Morrow's attention away from his self-pity when light spilled out into the basement as the bent door dislodged and slammed down on the ground in front of him. If his legs hadn't been amputated, the door falling on them would have done it, just not so cleanly. He quickly laced his fingers behind his back again, before anyone noticed the beginnings of his escape.

As his eyes adjusted to the bright light, he looked up to see the backlit outline of a figure that he hadn't accounted for. A stocky, muscular man, with the same hair as the kid that he'd expected to see, stepped out with an armful of mummified cadavers, and piled them onto a tarp below the elevated doorway. The woman that had accompanied the robot back at the lab followed him through the door and walked up to Morrow, standing on top of the fallen hatch in front of him with a furrowed brow and her head cocked to the side.

"Well, that was lucky." She snickered, looking down at his stumps. "Are you enjoying your modest accommodations? It's not too cramped for you down here, is it?"

"Cozy." Morrow responded, wiggling his shrugged shoulders and looking back up at her with a disingenuous shit-eating grin.

"How would you feel about getting out of here? Out of the dirt. Get cleaned up. Get some fresh air and a little sun?" she asked, with a softer tone.

"…Why? Why would you want to help me? Why don't you just pull what you need out of my head and be done with it?" he asked, suspicious of where her intentions led.

"Honestly? Because I don't want the repulsive shit that you've got floating around in *there*, floating around in *here*. I don't just look into your mind…I enter it. The psychic residue left behind by yours is…sticky. Think of it like this. I *could* wade through slop to get the truffle, or I could get the pig that lives in it to get it for me." She explained. "C'mon out and stretch your le- get some of that fresh air."

"Hmmph. Well, maybe I am a pig. Maybe I like it down here in the dirt, with my secrets. Maybe I want to watch that young man's face rot off, and the machine take over." he contested.

"Maybe. But, we've tried the stick, and that apparently isn't working. I'm offering you the carrot. I suggest you take it. It's the only chance you've got."

Morrow rubbed his chin with one hand and peeled back his bandages with the other as he mulled over her proposition. There was a spreading redness around the uniformly spaced sutures that was tender and inflamed, indicating to him that it'd become infected. He froze for a second, and looked up sheepishly, realizing that he'd just given himself away by showing his freed hands.

"I uhh...accept?" he said meekly.

"Good. And this half-assed little escape attempt? I'll keep that to myself, and you'll keep...whatever else Riley would cut off if he found out. Probably your hands?"

"What's in it for you?"

"You'll owe me. Big." She said, staring him in the eye, then turning away like they'd never spoken in the first place. "Rayn? Could you help the doctor up, out of the basement?"

He tucked his bandages back and brushed the dirt from his hands, offering one up to the baby-faced Hercules. His large hand reached past the doctor's and grabbed him by the bunched up material of his clothing, lifting him up so that they were eye to eye. Morrow's dangling stumps kicked as though he was trying to get his footing. Still coming to terms with his newfound handicap, he was more concerned with his inability to stand than the crash landing that he had ahead of him, as he was thrown across the room toward the pile of bodies.

A line was strung through the tarp's eyelets and pulled tight, bringing the edges of the canvas over him and together like a sack. The bag was heaved up, and bones jabbed at him from all sides. Bobbing and swaying as it was carried along, Morrow's stomach churned. The sack came down hard on the ground, unravelling as the brittle cadavers rolled out, leaving Morrow to crawl over them, covered in vomit and corpse dust with the bright sun stinging his eyes. It'd been some time since he'd felt the warmth of the sun, and breathed fresh, unfiltered air. Even before he was taken hostage and mutilated, Morrow hadn't strayed out from the subterranean facility in years. Crawling away from the pile, he felt a hint of relative freedom, even though he knew that there was no escaping now. That

feeling was quickly snuffed out when he was carried off again and locked inside of a poultry run by the barn. The chicken wire that it was wrapped in was thin, but the old man's frail hands weren't nearly strong enough to break it, and the frame was heavy enough that there was no danger of him lifting it to escape. He was stuck there, but at least he was out of the dark, dank basement and way from the dead.

"You weren't going to run away on me, were you?" Jessica chirped.

"Oh my dear, that's getting quite old." Morrow snarled.

"Hmm…You didn't seem to have any issue rubbing it in Riley's face. I don't think he likes being called 'Robot', and I think you know that very well. I'll let you think about that, before you two cross paths again." She lectured. "In the meantime, let me give you the grand tour of your new and improved living quarters. You've got four walls and a roof, with a lovely breeze, and your choice of sun *or* shade for *most* of the day, from this luxurious plywood awning." She told him, showing it off like a realtor presenting a new home to potential buyers. "This area here is your bedroom, bathroom, and living room." She said patronizingly, flaunting the ground Morrow was sitting on, as Rayn poured a large bucket of water through the fencing into a small wading pool that'd been used as a feeding trough inside the cage. "Now. What do you say?"

"Thank you." Morrow snorted begrudgingly.

"Here. A blanket and a first aid kit. Because you've been so well behaved. See? If you can be nice, I can be nice too…Clean yourself up doc, you smell like death…and shit."

She left him to tend to himself, heading back down into the basement. Rayn stacked wood for a fire away from their camp, with the skeletons he'd gathered piled in with it. When they'd both gotten on with other things, Morrow stripped down and cleaned the filth off of himself the best he could with his shirt as a rag, wet with his drinking water and some hand sanitizer from the kit, then got to work on his wounds. His eye twitched as he poured rubbing alcohol over the contusions, more so where there was any redness and swelling, then slathered them up with ointment and wrapped each with sterile pads and gauze. After digging through the pack, he found that the scissors, pins, and tweezers had all been removed, which came of little surprise. While he was in the sack of bones, he'd snapped off and pocketed a partial, hollowed out fibula. The bone already had a splintered edge that'd be simple to hone on the concrete beneath the straw bedding. The wire would be too strong for the bone to cut, and it was far too brittle to get any leverage using it as a prying tool, but there was one

thing it would be perfect for. For now, so long as he wasn't caught with it, his only option was to wait, observe and ponder why fate had been so cruel.

BEAST FEAST

They came upon a grassy clearing, tacky with dried blood from the massacre that'd taken place just minutes before their arrival. Bas was atop a pile of carcasses, gorging on meat and tossing the mangled scraps off to the side. It was a feast to compensate for the famine he'd lived through, and the alien's physiology was responding in kind. The bulk and mass that Bas was putting on was almost as drastic as the mutations, with his crown beginning to resemble that of the alphas, even at this young age.

Connor kept Fen from getting any closer while Bas was feeding, unsure of what would happen if they overstepped any boundaries. The growing hatchling's head popped up and spotted them waiting by the tree line, then shot back down, rushing through just one more. A few moments later, Bas rolled around, smearing himself in the glistening blood from his kills, then leapt from the pile, painted in red and wearing it with pride. Hopping around, excited to see them, he ran a figure eight, showing off his colour. "Ooohhh! Pretty!" Gaia praised through her shirt that she had held up over her nose.

Bas ran back to dig through the pile and picked out a body that had the least insulting amount of meat left, and brought it back as an offering.

Fen tried to keep his tail from wagging to hide his excitement, but no matter how stoic he succeeded in being, the hypersalivation and big wiggly rump gave him away.

"Hhhyuck! Ugh…Go for it Fen. Treat yourself, buddy." Connor said, gagging from the overwhelming metallic stench of the blood.

Before Fen got messy, Connor and Gaia hopped down to go look through the pile to see if they could find anything that they could bring back. By the time they found one that hadn't been too badly damaged, Fen was finished with his and had his head buried in the pile with Bas, revelling in the overabundance of food. Connor drew his knife and had Gaia watch the process so that she'd be able to do it herself. She knew that this was something that her father would have taught her one day when she was old enough, but that would never happen now, so she was thankful that *he* was there to teach her. She watched as he made a shallow incision near its groin

120

and brought the knife under its skin, opening it up along the way to the sternum, being careful to avoid any organs. He moved everything out of the way and cut through the connective membranes, then severed the esophagus, so that the entrails were no longer attached to anything inside of the body. After separating the groin and anus, he scooped its guts up and dropped them next to his little helper, who was starting to look a little queasy.

"You okay?" he asked, and she hesitantly nodded, trying to act tough. "You know, for a lot of people, it's tradition to eat the heart on your first hunt." He told her, cutting it away and showing it to her, seeing if she'd take the bait.

"...Really?" she asked nervously, kneeling down beside him and taking the thick heart out of his hands. She wanted to be included and didn't want to disappoint him. Slowly raising the dripping heart up to her mouth, she summoned her bravery and went for the bite. Connor was just about to stop her when she paused and looked at him suspiciously. "*We* didn't hunt this...Shouldn't *Bas* eat it?" She said, having figured out that Connor was playing a trick on her.

"I think it'll be okay, just this once. Go ahead." He said, egging her on.

Bas came over after hearing his name, and seemed pleased that Gaia looked like she was going to eat. She gave Connor a sly look, letting him know that she'd figured out his ruse, and stuck her tongue out at him. She laughed and tossed the heart to Bas, who caught and returned it to her like a hot potato, which put an abrupt end to her amusement.

"I think Bas wants *you* to have it. You don't want to be rude to the one putting the food on the table, do you?" Connor said, grinning mischievously from ear to ear, but it was clear that she wasn't buying it.

"I'm not hungry."

"For later then." he responded, packing it away as Bas huffed in disappointment, and went back to the pile. "Back to it then."

Connor wiped off his blade so that he could see what he was doing and went back to work on the gutted carcass. He cut around the elbow, through the ligaments, and snapped off the hoofed lower legs, then did the same to the top of the neck. Finishing off what he'd started with the esophagus, he severed the spine and decapitated it, since there were no antlers to hold onto for skinning.

Gaia seemed more at ease with the process now that she'd gotten some blood on her hands, and once the head was gone, she was able to

disassociate the animal from the meat that it provided. Peeling the hide back, Connor waved her in to help.

"Here, get a good grip and pull on this. Up and away from the blade, nice and steady. You keep it pulled tight, and I'll cut it away. Got it?" He instructed, giving her the flap of skin that he'd started. "I'll show you how to tan it later too, so we can use it for clothes, or blankets."

"Unnnhh- Like this?" she asked, pulling at the hide and leaning back with her weight into it.

"Perfect, just watch your footing. If you slip out here, you'll wind up looking like Bas over there." He said, looking over at the blood-caked mutant, who was now sniffing at the air with Fen, as a light breeze came through. "Speaking of…It's time to go. We'd better hurry and get this packed up. Looks like they're expecting company."

"Why?…It's not like we're helpless. What kinda dummy is going to mess with us, with *them* around?"

"Heh, not much I'd imagine, but we still need to be careful. Who knows what else is out there that we don't know about. Besides, sometimes it's just better to avoid a confrontation. No unnecessary fights. We've taken more than our share already, and we're not the only ones that need to eat out here." he explained.

Connor whistled, and the pair of bloody hell beasts came running, bellies full, and anxious to burn off some calories. He packed up their meat into a separate wrapping and loaded a few more of the cleaner kills onto the sled to finish later, since it was pretty apparent that Fen could handle the extra burden. Bas shot wildly through the overgrowth, bouncing around and trying to hold himself back to keep pace, absolutely teeming with energy himself, like a kid full of sweetened espresso.

All the way to their camp, they could hear echoes of the violent commotion back at the feeding ground. The scavengers that were encroaching on them before had converged into a battle royal for rights to the ample leftovers.

Ahead of them, a large plume of grey smoke rose from the pyre that Rayn had built while they were gone. They rode up and dismounted nearby, unstrapping the harness and letting Fen go off to get some water, while they finished prepping the meat for the grill, and the rest for preservation and storage. Rayn came to help, but chose not to mention the reason for building such a large fire during the day.

Fen made a beeline for Morrow's cage, sniffing around the corner that he'd been using as a latrine. Cocking his leg, he marked the area and

covered the scent of the old man's waste with his own. Once he was satisfied that he'd made an impression, he left to clean himself off with a swim in the moat.

As soon as Fen was out of sight, Bas, who'd been looking on, rushed the cage and shook it to intimidate the doctor. He cocked his leg, mimicking Fen, and urinated all over the side of the cage, further masking the prior scent and diminishing any territorial claims that may have inadvertently been made. Instead of cleaning the blood from his scales, Bas opted to bask in the sun, allowing it to dry out to a baked on crust.

Connor spent the next few hours tutoring the siblings on his preferred techniques for cleaning and preserving the meat, which they were both keen to learn. They took pride in the process, and the activity helped to reinvigorate Gaia's respect for him. She was no longer trying to impose upon him the position of a surrogate father figure and expecting his protection, but instead embracing his role of mentor and realizing that he was there to give them the skills they'd need to rely on themselves.

Later in the day, as the sun was setting on their camp, the air was rich with the pleasing aroma of grilled steak and ribs, with smoke from the drying rack upwind. They'd all cleaned up, and Jessica had joined Connor, Gaia, and Rayn by the smaller grilling pit to eat. Bas and Fen had bedded down by the embers of the pyre, having finally crashed after so much food. Riley however, was a no-show. He'd become more engrossed in his link with the ship. After updating the AEGIS and beginning to understand the technology, the more he explored what it had to offer, the more it was pulling his attention further and further away from anything else. His hunger didn't even register.

"Wow. I had no idea you were such deadly hunters!" Jess teased.

Gaia perked up, excited to tell her all about it, but her mouth was stuffed full, and when she spoke the words came out muffled, along with bits of food.

"More like gatherers. This is nothing compared to what we left behind. Riley's little murder machine over there slaughtered an entire herd before we caught up." Connor told her, nodding toward Bas. "He didn't need all that meat; not all of those kills were out of necessity. Don't turn your back on him if he looks hungry."

"Well…Thanks, I didn't want to sleep tonight anyway." She said sarcastically.

"Where is Riley, by the way? Why isn't he here eating with us?"

"He's still down there, messing around with the computer."

"Well, he'd better get up here. When I'm done eating, the old man's going to talk." Connor said sternly, plating up the steaks on to some old chipped dinnerware. "Gaia? Could you go get Riley for me, please?"

She nodded and hopped to it. Connor and Jess waited for her to get out of earshot before continuing their conversation.

"And if he doesn't? I mean, he's very likely still in shock." Jess reasoned.

"Then there's one more for the fire." he snarled, showing her the palms of his hands. One hand, rough, tough, and weathered from years of hard living, and the other, soft and smooth with raw blisters in place of built up calluses. "I have him and Gaia to thank for this. She gave me a new hand because *he* took my old one. He's responsible for what's happening to Riley. He tried to enslave the lot of us…If he doesn't give us anything useful, and I mean *damn* good, I'm going to slow roast that motherfucker and feed him to the boys when they wake up."

Jessica sighed, clearly uncomfortable with his intentions, and sure that Riley would follow with his sentiment. She looked at Rayn, trying to gauge his reaction to Connor's need for revenge, without intruding into his mind to read his thoughts. His dispassionate response for the old man concerned her, and she feared for the boy's apathetic mentality. Her thoughts turned to Gaia, who seemed to be the only one among them to retain any sort of innocence. She felt a strong desire to protect that.

"I'm going to go see what's taking those two so long." she told them, getting up and taking her plate with her.

She carried it over to Morrow's cage and dropped it off, in through the chain link door at the end, and locked it back up before she left to go down to the ship. Morrow looked confused and suspicious as she lowered the plate onto the ground, sitting dead still and making sure not to do anything that could be misinterpreted as aggression, then dove on the food like the starved animal that he was, as soon as the cage door latched shut.

"What'd she do that for?" Rayn asked Connor, "That guy sounds like a dick."

"…It's just misplaced compassion. It's not something you want to lose, but it can also lead you astray if you're not careful." He explained, sounding exhausted by the thought of it and eyeing up the cooling cooked meat. "What the hell are they doing anyway? I don't know about you, but I'm done waiting. I'm eating mine now."

"Mhmmnomnomnom!" Rayn mumbled back, stuffing his mouth full of steak.

TAKE OFF

When Jessica got downstairs, she could hear Gaia's voice from up in the cockpit, pleading with Riley. She ran in to see what was the trouble, and pulled the little girl away when she saw the condition that he was in.

He sat still in the pilot's chair, seemingly asleep, but with his eyes wide open, like he'd suffered a massive stroke. Light flickered rapidly in both eyes now, and the skin sagged lifelessly around the organic side of his face, drooping from his eye like an old Basset Hound. His skin had lost almost all of its colour, and if not for the activity in his eyes, she would have assumed his body to be vacant.

She could feel Gaia's distraught vulnerability and see the angst in her eyes, which triggered something of the same within herself. Her powers spontaneously activated in response to her level of stress and Gaia stood there like a mannequin as the world around her stopped, in a slice of frozen time. The computer kept working away, but everything else was still. Jessica had become flooded with emotions like the breaking of a dam. From what she'd perceived as a loss of humanity in both Connor and Rayn, she was seeing happen physically to Riley, and it was just too much to handle.

Looking at the greying flesh hanging off of his artificial bones, she knew that there was nothing that the doctor could do for him. Even if Morrow was telling the truth before about being able to fix him, that time had passed, and the only thing keeping him alive was gone. Jessica picked up Gaia in her arms and carried her outside to the cage, where the old man was kept. The plate she'd given him was nearly cleaned, and he was sitting still, mid-bite when she opened the door and pulled him out. She took Gaia's arm and placed her hand on Morrow's bare shoulder after pulling back the blanket that he'd used to cover himself. She entered her mind and took control, telepathically puppeting her into healing him.

Connor and Rayn sat locked in place by the fire as it continued to burn, unaware of what was happening at the time, though she could feel Rayn's mind adapting to her powers again and it wouldn't be long before they had no effect on him. A healthy fear made her blood run cold when she saw Bas, who'd woken up from the sound of the cage door swinging open,

but he'd noticed that Fen didn't seem to care about what they were doing and went back to sleep.

The fresh gauze bandages around Morrow's stumps stretched and pulled apart as his legs regenerated. His skin tightened and plumped, while his back straightened, as her healing powers corrected his scoliosis, and reversed the deteriorating effects of his advanced age. Because of the rapid healing, like Rayn, Morrow's mind was gradually becoming less and less susceptible to Jessica's power that kept them in stasis. He woke up from the daze, confused by the sudden shift in his location and situation, but soon calmed as he put the pieces together and became briefly distracted by the ability to wiggle his toes again.

"You have to go. Your leverage is gone, and they are going to kill you. I can hold the others for now, but I can't control the alien. Sneak out of here without waking it up, and you're free. What you do from there is none of my concern. I don't *ever* want to see you again." Jessica told him.

"W-why would you help me???" Morrow asked, bewildered and swinging his head back and forth between her and the scaly mutant.

"Make no mistake. We're neither friends nor allies. If anyone deserves to be punished for their crimes it's you...I'm just sick and tired of all the death. The world is full of monsters. We don't need to help them get rid of us by killing each other. Now get out of here, before I change my mind."

"T-thank... thank you! You beautiful, wonderful-" Morrow whispered excitedly, reaching out to take her hands in his as she cut his words short.

"Go!" she snapped, pulling away in disgust and throwing a folded up blanket at him that she'd found inside.

He stumbled at first, moving slowly and getting used to his new legs. He crept around the fire to avoid the beasts that slept on the other side. Moving carefully past the two by the pit, he was mystified by how they seemed frozen in place and completely unaware, like time had stopped just for them. His inquisitive nature compelled him to test his limits with their perception, but when the overgrown child began to move like he was cast in wet cement, wearing free of the hold Jessica had over him, Morrow snapped out of it and disappeared into the night.

Jess left the cage door open to legitimize the false notion of his escape, and brought Gaia back down into the ship, then called for help as she released her sway over the group, and time started back up again. Connor dropped his plate and ran over, following her into the basement without hesitation. Rayn sat by the fire for a moment, trying to work out

126

what it was that felt so off about the situation. It was like déjà vu, or a dream that he couldn't quite remember, but he shrugged it off, set down his plate and hurried to catch up.

Neither noticed that the old man was gone.

When they reached the cockpit, Gaia was on top of Riley, shaking him and trying to wake him up. Her eyes were full of tears as she tried to heal him, but nothing was happening. Jess stood behind her, trying to provide some level of comfort and keep her as calm as possible so that her powers didn't swing the other way. She'd already broken her promise to Riley, that she wouldn't use her abilities on anyone in their group, but with Gaia and her bipolar nature, she couldn't risk *not* using them again.

Rayn stood at the back of the room, trying to stay out of the way, while Connor was flying by the seat of his pants trying to help, but not really knowing what he could do. The AEGIS had interwoven its strange circuitry with that of the ship, physically connecting Riley to the pilot seat, just as his mind was connected remotely to the computer. He was becoming one with the ship, but losing himself in the process.

"Riley? Riley! Come on back buddy!" Connor shouted, leaning over him as Jess pulled Gaia back to console her. He grabbed him by the shoulders and shook him to no avail, trying to bring him back to reality. He lightly slapped Riley's face with an open palm, and everything from his cheek to his ear sloughed away into his hand. He flicked the pale flesh away onto the floor and reeled back in horror, speechless.

Gaia began rocking back and forth in Jessica's arms, her eyes growing darker, indicative of another incoming episode. Jessica looked to Rayn with dire urgency, and he knew what was about to happen. He sprinted outside to the camp and was back not more than a moment later with a heavy blanket that he wrapped around his sister. He took her out of Jess's arms, rushing her back out to the surface and getting as far away from the rest of them as he could, before she lost control again. As he ran with her, Jessica stayed behind, concentrating on Gaia's mind and doing everything in her power to soothe her volatile emotions.

The ship began to rumble and Connor backed off from Riley, out into the main deck where all of the equipment was booting up. The rumbling grew in magnitude, and he was knocked off of his feet and thrown back into the cockpit when the whole thing shifted. He slid into the base of the console where Jessica was crouched with her eyes closed. Looking up through the windshield, he watched the dirt that covered it, crack and fall away, revealing the auburn morning sky as the ship rose up. Lights were

flashing, and alarms blasted through the flight deck as they returned to the ground, settling down through the roof of the barn and flattening it under the ship's broad fuselage.

The mechanical connections that held Riley locked into the seat retracted, releasing him as the flickering lights in his eyes ceased. He attempted to stand, but fell to his hands and knees in his weakened and deteriorated state. He looked up, confused by the expressions on Jess and Connor's faces staring back at him, then down at himself trying to figure out why he was so weak. The AEGIS seemed to be fine, but his body had become frail and atrophied, like a geriatric patient. His once form-fitting bodysuit seemed baggy over his withered frame, and his throat felt powder dry with rotten breath wheezing out as he struggled to breathe. Riley tried to speak but lacked the energy to muster a word. He collapsed, lying motionless on the floor to conserve what little energy he had left, and used his connection with the ship to communicate with Connor and Jess about what they'd need to do.

The lights went dark, and the panel below Riley lit up with a faint glow, followed by the one ahead of him and another after that, creating a path out of the cockpit and leading to the large medical tank that had now opened and become illuminated itself. Connor left Jessica's side, whose mind was elsewhere, using her astral form to help Gaia to work to regain control. He picked up Riley with his cybernetic arm slung over his shoulders to support his near dead weight and followed the lights to the tank.

Once Riley was inside, Connor stepped back and watched as the AEGIS took over. Riley's eyes lit up, and the process began. The clear chamber sealed around him and a caustic fluid began to pour in. Connor pounded on the glass and tried to reopen the tank when it appeared that Riley was being dissolved instead of healed. As it filled, a second barrier closed over the glass, shutting him in and providing protection from tampering.

With no indications of how long the process would take or what was happening at all, Connor left after a few minutes of waiting for a change and went to check on Jessica, who was sitting in the cockpit sweating with her eyes still closed. A small trickle of blood dripped from her nose from the overexertion of buffering the lead up to Gaia's outburst and diffusing the situation.

"We're going to be okay...for now." She panted, rubbing her temples. "I couldn't help her regain control in time though, and I had to put her out."

"What do you mean?" Connor asked with concern his voice.

"She's unconscious. I had to- Well...I had to shut off her brain for a second to stop her. She's fine. She might be a little groggy when she wakes up, and she'll have one hell of a headache, but she'll get better soon, and we're still here." Jess explained. "She needs to learn to control her emotions, or else this *will* happen again. I can help. I can work with her and teach her some meditation techniques to keep her emotions in check, but her immaturity will be the biggest hurdle. But first I need to rest. That took a lot out of m-"

Jessica's head bobbed and dropped as she fell asleep, completely exhausted. She had put all of her energy and concentration into calming and containing Gaia's emotions. The constant threat of her untamed power was becoming more and more of a problem that would need to be dealt with.

Connor took Jess in his arms, carrying her out of the cockpit and over to a deep countertop connected to the rejuvenation chamber. Before he could set her down, it sprang into action, turning out to be some sort of fabrication bay, printing and assembling new mechanical parts, though it was too soon to tell what they were, or why they were being made. He resorted to what appeared to be a simple bench along the wall but knocked on it with his boot to be sure that it wasn't going to get tricky too, then laid her down and tucked his jacket under her head. Once he was satisfied that she was resting comfortably, he left them to go help Rayn tend to Gaia.

The view from the ship's missing hatch was quite a bit different now. Connor held onto a railing inside that ran around the edge of the frame, leaning out to take a look around. The drop from where he stood to the ground outside had to be twenty feet, he figured. It was a good vantage point over the area, but there was no way that he could just hop down. A quick whistle brought Fen bounding over, who stood up with his front paws on the ship, nearly reaching the bottom of the door.

"There's my boy! Comin' down."

Fen aligned his head with his neck and shoulders, inviting Connor to hop on and slide down.

"What a good pup." He said warmly, scratching and patting Fen's neck while he nuzzled into it.

Once he had his feet on the ground, what drew his attention was the size of the ship. The flight deck and the workshop were just the *upper* level, representing approximately one-quarter of its capacity. Below that was a whole other section to be discovered.

Sticking out among the smashed barn boards and beams that were pressed into the ground, Connor saw the cage that Morrow had been kept in. It'd been crushed under the ship when it came down, and all that was left was some crumpled metal with bloody bandages tangled inside. A nasty grin curled up for just a second before he let out a sigh of relief, believing that Morrow had been killed in the blind landing.

Over by the fire, Rayn sat with Gaia, wrapped up in a blanket and rocking her like a baby, while Fen laid as the big spoon around the two, setting his head on the bench beside them. Connor knelt down to look her over, then patted Rayn on the shoulder and laid down to rest.

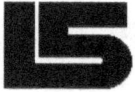

MORROW'S WILD KINGDOM

The sun was almost set over some overgrown remnant of the old world. They'd barely broken ground when it was abandoned, and now, nature had all but taken it back. The cool shadow of dusk chased the amber light across the vines and roots that had crept over large, unfinished concrete structures and woven through the cracks of rusted machinery. A deep roar echoed out from the forest, like crashing thunder.

He was in full sprint, and it was right on his heels, closing in on him like a charging rhino. Its snarling breath alone would make even the bravest man flinch. Unfortunately for the old man made young, bravery was not his virtue. His body trembled, even while he ran, as he watched the mountainous shadow begin to engulf his own. He dove into the opening of a concrete sewer pipe, narrowly escaping its snapping jaws, and there was a crunch as he landed on top of the old bones from the last poor bastard to take shelter in there. The familiar feeling made him nauseous, but the burning in his legs and chest pulled him back into the moment. The busted scope of an otherwise well-preserved rifle jabbed him in the ribs as he rolled over onto his back, and the skeletal hand that was still clutching the grip snapped off and fell away.

He was out of its reach for now, but it would be on him in seconds, once he crawled out of the other end. The pipe was slowly crumbling away as the ravenous creature tore at it, exposing rebar and jostling him around inside, making it hard to hold his position. The beast slowed its attack for just a moment, and Morrow reached for the gun. It was slung over the dead man's shoulder and laid by his side, pointing toward his feet. In one scrambled motion, he shouldered the rifle in an awkward crumpled sit-up, and squeezed the trigger.

The muzzle silently flashed, and the creature was gone. He didn't know where to, but it wasn't there, and that would have to do. He slid out of the old tube and struggled to pull himself to his feet, stumbling and staggering, unable to get his balance. A panicky feeling of dread swept through him, as he came to realize what he had just done. The shot rang out in that confined space, blasting out his eardrums, which now each had a

trickling stream of blood rolling down from them. There was no ringing, just silence. He was deaf, disoriented with vertigo, and the beast was still out there, wounded and angry. Now he couldn't hear it coming, and his equilibrium was shot. Something moved in his peripheral vision, and he spun around to see it, throwing him off balance, and he toppled over. He didn't need to hear, or even see it approaching; he could feel the ground beneath him shake as it charged full bore toward him. All he could do was drag himself into a shallow trench under the remains of the sewer pipe as the tremors quickly intensified. It was nearly on top of him, and he squeezed his eyes shut, praying to a god that he didn't believe in. The rumbling peaked and suddenly stopped as it smashed through the pipe, burying him in chunks of concrete. He felt something warm and wet spread across his back, dripping steadily. Then, he felt nothing and blacked out.

Morrow woke to a bright light. The sun was high in the sky now, and a beam pierced the cracks in the debris that he'd thought to be his tomb. Chunks of concrete and loose gravel covered him from the waist down, and what was left of the pipe had come down around him in a gnarled cage of metal and stone. After what seemed like hours, he was able to clear away enough of the rubble to pull himself out. He was battered and broken, but not beaten.

Upon inspection, he'd decided that he was certainly doing better than his pursuer. The hunched over behemoth had impaled itself on the rebar jutting out from the crumbling sewer pipe. Half blinded by rage, it had gone into a frenzy. Half blinded by the bullet that ripped through its right eye and left with a good portion of its orbital bone, it had no depth perception. He was covered in its blood, and the air was thick with its scent. Other predators would be there soon.

The carrion shifted, and three twisted monsters emerged from behind it. What looked like a horrifying cross between a mangy hyena and a myostatin-deficient chimpanzee, galloped around the corpse of the giant beast, which was beginning to stink of rot in the midday sun. The creatures dew claws had become functional thumbs, and their paws were heavily callused clawed fingers. They fanned out around him. On all fours, they moved the way a hyena would, but then as they grew closer and their pace slowed, the apparent leader of this pack reared up and began to walk on its hind legs, examining him. Morrow knew his own work when he saw it and was equally as inquisitive, hoping in the back of his mind that they didn't have some passed down memory of him and how they came to be.

"*Pan Crocuta*" he said aloud, reciting their genus, and finding out how much he was already missing the sound of his own voice.

One of them effortlessly sprung up onto the top of the broken pipe that the beast was slumped over and perched itself above him like a hairy gargoyle, menacingly watching and waiting for the leader's signal. Morrow was keeping a wary eye on both of them, which made it easy to lose sight of the third. In an instant, their body language went from inquisitive to vicious as the leader lunged forward with wild eyes and powerful gaping jaws. Morrow put the only thing he had between him and it, trying to hold it off. Easily overwhelmed by its power and dexterity, the hybrid clamped down hard into the thickest part of his forearm, grasping his wrist and shoulder with unimaginable strength. It thrashed back and forth, tearing meat from crushed bone and rag dolling him to the ground.

The second, perched atop the sewer pipe, rushed in for the kill. It nearly had him; just inches away from sinking its teeth into his skull, when it stopped. A spurt of blood spattered across Morrow's face, and it tumbled through the leader, knocking them both clear. They scrambled to their feet, and the snarling leader gnashed its teeth and raked its claws across the underling's face to reciprocate. The blood drizzling down its scar-pocked neck met that of the wound in its arm, which was dangling limp.

Just as quickly as it all happened, their voracity shifted to startled fear, as the two creatures took off into the thickly overgrown ruins of an unidentifiable city. The third was behind him, writhing in the dirt for a moment, before succumbing to the smoking, golf ball-sized hole through its torso.

A man in black gear from boot to helmet stepped out from cover with a familiar bladed weapon that was now trained on Morrow. He tried to call out a for help, but all that came out was a raspy gargle and a mouthful of blood. The man approached cautiously with the sun to his back. When he raised his one good arm to show that his hands were empty, a clean patch of the blanket that he'd gotten from Jessica revealed an embroidered logo, and the man took notice. Morrow recognized it as the one etched into the side of the bunker. He didn't understand its significance or the connections that this man might be making upon seeing him wearing it, but he hoped it could help. Instead of a helping hand, however, he met the padded knuckles of the man in black's fist, and he was knocked out cold.

16

NO ESCAPE

Morrow came to on a metal slab in a small, three-walled room with a flickering barrier of light that restricted his visible depth of field. He was separated from a larger dimmed area where the man clad in black stood, watching.

Morrow's arm was encapsulated in a glass and metal cast, filled with a clear solution churning with tiny metallic specks that seemed to move through him as well as around. The limb was completely numb and immobilized, unable to even wiggle his fingers. Sitting up, he discovered that he'd been cleaned and clothed in a one-piece jumpsuit. He felt a dull, humming pain at the back of his head when the man stepped forward and spoke through a deep electronic filter from his flat masked helmet.

"These men. Tell me where they are. I know you've had encounters with them in this region. I know that it was recent." his subjugator stated, as a holographic projection popped up in front of where Morrow was seated. He realized why the blanket was important now, but he didn't care, because he also realized, that he'd just *heard* what was said to him.

"I can hear you!" the doctor exclaimed, touching his hand to the side of his head and feeling something hard embedded in his ear canals. He hesitantly slid his fingers around the back of his head, feeling for the cause of his pain and discovered what he recognized as a sleeker version of his old implant. His head sunk into his shoulders when he realized that he'd left one group of captors for another. "Ugh, not again…" he muttered to himself.

Even though he was a prisoner once again, his situation had certainly improved. The cold, sterile cell was a significant upgrade from the dank basement, or pissy mud beneath the animal cage where he had been kept. His newfound freedom wasn't really working out for him as well as he'd hoped anyway, so it was almost a relief to be out of the wilderness, away from the monsters that he'd populated it with. The only troubling thought that he had now was that they might use the implant against him as mercilessly as he'd used it on others.

"Yes, you can hear, and your arm is being repaired as we speak. I'm sure you've also noticed that you're not currently being eaten."

"Mmm, yes. You have my thanks for that. Who are you anyway?" Morrow said with as much feigned graciousness as he could squeeze out.

"I'm not interested in your thanks, I'm interested in answers." He responded sternly.

Glancing up at the projections, Morrow was taken aback by one of the two mugshot-like portraits. He hadn't recognized the middle-aged man listed a 'Vonn', but the other was unmistakably a dated image of the one that destroyed his arena. He called himself 'Connor', but had no name listed on file.

"Connor." Morrow spoke up. "The younger one calls himself Connor. I've never seen the other one."

"So, you *do* know him."

"We've met, briefly. Why are you looking for him?"

"You can't protect him any more than you can protect yourself. I will find them. Tell me where, and your cooperation may grant you some leniency."

"Protect him? Oh no, you've got me all wrong." Morrow said, smugly. "He and his people...The things they did to me...They're monsters of the worst order. They're demons that need to be exorcised from this world with extreme prejudice. *Please*. Let me help you destroy them."

Morrow stood in silence, waiting for an answer, but the lack of response and faceless stare vexed him to no end. Stepping closer to get a better look at his captor, he heard a crackling static drone coming from the barrier, then a black-gloved hand came up and wagged a finger "No".

"Hear that? I know you can...Get any closer to the barrier and not only will it give you a nasty shock, but it'll overload the tech I've used to heal you." He explained, tapping the side of his helmet. "I've seen it firsthand. *Many* times. I can't imagine that having your brain turned into a lump of coal would be a very pleasant...or survivable experience. So, sit."

Another hologram appeared, replacing the others. It shuffled between overhead views of the other cells, all identical to the one he was being held in. The first two contained the charred bodies of alien juveniles, both flung back against the rear wall. In the next, was an alpha, burnt, scarred, clutching the sides of its head and holding itself as far away from the barrier as it could. The last cell didn't contain an alien, but the body of a man, dressed in a similar jumpsuit. His eyes had burst, leaving charred sockets and steaming dark fluid that bubbled out from his ears.

"For instance..."

"I see. Messy. Who gets to clean that up?" Morrow said, smirking. He sat back down, tapping his fingers anxiously.

"Tell me where to find him, and I'll let you live to do it."

"No need for the hostility, friend. I'll walk you right up to their doorstep, but first I want something from you."

"Of course. How about I fix your arm and restore your hearing. Oh, look at that, I did. *Where. Is.* He." He said, clearly growing impatient.

"That's all well and good, but not much use to me if I'm to remain a prisoner." he reasoned, "As much as I'd love to help you, if I have to spend another minute caged up like some lowly animal, I'd rather die. Gladly so, knowing that I've made my jailer's day even the slightest bit more difficult…Now, let me out, and we can work together as peers, on even ground, or you can get your mop, Buckethead, because this big brain is going to make more of a mess than the other guy, I promise you that."

"Just who do you think you are, old man?" he said, flabbergasted by his arrogance and already regretted asking before Morrow gave his answer.

"My name is Doctor Nathaniel Morrow. *I* am the one that brought life back to the wasteland. It is *mine* to create and *mine* to take. I am *Genesis*." He boastfully proclaimed, steeping in his own self-reverence. "If I die, so does all hope for this world."

"…You done?"

"Yes." Morrow said, contented by his own words as if he were being praised with them by another.

He slowly rose from the bench, taking a deep breath and crouching into a sprinters stance, using the back wall as his starting block. He shut his eyes and thought of his life and his accomplishments. He was ready to show them that *he* was the one in control, and that their power was nothing but a transitory illusion. Launching forward, resolute in his fate, Morrow threw himself at the force field. He felt a charge build in his head and the tingle of static electricity as it crackled over his entire body. In the split second before he fully connected, instead of the righteous justification that he'd imagined he'd feel, there was nothing but fear and regret. Those feelings were soon outweighed by confusion, when he passed cleanly through and landed on the other side, skidding on his stomach a short distance, until his cheek smushed into a pair of heavy black boots.

"Now you're trying to kiss my feet? Are you always this fickle?…Get up 'Doctor Genesis', you're embarrassing yourself." The man in black said, mockingly.

"W-What happened?" Morrow asked, confused and disoriented.

"I shut down the barrier, smart guy. Did you rattle that 'big brain' of yours?" he responded, taking his hand off of the controls. "Alright you nasty ol' prick, I don't like you, and you seem to have a general disdain for every living thing but yourself. But, I'm a fairly reasonable guy. I'm going to ask you a question, and you're going give me a suitable answer. Suitable answers will get you suitable rewards. In good faith, I've already healed you and let you out of your cell, like you wanted. You owe me your life and all I want is your help."

"And if I don't?" Morrow foolishly antagonized.

"You'll wish you had…I can heal your wounds and dampen the sensitivity of your nerve receptors, but I can also amplify it. I can make every cell in your body feel like it's on fire. I can make you wish that you were being torn apart by the creatures that I saved you from because eventually, they'd finish you off. I won't. I won't *let* you die. I'll make you scream until your vocal cords bleed. You'll *beg* me to end it, but the end will never come." He responded, cool and calm like he'd not only made the threat before but followed through with it.

"Ahem. Let's talk about these rewards then." Morrow said, climbing to his feet.

Before he could get off of all fours, a boot was planted on his back and pinned him back down.

"You still think this is a negotiation." He sighed, leaning over him and whispering, "You're only making this difficult for yourself. I'm *telling* you, I'm not a bad guy, but I *am* very good at doing bad guy shit. Play your part, and we can all come out of this better off than we went in. Or…"

Morrow nodded and took his hand when it was offered, getting back to his feet. Following quietly, he noticed some other familiarities than the weapon that this man carried. Like his lab, there were airlocks at regular intervals, but these were more akin to the broken door that'd almost landed on him when he was being held, back in the basement. It was only now that he realized that the bunker may not have been what it seemed. When he first discovered the facility under the mountain, he could barely wrap his mind around how such a thing could exist, but this was so much more. Considering the sophistication of the technology he'd seen so far, Morrow was beginning to wonder if what was under that dark helmet, was even of this world.

They entered a vantablack room that lit up with a fully encompassing holographic display as soon as the door closed behind them, so crisp and clear that it was nearly indistinguishable from reality. The floor

seemed to disappear and for a moment Morrow felt like he was falling. He flinched but remained where he had been standing, feeling embarrassed that he'd fallen for the illusion, and spiteful because he wasn't warned of it. He said nothing, knowing how any defensive reaction would seem silly to anyone used to this technology; his own pride wouldn't let him show it.

"*Heh*... What you see below you is a live streaming aerial view of what is left of the continent. The large green area in the west is where I found you."

"Yes, that's *mine*. I made it...I thought that all of the satellites were disabled in the invasion?"

"They were. What you see below you *is* below you, doctor. You are aboard my ship." he said, knowing full well how impressive that would sound to an Earth-born human.

"Hmmph, yes, as I've surmised. Go on." Morrow said, playing aloof and doing his best to hide his excitement.

"The radioactive signature that I used to find you matches that of the stolen craft I'm looking for. It belonged to Vo-" He tried to explain, before being cut off by a very agitated reaction from the doctor.

"I'm sorry, what was that about me being radioactive?!" he shouted.

"Well, you're not glowing, but it's still enough to detect. If I were to guess, I'd say that you've spent some time around a power core with a cracked containment vessel. From the look on your face, I'm going to assume that you weren't aware of it at the time...and doctor? Don't raise your voice to me again."

"Of course." Morrow said, shaking his head with a sad chuckle. "They get *superpowers* and I get cancer. I suppose it was inevitable, everything was great until those halfwits barged into my life. Ever since, it's been like the universe is having a contest with itself to see how high it can pile on the crap."

"What, do you want a fucking hug? Going to have yourself a little cry? Settle down sunshine, I never said that you had cancer. My people would never have lasted as long as they have if we'd been using the same primitive reactors or fuels as yours once did." He explained, slapping Morrow on the shoulder. "There was a spike of energy, which brought me back into the region. That energy disappeared soon after, and I was following the residuals when you got lucky, and I found you. You got that blanket from Vonn's ship, and it's showing signs of long-term exposure to the radiation that is evidently leaking from the core. Now, there was no massive, disastrous explosion from anyone trying to fly the thing, so It's

likely still where you last saw it. Possibly cloaked, or just hidden. You need to show me where that is. Now."

"It was a ship? I only saw part of it. I was in a basement, and one of its doors nearly crushed me when it was broken off. With the condition that thing is in, it couldn't fly, even if it was above ground." Morrow scoffed.

"So, the old man buried it. Makes sense why I couldn't find it. Sounds like it's pretty beat up. That's good stuff, what else can you tell me? Anything at all that we should be ready for?"

"We?" Morrow asked nervously.

"Yes, doctor. Helping me will increase your chances of survival if *we* find ourselves in the shit."

"Wonderful. Before I got there, it was an alien nest."

"Everything is a fucking alien nest…You said 'superpowers'. Tell me about that."

"It's as ridiculous as it sounds. There's a man that's part robot, a woman that can control your mind, a little girl that can heal any wound just by touching you, and a little boy that grew big and strong enough to rip an armoured door from its hinges in a matter of moments." He told him, reluctant to even say the words, feeling like a grown man trying to convince another grown man that comic books are real. "Connor; the one you're looking for, has a weapon like yours, that he used to blast out a chunk of mountain from inside my facility…How does that work by the way?"

"Ya, he does that. The power doesn't come from the weapon, it's just a conduit. The power normally comes from a miniaturized power core in our armour, like the ones that power our ships. He's different though. Much more powerful than I am, and he doesn't need a core; the power comes directly from him, somehow. These *powers*, originate from an ancient prototype that was stolen from my people, years ago. Vonn brought it to Earth, and my team was sent here to retrieve it. We were only able to track him down when the crazy old bastard activated it the first time. It's irreplicable and powerful beyond comprehension, but that power isn't free."

"What *is* the cost of the god-maker?" Morrow asked, rubbing his chin, and trying not to rub his pants.

"Whatever it is, no one was willing to pay it for thousands of years. Not until Vonn blundered his way into the picture… A tactical strike was out of the question. Our mission was *first*, to bring it back intact and *second*, to eliminate the target. We sent in one of our crew undercover, and we infiltrated his compound. 'Connor' was our man on the inside, but unfortunately for us, he'd gone native. Vonn had convinced him to join his

cause, and in exchange for his loyalty, he'd promised to grant him power beyond his wildest dreams. When he came through on that promise, Connor followed through with his, and came after us. He tried to tell us that he was just doing what he had to do, but it was evident that he'd become unhinged, ranting paranoid conspiracies and not responding to reason. There was a fight, of course. A big one, that didn't last very long. I got away, but the others weren't so lucky." He said remorsefully.

"So, we *both* want revenge for what he's taken from us." Morrow sneered.

"No."

"What?!" he shouted with disgust.

"What happened was unfortunate, yes, but I can't blame him for what he did…Not entirely." He said, removing his helmet.

"You're…twins?" Morrow asked, perplexed.

"My people have lived in artificial gravity for hundreds of generations, and as a result, their bodies have evolved differently. While their knowledge and technology is incomparable to the civilizations of Earth, physically, my people have grown more…delicate. Connor and I were built stronger and faster; altered to make us more formidable under these conditions. We're clones, though his physiology has been altered further by the catalyst, so I don't know how similar we are anymore. "

"You won't hold him responsible for his actions because blood is thicker than water. Is that it?" Morrow responded, rubbing the bridge of his nose.

"I won't hold him responsible for his actions because he was defending himself and the innocent people that our former leaders would have had us exterminate."

"Former?"

"When I reported our failure, they cut communications by activating a bomb, installed under the navigation console. I got a shield up in time to save my life, but not without being left with a few reminders." He said, pointing to the scars on his face. "The cockpit was destroyed and took years to get it to where it is now."

"So you're stranded."

"The arkstation isn't my home. I'm a clone. We were grown on this ship. Imprinted with a mission instead of parents. This is my home."

"Would they have sent more after you?"

"I can't believe that they wouldn't, but the Earth is a big place when you don't know where to look. If they're here, I haven't seen them."

"...If you have all of this next level technology, why wouldn't you use it to heal those scars and fix your face?" Morrow asked, holding up his cast.

"I want them to see what they did to me, so that they know why I did what I'm going to do to them." He said, staring at the reflection in his helmet.

"I'd sympathize, but waddling up on stumps would've put a bit of a damper on my rampage... They cut my damned legs off. Save me from your petulant sob story." Morrow snapped. "You'll get your revenge, and I just have to suck it up and help? Fix yourself up and stop behaving like an angsty, brooding teenager."

"*Excuse me?*"

"You expect me to set my feelings aside, after all they've done to me?"

"For now. We all have our part to play, and in the end, once our mission is complete, you'll be free to do as you please." he said reassuringly, but kept a stern tone, to remind Morrow that he wasn't letting anything else slide.

"Once we have them, then what?"

"It's we now, is it? Good." he said, almost smiling. "Then we convince them that we're the good guys. I'll recover the device and use it to lure in the people that sent me here. Once I do that, I'm going to destroy them."

"Oh, fuck me. We're going to die. We're going to die, then get fed to their pet monsters...If we're lucky, it'll be in that order. I made one from two superpredators, and the other is a juiced up alien with mutated DNA. Also, I hope you like shit in your pants, because that's what you're going to get!" Morrow rambled.

"Enough!" He shouted, then relaxed his intensity. "We'll be fine, as long as you keep your mouth shut and follow my lead. You'll be wearing Connor's old armour. They won't know it's you."

"The woman can read minds, remember?"

"Not as long as you keep your helmet on. It links with your implant and shields you from multiple spectrums. She should just get a static signal with it on. Trust me."

"It can block their powers?" Morrow asked, excitedly.

"If by block, you mean scramble, then yes. If you happen to be in the path of one of those mountain breakers though, well, our medical technology isn't quite that advanced."

"I wouldn't imagine so...What of this armour?" he asked, as the room seemed to respond, bringing up schematics and a detailed breakdown of its components and capabilities.

"It's an adaptive exoskeletal machine, designed for versatility in both combat and recon in most environments. You could survive in space with it for a while but avoid the urge to jump into an active volcano. It's got its own rechargeable power core, as I said, but because of its capacity, we won't need to worry about that anytime soon. Because of the extraterrestrial materials used to craft it, it's stronger and lighter than anything that could be forged on Earth. Once it's on and calibrated, it'll feel light as a feather. The suit will enhance your strength, speed, and reflexes. Its adaptive camouflage is what we'll use to get close, since bringing the ship down might make them run, and we can't have them attempting to fly anywhere with a damaged core. Not only that, but it'd certainly draw some very unwanted attention, especially during such a potentially volatile negotiation." He told him, rushing through the basics and switching the hologram back to the map.

"Show me where they are, then I can get you suited up. Help me get what *I* want, and then you can do whatever *you* want with them."

NEW YOU

The moon was big and bright in the sky, diffusing through the sparse fog, lighting up all but the darkest shadows and giving the newly unearthed craft a mystical glow. Their fire had gone out while they slept but still glowed with a bed of warm embers.

Rayn had laid down with the rest of them but was unable to sleep, enthralled by the *spaceship* that was unlocked with *his* touch. He felt like the chosen one, from so many heroic tales he'd read, and now that he had come out of hiding, he'd have the chance to be the hero of his own story. There was no way that he was getting any sleep, and when the bright light that shone out from the interior of the ship dimmed for a second, he knew that something was moving around in there. He got up, careful not to wake the others, and snuck away to investigate on his own. As he got closer, he could hear the busy, whirring chatter of finely tuned mechanisms in action, though he couldn't tell what it was from down there. He crept to the rear of the ship, below the open hatch, looking for a way to climb up and get inside, but the exterior walls were smooth and steep in all of the places that he needed them not to be. Taking a few steps back to get a better look, he noticed that the light was growing steadily dimmer. It became almost entirely blocked, aside from a thin ring around the edge of the hatch as a new door moved into place. The noise from behind the door elevated and then hissed, before being muffled silent when the airlock sealed itself. There was no more light coming from the ship, except for the short-lived orange glow along the edges where to door had been fastened.

From the silence, Rayn picked up a barely audible hum. He could feel it from the grass, through his bare feet, and watched the green turn a pale yellow as it dried out and crumbled in a spreading area around the ship. As the line moved past him, he felt a wave of heat all throughout his body. His skin began to discolour and blister as the temperature increased until he could no longer differentiate the searing heat from stinging cold. His vision blurred and went dark as the fluid in his eyes boiled. He went limp and crumpled to the ground when the strength went out of his legs as the

muscles deteriorated. Gasping at the tainted air, his throat and lungs had been burnt along with the rest of him, and he was too weak to form words.

Rayn tried to call out, not for help, but as a warning to stay away. He knew that he'd eventually heal like he always did, but if anyone came to help him, they'd suffer the same, but without coming back from it. Then as always, the maddening pain dulled and dispersed as his body began to remake itself accordingly in response to the damage it'd taken. His body hardened and turned dark like carbon. His skin cracked and buckled, creating fissures all over the surface as he moved. He opened his polished onyx eyes and saw the last thing he'd wanted to see.

His sister was standing near the edge of the dead grass, slowly walking toward him. She leaned in, and her feet dug into the ground as she began to sprint over to help her brother, but before she got the traction to carry her forward, she was lifted up off of the ground and pulled backward.

Gaia had been woken up by the sound of the airlock closing, and went looking for Rayn when she noticed that he wasn't with her. Connor had always been a light sleeper, and had gotten up to follow her and make sure that she didn't accidentally wander off in the dark. Lucky for her.

Connor had seen the ebony troll on the ground and noticed the stark contrast in the grass around him, in front of where Gaia stood. He scooped her up, swinging her around behind him to keep her from getting any closer. She was startled and almost shrieked when he did, but he'd covered her mouth when he grabbed her to keep her from drawing the others over and putting them in danger as well. She struggled for just a moment before Connor turned her around to show her his face and took his hand away from her mouth to point to the line in the grass. She took note, but was only concerned with her brother.

"Rayn?...I-Is that you? Are you okay?!" Gaia asked at the high end of a whisper.

"Stay back!" Rayn told her in a deep, gravely voice. "It's me...but you have to get back. Get away from the ship."

He stood up and walked at a sloth's pace out from the burnt perimeter, watching his path to make sure that he wasn't trailing any lingering radiation. Connor slowly backed away with her, looking up at the airlock door. The faint humming that could be heard before stopped, and another door began to open, but this one was no mere hatch. It ran almost the width of the stern, and came down like a drawbridge, forming a ramp over the burnt grass. A hardlight barrier extended out as a tunnel, beyond

the slowly expanding perimeter, giving them safe passage while a man-shaped machine stood at the top of the ramp, waving them in.

"Hurry! Get in! It's shielded!" The android instructed.

Remembering Riley's story about the other buried ship, Connor recognized it as the AI co-pilot/assistant that these ships were equipped with.

Rayn looked back and forth between Connor and Gaia, then back to where Jess was still sleeping. He didn't say a word, just took off back to the camp to get her, while Connor brought Gaia inside. Connor turned around, whistling at the top of the ramp, and seconds later, Bas and Fen came bounding up and entered with them, sniffing and inspecting every square inch of the cargo hold, frenzied by curiosity with all of the new smells. Gaia stood in the open, watching out for her brother to get back with Jess when the android spoke up again.

"I'm sorry, but the ship is only shielded if it is sealed. I have to close the door."

"So close the door, sympathy-bot." Connor told the otherwise faceless, two-eyed automaton that somehow still looked disappointed by what he'd said. The door raised up and sealed shut, protecting them from the radiation leak, but locking Rayn and Jess outside on their own.

"Wait! You can't just leave them out there! What are you doing?!" Gaia pleaded, visibly upset.

"He'll be fine, Gaia. You know that. You need to calm down. Now." Connor asserted.

Lights in the android's eyes flickered, and a hardlight barrier materialized around Gaia, about the size of a small bedroom.

"This will keep her contained in the event that she has another episode. It was intended for use in transporting radioactive, or chemically hazardous materials, and is based on a component of the core containment system."

"Doesn't seem to work very well though, does it?" Connor remarked.

"There are multiple components in different areas of the ship. That particular component is currently offline. This one is online." It replied, almost snootily, with a hint of condescension.

Bas and Fen's attention shifted to what they saw as a strange glowing box in the middle of the hold and were immediately drawn to it. Bas tried to claw at it and bite the frictionless corner without any effect, and Fen had taken to pouncing on it, using his mass like a polar bear breaking through ice, but making no progress either. This was a game to them, and they were

just playing with a new toy that could stand up to their roughhousing, but Gaia's view of it from inside wasn't quite as fun. From her perspective, it looked like they were attacking, and was more than enough to set her off.

"FEN! BAS! DOWN!!!" Connor shouted with authority, feigning anger, and they both flinched at his voice then scurried back to sniffing about the ship.

He turned to Gaia to try and talk her down, but it was too late for that. He was about to witness something that few would ever see, and live to tell about. Gaia's black sclerae were his first indication that things were about to pop off. He watched her hair dance as the air around her distorted and seemed to vibrate. An illuminated display within the barrier wall showed a series of graphs and information about its contents, with wildly spiking and flat-lining readings. A shock wave expanded outward, and the distortion in the air flowed in toward her, absorbing into her body. The readings on the display normalized as she dropped to the ground, unconscious.

"Incredible." The android said in response to the data coming in from the containment field.

"Incredible that nobody has died. These uncontrollable outbursts are becoming more frequent." Connor stated. "I need to speak to the ones we left outside, then I want to check on the tank upstairs. Can you help me with that?"

The android cocked its head and paused momentarily, then proceeded to lead him up to the flight deck. Up there, he could speak through a projection from one of the ship's orb drones, which was already on its way to their assumed location. He stood on the platform behind the pilot's seats, and dozens of metal eyes with lights for pupils hovered in an equally spaced semi-sphere around him. They were recording and tracking his gestures, but also panoramically displaying to him what the drone was seeing. As it hovered slowly through the camp, it became apparent that they'd left in a hurry. There was a clear line plowed through, with their supplies tossed and trampled. The vegetation all around the camp was dead now, and the range of the leak was still expanding, even beyond the tree line.

He knew that they were out there somewhere, and told himself that either the shielding that blocked out the radiation, or the radiation itself was preventing Jessica from contacting them telepathically. He didn't want to admit the third possible reason that came to mind. Feeling that there was nothing more that he could do for the time being, and wanting to check on Riley, Connor stepped off of the platform, and the floating eyes

automatically retreated. The android took his place, making tossing gestures and pointing in several different directions as its eyes flickered brightly, then followed Connor back to the medical station.

"I have assigned scouts to canvas the area. When they are found, we will be notified."

"...Where is he? Where is Riley?" Connor asked, staring into the empty chamber.

"The organic components had sustained far too much damage before receiving treatment, and could not be saved." The robotic voice explained, but lacked the inflection used in previous communication.

"He's dead?! I thought this piece of shit was supposed to be able to fix anything!" He shouted, kicking the machine hard enough to stub his toe from inside of his boot, though he was too upset to even flinch from it.

"While the organics did not survive, that is not to say that the mind was lost as well." The robot paused, waiting for Connor to process what he had just been told. "The AEGIS mapped and recorded every bit of information that it could about the existing organics from the moment it was installed."

"I'm listening." Connor said, furrowing his brow.

"It kept a history of everything, from the routes and activity of his neural pathways, to the composition of his gut bacteria, and fluctuations in bioelectric potential. All backed up to the AEGIS in case of catastrophic biological failure. Since there was already a partial merger, prior to the incident that disabled the autonomous repair protocol, the backup was only needed to fill certain gaps in the data, as opposed to serving as the primary source."

"I need a drink..." Connor groaned, rubbing his forehead and sitting down against the wall.

When he looked back up, the android was walking over to him from another piece of equipment, carrying what looked like two glasses filled halfway with a clear, amber liquid. It squatted down in front of him, passing over a glass and holding its own up to toast. He played along and clinked his glass with the android's, sniffing it before he drank. The smell was familiar, and the taste, unmistakable. It was the same rare vintage scotch that he and Riley drank when they met.

"Sorry, your stash got tainted. The ship can make as much as you want though. It's close right?"

"It's perfect... What's going on?"

"The AEGIS recorded everything, including the colour, flavours and aromas in the scotch when I tasted it. So, the ship took that information and created the recipe to duplicate it in that machine over there. It can make just about anything, *from* just about anything. It breaks down matter to the atomic level and reassembles it into other, more desirable things, like replacement parts and extinct booze." The android explained.

Connor took a sip from his glass, then gulped the whole thing back. He got back to his feet, taking the mechanical hand that offered to help. He leaned in, Looking the robot over and trying to find something in its lit up eyes. Tilting his head back and forth like a puppy hearing a new sound for the first time, he let out a sigh and patted the android on the shoulder.

"You going to drink that, or is it just for show?" Connor asked, eyeing up the other glass that the robot had used to mime sips.

"Be my guest." it said, handing it over in exchange for the empty glass. It waited for him to throw that one back too, but instead, he just held onto it, sniffing the contents occasionally.

"Thanks." Connor said with sincerity. "You're not the ship's AI...are you?"

"Yes and no." It told him. "I control all of the functions of this ship as an extension of myself, and I am compelled to keep it in optimal operating condition. If I were the AI designed to do so, maybe I wouldn't have tried to start the drives with only a software diagnostic. I skipped the manual hardware inspection protocols and endangered you all by doing so. For that I am sorry. We *will* get Jess and Rayn back."

"...Riley?" he asked nervously.

"AFFIRMATIVE." The android; Riley responded, as a caricature of a retro sci-fi robot voice, then lightly punched Connor in the shoulder and returned to his normal speech patterns. "Heh, ya man, it's me."

"Are you...okay? What you must be going through. Shit. I don't even know what to say. This is just so..." Connor trailed off into his drink, trying to find the right words.

"Actually, I'm not that upset about it. It was this, or dying, right? My new body isn't as frail as my old meat body. No offence. And if anything breaks, I can rebuild it. I can upgrade parts to make myself better, and I can do that on my *spaceship*! The boost I got before made me smarter, but this? Everything gets processed so much faster now, it's like time has been dialled way down. Again, no offence, but this conversation feels like an eternity."

"...None taken. Sorry to bore you."

"Shut up, you know what I mean. In the time we've been talking, I've also been working and learning in the background with no distraction between processes, or loss in performance." Riley said, shaking his head and rolling back the illuminated glass and metal spheres that functioned as his eyes. "Anyways, as soon as I can repair the damage to the core containment vessel, we can get out of here and find Jess and Rayn." he said, pulling up holographic schematics of the ship and showing Connor the problem. He extended his hand, and a small device came out of a compartment in his palm. "Neat trick, right? Take this and put it in your ear. It'll allow us to communicate."

"It's not going to bore through my skull and implant itself in my brain is it?"

"Nah, this one turns into liquid metal and worms its way in there through your ear canal."

"Ya, go fuck yourself." Connor told him and threw it away, revolted.

Riley laughed, then walked over to where it had landed, picked it up, and showed it to him. He then crushed the device in his hand and deposited the broken pieces into the machine that he got the drinks from. A second later, a new, identical copy came out. He took it in his hand and offered it to Connor a second time.

"That was a joke." Riley chuckled and sighed, "It's *pretty much* just an earbud."

"So, are you like, the evil robot version of Riley? Shouldn't you have a metal goatee or something?" Connor sneered, taking the device and putting it into his ear. He hesitated just before inserting it and winced, but nothing happened, and he was able to relax.

"Here, let me turn it on." Riley said, as a hardlight visor strip emitted from the earpiece and wrapped halfway around Connor's face, in front of his eye, making him jump. Riley slapped his knee with a clang, and shook his head, then wiped away an imaginary tear from his featureless face. "Now you can just about see and hear what I can, and vice versa. It'll also grant you access to some of the ship's functions, and a *massive* library. When we find them, I can't wait to give Rayn his. Every bit of media ever converted to digital format is on there, including every book, game, movie, song, and piece of content ever uploaded to the internet. He's going to freak out!"

"Focus. Let's get them back, and *then* you two can geek out over it all you want." Connor told him in a slightly irritated tone. "What do we need to do to get the core fixed so we can find them?"

"Nothing. It's almost done. Check it out." Riley said confidently, bringing up the visual feed of several orb drones sealing the breached containment vessel, then switching over to a cluster of POVs from the drones searching the area for Jess and Rayn. One of the feeds grew bigger and minimized the others as it had detected something ahead. "Here we go. Two heat signatures, travelling together, just through these trees. See? I've got it all under control."

18

OUT OF THE FRYING PAN

When Rayn got to Jess, he'd come crashing through the camp to get her as quickly as possible, startling her awake from a deep sleep. She was groggy and disoriented when she woke up, having been jolted from one of her power induced, ultra-lucid dreams. Being snapped out of one vivid reality and forced into another, harsher one was jarring, and having survived this long, had elevated her fight or flight response, which worked in tandem with her more basal abilities. Having no knowledge of Rayn's new form, or the urgency of the situation, she lashed out in self-defence, striking at his mind with the intent of making her perceived attacker catatonic. His legs wobbled like a fighter that'd just been clipped on the chin, but his power wouldn't allow it, and adapted a resistance to her influence once again. She tried to fight back and struggle free from the walking statue, but she may as well have been cast in iron.

Not knowing how far the radiation would spread, Rayn kept a steady pace to stay ahead of it as he carried Jessica away from the ship, hoping that the others were safe inside. His new body left much to be desired in terms of speed, and felt like he was running underwater. The density of this form made him strong; able to hold her with hardly an effort, but the energy that it took to use that strength to keep moving put a significant drain on his endurance. *He* would be fine if he stopped to catch his breath, now that he'd developed an immunity to the rads, but he had to keep pushing forward for her. She wouldn't heal like he does; she'd die a quick but agonizing death if he stopped and let it overtake them.

"Stop! Put me down!" she shouted, still futilely squirming against his grasp.

"Can't stop." He responded in a barely recognizable, gravelly voice. "The ship's leaking some kind of radiation, and I found out the hard way. It's spreading, and I need to get you away from it. The others are safe onboard, I think. It's shielded...I think...A robot told me."

"Rayn?! Oh no! I'm so sorry! I-" She gasped, reaching up and touching his face.

"I'm fine. I'm invincible, remember?" he said, trying to give the impression that he was unphased by his transformation. "So, where are we headed, navigator?"

"You mean that you don't know where we're going?" she teased.

"Hey, I came up with 'away' all on my own. How's the free ride?" he volleyed.

"Not bad, if you don't mind craggy bear hugs."

"Would you prefer to walk?" He asked, nodding to the ground.

Around his feet, the shadowed forest floor seemed to move with them as a flood of creatures scurried, scuttled, and slithered past.

"Nope. Nope. Nope." she said, monkey-climbing up to sit on Rayn's shoulders, repulsed by what she saw below.

"Comfortable?"

"Better. I feel like I should be wearing spurs though." She joked, tapping her heels against his sides.

"That's a good way to get bucked." he told her, trying to stay light, but clearly not impressed with this brand of humour.

"Sorry." she said, then squinted her eyes, trying to see through the trees into the sprawling field ahead.

Something was off about it, and Rayn saw it too. He broke his stride as they approached the clearing, as the creatures that had been moving in a straight line away from the ship were all making hard right angle turns where the otherwise tall grass and soft lumpy soil was flattened down. The space above the apparent crop circle seemed just as out of place. The trees in the distance looked slightly bent and warped, just so much that you wouldn't notice unless you were really paying attention. Neither of them could tell if the creatures were avoiding this area, or if they actually couldn't enter into it, but they knew it was bad news. Most living things tend to take the path of least resistance, which is why and how trails get worn and created. This large flat area certainly looked to fit the bill, but not a single thing crossed the boundary.

"What is it? Should we go around?" Rayn asked as they came upon the anomaly.

"Your guess is as good as mine." She responded, then looked back the way they came, seeing that they hadn't actually travelled very far. She could see through what had been thick forest just moments ago, but was now a sparse tangle of greyed logs and leafless branches, like the whole area was being consumed by an invisible wildfire. "We have to keep moving."

Rayn looked left and right, trying to decide which would be the shortest distance and quickest way around, but they'd found themselves right smack in the middle. Even with his best attempt at a sprint, he'd be hard-pressed to make it to either end before the ghostly flame reached them.

A third option presented itself as a rectangle of light from the edge of the empty space in front of them. The warp in the trees on the other side became much more apparent until it was identifiable as having its own surface, and jets of gas blasted out, repelling the hordes of creatures away. The line of light grew bigger inside of its perimeter, and more of the gas spilled out until there was a clear room on the other side, only visible through the doorway.

With no better options, Rayn went through the entrance and the hatch moved back into place, immediately behind them. He helped Jess down, off of his shoulders and she scanned the area for surface thoughts but heard nothing over the roar of fear from the creatures outside, which faded as the door closed. There was nothing, but it was a specific nothing. There was a void where there should have at least been echoes. She was being blocked, but not like with Rayn, who didn't even register anymore and blended in with the background noise. This was a noticeable absence, like a space had been cut out. She could see the hole, but not what was inside.

"You getting anything?" he asked, looking out the airlock porthole, which behaved like a two-way mirror, without the mirror. The radiation passed over them, and he watched the creatures that weren't quick enough to make it around, stop. They blistered and smoked for a few brief seconds, like hundreds of matches being lit, then immediately snuffed out. Their petrified husks peppered the field.

"Not exactly, but there's a strange nothingness that shouldn't be there...I've felt it before." she whispered back.

A light above the next hatch changed from red to yellow, and aerosol jets blasted them from all directions. A few seconds later, once decontamination was complete, the light switched from yellow to green, and the next hatch on the other side of the chamber depressurized. Rayn stepped in front of Jessica as the door opened up to a larger area, similar to what he'd seen inside of their ship, where the android had brought the others. He entered first, making sure that it was safe before waving her though. As she entered, a marble-sized glass orb flew over and hovered a few feet ahead of them at eye level, and a hologram of a man clad in strange armour appeared around it, with the floating orb stationed behind the eyes of its projection. They looked at each other, recognizing the gear of the figure standing before

them. It was, as far as they could tell, identical to that of the men that had attacked them back in the city, and Rayn instinctively moved to protect Jess, even though he knew that it was just a projection.

"What *are* you?" asked an intrigued voice from the intercom, matching up with the hologram's gestures as it moved around the room, inspecting Rayn. The hologram reached out and took his hand, feeling the rough surface of his arm and carefully manipulating his fingers to get an idea of his range and freedom of motion, surprising them both when it became evident that this was not just a standard illusion.

"Hardlight." Jess said under her breath, mostly to herself.

"That's correct! Very good." The hologram said, poking his head over Rayn's shoulder, then moving around him with his attention now focused on her.

"This is a hardlight projection. My suit gives me haptic feedback, so I can feel what it feels." He said, gently stroking it's hand up and down her arm. "…How do *you* know what it is?" She'd recoiled from his touch, but said nothing in response, and began to cower in shame as he continued. "Oh! What do we have here?" he remarked, running its fingers between her breasts, then snatching away the satchel by the strap across her chest and walking away, having lost all interest in her.

"No!" She cried, lunging forward and grabbing at the bag, trying to take it back. The hardlight hologram turned and caught her with the back of its hand, like he was swatting a fly. She was knocked back and collapsed onto the floor as though she'd just been cracked with a baseball bat.

"NOOO!!!" Rayn bellowed with rage.

His booming voice echoed and shook the room as he reached out to the hologram and grabbed it by its head with one hand, then squeezed with all of his might. The hologram flickered, and he wrapped his other hand around it as well, applying more, and more pressure until the light structure popped like a bubble, and the floating orb that was projecting it was crushed to sand. The bag fell to the ground, and Rayn turned back to Jess, trying to help in any way that he could.

Another orb appeared to replace the one that had been destroyed, creating an identical projection around it. The hologram stood several arm lengths away from Rayn this time and began moving its hands around like it was conducting an orchestra.

"That was very rude." The hologram told him.

A hardlight barrier appeared between Jessica and Rayn, splitting in two and sweeping across the room in opposite directions, pushing them to

separate corners. Each barrier closed around them until the space inside was roughly that of a shower stall. Jessica slowly climbed to her feet, heaving and gasping, still trying to catch her breath after having the wind knocked out of her. Rayn was hardly able to move at all. The proportions and rigidity of his body allowed for minimal movement inside of the construct. His arms were being compressed against his torso, and there was very little that he could do in such a confined space. His squirming did nothing to help since it was putting no extra tension on the barrier. It was doing what it was designed to do; constantly readjusting to keep its payload secure and undamaged.

The hologram wagged its finger at them, then faded away. A door opened, and the orb flew out as a helmeted figure in black armour, the same as the hologram, entered the room, wagging the same finger. He picked up the satchel off of the ground and tore the buckled leather straps off, then tossed back the flap and looked inside, curious about why it was so important to her.

A full minute passed as he stood frozen in silence, fixated on its contents, before snapping back out of it. He looked back up at them for a just second, clutching the bag tight, then hastily turned away and left, taking it with him.

Rayn was disturbed by the look on Jessica's face. Her expression was that of someone who'd just had their heart ripped out. She slouched back down and sat on the floor, running her fingers over her scalp and through her hair, over and over again.

"Jess?" he asked, concerned. "Are you okay?"

"No." She told him solemnly.

"I'll tear him apart for hurting you!" Rayn snarled, redoubling his efforts to escape, but only succeeding in tiring himself out.

"I-I'll be okay. But we have to get it back. We have to-" she panted through wincing breaths, hushing herself when the door reopened.

The man in black re-entered the room, walked over to Jessica, and deactivated the barrier around her. He offered her his hand, but when she didn't take it, he grabbed the hair at the back of her head, and pulled her up as she fought back, kicking and screaming. Rayn went berserk, watching as she was dragged out of the room, but the barrier that held him in place remained.

HIGH TECH

As the ship's repairs neared completion, Connor and Riley returned to the cargo bay to check on Gaia. Connor entered first, and both Bas and Fen rushed over from sitting outside of the barrier to greet him. Fen, nuzzling his head into him and wrapping a paw around the back of his legs, pulling him closer for a giant dog hug. Bas paced anxiously back and forth, still waiting for Riley, but when he arrived, he looked right past him.

Gaia was strolling around inside of the box, running her hands along the surface of the barrier and playing with patterns in the distortion that different levels of pressure created. When she saw them enter, she avoided Connor's gaze and quietly shied away to the far side of the enclosure.

"Hey, sweetie…what's wrong?" He asked in a concerned tone, trying to play the supportive father figure.

She turned toward his voice, still avoiding eye contact. "I'm sorry. I did it again. I'm so sorry." She told him, pouty and dejected.

"It's okay. We're okay. You don't have to be sorry. We can contain it now. Come on, I want to show you something. You're not going to believe it." he said, trying to comfort her, then turned to Riley and gave him a nod.

He reached out his hand, offering it to Gaia as the barrier flickered off.

"No!" she squealed, stepping away from him with her arms up in front of her, trying to keep him out, as her eyes darkened. "Put it back! You have to put it back!"

Connor paused, both shocked and disappointed, then sighed, and told Riley, "Okay…Let's put it back up, for now. She can come out when she's ready."

When the barrier was back up, and she felt that they were safe because she was properly contained, she spoke up. "Is Riley okay? Is he all better now?"

Riley stepped forward about to reintroduce himself, but Connor stopped him, shaking his head.

"Ya, I think so. He seems to be feeling better." He told her, "Riley's not the one I'm worried about right now though. I'm worried about you…I

know it's hard, feeling like you have no control over what's happening. Believe me, I've been there. I feel myself going there every time I use my power too." He tapped the conduit strapped to his thigh.

"But you don't kill everything when you get upset." Gaia countered as she started to cry, and the telltale signs of an episode started to show themselves.

"Sometimes I *do*. Depends on how worked up I get." He explained, "It's my willpower that keeps my power in check. It's your willpower that will eventually help you to control yours too. It's something we'll both have to work on, but we will get you there. I'm sure of it. I'll help you, and when we get Jess back, she can help you too, probably even more than I can. It won't always be like this, I promise."

The early onset symptoms of the episode dissipated as Connor's words calmed her back down to a manageable state. When Gaia realized that she had just come back from what she'd thought to be an inevitability, she was filled with something new that would grow inside of her; a seed of hope. Her eyes regained a subtle glimmer that Connor hadn't seen since back at the lagoon when she'd discovered the other side of her abilities. It was a step in the right direction for her, and they both knew it.

"Can I get you anything? Are you hungry? Thirsty? Bored? Anything you want, just name it."

She thought for a second and then asked bashfully, "Do you have anything for me to draw with?"

"Hmm...That might be a tough one." he said with a wink and a smile, "Let me see what I can find. I'll be right back."

Connor returned to the upper level with Riley, and walked over to the refabricator. He stood there staring at the machine, arms half folded and scratching his beard with one hand.

"Ahem...Lil' help?" he asked Riley with a puzzled look. "I need a nice big pad of paper and a bunch of pencils. Good ones, and some of those white erasers."

"I think we can do a little better than that." Riley told him boastfully.

Lights flickered in his eyes, and he tapped away at an invisible screen in the air in front of him. The machine started up and began constructing the assembled components of a device, similar to the earpiece that he'd made for Connor, but with ten tiny disks along with it. They were slightly cupped metal contacts with an adhesive layer on one side, barely a quarter inch across and paper thin.

"So uh, ya. That's not what I asked for..."

"What you asked for was archaic. We're on a spaceship." he said, patronizingly.

"Well, if you think you can do better…"

"I do. I can. I just did." He told him, both pridefully and matter of factly.

"Listen. Back there with Gaia…She's just dealing with a lot right now. I didn't want to give her anything else to trouble herself with just yet. You know?"

"BLEEP, BLORP." Riley responded, doing 'The Robot' dance.

"Heh, I knew you'd understand. Thanks, bud." Connor replied, "So, what're you making?"

"It's like yours, but with better peripherals. These stickers go on her fingertips, and they'll absorb eventually. She can digitally paint on anything with this, even the air, in 3D if she wants. Any tool or medium she can come up with is preloaded. It's got pretty much full access to the media library, and I've set up some lesson plans too."

"Wow."

"Or, we can give her a pencil and some paper…"

"Shut up." Connor laughed, punching Riley in his metal shoulder and immediately regretting it. He flailed his hand around to shake off the sting in his knuckles, trying poorly to not wince. "Motherf-!…I'm good. I'm good."

"How'd that feel? Are you bleeding?"

"I've had worse; I think I'll live."

"Want to give it another shot? I need a blood sample." Riley said, taunting Connor by offering up his shoulder again.

"…What do you need my blood for?" he replied, looking at him suspiciously.

"Evil robots are powered by human blood." He told him in as deadpan a tone as he could. Riley waited for a reaction, but Connor just looked slightly irritated. "I want to analyze a sample from each of you, to determine what gave you your powers, how they work, and if they can be replicated, altered, or enhanced in any way."

"Why? We *know* what gave us our powers." Connor said, defensively.

"For science, bro! " Riley said, again waiting for a reaction, but again getting the same irritated stare. "I might be able to help the kids control their powers better, for starters."

"How?"

"I don't *know* yet. That's why I need the samples so that I can figure it all out." Riley explained, with a hint of condescension. "Imagine if Gaia could use her powers only when she wanted to, or if Rayn could control his transformations, maybe revert back to his human form at will? There's a chance that you could use yours without going all Weapon X…But, I won't know until I do some tests. What do you say?"

"Weapon X?"

"It's from…classic literature. Old-world stuff. I'll show you when Rayn's back."

"Ugh, fine." He said, rolling up his sleeve and holding out his arm.

Riley took Connor's forearm with one hand and touched his index finger to the biggest vein that he could find. The area directly beneath the contact point went numb, while a sterilizing solution was applied, and a small syringe extended from the tip of Riley's finger to draw the blood. A few seconds after it was done, the numbness faded, and it was like nothing ever happened.

"All done. Here, have a cookie." Riley said, handing him one of the two that he'd just printed. "I wouldn't mind a sample from Bas and Fen as well."

"You got a cookie for them too?"

"Well, the sugar is to replenish your blood glucose levels, so you don't feel faint. Plus, it tastes pretty good, and I figured that Gaia could use a little treat…Didn't want you to get jealous." He explained jokingly. "The amount of blood I'm taking won't affect those two, because of their size and metabolism. I doubt they have the right taste buds to enjoy it anyway."

"Well. Good luck with that. Maybe you should make yourself a thick rubber coating before you try, because I've got- …Well, I haven't got much, but I'd be willing to bet that they're going to see you as their brand new chew toy as soon as you try it."

"Aww, shucks. Thanks for your concern, but I think I'll be okay."

"I just don't want them breaking any teeth off on you. Tame as they may seem, they're still technically wild, and I don't like the idea of having to deal with a couple of wild, giant, superpredators with toothaches." Connor told him. "Bas might just take a run at you anyway. You think he'll hear your voice and piece it together?"

"No, Bas has an implant. I'll use it to essentially hack his senses. I'll use his memory of my scent and make him think that's what he's smelling whenever I get close."

"If that doesn't work?"

"Rubber coating, I guess. Body by Kong sort of thing...It'll work. C'mon."

Returning to the cargo hold, Connor brought Fen over to visit with Gaia, trying to give Riley and Bas as much space as possible. As soon as Riley connected to the implant, Bas's head popped up, sniffing at the air, then swung around to face Riley. His tail began to twitch and sway back and forth, while his chitinous scales flared as he took a stalking posture. The mutant's toes spread wide under the pressure of tensed muscles being unloaded when he launched into a short, swift gallop, before lunging at Riley with his limbs splayed out, like an octopedal lion pouncing on a wildebeest. When their chests collided, Bas's arms closed around Riley, with his momentum carrying through as they tumbled and rolled to the ground. He was flat on his back with Bas standing over him, pinning down his arms and legs while he looked him over, trying to figure out where the scent was coming from. With his free talons, Bas searched Riley's body for a way to peel off what he perceived as a shell.

"BAS!" Riley shouted, freezing him in place. "Get off of me!"

Bas cocked his head to the side when he recognized Riley's voice, then stepped back, releasing him. As he stood back up, Bas swooped around him in tight circles, closely examining him and trying to find more sensory evidence to be certain that it really was who it seemed to be. Riley adjusted the signal until he was confident that Bas had calmed down enough that he could get his sample, but he couldn't seem to find a spot on him vulnerable enough to take it from. The small gaps between the plates and scales appeared to be soft and pliable due to the smoothness of his movements, but when Riley tried to penetrate it with the syringe, the metal kinked and broke off against the sinewy membrane that covered the flesh beneath.

While Riley attempted to get his sample, Connor stood on the far side of the barrier, with one of the walls taken down so that he could give Gaia her visor. Regardless of her protests, Fen romped over and gave her a slobbery, overzealous kiss, almost lifting her off of the ground with it. When she couldn't bring herself to drive the big pup away, Gaia resigned to the fact that she couldn't just stay locked away forever.

"Hey. Got something for you." Connor said with a grin, helping her apply the sensors to her fingertips, and seat the earpiece. "Just like mine, see? Tap the button, like this, and the thing turns on. Then you just...uhh. Actually, I haven't really had a chance to figure it out yet, so-"

"Whoa." She gasped, wide-eyed.

"It's really something, isn't it? Now, don't be too upset if you don't get it right away."

"Got it." She said.

The display over her eye flickered with activity, and she waved her hands around with fluttering fingers as she manipulated the virtual interface of the augmented reality overlay. She'd picked up on it much faster than Connor, and was flying through it like an old pro, while *he* was still getting used to the using the retinal tracker without moving his head.

"There should be some sort of tutorial or walkthr-"

"Doin' it."

"...And there's a great big library and art progra-"

"Found it."

"Show off." He said with a grin, and she smiled back before getting distracted by what it could do.

Gaia had gotten a feel for the software and was now doing what looked like a cross between rhythmic gymnastics and finger painting. Once Connor figured out how to view her shared canvas, the barrier cube lit up with coloured light that followed the path of her fingers, changing as she experimented with the different tools, filters, and settings available. He looked on like he was watching a performance, impressed by both her artistic talent and her ability to pick up on the technology so quickly.

Riley had finished with Bas and walked over to collect the remaining samples. His hand dripped with thick saliva that flung around in stringy spatter as he shook it off. Fen stepped up just to make his presence known, but since Bas gave him a pass and Connor wasn't behaving defensively, he remained calm himself. Riley reached up, slowly and deliberately, scratching and patting Fen on the neck.

"Good boy, Fen. You're healing up quickly." Riley said, sneaking the sample, nice and easy.

"Hey, Riley! This is so cool!" Gaia exclaimed when she saw him approach.

"How'd you know?" Connor asked, confused.

"He already told me with this thing, when it turned on. The tuhdoreal." she explained, then went back to her digital painting.

"Gaia, this is really beautiful. Are you sure you've never done this before?" Riley asked, encouragingly. "Come here for a second, I just want to make sure that it fits properly."

"Okay, but I think it's prob'ly good." She said, prancing over to him.

He knew it was perfect, but pretended to check it out anyway, using the opportunity to get a sample without having to worry about upsetting her. He placed a hand on her shoulder while performing the fake inspection and extracted a droplet of blood, completely unbeknownst to her.

Riley began running analyses on what he had available as high priority background processes so that he could tend to more immediate matters. The ship made a single loud ding, like the timer on a toaster oven, and he rubbed the palms of his hands together excitedly then ran out of the cargo bay.

"What, are you baking a cake?" Connor shouted after him, but got no answer.

"What's going on?" Gaia asked, not sure if she should be worried or not.

"I don't know, let's go check it out." He said, taking her hand to bring her along.

"No! I- ...I think I should stay in here." She told him, pulling away and stepping back into the containment cube, looking slightly ashamed and embarrassed by her own timidity.

"When you're ready." He said, resealing the barrier before chasing after Riley.

Gaia smiled, nodded, and went back to her art.

Connor followed Riley back to the flight deck where he was busy hopping around between consoles. Everything was lit up with holographic maps and interfaces whizzing around the dash.

"Ready to go for a ride?" Riley said giddily, looking back to Connor who was standing in the doorway, looking overwhelmed by all of the lights and sounds coming from inside the cockpit.

"This is an epileptic nightmare. What're you doing?"

"The repairs are complete! We can finally get out of here." Riley told him, sitting in the pilot's chair and patting the one beside him. "Let's take this thing for a spin!"

Connor made his way over and dropped into the bucket seat. He looked out of the large window in front of him, trying to find something that he recognized to get his bearings, but it was so dark out that he couldn't even see the trees, just a broad field of bright stars in the sky above. He stood up to get a better view and realized that he couldn't see the trees because they weren't where he'd expected them to be. Instead of being a few hundred feet ahead of them, they were a few thousand feet below. They'd already taken off, and he hadn't even felt it.

"Pretty wild, isn't it?"

"Thanks for the warning."

"Huh. I thought there was only *one* little girl on board." Riley laughed and explained, "The seats are really just so you don't have to stand the whole time. A luxury, if you will. The ship moves by isolating and manipulating its own gravity, which is also how it nullifies the momentum we feel inside of it. I won't bore you with the technical details."

"I appreciate it." Connor said dismissively. "So, where do we start looking?"

"Here's the thing. I had Rayn's DNA sample before yours, actually. It was his biosignature that got the ship going in the first place, so it's got him logged. Anyways, I had the ship tracking him, so that we could just swing by and pick them up, once we got it running. However, shortly after I sent the drones to repair the ship, they disappeared from the scanners, and I've been unable to track them since. I know which direction they were headed, and the speed they were moving, so I've worked out where they may have gone, but so far, all of my efforts have been fruitless."

"Shit. What could cause that? You think he adapted to block your scans?"

"I don't know. I doubt it, since the scans are completely noninvasive, but we're going to find out. What worries me, is that the spot where I lost the signal is now within the radiation zone. I just hope they made it out in time."

"Well, what are we waiting for? Let's go!" Connor urged.

"Jessica wouldn't last more than a few seconds of exposure down there, so either they made it out, or they didn't. Taking a few minutes to get a broader view of the landscape won't change anything, other than giving us the advantage of knowing what's out there."

The floating globe over the holomap disappeared and was now displaying a wide-angled bird's eye view from below the ship. The radiation zone was a diffused grey circle around Vonn's old compound that stretched out several kilometres in all directions, yellowing near the edges. Beyond that was a sea of green, intertwined jungles and forests, spreading out from the mountain where the arkship was buried. The coastline was completely unrecognizable from what Riley had remembered. Marred by carved valleys, craters, and sinkholes that had filled with ocean water and reshaped the landscape. From that perspective, it seemed evident that Connor's lagoon was not a natural formation. The inland horizon was comparatively bare and lifeless, befitting a desert.

"What do you think's out there?" Connor asked, pointing to the barren wastes beyond the overgrowth.

"My guess? Sandworms." Riley told him.

At this point, he'd come to accept that Connor wasn't going to be picking up on any of his references, yet he continued to make them, purely for his own amusement.

"Alright, we've had a look around, now let's go. I want to start where their signal dropped off." Connor said, taking charge.

The ship dropped and swooped around, hovering above the skeletal canopy along the edge of the clearing. Several orb drones had gathered in the area, skirting the perimeter, seemingly unable to enter.

"There's something here."

"Where? I don't see anything."

"Here, in the clearing. Look." Riley said, pulling up a screen full of data.

"There's...nothing." Connor said, staring at the glaring void in the display.

"Exactly. Whatever it is, it's cloaking itself, and doing *too* good of a job." Riley told him as he overlaid the display with Rayn's path before disappearing. "Their trail ends here. I'm almost certain that it's another ship...Stranger things have happened. I think they're inside."

"No kidding. So, let's say hello."

"Do you want to get out and knock?...No? Well, I can't hail them. Since they're cloaked, they're not broadcasting any comms."

"Then let's try something a little less neighbourly than knocking." Connor suggested, raising an eyebrow.

"Such as?"

"Got any weapons on this boat?"

"You want to attack them? Literally, shoot first and ask questions later?"

"Just a little mild provocation to get the conversation started." he said with a grin, making a pinching gesture with his hand. "Just a little?"

"You know, you're a bad influence."

"So, that's a no?

"That's not what I said." Riley told him as the weapons systems activated.

CAPTIVE

Jessica was being held in another part of the ship, separate from Rayn, though she could see him on the wall monitor. He was being compressed by hardlight barriers, and she could hear his childish whimpers over the audio feed.

"Let him go!" she shouted, trying in vain to break free from her bonds.

Two dark figures stood in the room with her. One fixated on the object from her bag, and the other on her. Neither spoke, until the one nearest reached out to brush away the hair that'd fallen on her face.

"Don't touch her." the other scornfully ordered. "What have you done to it?" he asked her, holding up the catalyst, unable to get it to work.

"Who are you?" she asked, recognizing his voice through the electronic filters, but unable to place where she knew it from.

"Read my mind." he responded, giving her the opportunity to figure out that she couldn't. "I'm Reave. Now, that we're acquainted, I advise you to accept your situation. Accept that I am in control here, and this can go smoothly. Tell me what I want to know, and please, I really mean this. Spare me the 'what if I don't' crap…What have you done to it?"

"I don't know what you mean." She said, defiantly alluding to ignorance.

"How do I activate it? Why isn't it working?!" He shouted impatiently.

"You know what it is?"

"It's the reason I'm here."

"Then you're wasting your time. It hasn't worked for years."

"Lies." He growled.

"It's the truth." She said, adamantly.

"Then why keep it with you? Don't you dare say sentimental value."

"If you know what it is, then you know exactly why."

He continued to examine the device, calling in orb drones to scan it. She could see the readouts scrolling along inside of the black glass faceplate of his helmet, vaguely illuminating his face, but not enough to identify him.

"There is a piece missing. Where is it?"

"If I knew that, do you really think we'd be having this discussion?"

There was a silence, and Reave began pacing slowly.

"Tell me everything you know about it. Every last minuscule detail, or your companion dies." He threatened.

"Do your worst." She said, half calling his bluff and half challenging him. "That's his power, moron. Anything you do to him will only make him stronger. You'll be digging your own grave."

"Hmm. Good idea. I'll let him know it was yours when I bury him. He can be invincible all he wants, 100 feet down, in a hardlight coffin. Do you have any idea how long our power cells last? Or, maybe we'll just go up, and space him. Then, when you look up at the stars every night, you'll know that he's out there floating, alive, and alone until he dies of old age...*if* he *can* die of old age. It's up to you."

Suddenly, the ship quaked violently, and alarms sounded. Jess looked to the monitor, expecting to see that Rayn had broken free and unleashed himself upon the ship with some newfound strength, but the screen was no longer displaying the room where he'd been held. Instead, it was flashing red with warnings, showing a diagram of the ship.

"What the hell was that?!" The other man shouted.

When he spoke, Jess almost gave herself whiplash as she turned to him in disbelief.

"You?!" she gasped, recognizing his voice.

"We've just been fired upon!" Reave yelled as the ship was rocked again, knocking him off of his feet. He switched off the alarms, and the ship began listing off a status report.

"Primary shields disabled. Recharging in 30 seconds. Backup shields at 40%. Cloaking disabled. Hull integrity at 100%. Weapons charged."

Reave hailed the attacking ship, and their image appeared on the monitor.

"Anybody home?" Connor said as he and Riley appeared on their screen, but he was the only one any of them recognized.

"Look who's decided to join the party! I've been looking for you for a while now. Today must be my lucky day. Everything just keeps falling into my lap." Reave said, looking back at Jess.

"Give us our people back. Give them back now, unharmed, and you can leave with your ship intact." Connor demanded.

"Is that a joke? You know this is a military vessel, and you're threatening us with a modded transport rig. You want your people back?

Nothing comes free. You know what this is." He said, holding up the stolen device.

Riley searched the ship's databases for any reference to the strange artifact the man in black held in his hand. He'd only seen it wrapped, and didn't recognize the catalyst uncovered, but Vonn's encrypted files would only take a moment to crack with the upgraded processing power that he now possessed. Communicating with Connor via his earpiece to keeping him updated, he explained that he was working on it, but for now, he'd have to stall for time until he could figure out what it was and why it was so important.

"Enlighten me." Connor responded.

"This is Pandora's box. You have the key. You can give me the key, or I can take it from you."

Riley detected a weapons lock on their ship and had to devote a portion of his attention to bolstering their defences. The shields could only take one, or maybe two direct hits before having to recharge, so plotting an emergency escape route if they began to take fire was of absolute necessity. It was true that this was a transport vessel, and its defences were designed to buffer meteoroids and accidental collisions while loading heavy materials, not active combat. To the same degree, its weapons system was really a mining tool used to blast apart mineral-rich asteroids. Though it was not entirely dissimilar to the technology behind their blasters and cannons, it was certainly not designed for combat purposes.

"Well, that's ominously vague." Connor said, furrowing his brow.

"Don't give them anything! Morrow is alive, he's one of them!" Jessica shouted from the background. "It's inert! They have nothing. Get out of here!"

"We have *you*...Shut her up." Reave ordered.

Morrow removed his weapon from its holster and held it to her head.

Riley had cracked the encryption of Vonn's restricted files and discovered the nature of both the box and the key. With their shields fully charged and the jump plotted, they were ready to escape with a single command.

"She's right. We need to leave." Riley told Connor over the private channel. "I know what it is. We do have the key. We can't let them have it."

"What?!" Connor turned to him, outraged at the idea of leaving them behind. His eyes began to glow white hot, and energy crackled around

his fists. Riley's sensors spiked, and he knew that he had to defuse him before he went off like Gaia.

"Listen. We have to go. Now." Riley privately implored, "They have the goddamn catalyst, but they can't use it without something we have. I don't know what it is yet, but we sure as shit can't let them have it. We need to regroup and prepare. We *will* get them back, but not like this. Trust me. It's what she wants. It's for the best."

Connor resisted the overwhelming urge to take his frustrations out on him for suggesting what he'd considered a betrayal in abandoning their crew. He took a long calming breath, and the light from his eyes dimmed as they returned to normal, and he loosened his fists as the charge dissipated.

"Always did have a short fuse." Reave taunted, before Riley cut the feed.

Over the course of mere milliseconds, Riley detected the discharge of the enemies cannons, and he executed the escape command. The blast ricocheted off of the shield, taking it offline, but spared the hull. The trees below bent toward the bow of the ship and the whole thing seemed to stretch as it shot forward, up and out of sight.

"Track and pursue. Notify me when the vessel is within hailing range." Reave ordered his ship's VI.

Connor's scarred doppelganger handed off the box to an orb drone that hauled it away and secured it in a small vault in their flight deck. He turned back to Jessica, who had her eyes closed tight with a vein bulging out from her forehead. Morrow stood next to her with his weapon on the floor, twitching with full body tremors and slowly raising his hands up to the sides of his head.

"What are you doing?! Leave that on or she'll-" Reave shouted.

"I already have." they said, in perfect synchronicity, as Morrow removed his helmet.

"How?!" Reave said, backing away from her.

"Come closer, and I'll show you." She told him, while Morrow worked at releasing her from the restraints. "You know what the others can do, and yet you underestimate my power. Your toys aren't nearly as impressive as you think."

Reave quickly tapped away at the holographic interface projected in front of him, and Morrow seized up, then went limp in his suit. Jessica's restraints were for the most part still in place, and she was pulled to the other side of the room.

A muffled bellow and a thunderous vibration pulsed through the hull. The lighting flickered and began to strobe red again.

"Hull breach detected." a computerized voice echoed over the PA.

Reave typed feverishly at his control tab while blast doors slammed shut between each section of the ship. Security feeds showing several different angles of the affected area cycled on screen, none of which contained their prisoner. The back wall that Rayn had been pinned against was torn and bulged outward, like the inside of a ruptured tanker. The projectors in the floor and ceiling spewed out black smoke that was being sucked out through the tears in the hull. The ship rattled, like aftershocks from an earthquake as the cameras went offline, one by one, until all of the monitors showed a constant stream of static.

"Where'd you go you big bastard?" Reave growled to himself as he switched from static channel to static channel.

"I told you, he adapts. Maybe if you'd have been a little nicer?" she taunted. "From the looks of it, that's exactly what's happened, and from the sounds of it, he's pissed."

Reave summoned a squadron of drones to scan the where his cameras had been disabled, and extended his arm with an open hand, remotely attracting Morrow's weapon into his grip. Now dual wielding conduits, he aimed one toward Jessica and the other toward the rear blast door.

"What makes you think that'll work?"

"These? Oh, these just make me feel better. I'm taking us into the upper atmosphere. While he's busy getting used to the lack of oxygen, I'm going to detach the rear compartment."

"I mean, you assume that he didn't absorb the energy from those force fields of yours and become it, himself. He could be shutting down those cameras like that because he's literally *in* the ship. He could be-" She said as it shuddered again.

"Primary cannons disabled. Switching to secondary weapons syszzz-tems" the V.I. reported with a glitchy distortion to its voice.

Jessica raised an eyebrow and shrugged her shoulders at Reave, who had dropped one of the conduits and gone back to tapping away at his controls. Visual feeds from the orb drones appeared on several monitors. One of which was headed outside of the ship, toward the main cannon to repair it, and as the drone exited the breach, the main cannon floated lazily past as it fell back down to Earth.

"Or maybe, he's not in the ship at all." Jessica commentated.

"Krzzzt! Subject l-l-l-located." the computer announced, as the orb panned around to reveal the damaged turret mount and the glint off the dark, geodic mass that was attached to it.

"Cut that growth away and let it burn up in re-entry!" Reave commanded his squadron, redirecting them all to converge on Rayn's location.

When the orbs made their first attempt to remove him, they'd fired at Rayn directly, toggling the camera feed off while they fired upon him in unison. When the cameras switched back on, a third of the orbs were gone, but Rayn hadn't moved. A single orb fired again while the others continued recording. When its energy beam made contact, it absorbed into him, then redirected back out, like a laser through a fractured prism. One of the random splinters of energy caught another drone on the other side of him, and another camera feed went static.

"Cut into the ship! Don't give him anything to hold on to!"

The drones circled him, moving faster and faster. Their cameras switched off momentarily as they cut a conical disk from the outer hull beneath him. When they switched back to camera mode, Rayn was clinging to the edge of the disk, reaching down to secure himself to the ship. His fingers penetrated the hull like it was made of dough, but as he steadied himself, the orbs made a second incision, removing his anchor point, and he drifted out of reach.

"Oh, this should be good." Reave said, grinning excitedly behind the mask of his helmet.

"*RAYN!*" Jessica screamed, watching him getting smaller and smaller on the screen as he fell.

"Yes. Hellfire and brimstone. You'd better hope that your friends aren't down there when he lands. If he's redirecting energy now, the thermal and kinetic force should have some explosive results."

"You'd better hope they're okay too. They have your key, asshole." She spat.

Realizing that the chances of them being anywhere near the projected landing area was small, but not impossible, Reave dropped the ship into a dive and accelerated down. Rayn appeared on the monitor once again as they caught up to him in reentry. With his back to the ground, flames shot up around his glowing body, like a comet burning up in the atmosphere. He reached out as they grew closer, but his hopes were dashed when Reave picked up the other ship on his scanners and veered off,

changing direction and speeding away toward them. The slingshot effect of their proximity accelerated Rayn far beyond terminal velocity.

"Fire a warning shot and pursue. When we come within range, volley fire with secondary weapons until their shields are depleted, then disengage." Reave ordered.

Riley had been monitoring their movement, so he saw it coming when the warning shot was made. He moved to evade and boosted shields, anticipating a battle that he wasn't ready to fight, then jumped away again before another shot could be fired.

Rayn's fall ended abruptly, in what had been an agricultural region of the Southern Great Lakes. A place that would have been known in future historical texts as the Great Northern Uprising, as an army of human resistance banded together to take back the land and water from the highest population density of alien nests on the continent. A story that would never be told, because there would be no surviving witnesses on either side of the battle.

Flying low and slow through the streets in the former city of Toronto, Riley took cover, trying to hide in the ruins until they were able to put up a real fight. Buildings moaned as beams bent, concrete buckled and glass burst outward, trailing behind them, trapped in the gravity well. He would bring the ship to rest inside of a large, domed arena that was opened just enough to fit the house-sized ship through. Powering down the flight systems, he did what he could to mask their energy signature and speed up other active processes. There was much work to be done.

Reave had broken off from shepherding them away, and stayed to watch the decimating effects of the impact. Hovering several kilometres above the Eastern portion of Lake St. Clair, Reave and Jessica watched the land around Rayn sink and burst with a shock wave, strong enough to push back the western tide.

"Whoa-ho-ho-ho! Did you see that?!" Reave howled, as Jessica looked at the monitor in disbelief.

"What?...What the hell is wrong with you?! Why would you do that?!"

"...For science." He scoffed at the ridiculousness of her questions.

Morrow woke back up from being shocked unconscious with a splitting headache and scrambled to put his helmet back on when he realized that it'd been removed. As soon as Jessica felt him return to consciousness, she made her move. She didn't have him try to grab Reave's

weapon, or physically overpower him. Instead, she quietly planted a mental seed and gave him a trigger.

"Doctor? Step away from her. How are you feeling? You had a little spell. Anything I should be worried about?"

"Huh? What?...Nonsense! I'm fine." he responded, shifting his legs to make sure that he hadn't soiled himself again.

"Hmm, good. I've got an assignment for you. Here, you may need this." he told him, handing back the conduit from the floor and directing his attention to the crater that was being displayed on the main screen.

"What happened down there? Where are we?" he asked reluctantly.

"Just tested a new weapon. That used to be Michigan."

"Of what nature?"

"That's what you're going to find out for us. You'll assess the damage caused, as well as the condition of the weapon itself, and how it can be contained for future use." he explained.

"It's *reusable*?" Morrow asked with immense curiosity.

"From what I understand, *very*." Reave gloated, raising an eyebrow and shooting a mischievous grin at Jessica.

They landed just outside of the glassy circle at ground zero, just long enough to unload him, then retreated back up, several hundred feet to observe. Morrow knelt down to examine the impact glass embedded in the densely compacted, smoking hot dirt. Reave wasn't lying about the armour's environmental resistance; what would have barbecued him otherwise, felt cool and comfortable inside the suit.

"Leave it. Proceed to the epicentre." Reave ordered over the intercom.

"Sure, let's see...Ambient radiation is normal, so this wasn't a nuclear reaction. No traces of residual hazardous chemical compounds, biological, or otherwise. I am picking up an increase in temperature as I get closer to the central cavity." Morrow reported. "Approaching the edge of the hole now. It's deep. The drop off is vertical, like a sinkhole. I can't tell how deep it is from here. I'm going to need to set up an crane arm and winch, and some more lights if I'm going down there."

"You are. I'll have the equipment ready in a few minutes and drop it off when you can confirm a secure area to receive it."

"There's nothing else down here, and the ground is solid. Put it down anywhe-" Morrow said, stomping his foot before the intercom went out. The previously round sinkhole had crumbled around the edge and

expanded out to where he had been standing, swallowing him up and belching out a displaced pyroclastic plume.

"Doctor? Are you there? If you can hear me, respond!" Reave shouted anxiously into the receiver in his helmet.

The radio crackled with garbled sounds for a few seconds before the signal cleared enough to make out his voice through the fizz of distortion. Morrow cried out in broken chunks as they listened on from above.

Inside of the deep cavern, Morrow aimed his glowing weapon up toward the dim light in front of him as he backed into the darkness, away from the keratin colossus in the middle of the pit. Its bulky, stout limbs swung around, feeling at the walls of the cavern, causing it to shake and crumble with every clumsy impact.

Morrow yelped out of panic and fear, discharging his weapon and sending a bolt of plasma into the golem's back. The point of impact lit up and bulged, absorbing the energy and erupting with growth. He did get its attention though, and it turned to face him. The weight of its heavy steps as it shuffled around shook the brittle walls.

In the dull light of its glowing hot core, Morrow could make out the orifices of its face, like holes chipped into a rough boulder. It growled with sooty breaths, and he couldn't imagine how it could see, or even breathe if there were any organics at all beneath the jagged monolithic exterior. Its arms came up, over their heads, and the light coming through the hole in the ceiling was blotted out as the earth around them shook.

Jessica and Reave watched the monitors from the safety of the ship as its scanners rang out with alerts about unusual seismic activity below. Fissures spread out from the pit, like cracking ice, and a geyser of dirt and steam shot out before the distended land collapsed in on itself.

Morrow's spotty comm link went dead.

REVELATIONS

Under the crippled retractable dome of the stadium, the new crew of Vonn's old ship used their downtime differently in preparation for the looming conflict.

The cargo bay door was lowered so that Bas and Fen could stretch their legs and get some exercise to ease the angst of being cooped up inside. They tore ruts in the artificial turf of the outfield as they chased each other around, doing laps and sparring in the much appreciated open space. While the bay was relatively spacious, to those two, it would have been bordering on claustrophobic.

Gaia was still insistent that she remained within her self-imposed prison to protect the others. She was unbothered by the isolation, thanks to the immersive tech that Riley had provided her with to help her learn, express her creativity and keep her entertained, but also, to try and take her mind off of the potential fate of her brother. It was doing its job well, and she was more than happy to discover what more it had to offer.

Connor did his best to make himself useful, but under the circumstances, there wasn't much that he could do at this point. He felt like a toddler in a machine shop and was just as much a liability as Gaia was. Even more so, in terms of potential destruction, but as long as he didn't use his power, he felt no more draw in using it frivolously. The only trouble he was bringing at this point was the production speed of Riley's new equipment.

"You're sure there's nothing I can do to help?" he asked, picking up what could have been anything from to an egg timer to a hand grenade, as far as he knew.

"Put that down!" Riley warned, stopping what he was doing to take it away before he broke something, or hurt himself. "Well I'm not using the fabricator *right* this second, so why don't you go make yourself a snack, while I get this done."

"So basically, get out of the way?"

"Basically. No offence."

"None taken. How does it work again?"

"Use your visor to interface with it. Just think about what you want, and the earpiece will pick up the electrical impulses in your brain, then use that information to create a physical copy. You'll figure it out." Riley assured him, then went back to work.

Skeptical of Riley's confidence in its ease of use, Connor squared off against the machine, ready for a fight. After tapping the button to activate his visor, he stared the fabricator down, thinking as hard as he could about what he wanted. He focused with as much clarity as he was capable of, yet the equipment remained dormant. Just as he was about to toss the earpiece and claim that the junk didn't work, Riley chimed in.

"There's a proximity sensor. Step a *little* closer, and it'll give you a prompt."

Connor flipped him the bird, then took a step forward once Riley had turned back around. Just as he'd been told, new options became available, and he found himself begrudgingly hesitant to admit, even to himself, how intuitive the user interface actually was. The process was quick, and once it was complete, he took a long sip from the brimming pint glass of peaty single malt and lit up a fresh Churchill, with a new level of appreciation for the technology at hand.

Riley had gone back to his secret project and was working away in what looked like a blur to Connor. The alcohol may have been partially to blame, but his rate of production with the resources of the ship and his full integration with the AEGIS had made his entire world different. He'd broken through into Vonn's encrypted partition and become able to use the ship for what it was meant to be, and more. With the capabilities of this technology, the only thing holding him back was his imagination, instantly justifying in all of the time he'd spent playing video games and reading comics.

"Why don't you take that outside? Go for a stroll; walk the bases or something. I need to concentrate." Riley told him, fanning away the lingering smoke and reiterating his point that he was only getting in the way.

"I'm going to take a walk. You should get back to work. You're too easily distracted." Connor jabbed back like it was his idea.

Taking his things with him, Connor went back down through the hold and stopped to see how Gaia was doing on his way by. While he was admiring the art that she'd moved on from, she turned to him, scrunched her face up, and plugged her nose even though she couldn't actually smell the smoke from the cigar hanging out of the corner of his mouth. He'd already been told twice to go away, and he didn't feel like hearing it a third

time, so he pointed toward her work and gave a thumbs up, then continued out and down the ramp. Outside, he took a long look around, along with another drink of his scotch, which was becoming much smoother the closer he got to the bottom of the tall glass. He watched the smoke swirl in the breeze, and wisp away as he took a moment to appreciate the calm. After taking a few steps out onto the artificial turf, he felt a vibration from the ground, that turned into a padded, thumping gallop as Bas and Fen came running around the field, and up to meet him at second base.

"Whoa-ho ho!" he shouted to Fen, stopping him from nudging his head into his chest and knocking everything out of his hands.

"Whaaa-ha-ha!!" Bas shrieked, mimicking Connor as he playfully circled around them, when a similar chatter echoed back from the stands.

Bas stopped circling and took a broad defensive stance in front of Connor, Fen, and the entrance to the ship. The fur on Fen's back stood up on end, and his lips curled back over his toothy gums as he whipped around to face the shadowy overhang of the upper deck. He stood tall with a puffed out chest as his head moved on a slow pan, scanning the darkness for movement. A rumbling growl rose from his throat, and Bas joined in with his own crocodilian mimicry.

"Hold..." Connor commanded, not sure of what it was out there. He didn't want to accidentally attack a group of survivors taking refuge here. It'd be over before they knew that they'd made a mistake, but from the postures of his two companions, whose senses were much better than his own, it didn't seem likely that whatever it was out there was friendly.

Bas flicked his tail anxiously as something moved in the shadows, and an exceedingly large, heavily scarred alien sauntered down the row toward them, taking steps on both sides of the handrails. Even though it walked with a slight limp, there was a clear confidence in the way it held itself. This one was unlike any of the others that they'd seen. It was much bigger, older, and more experienced in battle. Clad in grotesque adornments, it wore its defeated rivals as achievement badges and a warning to any future challengers. Skulls of its own species, and a few that seemed even more alien were broken apart and lashed back together with sinew, over a blood plastered tunic of scaly leather and mane spines. Following behind, a smaller adult with a severely bloated stomach and practically dislocated hips waddled into view. It was an alpha and its mate, pregnant and looking for a nesting ground.

On the next tier of seats above them, three younger aliens appeared, creeping along the balcony. A young female, a large male that was only

slightly smaller than the alpha below them, and a hamstrung beta of indeterminate gender followed behind. At first, it seemed like they were all one pack, with the younger aliens acting as lookouts for the big alpha, escorting the vulnerable female that was carrying his offspring. But, that would change when the alpha started to pick up his pace, moving toward the ship and leaving his mate in the stands.

As soon as they became separated, the beta male and female of the younger group leapt down from the balcony and converged on the pregnant broodmother. She yelped, calling out to her mate as they clawed into her sides, spilling out the eggs and nearly disembowelling her in a frenzy. Though her years gave her a slight advantage over the inexperience of youth, her physical state, and their timely ambush assured the finality of the situation. The alpha turned to them and charged in a rage, but its younger counterpart had been waiting from above, and dove upon him as he passed. The young alpha came down on the big alpha's rear hips, avoiding both its natural crown of horns, and the thick mane of spines that ran down its neck and upper back. Its hind legs buckled under their combined weight, and the sturdy metal handrail bent as they came down on top of it.

Slimy wet eggs rolled down toward the seats above the dugout, and the disfigured beta delivered one last slash across the mortally wounded female's face, before chasing after them. While the elder alpha struggled to stand and fight off its ambusher, it'd seen what the beta had done, and lunged for it instead. Powerful claws crushed the throat of the petty beta and hurled its spastic body at the young alpha, staggering it and delaying its attack, giving the more experienced combatant a chance to turn the tide.

During all of the brutal commotion, neither side had noticed a lone scavenger enter the stands from a few rows over. This one was very lean, about the size of the beta, but even more heavily scarred than the old alpha. The would-be egg thief wore no adornments, and seemed to have gone to the effort to instead make itself inconspicuous with mud and dead foliage to break up its body lines and hide its colour patterns. Instead of engaging the others, it snuck down toward the opposite dugout, using the seats and shadows for cover. It was going to try to quietly sneak away with its prize instead of establishing dominance for ownership, as was common nature for its species. This was certainly divergent behaviour.

Bas saw the sneak, and his instincts took over. The dirt shifted beneath his feet, and spooked Connor, setting him off like a nervous gunfighter with a hair-trigger. He dropped his glass and drew his weapon, charging the conduit with his own instinctive measure and unleashed it

before the drink hit the ground, stopping Bas just a few feet from where he started. The plasma beam punched a hole straight through the building, then arced over and upward before Connor could stop it. He was usually very accurate with his fire, but with the better half of a pint of hard liquor in him, finesse was no longer in his favour. He raised his hand halfway to his mouth before remembering that he'd lost his drink, which was sobering enough to harness his impulse to escalate. Holstering the conduit, he trudged back to the base of the ramp as the upper deck collapsed and brought down the lower tiers with it, crushing the aliens fighting below. A rolling dust cloud hurling chunks of metal, plastic, and concrete blasted out as the structure collapsed in on itself.

"Back in the ship!" he shouted to Bas and Fen while stumbling back up the ramp as it began to close. Both leapt up and took cover at the back of the cargo bay, fleeing the rushing wall of debris. As the door sealed behind them, he could hear the growing patter against the hull, and feel the building vibration until it all stopped when the shields came up.

Gaia was still playing with her new toy and hadn't paid attention to much of anything else going on. She'd barely noticed when they all came rushing back in. Bas was pacing, wide-eyed, and breathing heavily in the back. Connor didn't know what it was about, whether he was excited and confused about seeing his own kind for the first time, or angry because he'd just killed them. Whatever it was going on inside the mind of the agitated alien would have to wait. First, he needed a pot of coffee.

Riley was finishing up with his preparations when Connor came back. The refabricator had been disassembled, upgraded, and expanded throughout the main deck, which had been rebuilt to suit his progress and allow for the manufacture of his designs.

"What'd you do with the coffee maker?" Connor grumbled.

"I needed it. Don't worry, I'll have it back online before your hangover sets in." Riley told him, cycling through dozens of holoscreens per second as he automated the remainder of the operations. "In the meantime, I can fill you in on what I've found…That is, if you're done wrecking the place."

"Saw that, did ya?"

"I did. I see everything in and around the ship. I'm calling her the Aegis by the way. At this point, we're practically one and the same."

"We?"

"It's more than just part of me now."

"O-kay...So, what've you found?" Connor asked, diverting the awkwardness.

"I've been reading though Vonn's private journals since I got access to his encrypted files." Riley explained, pulling up holoscreens too quickly for Connor to actually read, but summarizing for him as he went. "What *Reave* is calling 'Pandora's box' and we know as the catalyst, is an ancient technology that had been locked away and forgotten until it was rediscovered not so long ago. This guy, Vonn, jacked the thing when he stumbled on to a clandestine meeting gone sideways. He'd believed that their leaders had planned to use it to quell a coming uprising. Not it's original purpose, but it would have done the job all the same. So, he took it and got the hell out of Dodge. He brought it to Earth, where he could lay low and keep it out of their hands."

"So, these guys from Dodge are here looking for a WMD that Jess has been carrying around in her bag this whole time?" Connor asked, squinting; trying to get the two blurry Riley's to stand still.

"Kind of. They come from a space station on the other side of the sun, not Kansas. What started as one of the escaped arkships has been expanded upon for well over ten thousand years. It's its own world by now. Dodge is...You know what? It doesn't matter." Riley attempted to clarify, "Vonn had planned to dismantle it, and scatter the pieces so that even if they did find him, they wouldn't be able to recover it. His curiosity got the better of him though, and he began studying it, putting off his original plans until he'd learned everything that he could from it. Despite what his former job assignment would imply, Vonn was a smart dude, and it was only a few years before he'd deciphered enough of its mysteries to get it working. But it wasn't just him. He had help." The monitors displayed a glitching time lapse of Vonn's property as Riley continued, "He'd never intended on using it himself, but the more he learned about it, and the more time he'd spent here, the more it tempted him. In his time here, he studied the people and our history and observed how little progress they'd made ideologically, compared to technologically. In his eyes, they'd simply gone from throwing rocks at each other, to being able to wipe each other out with the push of a button, while still fighting over faith and fiction. He wanted to help them, and knew that a bigger, badder weapon wasn't the way to solve their problems...but, you work with the tools you have. The power must have gone to his head just knowing what this thing was capable of, because his plan was pretty fucking nutty, to say the least. "

"He used it to make the aliens and unite the people through a common global threat?" Connor guessed.

"...No. I have *no* idea where they're from. He opened 'Pandora's box', or, more accurately, 'the *catalyst*'. He even used it on his own pregnant daughter. But first, he tested its capabilities and potential side effects on others that trusted him, before administering his tweaked formula to her unborn child. She would give birth to a new saviour; one true god to unite them. Faith would be obsolete when no one would be able to deny it. A life *he* would shape, using the knowledge of the mistakes of their past, to correct humanity's repeated follies, and bring them together on to one righteous path...I'm slightly paraphrasing his words, but you can see what was happening to his ego. Anyway, he wasn't expecting the zygote to split, which divided their power. With unforeseen complications arising so early into the pregnancy, the increased possibility of the project failing forced him to expand his efforts, but much of this information has been redacted."

"What about the team that Jess showed us in her memories?"

"There isn't much more to go on. But speaking of her memories, you were in them. I know you saw. At Vonn's compound, back before everything went to shit, you were there with him." Riley told Connor, hoping that it'd jog his memory, but he just stared back at him, like they were talking about someone else entirely. "If this is all true, then it was Vonn himself that gave you your power. You were the one that helped him to get it to work...it also means that you aren't from Earth."

"Wait. What???" Connor replied, seeming to sober up a bit, but only briefly.

"He says that the people that were sent to find him and recover the catalyst did finally find him, and were able to infiltrate his group. Their infiltrator defected when Vonn told him what he knew about what the leaders of the arkstation had planned to do with the device. Vonn gave him the power to fight off the wet work team that he had been sent with...This roughly coincides with the invasion, so the rest is on that, and he doesn't really say much more about it, other than the device disappeared shortly after he used it on you."

"You think that I was the defector?"

"Well, I mean...Ya. I'm certain of it. Aside from getting that glimpse of you from Jessica's memories, which she *could* have manipulated to present us with a narrative to fit her own needs, I've got all of the raw footage logs that actually place you onboard the ship and in Vonn's

company. She wasn't lying about you being there. It all matches up." Riley explained. "It was you, spaceman."

"Well, shit...I don't remember a fuckin' thing."

"That would make sense, considering the fallout."

"What fallout?"

Riley pulled up an old aerial photograph of the California coast from before the invasion and then overlaid it with images from the Aegis that he'd taken just before they began searching for Jess and Rayn.

"It looks like you found your old friends, and they wouldn't give back what we know they *didn't* have."

"They din'ave it?" Connor asked, slurring his words and bobbing his head around lazily.

"Vonn's *wife* stole it and gave it to Jess to hide, remember?...Ugh, you're barely going to remember what I'm telling you now, aren't you?"

Connor gave a wobbly thumbs up, then staggered to his feet and wandered over to what looked like a walk in shower.

"Wha's this?"

"That's going to be the coffee maker." Riley joked.

"Well, wha's taking so long? Looks done to me."

"I just need it for one last thing, then it's all yours. In the meantime, you might want to lay down for a bit and sleep it off." he suggested.

"Ya, but I think I'm going stay up here a bit, until Bas cools off."

"I'll find out what's going on with him. Since you're going to be resting for a while around here, do you mind if I run some scans on the conduit?"

"Huh? Ya, sure." Connor replied, taking the weapon from its holster and lobbing it at Riley, hoping *one* of them would catch it.

Riley's optical tracking system locked onto the conduit, following its path in perceived slow motion, and he caught the weapon in mid-air with one hand as he walked over to the new unit. The walls were based on the same hyper-durable glass polymer that was used for the quarantine dividers and the dome of the arena. A seamless window opened in the wall and Riley placed the conduit inside, closing again and sealing off, once he pulled his hand out. Gravity was nullified inside of the isolated area, and the conduit hung motionless in the air. A tint came over the glass, and bright orbiting lasers scanned the weapon, then began expanding its disintegrated matter outward as it continued to scan all the way through until the space was filled with glinting mineral dust, engrossed in laser light.

"What the fuck, man?!" Connor shouted as he watched his cherished weapon dissolve in front of him. He jumped to his feet with balled up fists and stormed toward Riley, swinging at the middle one, but missing when he easily sidestepped his punch.

"Trust me." Riley told him as he moved out of the way of his sloppy right hook.

As he stumbled past, Riley lightly touched the back of Connor's neck and injected a mild tranquillizer, enough to put him to sleep, but not so much that it'd adversely interact with the amount of alcohol already in him. He could have caught him as he dropped and set him down gently, but just let him fall hard for trying to punch him in the first place.

"Sorry, buddy, no surly drunks allowed at this party."

He loaded Connor's dead weight into an upright gurney that self-constructed from panels on the wall. Once he was secured, it carried him into the refabricator, same as the conduit.

"Gaia?" Riley called out, deactivating the barrier around her and pausing the functionality of her visor. "I need you to come up here. I've got something for you."

UPGRADES

With the new and improved refabricator online and fully operational, Riley was set to equip Connor, Gaia, Bas, and Fen, with the custom gear and enhancements that he'd prepared for them; things they'd need to get Jess, Rayn, and the catalyst back. Gaia had joined him after some mild protesting over him cutting off her visor before she could save. Riley wasn't too worried though, since he was confident that what he had for her now would make up for it. He handed her a folded bundle and turned around to give her some privacy while she changed into it.

The bodysuit that Gaia wore was similar to the one that Riley had on when they first met. Hers, however, was padded with modest armour that was spotted with hardlight projector nodes, built in and powered by a network of miniaturized power cores. The hardlight body shield fully enveloped her, protecting her from harm, as well as anyone in the vicinity if she had another episode.

Powering her suit up for the first time, she was taken aback when the shield sprung up around her, making her feel claustrophobic for a moment before it stabilized and she was able to calm herself as it became clear. The barrier conformed to her body and moved with her, making it fully mobile and effectively untethering her from the confines of the cube. It could be manually activated and deactivated, but would automatically trigger if her adrenaline and cortisol levels went beyond the set parameters so that she wouldn't accidentally forget to turn it on if she lost control. Riley did his best to explain, but she seemed more concerned with what shape her hair was in when the barrier came up, so he installed a tutorial to her visor, just in case she didn't catch everything he'd been telling her. Once she was geared up, Riley woke Connor and opened the refabricator.

Stepping out of the fog that he'd been suspended in, Connor looked himself over with a bewildered expression. He was wearing a suit that followed a similar design to Gaia's but lacking any of the projector nodes and armour. Jacob's ladders formed in the spark gap between each of his fingers and webs of plasma arced up his forearms until he closed his fist and reabsorbed the energy.

"What'd you do to me?" Connor asked in a low monotone voice.

"I cured your hangover." Riley joked, but quickly answered when he saw that he was the only one amused. "...Well, I figured out how the conduit works with your power, and then I disassembled it down to its core molecular components and infused your body with it. Basically."

"So what does that mean for me?" he asked, apprehensively.

"I believe it should correct some of the faults in your power set. It means that you won't have to worry about using your power unchecked because you left your only means of control at home under the damn bed. It means that it's part of you now. I'm seeing new activity in some atrophied neural pathways. It could be old memories resurfacing, but let's just pretend that it means you've gained some actual self-control. You've got to relearn the ropes, so start off slow. Your potential output hasn't been capped or dulled, so...baby steps. That being said, if you flip your shit, it's on you." Riley coached and cautioned.

"Huh...Why isn't my fancy suit as cool as her fancy suit?" Connor asked with faked seriousness, winking at Gaia, then looking to Riley with a sarcastically furrowed brow.

"The extra density has increased your relative durability and strength, but moreover, there is the added benefit of the conduit's properties of kinetic absorption and redirection, in which a large percentage of-"

"Wait...Can I punch things and make them explode?"

"... In theory. You might also be bulletproof. Who knows, it's not like I've done ever this before. We'll need to field test it, but-"

"That's so cool! Come on, there's a field outside!" Gaia chimed in, taking Connor by his hand with her shield up. The initial feedback was more than either of them expected but quieted when Connor focused on holding back his output and found a comfortable resting state. She pulled him down to the cargo bay and reopened the door with her visor. As the ramp lowered, they got a good look at the devastation caused by his previous sloppiness.

"Whoa." They muttered synchronously.

Sunlight poured into the stadium, brightly diffused through the lingering dust in the air, which carried off in a sweeping cloud of fine particulate on the gusting wind. Connor found his glass at the bottom of the ramp, chipped, spilled over and packed with dust. He kicked it away to be with the rest of the trash, but instead of skipping off harmlessly, the glass shattered in a shock wave of force. Shards blasted off in all directions, ricocheting off of him without leaving so much as a scratch.

"Come on, man!" Riley shouted, pulling up the stats on Gaia's personal shield. "You know how much of that glass defected off of her just now? Eighty-six pieces. Control yourself."

"My bad." Connor said, looking down at Gaia, who was trying to hide a mischievous grin.

"Is a little self-control too much t'ask for?" Gaia teased, which put a huge smile on Connor's face and would have done the same for Riley if he had a mouth to do it with. A polite golf clap would have to suffice. They were both just happy to hear something from her that signalled a positive state of mind. The comfort in the security that she felt now was freeing her enough to let her personality show through the wall she'd been building up around herself.

Bas and Fen cautiously descended past them, walking out into the heaps of trash and rubble that now covered the infield. Curiously suspended several feet from the exterior of the ship by its shields, the trash was piled up like snow drifts after a winter storm. While Fen hung back and stuck by the others on sentry duty, Bas made a beeline for the dugout, to search where he remembered seeing the stray egg roll.

Digging through the wreckage, he was drawn by the strong odour that was seeping out from beneath. After tossing away a slab of concrete like it was a sheet of plywood, he found the origin of the scent. The pregnant female, belly torn wide open with the smaller female inside of her abdominal cavity, crushed while feeding on the eggs still in her body. He would've scavenged the remains, but they'd been heavily caked in dust with everything else, and these scraps were not was he was after.

A gust of wind spun through, clearing the air some, and wafting up the clues Bas was searching for. The dugouts had been covered and only partially filled, creating pockets under the surface that he'd gone right past with the scent of still warm blood overpowering that of the dusty egg.

Climbing back down through the ever settling, unstable rockfall of blue seats and popped stadium lights, the scent trail came to an end at the mouth of the cave-like dugout. Bas entered, unhindered by the darkness, and excited by the prospect of finding the loot. One misplaced step a few yards in caused the heaping pile to shift and slide, opening cracks in the ceiling that rained dust, nearly collapsing the whole thing in on him. When it cleared, a ray of sunlight shone through, illuminating the tantalizing prize, and he impetuously hurried in to take it. As his hands wrapped around either side of the egg, his eyes caught the glint of another's, just beyond the light. A gurgling hiss was followed by a hard slap and the raking of talons

across the hybrid's tough armoured scales. The wiry thief *had* gotten to the egg first, but had been pinned down and trapped with it. Only part of the alien's upper torso stuck out from the crushing weight that had piled on top of it, swatting around with palsied attempts to keep the egg for itself. Its long tongue flopped out and hung from its mouth, dry of saliva and pale like its gums. Its demanding snarls turned into begging whimpers, as its life slowly slipped away, all the while still biting weakly at the air for whatever it could get.

Bas cupped the egg with his feet and moved it behind him, out of the dying alien's reach. He watched as it fought for its last breath, which never seemed to come, despite death's looming promise. The ne'er-do-well thief moaned gutturally, and its eyes rolled around in its bobbing head as it tried to remain conscious. It was suffering. Bas crept in closer, smacking the alien's noodle limp arm out of the way and taking it by the throat with a vicious but merciful curiosity.

"Bas?!" Gaia shouted from outside.

"BAS!!!" Riley's amplified voice echoed out through the stadium-turned amphitheatre.

The others had come to help when the debris shifted with Bas still inside. He heard their yelling and saw the dirt falling from the ceiling, just as the echo triggered another miniature landslide. Bas's decisions were as quick as his actions, and he finished his business in the cave. As the roof buckled and fell in, burying the dugout, he leapt out, once again covered in something else's blood and holding the egg triumphantly over his head.

Fen scampered over, hoping that he'd share, but was disappointed when he didn't crack it open and chow down. Instead, the egg was presented to Riley with great reverence.

"Umm...Thanks?" He said, confused, as he reached out to graciously accept it.

He looked on, waiting for Riley to do something, but no one but Bas knew what. He huffed and began pacing with frustration, trying to figure out how to communicate his intent. Though he seemed capable of limited speech, his inability to articulate was boiling up inside of him.

"I think he wants you to eat it." Connor said, leaning in.

Bas cocked his head back and hissed in repulsion at the idea. His pacing turned to a full out tantrum, tossing and stomping everything around him. His head popped up, and he stopped in place when it came to him, and he rushed back over to Riley to try and explain with fledgeling

pantomime. When gesturing between himself and the egg, then to Gaia and the western horizon didn't work, he tried using his words.

"RRRRRRRrrrrrrrrrrrrrrrrrrrrrraaaaayyyyynngh." He snorted, pressing his hand to the egg and looking Riley in the eyes as if he were trying to will his thoughts to him.

"Rayn? What the hell's he on about?" Connor asked.

"Brother; Sibling." Riley responded, gleaning Bas's thoughts through his implant.

"…What?" Connor grunted.

"Bas asked me what he was, so I told him. Straight up. I'm not a dad, and there's no Santa Claus answer for this, so I told him the truth as plainly as I could." Riley explained, understanding Bas's intentions. "He's not paying tribute with food, he wants me to do to this egg what was done to him. He's smart, but he only associates the pain with Morrow. He doesn't realize that it'd suffer just the same, even if I could do it."

"Can you?" Gaia asked.

"No. I'm not playing god." Riley said abruptly.

"Oh no? Well, then what the hell do you call this?" Connor said, holding up a glowing fist.

"An upgrade." He responded.

"Is Bas not technically upgraded from the baseline of their species? He's smarter and armoured and who knows what else."

"I'd need to-" Riley's voice trailed off, but his eyes were lit up with code.

"I have a lot of work to do. So do you." he told Connor sternly. "Bas, I need some time to think about it. It'll be safe in stasis for now."

Bas grumbled and stomped back up the slope to continue rummaging. As he turned, his bladed whip-like tail followed and flicked in front of Riley's face as it passed. He wasn't sure if it was unintentional, or Bas's way of flipping him off, but he held back the reprimanding and allowed him to go blow off some steam.

Nearly back to the dead females, the ground shook and churned as the big wounded alpha burst out, like a trapdoor spider, waiting for its prey to get close enough to attack. Though it was crippled from a shattered hind hip, it dragged itself along on its front legs alone as the trauma that it had suffered from both the ambush and collapse seemed almost inconsequential to the blood lusted alien.

Connor was the first to react but hadn't had the opportunity to relearn his power, and muscle memory had him reach for the holster that

was usually strapped to his thigh. The mistake was a quick one, but the moment was over before he could correct himself.

Like those of his birth species, Bas had an attack reflex, like a supercharged prey drive that supersedes any normal defensive reaction. In his agitated state, that reflex was triggered milliseconds after the alpha made its move. Bas curled his tail away from the target, then pivoted on his front legs and swiped with a wild claw that purposefully fell short of its mark, while his shoulder dipped and turned like he was going to run. Instead, the momentum carried through, and his tail came around with an upward chopping swipe. The sharp plates flattened out, cutting wind resistance and forming a blade edge that passed through the soft tissue between forelimbs, deep enough to notch the alpha's spine. The nearly bisected alien slumped down, unable to move anything below the diagonal gash in its torso, yet still swiping in vain as it died seconds later.

"Badass." Connor said, grinning.

"*Bas'*ass" Gaia said with an air of pride; new to being praised for her attempts at humour and acting like she'd invented puns.

"No. No. No. No. No. No. There will be none of that around here. I don't want to hear that kind of thing come out of your mouth again. Is that understood?" Riley said, adamantly.

"What? Why?!" she protested.

"Because puns are the lowest form of humour. We're better than that." He told her, walking back up the ramp.

"Ass." She shot back.

"Come on, let's go have some fun and blow some shit up." Connor said, stifling his laughter and guiding her away with him while Fen impatiently waited.

"Okay!" she said cheerfully, then turned around and stuck her tongue out at Riley before leaving with them.

"Where should we start, coach? Connor asked.

"*Cha-la! hey! Cha-La!*" Gaia sang, then awkwardly hummed through the rest of the song, since none of the words made any sense to her. She danced around, throwing uncoordinated kicks and shadow boxing like a maniac, as Connor watched on in confusion.

"Looks like you're in good hands!" Riley told him, while Gaia listened on their open channel.

He remotely activated Connor's visor and synced it up to hers. The look on his face when he saw what she was watching made Riley bust out in

giddy laughter over the intercom, hearing something that he recognized from his own youth, and seeing that it was sure to drive Connor nuts.

"What is this?" Connor asked with the hint of annoyance in his voice that Riley was waiting for.

"It's a cartoon."

"How exactly is *this* going to help?" he growled.

"Open your mind. Use your imagination…like *her*." Riley told him.

He looked over to the little girl, who was in a wide stance and staring intensely at what seemed to be an imaginary basketball in her hands.

"Alright." Connor sighed. "When do you want us back?"

"My estimated projections put the completion for the overhaul at just over two and half hours. If you're not back by then, I'll come get you." He said, pulling up a map of the city to Connor's HUD with their location tagged and tracked.

"Overhaul?"

"I'm scaling things up. Creating a Mass Assimilation and Refabrication System, which will take- …You'll see. I've got ideas."

"*Good* ideas?"

"I've got ideas."

"Fantastic."

"Ya, so if you're not back by then, don't shoot me down when I come to get you."

"I'll do my best to remember that."

"…Gaia?" Riley said. "Make sure Connor doesn't shoot me down when I come to pick you up later. Even if you don't recognize the ship."

"Kay." She responded, barely paying attention.

Riley lingered on the channel for a few seconds, deciding if he needed to reiterate, but cut out and left them to their unorthodox training. He wasn't kidding about having a lot of work to do, and production started as soon as they left the stadium. Every orb drone at Riley's disposal was dispatched throughout and around the Aegis, stripping, modifying and reassembling it all into something new. Arc flashes strobed out from the cavity and the sounds of grinding metal echoed out through the streets with an orchestra of clangs and whirs.

COVERT OPS

Reave's ship descended toward the crater where Rayn had climbed out, holding a very nervous Dr. Morrow, like a little, armoured action figure under one arm. Soot and steam wisped out from the cracks in the rocky shell that covered his body and was carried off in the wind as he slowly lumbered away with steps that made the ground rumble.

As the ship grew closer, its gravity drives' field of influence expanded outward, reaching down and engulfing his massive body. Rayn floated up, trailing with the ship as it ascended. A hollow sphere of hardlight was projected around him with a buffer zone that kept him from reaching or interacting with the barrier; immobilizing him without the need for restraints.

Jessica and Reave stared with their mouths slightly agape, at Rayn's new form on the central monitor. She thought of the poor boy at the centre of the thing before her, the struggles of his past, and what he must be experiencing now. Reave thought of the power he could gain, again seeing the incredible potential that the catalyst was capable of producing in others. What she saw as a side effect, he saw as a pure expression of unrefined power. Power that he wanted for himself.

"Oh, that's glorious." Reave said with a reverence for the power, but not one wielding it.

"…What do you want?!" Jess shot back with quivering spite.

"You know what I want." he sighed. "We've been over this."

"But *why*? Why do any of this? You *failed* your mission." She prodded.

"I was born for no other reason."

"But they tried to kill you."

"Exactly. I'm going to bring it back and shove it up their asses." He said, revelling in the thought of achieving his long-awaited revenge.

"Well, I'm guessing that you're not going to risk getting there in this ramshackle piece of shit, and you've seen the retro junker my people have. Hopes and dreams will only get you so far."

"You really think they'd let something like this, fall into to the hands of *anybody* else, and then just give up after the first try?" he said, holding up his piece of the catalyst. "They would have written us off and sent others. We're not the only ones after it, which means there's a ship here capable of making the return trip."

"Okay. Let's say that all of your *assumptions* are correct. Let's say you put the pieces together and you get it working. Then, let's say that the process doesn't kill you. Did you know that not everyone survives, and we don't know why? Forget that part. *Then*, you use whatever power it gives you, to commandeer a vessel capable of making the trip. You somehow get past whatever crazy space security they have. Then what?"

"Then I kill the people that failed to kill me."

"Who's that? Specifically. How do you figure out who's responsible? What about all of the innocent lives that'll be lost along the way?"

"Collateral damage. Not my concern." He grumbled, storming around and making manual adjustments to the ships navigation system. They would usually have been automated, but he decided to double check the overview himself, just for the distraction.

"Have you even thought this through?" She asked, digging her claws into his mind without having to use her telepathy.

Reave stopped what he was doing and paused for a moment before turning to her with his response. "…What do *you* want it for?"

"I-…" she stammered, not used to dealing with questions that she didn't want to answer without the persuasive assistance of her power.

"Hmm??" He prodded, turning the tables on her and sensing her discomfort.

"I-…" she stumbled on her words again before gathering her thoughts and regaining her composure. "I've been charged with the responsibility of keeping it out of the wrong hands."

"Is that so? Then whose hands are the right hands? Yours?"

"…It takes a special kind of person to use it for good. Believe me when I tell you that you are *not* that kind of person. You're no hero. Power corrupts, and absolute power corrupts absolutely. No one deserves that much power, and you've already proven that you can't handle it. You've only got a piece, and yet, you're already tainted by it."

"Easily said by one who's already received its blessing. What's the point of heroes after that world has ended?" He told her with a hint of spite seeping into his tone.

"The world hasn't ended. It's just going through a rough patch."

"Your intentions aren't as righteous and pure as you would have everyone think. If you really believe that it's a power no one should have, you could have destroyed it. Instead, you kept it close. You actively sought to complete it, after going so far out of your way to make sure they stay apart. The only reason that you haven't taken it for yourself is that you're not as powerful as the people you'd need to take it *from*."

"That's ridiculous. More assumptions." She scoffed.

"Is it? Which one is immune? Who can see through your tricks? Who's keeping you honest?"

"..."

"That's what I thought."

"..."

"Oh don't worry, I won't pry. I won't make you tell me anything you don't want to. I believe in free will, unlike some of us here."

"Then let us go."

"I'm not stupid. Sometimes you've got to circumvent your own rules and operate out of your comfort zone to achieve your goals."

"What do you need us for? If you drop Rayn on them, you'll destroy what you're after, and it'll have all been for nothing. You can't ransom us to them for it, I'll tip them off before you even see them."

"Will you now?" he said with some arrogance, as a drone entered with one of their helmets, open and ready to be worn.

"What are you-?"

"Can't let you tattle on me and ruin the surprise, now can I?" he told her as the helmet was lowered down over her head and closed back up, fitting itself to her proportions so that it wouldn't accidentally come off.

"There. No unauthorized communications in *or* out…Now, let's talk about how you're going to help me."

"You must be joking." She laughed.

"I'm deadly serious." He said with a cold harshness. "I'll ask you nicely. Once."

"And if I refuse?" she asked.

"Why does everybody have to-" he grumbled to himself, then snapped at her, "…Everybody dies."

"But then nobody gets what they want."

"If I don't get what I want, then I have no reason to live. One way or the other, I'm going to go out with a bang, and I'll take you all with me if I have to. This isn't a negotiation. That being said, if you cooperate, everyone lives. I'll take my toys and go home. You and your band of misfits won't ever

have to see me again, and you can live happily ever after, or whatever it is you'd planned on doing before I came along. Though you won't have the catalyst anymore, so I guess *you'll* have to make new plans." He assured her. "Oh, and sweetheart? If I tell you to do something and you ask me 'what'll happen if you don't', *ever* again...*Everybody dies.* You get me? Are we on the same page here?"

"..." she stared at him with a hatred that seemed like it could burn a hole through his armour, but she was backed into a corner, and she knew it.

"I'll take your silence as a yes. Here's how it's going to go down." He explained. "I'm going to go reintroduce myself. You'll remain hidden and sneak aboard their ship. You'll be nearly invisible standing still, but shifts in the way the light is distorted when you move will tip off anyone who's looking for it, so you'll need to use some finesse. Stay quiet, and stick to the shadows if possible. Get in, get it, and get out. I'll be monitoring you the entire time, so no funny business. Otherwise...?"

"...Everybody dies." She said through her teeth.

"You're so smart." He praised in a boisterously patronizing tone. "Once you have it, you bring it back to me. When I'm satisfied that you haven't done anything stupid, our transaction will be complete. You'll be free to go."

"All of us." She stressed.

"That's the deal, my dear."

Satisfied with their arrangement, Reave brought up another screen, displaying the two floating below. Working the controls, he targeted Morrow with a localized gravity well and the doctor fell upward into it, passing through a temporary hole in the barrier, and into the ship. Rayn, with his substantial mass, was unaffected by the excision, and remained ineffectually still, defeated, and retreating into his own mind.

"Do you have to bring *him* back?" Jess moaned.

"He's your decoy." Reave whispered playfully. "Shhh, you don't want to spoil the surprise."

She knew not to trust him and had a bad feeling that somebody was about to get royally screwed over. A moment later, Morrow came into the room, and though it was glaringly obvious that he was upset, he kept his mouth shut about it. He marched straight over to Jessica and began releasing her restraints as an act of insubordination.

"What are you doing??" she hissed through her teeth, afraid that Reave would hold her responsible for his actions.

"Ahem." Reave cleared his throat, attempting to get Morrow's attention.

"Screw you!" he shouted back. "That *thing* could have killed me. We're supposed to be partners. I'm an intellectual, not some bumbling labourer. From now on, you do your own grunt work."

"Oh come on now, it's called fieldwork. As a man of science, you should be able to appreciate that more than anyone. Besides, the armour I gave you kept you safe, did it not? Now get her out of those bindings for me will you?" Reave said, with a backhanded reminder that he was still the in charge. "We've spoken, and she's decided to help our cause."

Morrow paused in disbelief and looked to her for confirmation. She nodded meekly and rubbed her sore wrists after he'd freed her, then stepped down from the small platform without incident. Morrow was suspicious that something was amiss, but had learned that any inquiry would just bring him more trouble than the answer was likely to be worth.

"So…Can we get this over with?" she asked reluctantly.

"That's the spirit!" Reave exclaimed. "The doctor here will take you to finish getting suited up, and he definitely won't be a pervert about it. Then, we'll be off. You know what you need to do. Morrow, you'll be with me. We're going see if we can't pull off a little heist."

After Morrow pretended not to watch Jess getting dressed, he guided her into the vantablack room for their mission briefing. The holographic environment displayed a composite rendering of the terrain, tracking quickly toward scans of the dilapidated structures as they were at the time of Reave's last pass through the city. Information pertaining to their part in the mission was privately displayed on their personal HUDs.

"Our objective is simple, but easily complicated. Retrieving the rest of the catalyst is our only concern. Once we've made visual contact, the mission is a go. No turning back. " Reave explained, pulling up his old scans of the city and overlaying the live feed as they moved closer, cloaked for reconnaissance. "As you can see, they're dog shit at laying low. Either 'Connor' has completely lost his imprinted skills, or, we're walking into an unbelievably unorthodox trap. Best estimates to the former, but he's still stupidly dangerous, so we'll need to leverage for our safety. I'll disarm him, which will take away his ability to use his power with any measure of precision, and hopefully, make him think twice about using it with your friends around. That's where your friend, the nitroglycerin golem, comes in. My emergency escape shuttle has taken him to the mesosphere, above our area of operations, and will gravity assist him back down to us, if I release

194

this dead man switch." He said, showing them the button on his glove near his thumb. "While they try to negotiate a safe exchange, you'll be expediting the process. We'll draw their attention, while you sneak onboard and recover it, by *any* means." He told her, then shifted his focus to Morrow, and as he did, the volume of his voice dropped inside her helmet, and the ship's VI took over on her channel.

"Hello, I am the Systems and Operations Virtual Intelligence Assistant. You may call me Sovia." The digital voice introduced itself.

"Umm...Hi, Sophia?" Jess responded.

"*Adjusting for linguistic incompetence.* Hello, you may call me [Sophia]." It announced.

"Excuse me?!"

"*Adjusting levels.* Hello, you may call me Sophia." it repeated at an obnoxious volume.

"Too loud! I heard you the first time!" Jess shouted over it. Reave and Morrow didn't even flinch since her helmet had cancelled out both inbound and outbound audio.

"I will be here to provide on the fly mission support to ensure the highest potential for success." it told her, having normalized the volume. "This way." An illuminated route was layered over her environment, displayed on her HUD with a repeating animation, indicating direction.

"I-I'm just supposed to leave?"

"Yes." Sophia assured her. "I've taken the liberty of activating your suit's environmental sensors. You are now cloaked from part of the electromagnetic spectrum, most importantly, from the range of 400-700 nanometers."

"I feel like I should know that..." Jessica said as she followed the markers and left the room unnoticed.

"I feel like you should too. 400-700 nanometres is the limit of human visual perception. I will supplement data for your rudimentary optics." She explained, "It is quite effective. The arrogant one believes that we have already left, and has attempted to secure leverage against you by informing the commander of your apparent absence."

"That weaselly sack of shit." she scoffed.

"Indeed."

As Jess made her way toward the hanger bay, Sophia displayed a graphical representation of the completed catalyst device. Based on the modular components of the box, an estimate of the key's appearance was

extrapolated from the schematic and added to the helmet's live search function, scanning her field of view as she went.

The hangar looked more like a hallway full of man-door sized airlock hatches than the open spaceport she'd imagined. While Reave's ship was considerably larger than Vonn's transport rig, it was still just a recon vessel; a relatively small ship, built for speed and stealth. It was not nearly a carrier.

The hatch opened for her as she approached and stepped into the closet-like container. The airlock resealed as the floor opened beneath her, and she fell feet first toward the pavement, flailing and screaming all the way through the nearly five-second drop. Sophia activated the suit's built-in micrograv unit, decelerating her to touch down with an embarrassingly graceful step-in landing. Looking up, she could just barely see the distortion in the air from the cloaked ship continuing on overhead, and Sophia automatically highlighted the outline of the hull for the brief time that it remained in sight before completely disappearing deeper into the city.

She'd been dropped just outside of the blown-out stadium and could see the arc flashes coming from inside. Sophia applied UV, IR and audio filters as she crept into the building, trying to disrupt as little as possible, but began moving a little faster when her scans started detecting the alien biology littered throughout it. Approaching the practically unrecognizable ship, she stopped to look over the extensive mods that had been streamlined into the original boxy configuration. Distracted by the gaudy new pearlescent crimson hull with chrome trim and other superfluous design choices, she didn't notice that the construction had finished until the cargo door began to open.

"Be advised-" Sophia alerted.

"I see it...How could I *not*?"

They watched as a custom war droid descended down the ramp. Its matching garish paint job and tacticool modifications were completely illogical and distinctly human choices.

"What is that?" Jess asked.

"That is an older model humanoid co-pilot chassis with extensive non-standard alterations." Sophia explained., covertly scanning its systems. "Its software is-...[ERROR]"

"Sophia?"

"[ERROR]"

The HUD displayed inside of Jessica's helmet flickered and vanished as the android turned its head to face her. Like fur standing up on a dog's back, hardlight blades and shields emitted from its body, along with an array

of other strange armaments that had targeted her before she'd even appeared. She looked down to see that her suit's cloaking tech had gone down with rest. An electric chatter echoed briefly through the helmet's comms before clearing, and a familiar voice took over where Sophia's had previously been.

"Fancy meeting you here. Nice duds." Riley said.

She recognized his voice immediately, but the shock of his appearance didn't even register, as it seemed inconsequential with what she knew was about to happen.

"No. No! No!! NO!!!" she shouted, "You don't know what you've done!"

RAYN FALL

The downtown core of the crumbling city was silent, save the rustle of panicked footsteps from fleeing creatures that'd been using its buildings to hide from the aliens. From the silence, a crackling boom erupted, echoing through, then another and another.

Connor's fist slammed into the sturdy concrete pillar outside of an ancient looking train station, using them like heavy bags at a boxing gym. The impact would've broken his hand, if not for the bonding process with the conduit. Light glowed from his body, dimly at first but increasing in intensity as it travelled down his arm and out through his fist with a flash. The concrete fractured, spider webbing out from the point of impact as a charge carried through his fist and blasted out the back of the pillar. Gravely chunks pocked the wall behind it like buckshot into styrofoam, and a static sparked through the particulate.

"Heads up." He said, waving Gaia back as the top of the pillar collapsed down onto him. He bent his knees and launched himself up to meet it, connecting with an uppercut and obliterating the rest, turning it into an illuminated cloud of charged dust particles.

Gaia applauded and cheered him on, dancing in the shimmering wisps spinning around her, completely unconcerned by the shrapnel being sprayed all around. While searching her visor's library for more inspiration toward Connor's training, she found something that she wanted to try herself.

"Do it again!" she shouted.

"Okay, watch yourself." He told her, cracking his knuckles and winding up for the next one. Just like the last time, the bottom of the pillar exploded out, and the top broke away, falling like a broken stalactite.

Instead of doing as she was told, Gaia dropped her shield and held her hands up, focusing on the falling concrete. Weeds began sprouting from the cracks in the ground at an astounding rate. Doing in seconds, what would've taken years naturally as thick vines buckled the pavement, intertwining as they grew upward to catch what was left of the pillar. When Connor readied for the finishing blow, he caught Gaia out of the corner of

his eye and saw that she was unprotected. Without hesitation, he turned his momentum, throwing himself on top and huddling over her. Using himself as a human shield, he let his back take the brunt of the hit as the pillar fell on top of them and cracked apart.

"Gaia?! Gaia?!?" he pleaded through the thick dust that had billowed up around them.

"I-I'm okay." She coughed, reactivating her personal shield.

"Are you sure? What happened to your shield? Should we go back and have Riley take a look at it?"

"There's nothing wrong with it. I turned it off."

"What?! Why would you do that? You knew what I was doing. Are you *trying* to get yourself hurt??"

"*No.*" She said in a snotty tone to try and mask her embarrassment.

"Then please, tell me what I'm missing here."

"My powers don't work with the shield up." She began to explain.

"Ya, that's the point." He reminded her. "Why would you want to use your power while I'm standing right next to you?…Were you trying to hurt *me*??"

She was even more ashamed of herself now, having gotten caught up in the excitement and not considering the other end of the spectrum of her abilities. She wanted to explain what she was trying to do, but instead chose to shake her bowed head in silence as her breath began to flutter, and her bottom lip trembled.

Knowing better than to push the issue without a resolution in sight, Connor simply placed his hand on her shoulder and waited until she decided to voluntarily share with him. His wait was a short one, as the dust settled enough to reveal the tangle of smashed plant matter around them.

"Oh." He said with a sudden realization and understanding. "You were trying to use *that* power."

"Uh huh…" she whimpered.

"What were you trying to do?"

"I-…I was trying to catch the rocks with it, like in the show." She told him, before sending him another animated clip.

"You don't find out if you can fly by jumping off of a building. You start from the ground first and work your way up." He told her. "We'll work on it, just promise me that you won't go doing anything reckless like that again though, okay?"

"Okay. I'm sorry." She pouted.

"So tell me, what do you want to do nex-" He stopped, looking up past her as a large void moved toward them through the churning haze.

"What's that?" she asked, looking at the transparent distorted air mass after noticing the seriousness that washed over Connor's face.

"*Keep* your shield *up*." He ordered sternly, moving her behind him.

As it descended, the ship's cloaking gradually diminished, only fully revealing itself once it came to rest. Dust blasted outward, clearing the area between them when the main door depressurized, and its ramp lowered.

"Don't try anything." Reave's voice boomed as he walked down the ramp, holding his fist in the air with his thumb hovering over a trigger.

"I'm not here to start a fight, but I will end it if you make me." He warned, loudly and clearly, projecting holograms overhead of Rayn and the shuttle, as well as the results of a test he'd previously run. He removed his helmet so that they could see the earnestness in his eyes. "I'm here to negotiate."

"Let my brother go, you bully!" Gaia shouted, stomping out from behind Connor as her eyes grew dark.

"Shut that brat up, before I give her what she wants." Reave threatened, waving the trigger at them.

"Gaia...That's enough." Connor said with a calming tone.

She looked back at him like she was being betrayed. The blackness that had crawled out from her pupils swam over the sclera and spread out through the tiny veins around her eyes. Her hands trembled, and her breath fluttered as she struggled to rein in the hunger of the dark side of her power.

Reave watched closely, deeply fascinated by the tease of yet another power set. His mind raced with possibility and ambition, temporarily losing himself in the moment.

"Listen. I get it." Connor said, walking toward him with his hands up, showing him that he wasn't holding anything. "You want something we have, and you've got an overzealous ultimatum to convince us that you aren't messing around. It's what I would've done. I also admittedly know just how impulsive I can be...irrational even. So, I can understand some shortsightedness in your plans."

"Shut up and listen."

"No. You let me finish, or I make you more symmetrical...See? Always with the ultimatums, you and I." Connor said, casually dropping his hands and strolling to a stop, halfway between Gaia and Reave. "C'mon man, deep down, you're not a bad guy. You're just misguided. You've had some bad shit happen to you, and you're reacting. I get that. But you're

letting them win if you allow it to consume your life. You're going about this the wrong way." He chuckled. "…And this *'brat'* will grow a lovely little garden out of the compost that she makes of you. So, maybe watch what you say around her…Seems you've already had a taste of what *I* could do before, but *now*?" he said, shaking his head with a grin. Connor concentrated a charge to his hands, lighting them up like hot metal as he juggled arcs of plasma back and forth. "You're shaking sticks at the sun."

Reave took a moment to process, and countered, "You're right, I am outmatched. But I'm not stupid. Like I said, we don't need to fight. We have a common enemy. We can *help* each other."

"You kidnap and hold our people hostage. You attack and threaten us. Now you want our help?"

"…Yes."

"Go fuck yourself." Connor spat, channelling his energy into one hand, reaching out to his target with a thrusting fist to finish the job he'd started years ago.

Reave flinched but gathered himself when nothing of consequence happened. "What is this?"

"What are you doin'? Blast'm." Gaia whispered, loud enough to chirp him out.

"I can't." He whispered back, worried and confused.

"What do you mean?"

"I mean, I shouldn't have spent so much time *punching* things. It's not working."

"If *you* don't do it, *I* will!" she told him as she tried to storm past. He stopped her, putting a hand down on her shoulder and she just leaned into it, digging a shallow rut into the ground with her feet, but making no advancement.

"Ahem." Reave loudly cleared his throat, attempting to bring their attention back to him.

"Well, just go punch him then." Gaia lobbied impatiently, ignoring Reave and regarding him as no more than a noisy training dummy.

While they squabbled, he was becoming exasperated by their dismissal of the situation. Growing more and more frustrated, he eyed the trigger and his thumb began to twitch as it hovered over the button. Doubt suddenly raced through his mind, tearing apart his delusions of how it would play out, and undermining his confidence in the entire plan. While he was reconsidering the angle he'd taken, alarms began ringing out from

his helmet, indicating a malfunction of the VI, meeting a requirement of the override conditions and initiating the countdown ahead of the trigger.

He put his helmet back on and snarled, "Jessica? What are you up to?"

There was no response from her end, not even from the AI chaperoning her, just dead air.

"Doc? Change of plans. Get us out of here, *now*…Morrow?" Reave commanded but got no response from him either.

With the alarm getting louder as the countdown approached zero, he struggled to maintain his focus. Meanwhile, Connor and Gaia had shrugged him off and become absorbed in trying to figure out how to get his power to work the way he wanted it to. Without a real backup plan, Reave's only options now were to *try* and get away before the impact, *or* give up entirely and let the end come.

Hurrying back up the ramp on his way to the nav console, he was stopped short of entering and knocked clear of the ship. Their mammoth canine companion had come barrelling down a side street to intercept another alien that had crept up from behind the uncloaked vessel. Launching into the air and plowing through into a rolling tussle of gnashing teeth and flailing claws, their scrap had intersected with Reave's path and tossed him down another alley.

Thanks to his armour, Reave wasn't hurt by the collision, but his heart nearly stopped when he reached for the catalyst and found that it was no longer in his possession. He scrambled around on his hands and knees, digging around through the overgrowth and refuse, single-mindedly trying to recover it. While the monsters battled around him, he crawled deeper into the sidestreet. Glinting in the sole beam of light that reached down through the buildings, was the catalyst, waiting for him like a gift from the universe. His eyes widened as his vision tunnelled, and the only sound he heard was that of his heart pounding in his chest. As he grabbed it, the world came rushing back, and just then, the countdown ended. He knew that there would be no chance of escape for him now. Rolling onto his back, he clutched his piece of the catalyst to his chest and watched a tiny light grow in the sky as the EES began its gravity assist maneuver. A second later, Rayn flared up like a shooting star, heading straight for them.

Reave *tried* to accept his fate, sitting back to watch the brief light show before it all came to a close. The acceptance never came. He was another step closer, but it wasn't enough. He wasn't ready to go.

The sky roared as Rayn burned through the atmosphere, loud enough to stop Fen and the alien mid-battle, and draw everyone's gaze upward. The clouds burst away as the miniature sun passed through, instantly displacing them for miles, and windows rattled violently in the seconds before impact.

A drowned out sonic boom and the softened scream of jet engines raised, as another object appeared in the sky on an intercept trajectory. After a few quick, successive flashes and subsequent pops, the EES lost power and spiralled off, trailing smoke and crashing somewhere in the city. The noise from the jets intensified, and the glow coming off of Rayn dimmed as he began to shift course and decelerate.

An eerie second of quiet seemed to last forever before Rayn crashed through the roof of a nearby skyscraper. Each slab floor that he went through broke his fall, and slowed him down just a little bit more, while the kinetic energy that he was inadvertently redirecting with each explosive impact became correspondingly weaker. The cone of destruction shrank as he neared the lower levels of the building and the debris that came down after peppered the area with chunks of concrete, partially melted beams, and broken glass, laced with bits of office equipment for blocks in every direction. What resembled a controlled demolition behaved similarly when the remaining structure imploded and dropped the building straight down, burying Rayn and whatever he had become as a result.

Reave was frozen in place, astonished by the turn of events, and awestruck by the sight of it all, until the pyroclastic flow swept through the streets. If not for the filters in his helmet and the resilience of his armour, he would have been killed instantly.

Out from the clouded street, the alien that had crept up on them crawled down the same alley that Reave was knocked into, both fleeing the disaster area, and finding each other at a disadvantage. He was in shock, fumbling with the catalyst to make sure that it was safe, not considering that it would be useless to him if he was dead. He held onto it like a frightened child holding his favourite toy, while the alien scrambled closer. It pulled itself toward him, laying flat on its stomach, which trailed behind at nearly twice the length of its body. Its spine had been severed ahead of its hind legs, which were buried with its tail somewhere in the street. Dust fell between them as the buildings on either side seemed to sigh with relief before releasing their burden down into the alley.

Once the heaviest of the shaking stopped, Morrow crept through the dark interior of Reave's ship after pulling a fuse from the wireless power

relay on what felt like a whim. With the lights off and his helmet non-functional, he removed it to get some sense of his surroundings. Following the growing smell of sulphur and smoke, he felt his way through until gusts of hot wind blasted his face, and the tease of daylight glowed just beyond his line of sight. Morrow took one last moment to put his helmet back on and prepare himself, before using the chaos to cover his escape and finally be free. With his youth returned, his body healed, and an advanced set of armour to keep it that way, things were finally starting to look up for the good doctor.

SEPARATED

Connor pulled himself out of the wall that he'd been thrown through, laughing. He walked back to the ship, trying to wave the ash from the air as the particulate was ionized in his lungs, purifying it so that he could breathe. He was sufficiently impressed by the durability he had gained to forgive Riley for his benevolent subterfuge, and wondered if Gaia was having as much fun as he was.

As he searched for the little girl, a realization made his stomach knot up tight. He wasn't worried about himself, and Gaia had her shield, but Fen was out there too. Though his thick hide stood up well to thorny brush and the occasional scrap with competing predators, it was still just flesh and fur. Passing by an otherwise empty alleyway, he saw the alien that Fen had been fighting with, ripped in half, charred, and impaled by an I-beam. Connor's worry grew as his imagination began running wild on him, going through every horrible potential way that he might find his best friend.

Though the initial damage had been done, the danger was far from over. The surrounding buildings groaned and wailed as they burnt, spitting fire and ash, and pumping out huge clouds of thick black smoke. Their structural integrity had been weakened, and everything was coming apart, like sand castles at high tide.

Gaia woke up buried under a drift of smouldering gravel, lightly concussed, but otherwise unharmed by the weight. Thanks to her shield and its atmospheric generator, she could still breathe but was unable to move to get free. The darkness was absolute, and all she could hear was the rumble of the ground as the buildings continued to collapse. She struggled and panicked when she couldn't budge. She screamed for Connor's help, but no more noise was getting out than there was coming in.

She became embarrassed for a second, and almost glad that no one was around to see when she'd remembered that she could talk to him through her visor, which oddly wasn't lighting up.

"Umm...Hey, Connor? I'm stuck." she said, bashfully at first.

When he didn't respond within the span of her patience, she began to unravel. It wasn't that he'd been incapacitated, or that he was ignoring

her, it was because her visor had been slightly dislodged when she landed, but she didn't know that. Even if she did, she'd need to reseat it and press the button on the side to restart it, which wasn't going to happen, buried under several yards of gravel. Claustrophobia gripped her, and the darkness began to seep in when something grabbed her ankle and pulled her out like a rooted vegetable.

Outside of the ship, Connor waved his way through the smoke, tracing the dark, muddy, wet spots in the fallen ash from the dead alien, back up the ramp. Cracking of fibreglass and crunching of ceramic was followed by what sounded like the distress call of a wounded rabbit. The dust that was steadily falling was being sucked into the dark loading bay and blasted back out in hot gusts, which came with a rhythmic thumping that gained tempo as he approached.

Connor raised a charged hand, illuminating the bay with light from his palm and what he saw made his eyes well up as he dropped to his knees, overwhelmed with joy and relief. Fen had taken refuge in the back of the small loading bay, crouched down with barely enough room to turn around. A smirk grew on Connor's face when he saw that Fen's wagging tail was the source of the thumping, but he burst out howling with laughter when he saw what Fen had been chewing on and where the strange noises were coming from.

Because of the full face coverage of the helmet and the similarity of the black armour suits, Connor was under the impression that it was *Reave* being used as a chew toy, with no thoughts to an alternative. The armour was strong, but Fen found the weak points where it hinged and was working his molar like a big pearly can opener, while Morrow's muted helmet couldn't completely block out the top end of his shrieks. The squeaky wails that made it out were music to Fen's ears and gave him a little dopamine hit with ever squeal.

"Hey buddy, you got yourself a new chewy?" Connor said, glad to see his friend safe and his enemy neutralized.

Fen wagged his tail faster in response, but growled subtly when he approached, protective of his crunchy new squeak toy.

"Easy bud, all yours. Try not to break it *just* yet, okay? Leave the head on." he said, backing off with a smile. "Reave, I promise, you're in good care."

"No! I'm not Reave!" Morrow shouted, spitting all over the inside of his fogged up helmet.

"...Fen, drop it." Connor ordered. "...Fen!"

206

The big dog's tail stopped wagging, and he let out a growly breath. He took a few good last chomps, then opened his jaws and obediently dropped his drool covered toy. He groaned with frustration, cocked his leg, and proceed to loudly clean himself in front of them in lewd protest.

"Lose the bucket, Not-Reave."

Morrow knew better than to test his patience, and hastily removed his helmet as he was instructed. He pulled it off and cowered, with his hands up, trembling, and begging for mercy.

"Huh. You *are* Not-Reave." Connor said. "You look nothing like us. So, who are you then?"

Morrow slowly dropped his hands and looked up at Connor, as he put two and two together. His voice had lost its hoarse raspiness, and the wrinkled valleys that marred his face had been smoothed out since they'd seen each other last. Connor didn't recognize the younger man, and had no reason to make the connection; he was a stranger again, so long as he didn't reveal his true identity. He saw his opportunity to start over, or at least get a head start.

"Where did he go? Speak up." Connor demanded.

"He's gone to commandeer your ship." Morrow said nervously, expecting Connor to recognize his voice.

"Pfft. Good luck with that. Besides, from what I've heard - the way I understand it …*this* is my ship." He said with a tone of arrogance that Morrow had also noticed in Reave.

"Umm, of-of course."

"Why'd you bust up my ship, Not-Reave?"

"I-I don't know. I just- …How did you know?"

"I know all, and I see all…or, I guessed. Take your pick. Why are the lights out? Start talking."

"It wasn't me. I mean it *was*, but I wasn't in control. Something came over me. I blacked out, and when I came to, everything was off." Morrow blubbered, pathetically. "I'm…sorry?"

"Have you met my friend, Jess?" Connor asked, familiar with her modus operandi.

Footsteps outside interrupted them when Fen shot up and ran out to investigate. Morrow retreated back into the darkness, while Connor followed Fen outside. Once they'd reached the street, Morrow closed the ship up tight behind them. With the air clearing and visibility extending, Connor could just make out the silhouette moving toward them, slowly, and under load.

"Gaia?" Connor sighed, speaking apologetically into the mic of his visor.

She didn't respond, but he could see the shimmer of her shields as the strange silhouette took shape. Bas walked out from the dust, holding a collection of alien eggs bundled in hides, and tucked under his arms. Gaia rode in on his back, using his crown like handlebars, her shields actively protecting her from his spikes and scales.

"Hey, where were you?" he called out with a light-hearted tone, pointing to his visor.

She let go with one hand and held it out at him, palm up, and shouted back, "Where were *you*?"

Bas snarled, and barked a poor attempt at repeating her, but lost interest in their conversation when he picked up a familiar scent. He dropped off Gaia and his bounty with Fen, trusting him with their protection, then left again to find what he was smelling.

"I uhh…What's *that*?" Connor said, changing the subject and pointing at something shiny hidden in the bundle with the eggs.

Gaia's curiosity derailed the scolding that she had planned, and she ran over to them to check it out. Fen was digging through the pile, inventorying potential snacks, and pulled out a new toy to replace the one that Connor had made him drop.

"Fen! Drop it!" Gaia commanded, stomping her foot, and pointing at the ground assertively.

Fen whined and cried in protest, but he was a good boy, so he let them have it. He rolled over and pawed his way through a frustrated begging session, upset that all of his toys kept getting taken away. A sad display for such an imposing beast to resort to, but he wasn't used to being refused, and his nose was put out of joint by it.

"Good boy." she praised, reaching out to pet him, but he wasn't having it, and ran off to find Bas before she could.

Nestled in the bundle of rough-shelled eggs, was the smooth metal armour of a burnt out android, lying face down. Its missing and mangled appendages, scorched plating, and chipped post-showroom paint job made the robot look like it had just walked off of an assembly line, then pulled all of the pins from a grenade belt and forgot to throw them.

"Another robot?" Connor said, squatting down beside it.

"Help me flip it over." Gaia said, straining with a rounded back as she tried to lift it.

Connor stood up and moved her out of the way, then grabbed the mech by the shoulder, and flipped it like a dysmorphic masochist with a tractor tire. When he made contact with the metal frame, it turned back on, but immediately lost power again when he let go and backed off.

"Do that again." Gaia said, grabbing his forearm and pressing his hand back against the metal.

The one remaining optical lens was cracked, but still lit up with his touch, and the socketed orb swivelled to look up at them. It tried to look itself over, but it was basically just a torso with a head. Points of articulation shot sparks and whined as they tried to move, but with nothing left to control, they were just a bunch of wiggling mechanical stumps.

"Oh g-g-good, it worked!" Riley's voice came through, crackling and full of static.

"Riley?"

"How do I l-l-l-look?" Riley asked.

"Not being able to tell, should tell you something." Connor remarked.

"Yep. I'm busted." He confirmed.

"Well, thanks for taking one for the team." Connor said.

"You were flying!" Gaia chimed in.

"Ya, you should've seen me. Jet-boosted 'Gundam' wings, hardlight swords and shields, m-m-mobile projection fabricator, and a *killer* paint jo-o-ob...It *was* awesome."

"*Cool.*" She responded in awe as she cycled through image catalogues of cartoon robots that her visor had brought up for her.

"Seems kind of wasteful, going to all of that trouble to just blow it up." Connor said.

"Didn't know I-I-I was going to have to blow it up, did I?" Riley retorted. "How long have I been offline? I d-didn't transfer back to the Aegis like I t-t-t-thought." Riley told him, sounding a little worried.

"Not long."

"Any sign of Rayn yet?"

"Rayn!" Gaia shouted, remembering that it was her brother that had done all of the damage, as she got up and ran off toward ground zero.

"Ahh, shit." Connor grunted, watching Gaia leaving on her own. He tried to hail her on comms, but she'd declined the call and the HUD on his visor then popped up to notify him that he was now the only one active on the network.

"What is it?" Riley asked, trying to look around with one eye.

"Gaia just took off by herself to look for Rayn. I can't get her on comms. I'm going to have to go after her."

"I wish I c-could help. Seems that my remote link w-w-w-w-was severed. Meaning, not only do I not have a p-p-power source, but I won't be able to access the ship's systems, and I'll be locked out until I can re-establish a direct c-c-c-c-c-c-c-c-c-c-connection." Riley explained. "I need you to take me back to the Aegis."

"I'll carry you. But, we need to get her back before we lose her."

"Agreed. Let's make it q-q-q-q-quick."

"Tell me something. You've got no arms, or legs, or whatever other gadgets that you had before, but you're still working...kind of." Connor said, fidgeting with the connections between Riley's head and torso.

"Y-y-yes?"

"So, would you still work the same if you didn't have this heavy, awkward body?"

"Oh, this is going to be weird."

"Ya, I imagine it will be." Connor said, adjusting his hands so that one was on the clavicle area of the frame, and the other, under what would have been the jaw.

"Wait! Wait! W-w-w-w-wait!" Riley interrupted.

"No time." Connor told him, pulling Riley's head from his body like he was removing a bandage.

Riley's voice glitched out, and his protests became scrambled as he was disconnected from the rest of the machine. The stumpy limbs on his torso flailed, then froze when they stopped receiving signals from the processor.

"Y-y-y-you a-a-a-assho-o-ole!" Riley stuttered.

"What? Quick and painless."

"I w-w-was going to tell you to insulate your hands. I could have been o-o-o-o-o-o-o-o-offline when you did it, like a-a-a-a-anesthesia." He explained.

"Want to try it again, or can we get going?"

"No, no, I'm g-g-g-g-good. Let's go round up the kids, then I can get my body back...P-p-p-p-p-prick."

CHANGES

When Riley took off to intercept Rayn, Jessica was left alone with the ship. It was wide open, and the catalyst's missing component was ripe for the picking if she could find it. Just a few seconds later, the explosions and quakes from the city had her taking refuge onboard. She hadn't seen Rayn fall, but she felt him land, and now she was left wondering if finding the key was still a priority.

With Sophia offline and the locks disabled, the helmet was only serving to dampen her telepathy, so it had to go. Despite the renovations, Jess was able to find the tools she'd needed to pry open the clasps that connected it to the rest of her suit. She pulled it off to get a breath of fresh air and immediately felt a presence behind her. She didn't see his face but knew that it was Reave and that he wasn't happy.

A sharp blow to the back of her head knocked her unconscious.

When she woke up, everything was spinning, her vision was blurry, and she had a splitting headache. The helmet was back on and secured with ratchet straps. Confused and uncoordinated, she fumbled helplessly trying to figure out the releases, but couldn't get her fingers to do what they were told.

"Sorry about that. I hope I didn't hit you too hard." Reave said once he noticed that she had woken up.

"Wha-?"

"But to be fair, you *did* break the terms of our agreement."

"Huh?"

"Uh-oh. That *was* too hard, wasn't it?" he said in a tone only slightly more sympathetic than patronizing.

She felt her conscious-self shrink away, flowing in and out of reality; drifting through the dream state, and into the astral plane, then back again, like a drunk driver, veering across lanes on an empty highway. Meanwhile, her mind unconsciously lashed out with psionic assaults against the psychic barricades built into the helmet.

During her more lucid moments, she'd watch Reave rummaging through everything he could access, searching for hidden compartments,

and eventually resorting to tearing up seats and busting out light lenses as he grew more and more frustrated.

"Where is it?!" he shouted at her, losing his temper along with his patience.

"I don't...I-I don't know." She managed to get out.

"What did you say? Where is it? Tell me!" he grabbed her by the shoulders, trying to shake the answer out of her.

His anger had made him sloppy, and he'd overlooked the proximity issues that Morrow had previously revealed. A special mistake, considering it was the first domino to fall in the sequence of events that unravelled his plan. He'd stopped shaking her, but couldn't move his hands from her shoulders, or stand back upright. He couldn't move, or speak, or think on his own. Reave had gotten too close, and now he was in her domain.

His consciousness floated in darkness and was approached by the light of her astral form. The calming glow flickered out as she began to lose control, and a growing storm flashed around him. Another presence swirled in with malicious intent, infecting him with cuts of anxiety and fear. Just as he thought that the dark essence was about to overtake him, it dispersed, and the light returned, freeing his mind and pushing him away before the darkness could reconstitute.

Jessica knelt on the ground, pinned by vertigo, fighting to regain control of herself and to find an anchor in reality. She wouldn't be a problem for anyone but herself for a while.

Stumbling back, dazed by the experience, Reave leaned up against the locked out bio unit to collect himself after another in a long line of mistakes. On top of not being able to find the rest of the catalyst, he couldn't access the ship's systems, because Vonn's original administrator account that he had backdoor access to had been overwritten.

Frustrated by the mounting losses, he punched the wall of the bio-unit, and a hidden panel slid open. Luck hadn't been on his side in so long, that he almost didn't recognize it. He just stood there, staring at it, unable to convince himself of what he was looking at. An indicator lit up on his HUD, confirming the detection of the catalyst's missing component, and his pants got a little tighter.

To retrieve the module, he'd have to insert the device into the panel before he could extract it like a fuse. It was just sitting there, waiting for him. It was too easy; too good to be true. He knew that any brief luck that he might have come across couldn't last, and he plugged it in hoping that his hadn't yet run out.

A red light lit up on the console, and the completed device was pulled in and sealed. Reave flew into a panic and started pounding on the machine trying to get it back. Something churned inside of the sealed tank, and when Reave stopped, so did it. He was waiting for some monster to burst out, or another trap to go off in his face, but only two things happened. The red light turned green, and the completed catalyst ejected, like a cassette from a tape deck.

A horrid bellow from the city shook the stadium and rattled the ship, putting this victory on hold while he went to close the cargo bay door. He may not have had access to the systems, but this was a spaceship. All spaceship doors are airlocks, and all airlocks have a manual override in case of system failure. He'd secure the ship, and then he would finally get what was coming to him.

With the completed catalyst in hand, he took the long way around Jess, still feeling the darkness reaching out to him as he passed. It strained to find him, searching for weaknesses in the helmet's defences, and seemed even more agitated by the catalyst's presence than by Reave alone, making him crave its power all the more.

Once he'd made it to the ramp, he could see out into the city and watched bright lights flashing off of the buildings and refracting through the dust clouds. He knew that it was Connor, and took a moment to revel in the prospect of finally being his equal once again. The door closed, sealing the ship as he moved to the centre of the hold and removed his armour.

Upon making skin contact with the catalyst, the surface lit up with glyphs. Reave hadn't been imprinted with the languages of his creators or their ancestors, so there would be no comprehending of any instructions or warnings; he'd be taking a leap of faith. Illiteracy wasn't a concern of his at that point, but the amount of information being thrown at him was somewhat troubling. When the flood of glyphs finished, he was prompted with two icons, one green, and one red. He touched the green symbol, and the catalyst unlocked and opened, presenting a liquid filled vial, loaded into an auto-injection device. He removed and inspected it, trying to get some idea of what he was about to put into himself. The liquid inside moved like nanites, but instead of a metallic shimmer, this substance seemed to be swimming with microbiological bioluminescent organisms.

He took the injector in his hand, raised it up, and drove it into the side of his neck. The glass tank emptied as the catalyst was pumped into his veins, and he felt the warm rush as it spread throughout his body. Closing

up the device, Reave set it down in front of him and meditated on his revenge, waiting for the transformation to begin.

The cargo bay's hardlight barriers activated along the walls, indicating that the automated systems had detected a change in the environment, though he felt no different than before. After several minutes of nothing more, Reave was beginning to think that the catalyst he'd injected was a dud or worse; if it had been damaged or tampered with, the catalyst could be inert, or even toxic. With a full dose of it already in his blood, if it was going to kill him, he figured that he would have felt something by now, good or bad. But, still nothing. It was too late for half-stepping. With nothing to lose, he reset the device, repeating the steps he'd taken to activate it, and loaded another vial injector with a second dose. After a moment of contemplation, he did it again, loading another, and another, and another after that. Holding the bundle of injectors together, flush at the ends, he pressed them into the other side of his neck. The needles extended from the auto-injectors, piercing his skin in a tight cluster and simultaneously delivering their payloads.

Reave felt like he'd been put in a choke hold with the sudden localized influx of fluid. His eyes went bloodshot, and his veins swelled, asphyxiating him with the added pressure. Pins and needles swept his body in electric waves as he became feverish and his muscles spasmed. He wasn't sure if the catalyst had finally started working, or if he had overdosed, and this was what dying felt like. His sight went blotchy and blurred as darkness closed in from his peripheral vision, and he blacked out on the floor.

BLINDED BY THE LIGHT

Connor walked toward ground zero; the caldera of rubble where Rayn had fallen. Carrying Riley's head under his arm, he kept him powered while he scanned for the twins. The ashy streets made it possible to follow her tracks, but the wind and constant settling of the dust in the air filled them up or blew them away quickly. They'd have to hustle to keep up. Even though the area they were searching was only a few a blocks, finding two kids in that mess made a needle in a haystack seem easy.

The skyscraper that Rayn had been redirected into was now reduced to only a few stories tall and kept shifting like a giant botfly mound. The creaky buildings sounded like moaning giants, but the sounds coming from inside the crater were even more haunting.

Climbing to the brim of the mound, Connor spotted Fen crouched at the opposing rim, apprehensively whimpering at something inside. Riley had Bas locked on as he paced along the perimeter, further along. He whistled, calling them both over, and they fell into rank as he moved closer to find out what was causing their curious behaviour. Inside of the pit, the steep, unstable walls sloped down to a lower gorge, where the ground cracked and moved like cooled rock on a lava flow.

"Hey, Connor?" Riley said, through modulating distortion.

"Ya? You see them?" he asked, looking down through the steam, rising out of the gorge.

"Nothing yet. I was just wondering if you've put any thought into why Jess would w-w-w-w-wipe your memory."

"What are you talking about?"

"Remember, b-b-back at the beach? Fishing?"

"Heh. Ya that went well." Connor shook his head, grinning while he searched.

"You told me before, that without the c-c-onduit, you couldn't control the output of your p-power and it would scramble your brain, wiping your m-memory."

"Ya…"

"No."

"No?"

"When we were on the water you used your power without the conduit…You definitely annihilated a few generations of sea life, but you d-d-do remember."

"…Well, I was a little groggy, and I don't remember it as clearly as I probably should."

"That's not amnesia." Riley told him. "That's a hangover. Back when you got your powers and f-f-f-fought Reave, you really *did* lose your memory."

"Right…?"

"If you didn't remember anything, how did you know that it was your power that caused it, or that you'd n-n-need the conduit to control it? How did you know what the conduit was, or how it w-w-w-w-w-w-worked?"

"I don't know. I just knew."

"W-w-w-w-w-hat else d-d-d-did you know?"

"Ugh." Connor grunted as he came down with a light hammerfist, trying to rattle loose whatever was binding up Riley's works.

"Kzzrrzt!…Thanks, I was getting tired of the Max Headroom schtick, myself. You were saying?"

"I knew that this power was dangerous, so I should keep my distance from other people. I knew how to hunt, and survive on my own…"

"That sounds like an implanted suggestion, like I did with Bas, so that he wouldn't turn and eat us when he got the munchies. Why would Vonn trust a known double agent with that much power? I think Jess figured you out, and dealt with it in the way that only she could. I think she got inside your head and *made* you turn on your team." Riley suggested. "Once it was over, she made you forget what happened and where you came from, so that you wouldn't find your way back. Making you believe that your power was the problem, was just a deterrent."

"You know this for a fact?" Connor said, growing more serious.

"No."

"No?!"

"Well, not for sure. Try not to lose any sleep over it. Just something to keep in mind."

"I just have to let you go, and you'll stop making noise, right?"

Riley stopped trying to make conversation and continued visually scanning for Gaia and Rayn, in what *he* felt was an awkward silence. Connor, perfectly content with the peace and quiet, looked to Bas and Fen

for any cues that might point him in the right direction. Fen's ears perked up and his gaze shot down into the pit. He crept toward the edge, but every time he got closer, Bas would throw a hissing fit, warning him to stay back. Each step closer was making the ridge crumble more, causing concrete rock slides and further destabilization of the mound.

"Careful, bud-" Connor said, then heard Gaia shrieking below.

"There!" Riley announced, forgetting that he had no arms to point with, but Connor had already spotted her.

Directly below them, in a precarious position, Gaia had climbed half of the way down and was getting pummelled by the rubble that was being dislodged from the weight of their steps. Her shield protected her from impact trauma, but the continued barrage made it difficult to keep a grip on anything as the loose debris moved like white water when it flowed, threatening to pull her under.

"I'll let you know how the ride was." Connor told Riley, leaning over the edge.

"Wait, Wha-" Riley said, powering down before he could finish.

Connor whistled, and tossed Riley to Bas. Snagging his lifeless metal head out of the air, he held it close, ineffectively trying to power him up by pressing a hand to his face a few times. Fen saw the toss and got excited, rearing up and barking, doing his best to fight the urge to run over and catch it. When he came back down, his tremendous weight compacted what was under his feet and pushed away the surrounding plateau, releasing the avalanche that was waiting to happen.

Connor made a rough guess at the trajectory, and jumped, aiming to add as little to the slide as possible before he could reach her. By the time he landed, she was already starting to disappear into the flow. He reached for her hand, and she reached back for his, but the wreckage that Fen had accidentally released, crashed over them, burying them both under tons of man-made talus and scree. They were only a few metres from each other, but unable to move or communicate. They may as well have been miles apart.

As soon as the light was blocked out, Gaia went right back to the same despairing headspace that she'd found herself in when she was buried before.

Connor's improved durability kept him from being immediately crushed to death, but his new strength was doing nothing for him under such a load. He was just as stuck as she was. Though the particulate hadn't impeded his breathing, the lack of available oxygen in the confined space

had him heaving for air that couldn't reach him, and with every exhale, the pile tightened around his body. He was suffocating, and his power reflexively activated to free him.

Gaia felt the heat, even through her shields, which were bolstered and expanded by the power surge. Light returned in the form of billions of tiny arcs, jumping between the conductive materials around her, as well as the glow that her shields emitted when under stress. The bits and pieces of the buildings that entombed them vibrated with the current passing through. In a flash of intense light, Connor's energy caused an explosive disintegration, breaking the molecular bonds of what was around him and welding together a shell around the blast zone.

Hovering at the centre of his orb of influence, he slowly descended through the lingering static. As soon as his feet touched down, he sprinted to Gaia, who was still only a third of the way uncovered. Her head and one arm had been exposed, sealing the rest of her body in the wall. Her shield had grown with the increased power supplied to it, leaving enough of a buffer that he could pull her out, but she'd need power it down first.

When he freed himself with the blast, he'd done so accidentally, in a moment of inept panic. He was still discovering what he was capable of, and his body reacted to the survival situation with a subconscious override, activating his powers and doing what he couldn't. This, however, wouldn't protect him from the feelings of guilt and remorse that hit him when he saw Gaia's eyes.

Though Connor was invulnerable to the full effects of his power, Gaia was not. Her shields protected her from the most of the heat and the force of it, but as the concrete blocks lit up like the filament in a light bulb, it was easily enough to bleach her retinas. She had been blinded, and her skin burnt in the second degree. Gaia was trapped by the dark side of her power that was pouring out uncontrollably, like a broken fire hydrant.

The blast had freed Connor and trapped Gaia, but it had also stabilized the quicksand pit at the bottom of the depression. The fused rubble crust cracked and burst open near the edge of the pit, as a huge geodic appendage reached out and slammed down onto the bank.

"No…No!" Rayn shouted, looking up at them, freshly emerged. His rage shook the walls, nearly causing another section of the shelf to break away.

"I- I didn't mean to…I had to…I'm sorry. I'm so sorry…" Connor rambled, barely registering anything else around him, paralyzed by the look of helplessness on her face.

Charging like a tiger on attack, and scaling the slope, Rayn put himself between Connor and his sister with incredible speed for his size. A swiping backhand that was meant to incapacitate, instead sent him sailing over the plateau.

"Gaia…Gaia, it's me. It's Rayn. I'm here…Gaia?" Rayn said in his booming growl, trying to comfort her, but she wasn't responding. He reached out to her, to hold and protect his sister, but pulled back when he realized that it would've been a mistake. Looking at his own monstrous hands and considering the unwieldy power that they'd exhibited on Connor, he was afraid that he'd just make things worse. Rayn would instead take up a guard post by her side, to watch over her, until he could figure out how to better help.

Connor felt like somebody had taken a percussion mallet to his eardrums as a kindness for what was done to his body. Rayn had hit him with the force of a speeding railcar, which should have liquefied his internal organs, if not for the durability of his new conduit-laced form. While he had been protected from fatal wounds, he certainly wasn't in any condition to be charging back in for a fight.

Bounding down the exterior hillside, Fen came to Connor's aid by slapping him with a hot, slobbery, couch cushion-sized tongue. Bas trotted down behind him, skipping the greeting altogether and impatiently grabbed Connor's arm, like Gaia had previously, pressing it to Riley's face to power him back up.

"Okay. Okay! I get it." Connor barked, snatching Riley's head back and giving him the power to function.

"Zzzrrttk- …How'd it go? Riley asked, booting back up.

"Bad. It went bad."

"What happened?"

"We got trapped. I panicked, and my power went off on its own. I got free. Gaia didn't. She's still in there…Blind."

"…*Blind*??"

"The flash."

"Oh no."

"Rayn is down there with her. I think." Connor said, rubbing his shoulder.

"We need to get them both back to the ship."

"You can help?"

"I need a body before I can do anything. We need to get back to the Aegis."

"Reave's ship is a lot closer. I'm sure I can pry it open."

"No. I'm not that heavy. It's of *vital* importance that we get back to the Aegis."

"Okay, wha- Whoa! Did you feel that?" Connor asked, stumbling on his words as a strange feeling washed over him in a flood of confused emotions that were not his own.

"I'm a disembodied metal head. I don't feel anything. What was it?" Riley chirped back.

"I don't know. It was like a eureka moment, muddied with fear and confusion. It's hard to explain, I've never felt anything like it."

"Could it have been Jess?"

"If it was, I don't know what she was trying to tell me. We should find her."

"Add it to the list."

Connor nodded, and Fen laid down. He grabbed a tuft of fur from his back and flung his leg over to pull himself up, still carrying Riley under his other arm. A quick pat on Fen's neck let him know that they were ready to go. He ran through the streets with a wild look in his eyes, thrilled with a chance to go all out. The city ruins were like an open track, compared to the thick woods that he was used to. They were back to the stadium in under half of a minute.

"Something's not right." Riley said as they approached.

After dismounting and Bas caught up, Connor whistled and made a circling gesture with his hand, giving the order for them to go patrol the area. Once Riley was plugged into the exterior access panel, he immediately became more lucid and lively. The ship came back to life, and he'd only have to deal with being dumbed down for a just a little longer, while Connor boarded and found a terminal to hook him into. As they entered the cargo bay, a beam of sunlight shined in through a round hole in the ceiling with edges frayed outward.

"What th-…Why is there a hole in the roof?" Connor asked, hoping that it was something simple that Riley had already known about.

"This is new. Guard up. We may not be alone." Riley told him.

Sparks rained down from the severed lines in the ceiling and alarms rang out, alerting them to the hull breach. With the cargo bay clear, Connor continued up through the ship.

"There." Riley said, "Put me down there. I'll handle the rest."

Following his instruction, he set his head down on the central control pedestal and stepped away while he did his thing. The light in his eye went out, and a cluster of holoscreens popped up around the sealed pod.

Walking over to view the readouts, Connor moved around the island and found Jessica laying on the floor behind it. He hurried to help, hoisting her up into a seated position, and released the straps that kept her helmet in place.

"No! Please! I can't turn it off." She shouted, grabbing the top of the freed helmet and pulling it back down as he attempted to remove it, wincing in pain as she did.

Before he could ask what she was talking about, he felt an ominous presence lingering at the boundaries of his perception; an odd feeling of being in the company of an old enemy, long forgotten. Connor was sucker-punched with an unintelligible onslaught of thoughts and memories that disoriented him, as they tried to find a place in his mind to hunker down and unpack.

"Stay away." She snapped, waving him off with one hand and hugging the helmet down with the other.

"Are you okay? There's something I need to tell you." He told her, sombrely.

"It's overwhelming. I just- …can't. I need to be alone." She protested, leaning away and rocking in place.

Whatever she'd done, seemed to trigger something inside of him. Being pushed away after what had happened with Gaia, and then with Rayn, his compulsion to withdraw into exile was reignited. After checking that the cockpit was clear, he made a quick trip to the refabricator for a fresh Cuban and a reasonably measured glass of the highland spirit, then retreated to the cargo bay to think.

Riley's consciousness had left its broken container and rejoined with the ship. With his faculties fully restored, he queued himself up for the next transfer.

The Aegis showed him what had happened in his absence, from Jessica suspiciously nosing around and being ambushed, to Reave's worrisome transformation and disappearance. While he reviewed the data, Riley deployed a squadron of drones to assist the ship's new repair functions, diverting a small detachment to keep on eye on the kids.

The backup that he'd collected from Morrow's files on the arkship had contained the raw data from the tissue samples taken from him while he'd been held hostage. Having integrated the refabricator throughout the

ship, he'd been using the bio-unit to construct a new body. Developed with a symbiotic marriage of nanomachines and stem cells created from his own DNA profile, Riley was able to design something new. He would retain the functionality that he'd become accustomed to, while regaining the ability to feel something more than a simulated response to stimulus. He'd been a man, a cyborg through prosthetics, an android through digital transcendence, an intelligent essence existing as a spaceship's processor, and now, he would be all of them at once. The merger between man and machine was to be elegant in its seamlessness. He hoped.

GONE

Reave woke up twice after injecting multiple doses of the catalyst. The first time, he was still deep in REM sleep when his dream state became a lucid reality. Eerily similar to the astral plane, his first thoughts were of fear. Thinking of the monster dwelling in Jessica's subconscious, he felt like he'd been dropped into a dark sea with a peckish leviathan swimming just out of sight. He could feel it out there, somewhere in the distance, just beyond his perception. He tried to escape, or at least put some distance between them before it noticed that he was there, but with no point of reference, he was just flailing around in the nothingness.

Cascading portals opened themselves to him in every direction, offering a trade of one unknown for another. Through one, he saw himself, lying unconscious, with his veins bulging and pulsating in rhythm with his heartbeat. Within this window, as with the others, barely discernible flickers and flashes of future potentialities hinted at what was to come. With only a brief glimpse of what he believed to be the arkstation and the location of his targets, he reached out and fell through, landing in his own body and waking up in the physical world.

He woke up for the second time to the crackle of sparks from the overloaded containment projectors. The room spun, and every nerve in his body throbbed with an electric ache. He searched with tired eyes, until he found the catalyst, laying on the ground *below* his feet. Reave blinked hard and rubbed his eyes, then took a deep breath and looked again. Working through his excitement with huge calming breaths, he stared at the catalyst with great intent. His finger twitched, and the device hopped like a Mexican jumping bean, making his heart race. Another long breath and he was able to lower himself to the floor. A Cheshire grin grew across his face as the catalyst practically leapt into his outstretched hand, and the gear that he'd removed orbited around him, waiting their turn. His eyes grew wide, and his grin became manic. He hadn't noticed until just then, that the sparks flying out from the walls were not falling in their proper arcs, but instead ricocheting off of an invisible barrier. This was when he realized that he could feel it. He could broadly manipulate the barrier's size and density, and

with a little concentration of will, he was able to form constructs of hardlight from it. Fully absorbed in the exploration of his new abilities, Reave's thoughts drifted from his mission. With his powers in their infancy, he could only imagine what mastery would bring.

The psychic monster from Jessica's subconscious had grown bold, mistaking distraction for defencelessness, and crept into the expanded reaches of Reave's mind. Even though it was the weakest of his new power set, his psionic defence was enough to instigate the monster's hysterical retreat. He got the impression that it'd never been challenged before, but he wasn't yet confident enough in his own ability to take it on again.

A surge of emotion made its way from the inner city and alerted Reave that company was on its way. More determined than ever before, he refused to let everything he'd earned be taken from him. Though he thought that he'd accepted the fact that Connor wasn't solely responsible for his actions, deep down, he still felt that he was owed a reparation, and he couldn't think of a test more befitting of his new powers.

Preparing for battle, Reave suited up and checked his gear. He focused his energy on the density of his shield, in the event of his worst-case scenario. He'd seen firsthand the damage that Connor was capable of, and he needed to know that he could tank his blasts. He had confidence and determination on his side, along with a handful of powers that his opponent did not possess. In a one-on-one contest, he was convinced that Connor would fall. He told himself that he'd show mercy and let him live. He'd offer him a place by his side, like the way things were. But, this wouldn't be the honourable competition of his idealized vision, and he knew it. He wouldn't be alone, and the others were as unpredictable as they were powerful - a department that he was certain none of them were lacking in. His confidence began to feel like cockiness, and he knew that escape was the only real sane course of action. He believed that he could win, but on his own terms, which was neither there, nor then.

Taking to the air with shields up, if he could get out quickly enough, keep moving and avoid any nasty surprises, there was a good possibility of a successful escape. Once he was away from them, he could return to his ship and rework his plan to get to the arkstation.

"There goes another plan...as is tradition." He grumbled to himself, and suddenly, the ceiling warped and dematerialized, opening up to a dark starry sky in the middle of the day.

The hole wasn't just in the ship, but in space-time itself; a wormhole, created by his intent on escape, and guided by forces that he didn't yet

understand. Staring pensively into the calm centre of the vortex, he triple-checked the life support systems in his suit. He'd never actually seen the arkstation before, but he knew exactly what he was looking at when he saw it through the portal. Gathering his courage, he bolstered his shield and entered the unknown.

Passing through the tunnel, he watched the entire expanse he was travelling, compressed down to the depth of only a few metres. He watched the Earth fall away until it was a speck in the dark, and the Sun passed by like a blazing rocket, bigger and brighter than anything he could have imagined. Nearing the point of juxtaposition with the Earth, Reave came out of hyperspace and was greeted by a spacecraft cemetery, instead of the thriving world-ship that he'd envisioned.

The wormhole closed, and he was left with the wreckage of what he'd come to destroy. Dead ships were tethered in orbit, all around the fractured artificial world. Huge sections of the station that had broken away were now floating islands in a field of scrap, silently crashing together and bouncing off of each other, like giant slow-motion bumper cars.

"…Asteroids?" He asked himself, looking around cautiously and wondering what could have caused so much destruction.

"No." An ethereal whisper echoed in his mind. A wisp of light appeared, taking a vaguely humanoid form and flew away, into the debris field. "Come."

Reave followed the light, which gained in speed the farther it went, making it difficult to track through the maze. Just when he thought that he'd lost it, the voice returned, beckoning him forth, begging him to continue.

"You must hurry."

He slowed down despite the urgency, to survey the area before entering into what his gut told him was a trap. Though he'd just arrived, and no one could have known that he was coming, a trap was a trap all the same, and not something that he wanted anything to do with. He watched every vantage point and shadowy hiding place for movement that would reveal an ambush. There was nothing there, but tricks of the light. He could still feel the presence that had called to him and ventured on in search of it.

"Where are you?!" He telepathically shouted in frustration, and a feeling of fear and anxiety that wasn't his own echoed back. "…I'm yelling at ghosts, aren't I?"

"Not yet." It told him. A tiny light flickered through the porthole of an exposed, internal airlock. As the door opened, the voice returned. "Inside. quickly."

The dancing light was devoured in a shadow that swept through the flotsam, and Reave hurried into the provided cover. The airlock sealed and repressurized behind him, and the cast shadow quickly overtook the window. Inside was just as dark as outside; pitch black, if not for the light he'd created. Ball lightning materialized around him and floated up to the ceiling, illuminating the area as he explored the equipment. Whispers in the dark drew him down a broad corridor to a medical centre that he could have parked his own ship in. Even though most of it had been salvaged for barricades and blinders against the windows, he could tell without a doubt that their tech was much more advanced than his own, and decades beyond what Vonn had appropriated.

With the level of medical tech they possessed, Reave's thoughts went to their military arsenal and what he might be up against. A cornered animal was one thing, but a cornered animal with the power to tear apart the station was another.

A single room in the infirmary was powered and lit, hidden away from the covered windows of the exterior. Packed inside, huddled up close around the only active pod, were dozens of women and children, with the older boys holding a defensive line around them. Though their faces showed conviction, he could sense much fear in their hearts. But what bothered him, was that he couldn't sense their minds at all until he was almost on top of them.

As he approached, the huddled youths divided the room to make way. A path was formed, leading him to the tank, where a middle-aged woman floating in liquid watched him through the glass.

"Please, we mean you no harm. We need your help." She told him without moving her lips.

"You speak English?" he asked, puzzled by his ability to understand her.

"No, but *you do*."

"You have powers too…" He said, warily.

"Yes. Our people carry an inherited mutation, passed down from our ancestors. Dormant in most, but the direct descendants of the chosen were able to rekindle these latent abilities. I've trained my entire life in order to wield the power of my bloodline." She explained, casually eyeing the device strapped to Reave's armour.

"Uh huh…What happened here?"

"We were found by the cosmic scourge that we've been hiding from for thousands of years."

"I've had encounters with these beasts on Earth. With your technology, this cou-"

"No." The woman in the tank communicated with only her thoughts, as it was evident that her corporeal form was far too weak to do otherwise. "*This* scourge is both a new and ancient threat…The beasts you've encountered are…familiar to us."

"Familiar?" he asked.

"They were created off-world, as a weapon against the scourge. But, it fell into the wrong hands and was used against us instead. A device was created to empower us, and give us the strength needed to fight back. But, it too was lost. The *catalyst* is ancient and was the origin of our mutations. Something *you* seem to be *quite* familiar with…"

"You know who I am?"

"I know *what* you are."

"Then you know why I'm here?"

"I know why you *think* you're here. The ones that you believe to be responsible for your misfortune are neither guilty of your accusations, nor are they alive to face your judgement. They are gone, and the war you're after is bigger than you. Your enemy is out *there*."

"You're lying!" he shouted, clenching his fists and grinding his teeth, creating a bladed arsenal of light all around him.

"Use your power. Look deep into my thoughts and my intentions. You'll see that what I tell you is true. *Join* us." She said to him with a comforting wink.

Diving into her mindscape, he found more truths than he'd anticipated. Her comparative mastery allowed him to gauge where on the telepathic spectrum he fell, and was humbled in the context of his own ability. The potential granted to him by the catalyst may have been beyond that of her inherited ability, but it was nothing without knowledge of how to use it. The old woman sensed this in him and acted as a guide, first showing him what he needed to see, but also opening the doors to the residence of her mind, allowing him to explore unimpeded.

A moment for everyone else stretched out unquantifiably for Reave, as the time dilation effects of her power allowed for a crash course to remedy his ignorance. Probing his memories to find out what he knew and what he thought he knew, she would set the record straight. If he was going to be the saviour they needed, she'd have to show him that his lust for revenge was misplaced and unfounded. They needed his power, so they'd need his trust and devotion as well.

Their consciousnesses merged, and ambiguous visions of a sacred relic stirred with feelings of dread reaching out to him like phantom claws from the cold, dark void of deep space. Offended by its existence, with the hate of a zealot for a heretic, darkness began snuffing out any life it found. The relic imbued his essence with its power, and projected its light into the dark. Drawn to it, like moths to flame, the shadows recoiled from the radiating energy. Before it could regroup, the relic vanished from its perception and was hidden within the heart of a star going supernova. Like spores on the wind, its power spread out with musings of rigorous inspiration. While driving weaker minds mad, it would eventually lead to the creation of the catalyst.

She showed him their history in flashes. From the first remote evidence of their dark nemesis, to the as yet unrivalled arms race that resulted from the fear of its arrival. Unsure of which faction triggered the initial invasion from the so-called aliens, or of their intent, she speculated that they'd been called to Earth early, as a trap for the scourge, though she made it clear that humanity's perpetual infighting could have nullified any logic to their actions. False unification and the subsequent sabotaged launch of the other factions' arkships had ingrained a common paranoia in their genetic memory.

"The catalyst was smuggled off-world by the first leaders of the arkstation, who knew that whoever commanded its power, could rule unopposed. Kept locked away in secret and used only with the greatest of restraint, their faction's reign spanned millennia. It wasn't until a familial dispute lead to a fracturing of their oligarchy, that spawned new rival factions and a war for power that few of them understood." She explained, showing him what their world once was. "The catalyst was stolen from their leader's vault by his own son, in an attempt to trade it for peace. When his proxy agent never returned from the exchange, it was assumed that they'd been betrayed. We had suspected the same, and the scramble to recover it drove both sides to unconscionable acts that set us on the path of our mutually assured destruction."

"…*We?*" he asked, even though he knew that she was likely part of the rival faction's leadership. She saw the rhetoric in his query and gave no direct answer.

"When a seeker clone ship was discovered on its way to Earth, our forces were already spread too thin to send our own equivalent. Instead, I sent my best asset after them. Alone." She told him, pausing to glance through his memories. "Hmm, I see you've already met my niece. I'm

pleased that she is alive and… well, alive at least. I could be angry about your actions, but I choose forgiveness and to thank you for your attempted restraint. I sent her because of the prowess in her ability, and to keep her from what I knew was coming for us."

"You sent her away to protect her from the consequences of your mistakes." He inferred.

"In part. Though we were headed toward that inevitability, neither side was responsible for the destruction you've seen here."

"Then…"

"They've found us." She said with great dismay.

"How?"

"Whenever the catalyst is activated, there is a surge. A brief flare, like a twinkling star that guides them."

"…They've been followin-" Reave was cut short when the hull behind him was torn open from the outside.

HARMFUL HELP

Connor trekked toward the ridge of the mountainous crater at ground zero, fiddling with the gadget he'd found in the back of a maintenance locker. The precision tool simply consisted of a hardlight emitter in a durable hilt, projecting a blade designed to carve through even the hardest of materials by cleaving their atomic bonds. Charging the tool expanded the blade from knife to sword, which would allow him to cut around Gaia, and free her from the welded shell that she was trapped in, with relative safety.

"Don't worry, kid. I'm comin'." He said with whiskey fuelled determination.

The earth quaked and a cone of haze blasted out from within the crater.

Sludge puddles rippled from heavy footsteps that felt like aftershocks, growing with intensity as Rayn summited the crater ridge, holding Gaia in his arms as if she were a tiny glass ornament. Her shields were down now, and she'd passed out from overexertion. Immune to her power, he was able to gently pull her free and gave no care for Connor's safety as he brought her to him.

"You did this." Rayn growled.

Reluctant to take a chance after their last encounter, Connor gripped the energy sword, ready to power it on in case he was forced to defend himself. Though his own durability had been greatly improved, the plausibility of organ liquefaction during a fight with Rayn made it a theory that he had no interest in confirming. However, Rayn's demeanour told him that he may not have a say in the matter.

Stopping directly in front of Connor and glaring down with burning eyes, Rayn extended his arms and presented his sleeping sister.

"Help her." He demanded.

"I- I don't know how..."

"*Please.*"

Surprised by the timidness of Rayn's inflection, it took a moment for Connor's head to clear and realize what could be done. Hailing Riley on the

comm brought nothing but frustration, as there was no answer from the other end.

"Useless." He grumbled at the tech, pulling the visor from his ear, but stopping himself before throwing it away. "Here. Peace offering." He told Rayn, remembering the joy that Gaia had gotten from hers.

Rayn looked at the fragile piece of technology, then to his huge stubby hands and back to Connor. A displeased grunt was the only response he'd give. Trying to hide his shame, he pocketed the ill-conceived gift and put the cutting tool away with it. Connor sighed, then turned back to the stadium and waved Rayn on to follow.

Although his movements were sluggish, his size and long-striding gait kept him right on Conner's heels. A rocky forearm held above the sleeping girl kept her safe from the falling rubble, loosed by the rhythmic tremors from each step taken.

Having completed their patrol, Bas and Fen came running when they arrived at the stadium. With the hair on Fen's back standing on end, and Bas's scales clattering, they were primed for a battle with the monster that seemed to be chasing Connor.

"No! Back off!" he shouted at the two, trying to protect them from starting a very one-sided fight that could easily get them both killed.

While Fen's obedience kept him from attacking, Bas became bloodlusted at the sight of Gaia's limp body. He leapt over Connor with talons spread and drool spraying from his wide, hissing jaws.

"Bas, no! It's *Rayn*! Stop!"

Rayn straight-armed Bas in mid-air with the hand he'd used to cover Gaia, knocking the wind out of the reckless mutant and tossing him aside. Fen gave Rayn a wide birth and hurried over to his downed friend, but before he made it there, Bas was back up and making another attack run.

"He doesn't know it's you! He's just trying to protect Gaia. Don't hurt him." Connor told Rayn, pleading with him to pacify the situation without harming his misguided attacker.

Bas pounced onto his back, attacking in a mindless rage. He barely flinched while snapping off the sharp tips of his claws on the rocky surface that was redirecting each blow back at him. When his claws failed, he tried to sink his teeth in, with the same result. For all of his intelligence, this had been the dumbest thing he'd ever done. Rayn reached over his shoulder, and picked Bas off of him, holding him again in one hand. Struggling like a cat in a bath, Bas suddenly froze with saucer eyes when Rayn let out a frustrated

roar. Humbled for the first time in his life, he became submissive and ran off to lick his wounds, having learned a definitive lesson in self-control.

Connor entered the ship, and with no signs of activity from Riley's severed head, or the systems at all, he had to assume that something had gone wrong. He looked over the medical unit in the hopes of being able to get it going on his own. With no working knowledge of the system, and with Jessica still incapacitated, he felt a hopelessness growing that was matched by his restlessness to resolve the situation. Mindful of what he was capable of, Connor had to tell himself, over and over again, to not just rip off the lockout shielding for fear of damaging the equipment.

"Come on. *Come on.*" He fretted, storming around and looking for anything that might indicate a lockout release, or at the very least, related controls that he could even vaguely understand.

Reaching the limit of his patience, he threw out his reservations and stormed over to pry it open. As he buried his fingers into the metal of the shield, like soft butter, an alarm sounded. Stepping back and hoping that he hadn't broken it, Connor watched the lockout disengage and retract. An opaque liquid that filled the tank drained and gas was pumped in to repressurize, leaving the glass foggy as the cycle completed. To his great surprise, he watched *Riley* climbed out of the tank, not in a new mechanical frame that he'd built for himself, but in what seemed to be an organic body that he'd grown. A juvenile, shit-eating grin spread across his oddly symmetrical face as he looked himself over. He stood taller and hung lower, built like an obscenely endowed comic book superhero.

"Check it out!" Riley said unabashedly, striking several cheesy action poses.

"Congratulations, you're the embodiment of a teenagers ego. Stroke it on your own time." Connor said, rolling his eyes. He put a hand on Riley's shoulder, then tossed him aside and looked in the tank to make sure that it was clear.

"What the f-? ...Shit, what happened?" Riley asked.

"Don't worry about that right now. Gaia's hurt. Worry about helping her."

"Right." He nodded, standing back up and helping to prep the chamber.

"Ahem...Pants." Connor insisted.

"Oh ya, sorry."

A dark fluid secreted from his pores as he worked, spreading across his skin and solidifying into an armoured material, similar to the suits he'd

made for the others. Light flickered in his eyes, just like it had with his robotic optics, and the systems responded through organic technopathy, instead of a digital transmitter.

"What happened to her shields? They should've been…oh man, I messed up didn't I? I was too distracted by my own-" he rambled before Connor interjected.

"It's on me. I did this." He tried to explain, but was cut off by a terrible wail, deep as a lions roar. The entire ship rocked, tossing them around inside, and Connor scrambled for the door while Riley finished resetting the unit.

In the open cargo bay, he found Gaia laying limp with new injuries that he hadn't seen before. He scooped her up and rushed her back to Riley, who helped him ease her into the chamber. Her lips had started to lose colour, and her breath was weak and rattling. Her suit had been torn, and her skin was bruising from recent trauma. Once she was in, the medical unit sealed and refilled, suspending her in liquid as the machine scanned her body before starting the healing process.

"Burns to the eyes and face. Fractured clavicle, sternum, four ribs, and a punctured lung. Internal hemorrhaging at multiple sites throughout…What the fuck happened?!"

"What the-" Connor said, looking over the scans.

"What did you *do*?"

"I didn't do all of *this*. We were trapped, and I reacted. The flash made it through, but her shields were still up. This happened after." He explained, partially defending himself, but mostly trying to work out what happened.

He thought back to the scuffle with Bas, and the noticeable effort it took for Rayn to pull his punches enough to avoid crippling him. With their emotions running high, and Gaia so delicate, it was easy to see how an accident could've happened. More rumbling, crashing, and crying from outside told him that Rayn may well have come to the same conclusion and was blaming himself.

"Rayn?" Riley asked in a hesitant whisper.

"We don't tell him that he did anything but help. Let him blame me."

"It was an accident though, right? If he believes that you're at fault for *all* of this…" Riley said, showing Connor a live video feed that he'd been using to monitor Rayn.

He'd left to take out his aggression on the city, where no one would get hurt. He roared in pain, and smashed the ground, levelling what was left of an office building and destroying the drone with the shock wave.

"Connor, that's noble and all, but if you put a target on yourself and give him an excuse like that…He'll kill you."

"Then I'll leave." He said, staring remorsefully into the tank.

"You'll leave…" Riley said rhetorically, shooting him a sideways look. "Sorry to burst your bubble, but when you took her in, she became your responsibly. If you leave now, that makes you a deadbeat."

"I'm not her dad." He rebutted with shame in his words.

"No shit. But we all lost our families, and now all we've got is each other. If you leave, you'll be adding insult to injury. You can't just abandon your family when things get rough."

"Back off. It's not your problem. You said it, it's mine."

"Who's problem do you think it becomes when you're gone? I'll be the one to heal Gaia. I'll be the one to help Rayn. I'll be the one to find out what's wrong with Jess, and get them all through it. I can't take this burden alone. We need to help each other to help them. That's what a family does."

"Riley, I'm sorry. I didn't think of it like that."

"That's right, you didn't. Now quit being so selfish, and man up. We need to figure out what we're going to do about all of this."

"Well, how long is this thing supposed to take to fix her?" Connor asked.

"It's already begun, but it's going to take time. The healing process will speed up more and more as the system refills its stores of the nanomachines that do all of the work."

"What happened to them?"

"…" Riley waved his hands over and around himself.

"Huh?"

"I used them. They're part of me. I learned from the samples that I took from all of you, compared to mine, that was never exposed to the catalyst. I'm oversimplifying the shit out of it here, but…the catalyst adapts the cells and microorganisms in the body that make it all work, to do things that only super advanced technology normally could. I took that concept and reversed it. I took the nanomachines, which already know the biological functions that need to be reproduced, and gave them my genetic code with some …minor tweaks. Without any living tissue to regrow, they took the role of the microorganisms and started building new cells off of that scaffolding. You follow me?"

"So, you're telling me that you used up all of our medical resources, and you're still basically a 'bot, but now you can express your vanity issues. Am I getting that right?" Connor said, annoyed by Riley's explanation.

"Umm, no. That's just a bonus." He chuckled awkwardly before taking a more serious tone. "This isn't just another vehicle. I'm *alive*. My body may not have been made in the traditional way, but neither was yours. I can *feel* again, both physically and emotionally. Not through sensors and algorithmic simulations, but *real life*. Until you have that taken away from you, you have no idea what you take for granted. I was a ghost in a machine, but now I'm so much more.."

"...I'm happy for you bud, but-"

"But, nothing. I had no way of knowing that this would happen. I did everything in my power to protect all of you so that I could do this without having to worry about temporarily depleting this one resource. No one is at fault here. Shit happens. End of story."

"Point taken. What can we do about Jess? She seems pretty messed up."

"You talked to her. Any idea what happened?"

"No. She wouldn't let me take that thing off of her head though. Said she can't turn 'it' off and needs to be alone."

"Let me give it a try." Riley said, making sure that the Aegis's telepathic defences were still intact and up for the task before walking over and kneeling down beside her. "Jess? It's Riley. What happened? How can I help?"

When he approached, she recoiled and tucked her head into her knees, tightening her grip on the helmet. She was conscious and aware now, doing breathing exercises to keep calm, but not allowing herself to move or respond. She feared losing the tenuous grasp on reality that she'd been fighting to regain.

"Don't worry, I'm not going to take it off." he assured her. "...But I am going to need to interface with it, so just bear with me, okay?"

Taking her lack of response as a go-ahead, Riley established a technopathic link with the systems in the helmet. Booting it back up to run a diagnostic scan, he was confronted by a very unwelcoming VI that was just as confused as they were about what had happened.

"Warning: Improper shutdown may result in file corruption and operating system malfunction. Warning: User vitals irregular. Immediate medical attention is required. Warning: Malicious software detected. Initiating quarantine and deletio-"

235

"Oh no, you don't." Riley said, overriding the VI's directives and disabling her malware detection. "Feisty, aren't you?"

"What's going on?" Connor asked from over Riley's shoulder.

"I just got tripped up by the VIOS, but she should behave herself now." He explained, looking through her diagnostic logs.

"So she's going to be okay?"

"I meant the VI" Riley explained. "Jess is in a real bad way. Severe concussion, fractured skull..."

"How could things possibly get any worse?"

"Do me a favour and *never* say that out loud again. Okay?"

"Well, what can we do? Can you build another med unit for her?"

"Not until the nanite stores have been replenished. Reave left his ship behind. We should be able to use his-" Riley said, pausing after a tremor from the city sent vibrations through the floor. "...Scratch that. There it goes."

"There what goes?"

"Reave's ship. It just took off. That sneaky prick must have circled around."

"Son of a bitch!" Connor growled, clenching his fists. "Not necessarily. He had another one with him. I got distracted; let him get away. Can we go after it?"

"Sure can. It cloaked almost immediately, but I can trace the energy signature from its gravity drives. Let's go round up the goon squad, and then I'll show you how this baby moves." He said as his eyes flickered. "And we're off!"

"Let's uhh...Let's grab our four-legged friends first. Give Rayn as much cool down time as he needs." Connor suggested.

Popping up on the display, Bas was cleaning his sores, and Fen stood guard over him. He was bloodied himself, but not of his own. A ravaged alien corpse was in several pieces nearby, missing chunks that matched Fen's bite pattern. Riley lowered the ramp to the Aegis and hovered just above them, while Connor waved them in from the entrance. Once Bas made it on, he shuffled past with his head hung low and headed to a dark corner to wallow. Fen leapt on board once he was certain everyone was safe and hit Connor with a sneaky kiss on the way by, then laid down to rest with his wounded buddy.

Finding Rayn wasn't difficult. The path of his rampage resembled the aftermath of a carpet bombing. Even though he was winding down, his

continued outbursts and the potential for catastrophic accidents made it extremely unlikely that he'd be able to come aboard.

"Rayn...you got it all that out of your system?" Riley asked. His amplified voice echoed out from the PA, as he brought the Aegis around.

The sudden appearance of the gaudy ship and loud voice startled Rayn, causing him to react without thinking, and the front end of a rusted out SUV flew through the hazy air, directly at them. Riley's enhance perception and reaction time allowed him to weave out of the way unscathed, and reposition the ship at a safer distance.

"That's *enough!*" Riley's voice boomed like an angry god. A holographic projection of Gaia in the tank appeared over Rayn, and he stopped everything. "We've got your sister stabilized and she's getting the treatment that she needs, but that won't mean a damn thing if you destroy the ship she's on. I know you're a smart kid, so start acting like it."

"I-I didn't mean to! I thought it was the other one, that just flew by. I promise you, I didn't-" Rayn pleaded, getting more worked up than Riley had intended.

"I believe you." He assured him. "I get that you're upset. But we don't have time for that right now. Something's happened to Jess. We aren't sure what exactly happened, but she's hurt pretty bad, and the only thing that I know of that can help her was on that ship."

"What?!" Rayn shouted in pain like he was being kicked while he was down. "No. No. No! Not her too!" he wailed, stomping quakes into the Earth that could be felt for miles.

"Rayn! Listen to me. We need to go now, and I'm not leaving you behind. I need-...They need you to man up and work with us. Can you do that?"

"I uhh...Y-ya. I can do that." He said, through trembling breaths as he stood as tall as his frame would allow. "I've got this. I can do this. They need me. I. Got. This." He told himself to build the confidence that he needed.

"Good man."

"I've got this. I want to help. Open up, I'm ready to come onboard."

"...Ya...About that." Riley awkwardly hesitated to fill him in on the details of the seating plan.

"Oh." Rayn sighed as the wind went left his sails. His awareness became clear and he knew that they couldn't risk having him on board with Jess and Gaia already in such delicate states.

"Try and think of it this way…" Riley said, seeking to boost him back up. "You'll have the best view of the landscape, and it's something that nobody has ever done before. I'm actually a little jealous that *you* get to do it first."

"Ya?"

"Ya, I can't wait to try it myself, once we get everyone taken care of. But, first things first."

"Alright. Let's fly." He consented with a barely distinguishable grin and a nod.

Riley swung the ship around and lowered it, activating the antigrav modules and projecting a hardlight windshield around him as Rayn became weightless and floated off of the ground with the ship. Ascending gradually before accelerating, he wanted to be sure that Rayn was relatively comfortable with the flight, and took it easy to start. Riley knew where they were headed and once he was sure that this method of transportation would work, he kicked it into high gear and hauled ass after the runaway ship.

MONSTER MILL

Reave's flopped plan required a getaway driver. With the basic instructions that Morrow had been given, he was able to operate the flight controls and perform some basic maneuvers, enabling him to pilot the ship out of immediate danger and escape. His most difficult task was figuring out the repair commands to fix the mild damage that he'd done to the console. By then, he'd pieced together the source of his compulsion and had been working relentlessly to get it back up and running, so that he could do the same. He had no care for Reave, or his plans, regardless of what he may have owed him. His primary concern was to save his own ass and get away from the people that had caused him so much suffering.

He could hardly believe his luck when he made a supposedly clean getaway, and out of pure happenstance, he was able to engage the ship's cloaking on the way out. Based off of the limited knowledge that had been bestowed upon him, the ancient language he'd decrypted from his lab, and what he was learning as he went, Morrow was beginning to discern the symbols that everything here was presented in. His unique intellect had been going to waste for so long now, he was soaking up the challenge of deciphering the new language like a dry sponge. Though he was nowhere near fluent, by the time he'd reached his destination, he had discovered a translator program but declined to use it, opting for a better understanding of what he was working with in its native format.

With the ship having escaped in stealth mode, and only Reave and Jessica knowing *for sure* that he was still alive, he'd have time to prepare for when their paths would inevitably cross again. While he could have disappeared to a lonely corner of the world and lived out a simpler life, Morrow knew that he'd never be satisfied with that existence, letting his hatred eat away at him and knowing that his retribution would never come to pass. The mere thought made him sick, driving him to more perilous endeavours. A straight shot back to his lab would ideally buy him the time to refortify the facility, and begin the production of the army he was destined to raise. He knew that Reave would never let this betrayal or the theft of his ship slide, but without the means to get back, the travel time would provide

enough of a buffer to temporarily nullify him as a threat. His only concern was that Jessica would somehow rejoin her crew and lead them back before his reinforcements were fully grown. He had no intention of waving any banners before he was ready to flaunt the might of his backing, though when he arrived, seeing the damage done to the entrance and surrounding area gave him a renewed motivation.

After backing the ship into the blasted out tunnel, and blocking the entrance to his lab, Morrow toggled the stealth mode from cloaking to camouflage, making it blend together with the rest of the overgrowth. He disabled the restrictions that Reave had put on his suit and armed himself with a pair of bladed conduits. When he was certain of his preparedness, he exited through the rear of the ship to clear out and reclaim his lab from whatever infestation had taken over in his absence.

"Hello my lovelies, Daddy's home." he called out into the darkness, flipping on the headlamps built into his helmet.

Even he was surprised by how quickly the mutated flora had taken over. Hanging moss and fungi grew from everything but the shallow water, which was teeming with creatures that he'd recognized as *Paraponera Bathynomus;* highly venomous, bug-like organisms with incredible strength for their size. One of his earlier creations, and a hybrid of bullet ant and giant isopod genetics, he'd initially used them in swarms to clear out the arena of anything living or dead that remained after his tournaments. His armour was immensely durable, tried and true, yet he still moved with caution in respect of their potency, but also, as an act of masturbatory reverence for his own design.

Thanks to Connor and Riley's vandalism, Morrow had very few locked doors to bypass, since the majority were now either so damaged that they were unable to reseal themselves, or entirely absent. Through the dilapidated corridor of breached enclosures, he'd come to the old arena. Every crack and fissure in its distended walls was filled with thorny vines, that writhed and grew with every bit of stimulus to their sensory receptors. Seeking out the source, like hundreds of intertwining serpents, they quickly found him. Fibrous tendrils coiled around Morrow's ankles and up his legs, trying ineffectively to constrict his armour, but only succeeding in taking him off of his feet.

"I can't play right now." He told it, hacking away at them in an attempt to escape.

Severing the vines caused the detached ends to harden into wood, while multiple duplicates regrew from each stump. His actions incited a

further response from behind the wall, which crumbled as the central mass of the carnivorous megaflora emerged. Thorn-toothed lobes snapped like bear traps and oozed digestive acid that eroded what was left of the metal floor on contact. Seeing the smoke rise up from the hissing puddles and dissolving protective materials from where it spattered onto his boot, anxiety gripped him and squeezed tighter than the plant ever could. He'd discovered a weakness in the armour that Reave had failed to mention. Pulling him closer, a belching maw gaped open, spewing its corrosive fluids like a salivating glutton, struggling to consume everything in its grasp.

The shift in its priorities allowed another recent near-victim of floral predation to escape from the plant's clutches. Though much of its hide had been digested; slimy pink and raw, the wounds only served to agitate the tenacious creature. *Isurus Mellivora*, possibly the most voracious of his creations, was never one that Morrow thought he'd be glad to share space with, but in this rare instance, he couldn't think of anything more appropriate. Ignoring the spines, and seemingly impervious to pain, the mako shark-honey badger hybrid tore through plant matter, like a tornado of sharp teeth, thick claws, and dense muscle.

Using the distraction to chop himself free from the rigid coils that bound him, Morrow hesitated before retreating to the segregate refuge of the genetics lab. He could have kept with tradition and let his hybrids fight to the death, but instead, turned back and charged the conduits until he felt their weight in his arms as the suit began to lose power. Twin arcs of plasma shot across the arena and connected with the plant, which tossed the hybrid's stiffened body away as the current reached it. Its spiny tentacle appendages shook violently, and the centre mass bloated with tumorous growths, while acid glands ruptured, like kernels of popcorn as it cooked. Holstering his weapons, he quickly grabbed the stunned creature by its twitching hind leg and dragged it with him into the lab. As he turned to hit the panel and seal the bio-hazard resilient door, the swollen plant-monster burst, spraying its acid blood, and painting him with it before the airlock slammed shut.

Morrow threw himself back, screaming, and desperately clawing at his armour, fighting to remove as much as he could. He careened into the emergency wash station and pulled the big lever, releasing a neutralizing agent which stopped the chemicals from burning through further and delivering a temporary nerve blocker to mitigate the pain.

The cranial implants that he'd received were still functional but had fused with the components in his helmet. Blurred vision from one eye was

the result of a portion of composite glass from the helmet's visor, warping as it melted onto his face. Cutting away the now stable, failed face shield, he regained binocular vision, but with deadened nerves, he didn't feel the layers of burnt skin peeling off with the glass. Of the armour that remained, what had been burnt was similarly grafted to his skin and seeped into his muscle tissue, through to the bone, before re-solidifying. With his mobility hindered, Morrow's crooked gait returned to the state that old age had brought him in the past.

Using the lab's refabricator to craft a new implant controller and a transdermal nerve blocker pump, he'd be able to continue without the interruption of his body's natural alarm system. Without the inhibitions of active pain receptors, Morrow was able to use his fear and anger as fuel to drive him, but before he could begin creating his army, he'd have to do something about his debilitation. He had never had the courage or the cause to experiment on himself, but things were much different now.

Splicing in selected genes from planarian and octopod samples, the goal was to assume their abilities to regenerate and utilize soft tissue as a decentralized extension of his brain. Disoriented by the process, but pushing through with his objective, he gave the stunned hybrid a slave implant before it recovered, and administered a mutagen that introduced his own mutated genetics to the hybrid genome. The transformation would repair its wounds at the very least, but most importantly to Morrow and his pettiness, he'd now have his own personal minion to fill that particular jealous void.

With access to the updated tech from Reave's ship, he was able to accelerate the growth process in the same way that Reave himself had been made. Selecting saved profiles of the arena's upper echelon and automating the process, he would have the first wave of hybrids grown to maturity in a fraction of the time that it would have taken with the arkship's previous capabilities. With each creature receiving an implant, they could be released into the wild without the need for private habitats, which were running a list of bypassed contamination and viability error codes. He would be able to recall the horde en masse, and with their inhibitors activated, they'd be unable to enact any aggression on others with a similar implant. With his monster mill in production, all that was left to do was move the ship and open the floodgates.

WHAT DOESN'T KILL YOU

"Son of a- ...What are we doing back *here*?" Connor complained, looking out from the Aegis' cockpit.

"This is where the trail ends. We should be staring right at it." Riley told him.

"Well, *I* don't see it. Are you sure you didn't just retrace their path? You know, like a residual energy signature from when *they* were chasing *us*?"

"Of course I'm sure." A deep crease formed on Riley's brow as he scanned the area and quietly double checked his tracking data to make sure that there really was no mistake. "It's here somewhere."

As the epicentre of contamination, the plant life in and around the region hadn't stopped its advancement since they'd last seen it. The overgrowth was healing the environmental damage at a staggering pace, but one area stood out, as it seemed much further along than the rest.

"What do you see?" Riley asked.

"Same as you. Nothing."

"Humour me. What do you see?"

"Trees. Mountain. More trees. Pond with a big ass trench. Heh...I don't know, what's your point?"

"What's missing?"

"Spaceship." Connor said tediously.

"And?"

"...Big-ass hole in the mountain." He said, realizing what Riley was getting at.

Riley hopped up from the captain's chair, waving on Connor to follow as he headed back down to the cargo hold. Connor grabbed his blade emitter from off of the dash and followed, eager to try out his new toy.

"How're ya doin' down there, bud?" Riley asked Rayn through the intercom.

"That was *amaaaazing!*" He shouted back.

"Haha, glad to hear it. Just a heads up, we're going to land, so I'm going to set you down."

"Nice and easy, okay?"

"I gotchu, fam." Riley told him, as Connor shook his head.

The Aegis lowered, ever so gently setting Rayn down on the soft marsh near the water's edge, then landed nearby, on a broad area of partially exposed bedrock. Shallow-rooted plants pulled up from the loose soil, trapped in the gravity drive's field of influence. Most floated about inertly, while others stretched out, reaching for the ground, like drowning victims struggling for the surface. When they powered down, only those that had fought for life were able to reroot and survive.

Bursting out from the swamp, a crocodilian behemoth mistook Rayn for an easy meal and threw its weight at him, headlong and hungry. Rayn barely flinched as its jaws closed around him for the takedown. Its body crumpled like a derailed train, and its jaws blew apart from the returned force of the attack. The gurgling mess twitched at his feet, and Rayn kicked it back into the pond, putting it out of its misery and giving the more patient wildlife the buffet that it had been looking for.

The trees where the mountain entrance should have been flickered and faded as the camouflage illusion was deactivated. The ship they'd been searching for launched above them and hovered in place, training its weapons on Connor, Riley, and the Aegis. A distorted projection of a man in a damaged helmet with a half burnt face was displayed to them as it spoke.

"That was meant for *them*. I have no quarrel with *you*." He said in Rayn's direction.

"Reave, you two-faced bastard." Connor shouted. "We're not here to fight. We...*Ugh*, we need your help. We have wounded."

Morrow paused, realizing that his appearance must have been confusing for them. With Connor, Riley, and Rayn presently accounted for, and with the exception of any unknown crew members, he'd quickly deduced the identities of the wounded that they spoke of. The girl, whose power had restored his legs and the beautiful young woman that made it happen. They had made their way off of his shit list, just as the boy that Reave had weaponized did when he rescued him from the crater. Connor and Riley, on the other hand, were still very much in his crosshairs.

From the dark hollow that the ship flew out of, Riley spotted a light from the partial mask of the man being projected above. He was remotely piloting from the shadows and hadn't yet known that he'd given away his position.

"Don't look now, but I found the big asshole in the mountain." Riley whispered to Connor.

"I said 'big-ass' not- Oh. Heh." Connor replied, spotting him himself.

"If this doesn't go smoothly, which I'm guessing it won't...I'll create a distraction, and you rush him."

"Can't we just do that anyway?" He asked with a devilish grin.

"In exchange for your ship and your lives, I'll take the woman and child, and give them the care that you cannot." Morrow told them, patronizingly laying out his stipulations.

"Ah, fuck it. Go." Riley said, already tired of the games.

The Aegis's dorsal shield expanded, with power diverted from everything but the medical and operating systems. The stolen ship bounced off and crashed into the swamp before it could stabilize, sinking into the muck and resting partially exposed on the bottom, like a hippo in a mud bath.

Connor moved like lightning, using his power to enhance his speed, and covering the distance in a flash. Catching Morrow by surprise, he pinned him to the wall and immediately noticed the slimy texture of his flesh. Up-close and personal, he could see that the mutilated face wasn't Reave's, and the grin looking back told him that he'd just rushed into a trap.

"What th-" Connor mumbled, trying to figure out what was going on when his feet were swarmed by bugs, and he was ferociously tackled by something much bigger that had been waiting in the dark.

Tumbling out of the cave, Connor discharged his power. The bugs sizzled and popped, dying instantly. The larger creature had latched on, shaking its head, trying to tear off chunks of Connors augmented flesh, but had its head vaporized instead. Blood from its stumped neck coagulated within seconds and a jelly-like slime enveloped the wound. Even without a head, it tried to stand and fight, as if decapitation was only an inconvenience.

Fen rushed to defend his master, ripping apart the creature that attacked him, and flinging pieces of it all over. Bas tried to help, but was still sore from his recent misfortune, and settled for eating whatever was thrown his way that didn't fight back. Initially gnawing on the dense meat with broken teeth, he eventually gave up on chewing and swallowed the chunks whole. Unlike Rayn, he'd need all of the nourishment that he could get to fuel and speed up the healing process. Fen saw this and left the rest for him, rejoining Connor and keeping an eye out for any other surprises.

"Hahahahaha!" Morrow cackled as he watched on.

"I know that laugh." Riley growled, igniting a light blade that matched Connor's in every way, shy of the boost his was receiving. He

grinned bashfully and shrugged when Connor saw it, then they both turned back to Morrow. Neither was sure how it could've been him, but both knew that it was.

"I hardly recognized you! Is '*Robot*' still applicable, or are you a real boy now?"

"Morrow?!" Connor shouted, reaching for his blade emitter and finding nothing.

"How astute!" he chortled, slinking out from the cave with Connor's new weapon in hand.

Bas hissed, with his plates and spines standing on end, vibrating with hate. He tossed what was left of the carcass, oddly full after only a few mouthfuls. He could already feel his strength returning, and couldn't wait to get a piece of *him* too.

"Ugh, you're like a cockroach. I don't know how you've done it, but I guess it's on me for being so lenient with you the last time. If you won't help us, then you're going to lose more than your legs this time, I promise you that."

"You can't hurt me anymore." He responded, igniting the tool with one hand and holding up the other. "In fact, let me give you a hand. I owe you one."

Morrow took the blade to his bare forearm without so much as a grimace, cutting it off at the same point that Connor had lost his in the arena. The severed hand dropped to the ground, still wriggling as he picked it up and tossed it at Connor's chest. Both stumps oozed with slime and began to regenerate before their eyes. Connor kicked the amputated appendage back at him in disgust, and watched as a gelatinous hand reformed in place of the old one, perfectly replicating the bones and tissue that had been removed. Morrow tossed the weapon back to Connor and wiped the jelly from his face, which was now fresh and unscathed.

"Do your worst." Morrow told them, holding out his arms, and offering himself up without resistance.

"With pleasure." Connor said, marching at him with his blade extended.

"Wait...Stop!" Rayn shouted, but it was too late.

With a few quick swipes, Morrow's body fell into pieces and his head rolled from the top of the pile. Even decapitated, he looked up and winked, laughing silently, without attached lungs, or a larynx to make the noise.

Connor put a foot over Morrow's face, channelling energy into his heel, then stomping his head into charcoal dust.

"Heal from that, asshole."

Bas groaned, clawing at his aching sides, but with broken talons, he wasn't able to pierce his scales. Riley scanned him to learn what was causing so much discomfort, and the source was abundantly clear.

"Maybe something it ate? Hahahahaha!" Morrow's voice echoed out from the cave, where his other hand had been kicked.

With the traits he'd acquired from the mutations, his body had completely regenerated from the severed hand, retaining the memories and personality of his original self. As he stepped out of the cave, naked and dripping with ooze, he directed their attention to the sliced up bits of himself on the ground. Each piece, percolating with the same jelly, and regrowing…individually.

"Connor, fry'em! Things just got a little more complicated. He's not the only one that's multiplying." Riley shouted, pointing out that the leftovers of Morrow's hybrid minion had been regenerating all the while, just as he had. What was once a single nuisance, was now an accumulating cause for concern.

"Didn't Bas just eat some of that?" he asked as he buried his hand into the growing cluster, burning them out before they had to deal with any more Morrows.

"Ya, he's regretting it now, but so far, he seems to be digesting it as fast as it can grow. Who knows? Maybe it's the world's greatest appetite suppressant."

"Fen, no eats." Connor ordered, receiving a compliant whine in response.

Connor, Fen, and Rayn gathered around Riley and Bas in a defensive semi-circle, with Morrow's snarling creatures creeping up around them. He'd have to keep them in one piece or destroy them entirely to prevent them from propagating. Passing his blade emitter to Riley, Connor cracked his crackling knuckles and prepared to take them on with his bare hands and the tsunami of energy that churned inside of him.

Piling over each other, in a single-minded frenzy, they attacked like a rabid hydra. Rayn's thoughts went to the mythical beast and the stories he'd read so many times in the different tellings of the Labours of Hercules. His mind raced as they drew closer, thinking of how Hercules would cut off the Hydra's heads one by one, while his comrade-in-arms, Iolaus, would cauterize them before they could regrow, until Hercules finally found the mortal head of the beast. Rayn looked to Riley, who held two blades that

were sharper than any sword, then to Connor who seemed to carry the thunderbolt of Zeus.

With no time to lay out his plan, Rayn took it upon himself to repel them. He drew from the tales of another great mythological hero of the lost world: The Incredible Hulk. He lunged forward with his arms spread wide, and brought them together with a thunderous clap, blasting the creatures back with a shock wave, stunning them, and giving him time to tell his teammates how they could defeat the monsters.

"Alright guys, I know how to beat these thin- ...guys?" Rayn said with dwindling confidence, as he turned to see them running up the ramp to the Aegis, leaving Bas, Fen and himself behind. "...Guys?!"

"You're doing great kid, keep it up." Riley told him over the PA.

"Where are you going?!"

"We aren't going anywhere. Just keep them busy."

The Aegis lifted off, sweeping over the water and holding position above the submerged craft, splitting along the keel. What was previously the underside of the cargo bay, opened up as feeding arms, like the mouth of a giant mechanical crab. The sunken ship ascended from the swamp, tractored-out and into the Aegis's embrace. The arms wrapped around, clamping onto its hull as a swarm of drones flooded the gap and began fusing the crafts together, assimilating both its hardware and software. Within minutes, the rough expansion was complete.

Connor manned the core, boosting the Aegis's power for the conversion, and subduing fluctuations that could damage or disrupt delicate systems. Riley took care of the rest, technopathically administrating the entire unification process, and at once, bringing Jessica down to the infirmary as the ship reconstructed around them. While they were previously on the ground attempting to solicit aid, she'd lost consciousness from blood loss, and was now limp in Riley's arms as he carried her.

Below, Rayn and Fen were holding their own. Rayn's nearly monolithic bulk began to crumble away as he fought, giving the dexterity that he needed, but retaining the protection he required. Fen was intelligent enough to learn and understand the necessity of restraint, after ripping three in half, and they came back as six. Bas, still debilitated by what was happening inside of him, was growing in angst while healing at an unprecedented rate. Bombarded by wave after wave of enemies whose numbers continued to grow, despite their best efforts, they'd soon be overtaken.

"HA! Haha!" Morrow's incessant laughter carried on maniacally as he climbed to the plateau above the cave entrance. Box seats for the initial rollout of his mutant army.

The cross-breed progeny of the arena's best wandered out, surly and confused. An indistinguishable genetic amalgamation of the world's apex predators, the only thing that it lacked in was experience. With its emergence drawing the attention of the regrown hydra-like horde who'd lost their implants, Rayn's workload lightened when they switched targets and swarmed the newcomer.

"Wha- No! No, you fools!" Morrow shrieked, as his arrogant cackle came to an abrupt stop.

His frustration with their disobedience turned to dread when he realized that it wasn't only *their* implants that had been destroyed. Each new duplicate would be uninhibited, allowing their natural instincts to drive them, and turning the cave opening into a steady supply of fresh meat. With blood, bones and fur flying, like the discharge of a misused wood chipper, Morrow knew that his plan was FUBAR.

With the nerve blocker pump and his implant controller destroyed, he had no more protection from any of the monstrosities he'd created and would be doomed to an eternity of pain. Unless a miracle happened and he was able to find a way of escaping it, he'd soon be ripped apart, consciously experiencing the entire process through each separate piece of himself, being eaten, digested, and defecated, over and over again. In his hubris, he'd created his own hell and was about to be taken by it.

The newly expanded Aegis swept overhead, having functionally completed its transformation. A hardlight barrier was projected down, around Rayn, Bas, and Fen, protecting them from the surrounding carnage, as an isolated gravity well lifted the trio up, and dispelled as they boarded. The ship hovered for a moment, floating closer to Morrow and giving him a brief glimpse of hope, before jumping away in a blink.

REBIRTH

Onboard the expanded Aegis, Rayn stood nervously still, afraid that he might accidentally break something, or hurt someone. The texture of each surface inside this spacious hold stood out to him as something he'd seen before. It responded differently, in that it seemed resilient to the impact of his steps, though he kept them light, and was reluctant to give it a thorough test.

"This section is made from some of the same stuff as the conduit, with some other goodies mixed in." Riley said, as he entered the room with Connor. "It'll absorb your surplus kinetic energy, and redirect it into our new reserve power core."

"What happens if the reserve fills up?"

"We'll need to vent the excess. Maybe we see how fast we can get this thing going." He suggested.

"Cool."

"Ya, *or* we blow up. Let's not test that theory *just* yet."

"Heh. Ya, okay." Rayn laughed awkwardly, not sure if Riley was serious or not.

"Hey, you did good down there." Connor told him. "You kept the boys safe. Thanks."

"I've got something for you. I can't imagine the standard earpiece would fit, so I've customized your own personal orb drone with the same tech as our visors." Riley told Rayn as it flew in and hovered in front of him, projecting its display and showing samples of what it had to offer. It had been set up so that one of the first things that he would find was the interactive virtual museum tours that were available before the invasion. He'd get to see the things that he'd loved, the way they were when they were still intact.

"You control it with your eyes. Just look at what you want, and it'll know what to do. It'll also take voice commands. You can set it up however you'd like. Gaia's gotten pretty good with it, so I'm sure she can fill you in on anything you might have trouble with."

"Gaia…is she-?"

"She's coming along. Shouldn't be long now." Riley assured him, and Rayn let out a sigh of relief.

"...What about Jess?" he asked, optimistic that he'd get a similar answer.

"I'm working on it. I promise you, I'm doing everything I can." He said, trying to sound encouraging, but even *he* wasn't buying it.

Riley left for the infirmary and Connor followed. Bas and Fen found their own separate lodgings in the back, like over-sized dog houses, made from the ship's old holding cells, where they happily made themselves at home. Hearing that his sister was on the mend was a weight off of Rayn's shoulders, and he was grateful for the device that he'd been given to help keep his mind from drifting to the stressful thoughts that were constantly trying to creep in. Just like his sister, he was entranced by this technology that seemed like magic, and he allowed himself to escape into the entertainment that it provided.

In the infirmary, Riley did as he'd promised, exploring every possible way of helping Jessica. Connor looked on, holding the bloody helmet that she'd insisted on wearing after they found her. Grinding his teeth, his mind cycled through every conceivable scenario of what could have happened to her, always coming back to the same conclusion: Reave.

"Blunt force trauma has caused severe brain damage." Riley choked. "She's *technically* alive, but only because the equipment here is keeping her that way. Her autonomic nervous system has shut down, meaning that her organs are no longer functioning on their own. The only brain activity I'm picking up is in her frontal lobe."

"So, she's not brain dead. You can fix her?" Connor asked, desperately.

"Her consciousness is alive in there somewhere, and I've expressed the pineal gland to stimulate whatever's left. She's dreaming. Hopefully it's of something good."

"But, can you fix her?"

"I can repair the tissue, but the neural pathways she's formed throughout her lifetime can't be. She'll be an invalid. She'll require constant care and extensive rehabilitation." Riley told him with a heavy heart.

"But eventually she'll get better, right?" Connor asked, growing impatient and frustrated.

"There's no way of knowing. Either she will, or she won't. She could end up fully conscious, but completely immobile, hooked up to dialysis

machines, and breathing through artificial respirators for the rest of her life."

"...That's no life." Connor sighed.

"No, it's not. There is an alternative, but it's just as risky, and I feel shady even suggesting it." He cringed.

Riley opened his hand and held out a slave implant.

Connor looked at the device with animosity. He swallowed the lump in his throat and took a deep breath before asking his intentions. Riley knew better than anyone that those things were bad news, so if it was an option that he was willing to consider, he must have had a good reason.

"What exactly are you suggesting?"

"In theory, I could wipe the software, and completely scrub the implant of its code. With the blank slate, I could upload the VI from the helmet into it, along with the algorithms and subroutines I'm using now to simulate her brain's autonomic functions. Kind of like a pacemaker for her nervous system." Riley hesitantly explained.

"Even after Morrow used it to make you a puppet?"

"She won't be anyone's slave. I couldn't do that to her, or anyone else for that matter. My concern is with the overlap in personalities, between hers and the VI. The artificial personality is an essential part of its program. It allows the VI to make vital administrative decisions, optimizing its performance, and allowing it to function to the best of its ability. It's her best shot."

"I trust you. We all do." Connor told him. "If this is her best shot, what's stopping you?"

"I don't know how much of her is left in there, or what the damage has done to her power. If the VI is dominant, we could be giving something that has no experience with empathy or emotions, the power to influence our minds." He warned.

"But what about you? Why weren't you corrupted by it?"

"I- ...I'm not entirely sure that I wasn't. The Aegis was a sentient AI, designed to protect humanity. This VI was designed to simulate it."

"But if you do nothing, she's a vegetable. Rayn was- Rayn *is* the closest to her. Maybe he should decide."

"Rayn is a *child*. He may not look like it, so it's easy to forget, but he's just a boy. A boy with incredible power, who's got more to worry about than anyone his age ever should." Riley said. "I'm not going to put this burden on him. This is on us."

"I need a drink."

"So do I."

Connor and Riley went to the vantablack room to deliberate, carrying two glasses and a full carafe. The room illuminated, displaying the Earth turning below them. From this perspective, it was hard to tell that anything had changed. Pouring tall drinks, and taking long sips as they passed over the ocean, they both looked down on the blue globe with reverence.

"What are you thinking?" Connor asked, looking for some insight.

"What's next. If this works out, or it doesn't. I'm thinking about the what we do next, hoping what to do *now* will come to me."

"So, what *do* we do next?"

"We take it back." Riley said, gesturing with his glass to the Earth below. "It's ours, and it was taken from us. There are still people down there, surviving, for now. Every day their numbers are dwindling, while these aliens keep growing *their* population unchecked. It's a losing battle; it's not a fair fight. We have the power to change the odds, so we have a responsibility to help them."

"Is that Riley talking, or the Aegis? I was thinking about something smaller, like taking a vacation." Connor half-joked.

"Does it matter? I can't find the line between '*Riley*' and the '*Aegis*' anymore. To be honest with you, I'm not even sure that I'm still the same iteration of my original self. It's entirely possible that the original Riley died, and what I consider to be my consciousness is just a perfectly indistinguishable replica, with all of his memories and mannerisms. Consciousness may just be the way that energy reacts when it flows through the physical structure of our brains. Like water in a river; if a river dries up, then starts flowing again with new water, it's still the same river. Right? There is nothing metaphysical about it. The issue comes with cell degeneration in the biological vessel, once the flow of energy has ceased."

"But you'd know if you were really you."

"How? If memories are replicated with the rest, how I would differentiate?"

"So…maybe?"

"It's a shame that you don't remember coming here. To Earth, I mean. I would be interested in knowing about the process. I imagine that you would have been implanted with your skill set and knowledge base while you were being grown, and when you were ready, you'd wake up believing that you were already mid-mission."

"As opposed to?"

"As opposed to waking up one day on a spaceship, and wondering why you're a baby in a man's body, that knows how to fly said spaceship. You wake up like it's any other day, and you go with it because your memories tell you that it's all real and business as usual. You wake up in the morning, assuming that you're still the same 'you' as when you went to sleep the night before. You're in the same body, in the same place, with all of the same memories, but we know that memories can be altered, created, and erased. How do you know that the last time you woke up, wasn't the *first* time you woke up?"

Connor took a sip and stared at Riley like he'd been speaking a different language. "If it's all just electricity *in* the brain, then how do Jessica's powers work?"

"Oh, I'm just speculating. Maybe we do have magic spirits that we like to call souls, but as a quantifiable entity, it's unfounded. Or, maybe it's like wifi."

"I don't think that was what I asked."

"You kind of *did*. *Anyway*, I like to think that I'd want to help them, regardless. We have a moral obligation from the means and the know-how to do something. So that's what we're going to do."

"Ya okay, that's a good idea too..." he said, resigning to Riley's persuasion.

"The problem is, I've got this ominous feeling that this isn't it." Riley told him, drinking deeply.

"This isn't what?" Connor asked, doing the same.

"I've got this constant nagging feeling, like something *worse* is on its way. That feeling, like something is staring at us in the dark, has been getting stronger."

"What could be worse than all of this?"

"I think that we're going to need all the help we can get." Riley said, handing off his empty glass.

He left the room and headed back toward the infirmary with his mind made up. Connor followed, tipping his head back, as he threw the rest of his drink down and clumsily walked into Riley, who'd suddenly stopped in the hallway. He wiped the spilled liquor from his beard and looked to see why he wasn't moving.

"Come on man, you couldn't have warned me? I spilled all over-"

"Did you see that?" Riley asked, slightly unnerved.

"Ya, I saw you stop for no reason and walked into you *on purpose* because I *like* whiskey in my beard." Connor sneered.

"You aren't afraid of ghosts, are you?"

"What? No. I don't believe in ghosts."

"Ya, good. Me either."

"You're drunk."

"I'm hardly buzzed…That being said, I just watched a little glowing person, float down through the ceiling and pass through the wall, like they weren't even there." Riley told him as they followed it into the infirmary where the luminous spectre held Jessica, floating outside of the tank and transferring its energy into her.

"Whoa…There's a *lot* of energy coming off of that thing." Riley said, scanning it. "Not so sure about my ghost theory. Any thoughts?"

"'Holy shit' comes to mind. Also, 'what the fuck?' and 'I need another drink'."

"I hear ya."

They watched as the light dimmed, and Gaia revealed herself. She'd completely recovered from her injuries, with no cybernetics involved, and more so, attained a gamut of new abilities in the process. She levitated in front of them, with a look of distraught confusion on her face, as Jessica appeared to be fully healed, but remained limp in her arms.

"Gaia?" Connor asked, looking just as confused as she did.

"It's still not working. Why can't I fix her?"

"I think you did, but the brain is a complex thing." Riley explained.

"How do we make her better? Do what you did to me."

"Gaia, are *you* okay? How are you doing…this?" Connor asked.

"I don't know. I feel like I can do *anything*, but-" she trailed off, looking between them for the answer.

"Nobody can do everything on their own. Here, let me help." Riley said, holding out his arms as Gaia lowered Jessica down to him. He set her down on a tabletop that constructed itself beneath her, making sure that she'd be comfortable for the procedure to come.

"Riley, you're back!" Gaia said, suddenly noticing his new face.

"So are you." He smiled and held out a new visor with a backup of her old data. "Rayn's here with us; he's downstairs. He could probably use your help if you're up for it. Nothing quite so serious."

"I know, I can feel him…You're *sure* you can help her?"

"I'm going to try my best."

Gaia smiled back and nodded, drifting over to hug them both, then passed through the floor to reconnect with her brother.

Riley waited until she was gone before pulling out the implant, and Connor handed him the helmet. His eyes flickered as he wiped the software and transferred the VI, with its new code, into the implant. When everything was ready, Connor gently lifted Jessica's head and folded away her hair. Riley placed the device at the base of her skull and allowed it to do the rest. There was a dampened crunch as it passed through the bone and began meshing with her brain. Her eyes rolled back and her body seized about through the installation. When she finally stopped, they left her to rest and recover for the unknown time that it would take for the VI merge.

Before either of them returned to the others, a quick trip was made to the medical unit that Gaia had used. Under the guise of checking the logs, Riley secretly wanted to be sure that she wasn't still inside. He was relieved to find that the tank was empty, but the logs were full of anomalies. Not only had the process not completed, but it hadn't even started. She'd been kept in stasis while the nanomachines that Riley had depleted were replenished. The fluid that filled the tank had been substantially laced with a substance compatible with her DNA and known to the system, but any and all information on it had been encrypted, even from him as the administrator.

"All good?" Connor asked, ignorant to the details of the scan. "Any idea why she's...you know, glowing and flying and all that?"

"Yep." Riley said, not sure how to answer, and leaving it at that.

His focus zeroed in on the diagnostics and attempting to decrypt the redacted information, practically forgetting that Connor was there with him. He became obsessed again, like he had with the ship's systems in the first place.

"O-kay...Well, I'm going to see how Fen and the others are settling in." Connor said, though Riley was too absorbed in what he was doing now to respond.

Returning to the lower deck, Connor entered to witness Gaia's second attempt to put things right. Taking on her luminous form, she pressed her hands to Rayn's chest and channelled her energy into him, just as she had with Jess. The energy spread through his body, glowing from within as it worked. The initial response was the same as it was for anything else; rapid adaptation to combat the outside influence. Light poured out from crystalline veins, growing from the fissures in his exoskeletal armour that allowed him to move. The quartz mortar spread, fusing his rocky skin in place, muting the light, and entombing him in his own body.

"Gaia, what-" Connor said, baffled by what he saw.

Taking her hands away from the statue of Rayn, Gaia turned to Connor with a zen smile and waved him over, presenting him with what she'd done. Nervous of the implications of her mysterious transformation and the new powers she'd obtained, he complied and joined her.

"Why are you afraid?" she asked, seeming to have read his mind.

"I'm not." He said, maintaining his stoic composure to mask the anxiety inside.

"You are. Don't be." She told him, tapping her finger to his forehead and taking it all away.

Gaia turned back to Rayn's living sarcophagus as it began to crack and crumble, like delicate shale. She blew a gentle kiss that shattered the brittle husk, though the fragments remained, floating stationary until she casually wafted them away. Underneath, Rayn was suspended within a shimmering barrier, having been restored once again to his human form. As he slowly descended to the deck, and the barrier dispersed, the twins hugged each other tightly with tears of joy running down their faces.

"Wait! Remember what happened last time." Connor exclaimed, recalling the side effects caused by their close contact before.

"It's fine. You don't need to worry anymore." Gaia told him.

"But...how?" Rayn asked, puzzled.

"I think there's something wrong with our powers. Like, something was missing. Now it's not." She tried to explain.

"Something in the med unit?" Connor asked, thinking of how easily Riley had been distracted by the readings from it.

"The thing I was in? I don't know, maybe. When I woke up in there, I was all better, and there wasn't anything missing anymore...Now I can do all kinds of stuff!" she told them, levitating and surrounding herself with a display of dancing light without activating her visor. "Rayn, you should do it too!"

Before anyone could respond, they all turned toward the galloping beast charging toward them. Fen had picked up the new scent from Rayn and came running to greet him. All three were bowled over and caught in Fen's enormous paws as he slid across the floor, enthusiastically doling out his love. A deluge of excited, slobbery kisses covered them, like splashed bathwater, until Connor wrestled him off.

"Ugh...That is some serious stink breath you've got there, pal." he laughed, patting Fen's head, and wiping himself off on his fur.

Gaia briefly lit up, and the slobber came off as steam. She looked to Rayn, pleased with herself and her new party trick. While he *was* impressed,

there was also a hint of jealousy, as he stood there, still covered. A few seconds later, he realized that the slobber was the *only* thing that he was covered in, and became embarrassed for both himself and his sister, who were both, still in their birthday suits. Gaia, though not quite as concerned, noticed this as well and simply created herself some temporary attire, turning her hardlight barriers opaque and wearing them tightly, like fanciful armour with shifting designs. Blushing and trying to cover himself, Rayn hid behind Fen, who thought that he was playing and spun around with him, like a puppy chasing his tail. She giggled at her brother and his buffoonery, who conversely, did not find it funny at all.

Bas, who'd been quietly secluded, was beginning to get annoyed by their antics. While his stomach continued to rumble, his deep grunting breaths turned to angsty growls as his patience wore thin. Refusing to come out of his hidey-hole, like a broody teenager, he'd let them know of his distaste for their noisy shenanigans from there. Peaking his horn-crowned head out from the dark, Bas let out several vexed huffs, blasting away the bits of Rayn's husk that had been scattered about while they'd played. Baring his chipped teeth, which were being pushed out of the way by new ones, Bas groaned and returned to the back of his dark shelter, giving them a brief glimpse of what he was becoming.

"Killjoy." Connor taunted.

"I can make him feel better." Gaia said, heading over to do for Bas, what she'd done for Connor.

"No." Connor told her, taking her by the arm. "Leave him be. You can't fix everything. Even if you can, you've got to ask yourself if you should. Bas is very young. If you just solve his problems for him, he'll never learn how to work through them on his own. I know you just want to help, but you'd be doing him a disservice. Do you know what I mean?"

"I think so." She replied, a little disheartened.

"Lighten up, he'll get over it. Let's give him some peace and quiet. What do you say I show you how to use the refabricator, so we can get you and this little streaker here some proper clothes?" Connor said, making Rayn blush again.

"Can we? It's uhh…cold in here." Rayn said, sheepishly.

"Heh. Come on." Connor waved them on to follow.

As they left, Fen gave Rayn one last sneaky kiss, making a sloppy cowlick in his hair. Returning to his oversized doghouse, he sniffed around the entrance of his grumpy neighbour, who was shuffling and grumbling, but pulled back when he began to hiss. Climbing inside his own, he lapped

up some water from the dispenser and laid down. He was going to watch over the ship, but the weight of his eyelids grew burdensome, and he went back to sleep instead.

INTO THE DRINK

"There's something different about you…Don't tell me, I'll figure it out." Riley joked, looking over Rayn after he was outfitted with his new gear.

"Gaia hel-" Rayn started to say.

"No, no, no. I'll get it…New haircut? It's the shoes! You got new shoes, right?…Ya, it's the shoes. Very nice."

"I fixed him! And look…" Gaia told him, excitedly grabbing Rayn's hand. "Nothing bad's happening."

"Oh ya! You're not covered in rocks anymore! How'd I miss that? Congratulations, kid. It's a good look."

"Did you find out what happened with the equipment?" Connor asked.

"I think so. A lot of the info is blocked, but I did some digging and found some pretty interesting stuff. It goes without saying, but you've all got a little something extra in you. The other half of the catalyst; what it was that gave you that something extra, was kept hidden in with the nanomachines that do all of the work…The ones that I used up to build this beauty." Riley explained, vainly showcasing himself. "It was in the soup, dormant until something activated it. When Gaia was exposed, she got a mega-dose of the stuff."

"Which is why she could heal herself without the nanomachines." Connor deduced.

"Heal, fly, create hardlight constructs, pass through solid objects, and I'm betting there's quite a bit more that we haven't seen yet."

"I'm in control now. It fixed me." She added.

"I imagine that it patched whatever flaws there were that made your powers unstable. Which, if I don't mind saying, is a major bonus." Riley told her.

"Do it to Rayn now, so it can fix his powers too."

"I, uhh…don't think that's going to happen, unfortunately. You absorbed the whole thing; you got it all."

"Then take some back!" she pleaded.

"I'm sorry, I can't. I know what it did, but I don't really understand how it works. This is mostly conjecture...err- guesswork based on what little I was able to interpret. The completed catalyst *was* here, but now it's gone, and I don't know where it's been taken."

"So, when I change again, I'll be stuck like that?" Rayn asked, saddened.

"Let's just say, that it's a good thing you've got an awesome sister that can help you with that." Riley told him, trying to soften the blow.

"I'm so sorry. I didn't mean for this to happen. I'd share if I knew how." Gaia apologized, feeling guilty for what she'd been given.

"It's okay. Just means that we'll have to stick together." Rayn told her, gently squeezing her hand, and forcing a little smile to show her that he wasn't upset. He put up a decent front, but she could sense how he really felt.

Breaking the calm, alarms began ringing out through the ship, throwing everything into a state of emergency. Sensors were detecting sporadic tracking locks and a massive inbound energy source.

"What the hell's going on?!" Connor shouted over the sirens, following Riley, and bringing the twins into the vantablack room where they could see what was happening.

"I don't know. These readings are crazy. It's telling me we've got something massive, like, asteroid massive, right outside. But, as you see..." Riley said, illuminating the room with an immersive display of the outside of the ship, but the skies were clear with no signs of the attack that the Aegis insisted was imminent. "...Nothing."

"Is the Aegis malfunctioning? ...Could it be Jess?" Connor asked Riley, suspicious that the VI they installed may have been the one causing the disturbances.

"Diagnostics are coming back clean, and she's still out. Whatever this is-"

"Whatever what is?" Jessica asked as she wandered in, catching everyone off guard. "Hi. I think I'm lost. Can somebody help me?" she said, innocently and apologetically.

"Still out, huh?" Connor sneered. "Maybe rerun those diagnostics."

"Jess? I'm thrilled that you've come back to us, but we've got a bit of a situation right now. I'll explain everything when shit calms down."

She looked around, trying to keep up with the conversation and figure out who he was talking to. When nobody else responded, she asked, "Who *me*? My name is...is *my* name Jess?"

"You don't remember? I can't possibly imagine how frustrating that must be for you." Connor said with heavy sarcasm and a hint of vindictiveness.

"Something's happening." Rayn pointed out, noticing a growing distortion on the display.

"I can feel them." Gaia said, confused by what she was experiencing.

"They're afraid." Jess added, feeling it too.

The distortion quickly expanded in diameter, pouring in and creating a hole in the sky. An orb of light passed through, tiny in comparison.

"Who is that?"

"That's a person?" Riley asked, zooming in for a better look, but stopping when a second, much larger object began to emerge. "Here we go."

A heavily damaged, skyscraper-sized section of a vast ship came in tow, barely held together as it passed through. The portal closed immediately behind them, and Riley armed the Aegis's weapons. Targeting already weakened sections of the hull with cutting beams, and focusing in on the leader with precision ordnance, they were prepared to take it down with a heavy bombardment.

"We're being hailed. Bringing it up on screen." Riley said, answering the call in a partitioned display.

Connor's fists clenched, and Rayn audibly ground his teeth when Reave appeared in front of them. Both Gaia and Jess could feel the surge of animosity, but only Gaia was able to understand the cause. A darkness swirled around her, and her eyes turned pitch. Picking up on it through Rayn's orb drone, Riley turned to her with grave concern.

"Keep it together, Gaia. Remember, you're in control. Don't go losing it on us now." He told her.

"I *am* in control." She said, hovering off of the floor.

"Gaia? I want to believe you, but we've seen this from you before. You're making us all a little nervous." Connor corroborated.

"I won't let him hurt you again." She told Rayn, looking around to the others. "I won't let him hurt anyone, ever again."

Before anyone could say anything else, she leaned forward and vanished, similarly to the way that Reave had appeared.

"Don't fire!" Reave pleaded. "I have refugees. You'll be taking innocent lives and destroying a trove of incredibly advanced technology. They are *not* my hostages, and I am *not* the same as when we last met. Please, hear me out!"

As they tried to process what he was telling them, and judge the validity of his statements, Gaia appeared on screen, hovering face to face with him, within his spherical barrier. Wrapping her tiny hands around his throat in a purely symbolic gesture, she scoured his mind for an explanation of his previous actions.

"Brace yourselves, things are about to get nuts." Riley muttered.

"*Revenge*?! That's *it*? You did that to my brother 'cause you were mad at people that you don't even know?! …*You're* the one that hurt Jess?"

"Our priorities have changed…Where did you get this power, little one?" Reave asked her, touching his hand to the catalyst and reassuring himself that it was still his.

Gaia's eyes lowered, and the darkness left her, as she too became fixated on the catalyst. Pulling the information from his mind, she confirmed what it was, and what it was capable of. She released her grip on his neck and lunged for it. Reave sensed her desire before she even moved and gripped it in one hand, countering with both gravity and light. Swatting Gaia away with his free hand, he blasted her back with an inversed gravity wave and hurled a salvo of hardlight spears out of defensive reflex.

Pierced through her chest, Gaia tumbled in the air, falling uncontrollably toward the open ocean.

"Nooo!" Rayn screamed with tears pouring from his eyes.

"Shoot him out of the fucking sky!" Connor shouted, crackling with power.

"I can't! He'll drop them." Riley said, overlaying the bioelectric signals detected throughout the wreckage, and showing all of the people onboard. "We're diving now, and I'm prepping the infirmary. The best we can do is recover her before it's too late."

"They're not my problem. If they're so much more important to you, you'd better figure out how to hold them up, right quick." Connor told him, storming off to get Fen for the aquatic retrieval.

As the Aegis flew low over the water, Riley tracked her dipping vitals. Large bomb bay doors opened, and Fen leapt into the deep blue abyss. Without hesitation or regard for his own well being, he dove down to rescue his tiny friend.

"*NO!*" Connor heard Reave shouting over the comm, from the deck above.

"Ya. You just made a *big* mistake." Riley asserted.

"If you take me down, these people will all die." Reave warned him again.

"They won't let them die. *She* won't anyway." Jess mentioned.

"They? *She*?" Riley asked, perplexed by the nonsense that she seemed to be spouting.

"He is…possessed? More than one mind is using his brain. A mind without a body is waging a one-sided war of attrition that he is unaware of. Even if he wanted to, he's not going to let them die."

"You're sure?" he asked, dumbfounded.

"As sure as they are. They would give their life to save them."

"I'm going to ask you one more time. If you're wrong, you're going down with him. Do you understand?" Riley emphasized.

"I do." She told him in earnest.

Riley hesitated, contemplating the repercussions of both his actions and inaction. What was a lengthy introspection for him, passed in seconds for everyone else.

"Connor?" he said over the intercom.

"What?" he snapped back.

"How are we doin' down there?"

Connor looked out over the water, trying to spot either of them in the shadow of the Aegis, but all he could see was more blue. His anxiety built until something finally moved in the deep. The water churned as Fen rushed to the surface and breached, launching himself out and landing back inside the open bay.

"Fen's back." Connor reported.

"How's Gaia?"

Fen shook the water from his fur and cowered in disgrace, having failed to bring her back with him. Connor nearly dove into the water himself, but just as he reached the edge, another burst of water erupted from below. Gaia seemed to be thrown up through the open doors and crash landed into Fen, rolling off of his back, and coming to rest on the deck. Rayn hurried to her side and checked beneath her suit, which was torn wide open. Scar tissue had already filled the hole in her chest, and as she laid there, catching her breath, they watched as even the scarring reverted to what appeared to be untouched skin.

"We're all aboard. Cancel the infirmary; she's healing herself." Connor reported, with great relief.

"Beautiful. So we're going to let this slide?" Riley asked, rhetorically.

"Not a chance."

"I agree. Give me some juice."

The Aegis accelerated upward in a wide flanking run, changing focus, and locking everything they had onto Reave. Connor pressed his hands to the conductive material on the floor, and pumped his energy in through it, overcharging the Aegis' reserve power cores. The excess energy bolstered the output of their weapons, all firing simultaneously on their single target, and the resulting fireball made all of the cameras show white before the burst subsided.

"Did we get him?" Riley asked Jess.

"...No, but they're dazed, and panicking. They've lost something very important, and they're afraid of further collateral damage." She told him.

"Further?" Riley mumbled, looking on as the smoke from the explosions cleared.

Reave's personal shield was down, having been popped like a bubble, but not without absorbing and deflecting the some of the attack. His armour was pocked and scorched, lit up with burning embers from what had gotten through the barrier. Much of the damage, however, came from the unintended ricochets that found their way to the refugee carrier. Fires burned along its hull, spreading inside and threatening the survivors.

"Hit him again! Light him up and finish him off!" Connor shouted as they watched through the open bomb bay doors.

"If we do, and he brings up his shield, those people in there are as good as dead." Riley explained. "Our guns aren't going to help."

"Then put me above him. I'll do it with my bare hands."

"No. I need you here. If he drops the carrier, I'm going to need you to boost the gravity drives, so we can try and catch that thing."

"I'll do it." Rayn interjected, standing up and cracking his knuckles.

"Not like *that*, you won't. Stay with your sister." Connor immediately shut him down, knowing that he wouldn't last a second in his current form.

A crash came from Bas's shelter, and he let out an irritated roar. Having undergone a rapid transformation while hidden away, he now carried himself on six limbs and had a pair of budging growths running along his spine. Clawing his way along, Bas stormed past them and threw himself out of the ship.

"Where's he going?! Can he even swim?" Rayn screeched.

"What the hell happened?" Riley shouted.

Connor, Gaia, and Rayn, hurried to the edge of the open doors that he'd just run through, watching as he fell like a rock. His scales spread, and

the skin between them fissured, tearing open as the growths burst. Shaking off the bloody serum that covered them, Bas unfurled expansive, bat-like wings that caught the wind, carrying him with great speed, and force.

"What happened to him?" Gaia asked as they watched in awe.

"He just turned into a dragon." Rayn answered to the best of his understanding.

"He's *not* a dragon." Connor said, trying to be realistic about it.

"What would you call a giant flying dinosaur?" Rayn shot back.

"He's *not* a dinosaur." Connor added.

"Will somebody tell me what the hell just happened?!" Riley pleaded.

"Bas just, uhh…" Connor tried to explain, unsure of how to do so in his own words, but settled for the only explanation that he had available and sighed, "…Bas just turned into a dragon and flew away."

Soaring through the sky with terrifying majesty, Bas flapped his new wings, stretching them out and building their strength, doing laps around the carrier. As Reave regained his composure, the barrier around him began to weakly flicker and reform. Before it was strong enough to be of any use, Bas slammed through it, piercing both Reave's shield and his armour with outstretched talons, like an eagle taking down its prey in mid-flight. Sinking in every claw that he had, Bas wasn't letting him go. They plummeted faster and faster, and just before hitting the water, Bas unhinged his jaw and took Reave's entire head into his mouth.

Riley took the Aegis above the free-falling carrier, and directed all of the power from the weapons into the gravity drives, using them as tethers. Connor took his cue and strained to give Riley all of the power he would need to keep them aloft until they reached a nearby island chain. They were barely able to take the weight and stay in the air themselves, but Vonn's ship was originally designed to do just that, albeit outside of the atmosphere in a near zero-g environment. Setting it down as gently as possible in the lush ravine, Riley landed the Aegis and immediately deployed the full fleet of his orb drones to put out the fires and assist the survivors.

"Tell me we got him this time, Jess." Riley said.

"I don't feel *him* anymore, but I can still sense *her*. She is in the minds of the refugees."

"They're all possessed too?"

"Possessed may have been the wrong word. Even still, that was two minds struggling for dominance. These are tiny splinters of her psyche, spread across their population. She has no more sway on them than their own gut bacteria. Besides, when I connected with their shared mind, I felt

that she was a benevolent influence. Honestly, I wouldn't give it a second thought." She told him with a comforting wink.

Riley would take her advice into consideration but remain wary of misplacing his trust. With his drones tending to the refugees, he was able to monitor for any suspicious activity, as well as satisfy the Aegis's need to protect them. Setting a rallying point on everyone's visors with a priority notification, he would have his crew meet him on the beach. They needed to discuss the current state of affairs and their plans for the future, not just each other's, but that of the other survivors as well.

34

A NEW BEGINNING...

Riley's drones were busy at work, flying in and around the caffeinated beehive that was the now-displaced section of the arkstation. Assisting the refugees out of the wreckage, while reinforcing its structure and giving support to the wounded, casualties were minimized. Outside, they recuperated in the shade of the palms, while the smoke from recently extinguished fires was carried away on a tropical breeze.

Gathering on the beach, despite the smouldering heap in the ravine, the whole crew took a moment to appreciate the beauty and tranquility of their new surroundings, soaking in the time of relative peace that had become so unfamiliar to them. Gaia, Jess, and Rayn enjoyed the sun on their faces, and the sand between their toes. Connor sat in the shade, relishing a frosty pint of stout that he'd grabbed before leaving the ship, and watched Fen bounding through the surf. Meanwhile, Riley scanned the horizon for any sign of Bas, or Reave. He knew that there was still much to do, and he could still feel a coming storm, but he also knew that they'd need bits of good like this to give them something to fight for, when the bad times came again. They'd earned it.

As the prime sunlight passed, and the afternoon came to a close, Riley gathered his team together around a bonfire that Connor had built on the beach, accompanied by flocks of refugees that were brave enough to venture near. None had ever been planet-side or experienced it through anything but stories. They left their broken home to warily join the crew around the fire, while Gaia and Jess did what they could to settle those that couldn't handle it. Riley climbed on top of a boulder in the sand and called for everyone's attention, which they gladly gave, hoping for anything to go on. Having learned their languages from what functioning technology was available in the wreckage, Riley used his drones to broadcast translations as he spoke.

"Your home was taken from you. So was ours. Though it may seem like it, this is not yet the sanctuary that you'd hoped for. We face an infestation, from an alien species that would hunt us to extinction. This is a threat that we have faced before and survived. We *will* do it again. We may

be few in numbers now, but there are others out there, all over the world, surviving, as we do. We have the power to overcome our enemies, so long as we remember who the real enemy is." Riley's voice echoed through the translators.

Gaia joined his side in her light form, uplifting their spirits and rallying them with her god-like appearance, unaware that she was playing the role that Vonn had intended for her. She handed him the coveted relic that she'd taken from Reave, and as soon as he touched it, he too knew what it was. With his eyes full of excitement, and hers brimming with hope, he took her hand and raised it above their heads, declaring to all of them, "As individuals we have the power, but only together, will we persevere!"

Regardless of what may have been lost in translation, he was successful in getting his basic message across to them. A clamouring applause came from the nervous audience. As the crowd settled, one of the refugees shouted to him, and their translated question was relayed back so that everyone could hear it.

"Are you our new rulers?"

The question made Riley pause, and he looked to his crew, who were also very interested to hear his answer.

"No." He told them, causing a mild stir. "We will protect those who are unable to defend themselves, until they can. We will help those who need it, until they don't. We will use our experience to guide you on the path to gaining your own. What we will not do, is abide anyone, or anything that assumes dominion over the sovereign people of our free world. We will work together. We will take back what is ours. We will rebuild a better world, and we will start right *here*." He told them, sweeping a hand over his view of the islands.

An ovation erupted from the people and his crew. They weren't just cheering for him and what he'd said, but for themselves as well, and what it meant going forward. It was a monumental occasion for everyone in attendance and even though they didn't yet know it, for all of those around the world that would soon be saved as well.

Though they had cause to celebrate, their enthusiasm died down, and everyone's gaze shifted to the horizon. Squinting against the setting sun at what looked to be a mirage, Riley adjusted his filters and focus to see what they couldn't. Against the burning orange sky, a dark, winged silhouette appeared in the distance, racing toward them.

"Don't worry, it's a friend." Riley announced with a sigh of relief that turned to dread when he saw what was behind him.

The ocean swelled on the horizon, and the Earth quaked. The tide rushed out, exposing the ocean floor for miles, before the swell burst, exploding upwards in a pillar of steam and light, like the mother of all nukes had just been detonated. When the shockwave hit the beach, it wasn't the pop of a sonic boom, but a roar of unbridled fury that stung their ears.

35

...AND THE END OF ALL THINGS

As the air cleared, Reave hung in the sky at the centre of an ethereal inferno, blasting out from the core of his being. Instead of the ocean water returning as a tsunami, it stayed with him, gathering in a great storm. The sky became dark, as billowing black clouds swirled and expanded, crackling with bright lightning and rumbling with constant, building thunder. When the supercell's growth finally plateaued, it launched itself toward the island and its precious few inhabitants.

Bas flapped his new wings with the tenacity of a sprinter, but his fledgeling aptitude was shortening the gap between him and the elemental carnage in chase.

Jess could feel Reave at the centre of the storm, but he was no longer the man that held them hostage, or the amalgam that wouldn't let the refugees die. That part had been violently torn out of him, leaving his fractured psyche overwhelmed, and spiralling in chaos.

As the survivors retreated, Rayn was the first to stand and run toward the problem, despite his current vulnerability. Gaia powered up, and Connor transmuted into the living conduit that Riley had originally intended. Turning the sand to glass as he ascended, the stray arcs that escaped him miraculously avoided all friendlies.

Riley felt a disturbingly strong presence in his mind, dancing around his psychic bulwarks, but making no attempts to influence him. Before he could alert the others, an island-wide barrier of hardlight with no discernable point of origin materialized, stopping their charge, as a stable portal opened on the beach. This aesthetically streamlined, yet unfathomably complex gate held the slipstream stable as a solid crystalline corridor, bridging their worlds. Unlike the holes Reave was spastically blasting through space-time when he'd conjured his, this gateway displayed the master craftsmanship of a fine artisan to even the lamest of laymen; this was the Leonardo da Vinci to Reave's Kool-aid Man.

A masked woman emerged, leading a group of strange beings with silent authority, surveying the area they'd captured, and those trapped within it. A bipedal insectoid, with natural chitinous armour and sheddable

spikes, fluttering its covered wings as though it were a nervous tic; a floating, polymorphous cluster of semi-transparent tentacles, like a sentient sea anemone mimicking the form of their leader, and flaunting its caricaturized feminine wiles; a classic grey alien, complete with super-sized cranium and globular eyes, overcompensating for its frail body using an assortment of gadgets and tech-based accoutrement; a taller, almost elfish cousin of the grey, tattooed with gold, cloudy-eyed and emaciated from the symbiotic mass of fibrillating muscles and teeth growing out of it; and a cluster of vapourous lights that moved like a flock of starlings assembled into a vaguely humanoid formation.

Their stoic demeanour was rattled when the otherwise awe-inspiring barrier nearly overloaded from Connor's first attempt to break through, but remained calm when it held. As they were about to make themselves known, Bas reached the island, barely ahead of the storm. Desperate to escape, and blinded by hail, he flew into straight into the dome, like a bird hitting a window.

"NOOO!!!!!" Riley screamed as microgravity nodes flared up all over his body and he took flight, speeding off to give what aid he could, despite this new potential threat.

"Let him in!" Jess pleaded, but her cries seemed to fall on deaf ears.

Without a need for direction, the frightened refugees sought shelter once again in the now fortified wreckage, as the dome overhead was disrupted once more. This time, Connor's output was enough to breach the wall, but not take it down completely. The hardlight ripped open, blasting the shoreline with cannonball hail and hurricane-force winds. Riley activated his personal shields and used his proximity to take the weight that Bas had been steadily putting on since his last meal. Even uninjured, the constant pain of growth must have been unbearable. The Earth shook again, and the barrier regenerated just in time for Reave's onslaught.

The swirling clouds turned black as night, and wormholes sporadically formed like waterspouts, as the bare ocean floor cracked open with a fiery wrath of a waking titan. Flash-frozen icebergs whipped through the air, and geysers of lava erupted all around.

Meanwhile, on the relative safety of the island, Gaia assisted Riley with Bas, while Rayn followed Connor to confront the new arrivals. An impressive group of freaks with an err of order and control to juxtapose his own. He decided he'd try a new approach and powered down completely.

"You doin' that?" he asked them with a restrained aggression, pointing upward to the struggling shield.

The density of the hardlight projection began to waver under heavy bombardment, and the Lights started to lose their cohesiveness as their power and attention was being focused on maintaining the barrier's solidity.

"How do I help? Anything." he offered, recognizing the effort.

With his show of peace, their telepath made direct contact, familiarizing him with the team and their capabilities. Suddenly, the Lights dismantled their pose and reconstituted as a blazing swarm around Connor. He felt a warm static as they passed over his skin, that built to a surging of his own power as he allowed it to use him. The conduit was drawn to the surface, and with it, all the energy they'd ever need to hold the shield in place.

"What can *I* do?!" Rayn asked, looking to each of them for an answer, unsure of what he could offer now.

Their leader, who had become fixated on Rayn, cautiously approached him as if she were afraid he'd break. She dropped to her knees before him, and her chest heaved as she reached for his face, gently caressing his cheek.

"Oh, my sweet child..." she sighed, as her mask disengaged and retracted. "You were born to save the universe."

Rayn cocked a skeptical eyebrow at the strange woman and her pandering, but found himself intrigued by whatever it was that she was trying into sell. She had his sister's eyes, and a kind smile that gave him a feeling of nostalgia that he couldn't place.

"Holy shit." Connor blurted out from beneath the swarm of light.

Jessica was filled with a conflicting rush of emotions, and ran from her old friend to retrieve something much more important than their immediate reunion. In her place, Fen approached them, growling with flared nostrils and fur on end, but having learned Bas's lesson, he waited for a clear cue before getting onto it. Fen cautiously approached each individually, sniffing them over to get a better idea of what he was dealing with, but their leader was the only one that he had a gauge for, and the bug's secretions were throwing off his senses even further. As he began to back way, Fen bumped into something nearly his own size, but Gaia was there to help him understand.

Gaia lit up, and lifted off of the ground, while Bas stood behind her, reared up and fanning his wings as he looked down at them, curling his lips. Riley lowered himself into the fray, scanning them all, and making certain that Connor wasn't being harmed before acknowledging them as non-combatants.

"Holy shit." Riley blurted out when he too recognized their leader.

She smiled as a tear rolled down her cheek, looking into the bright light without squinting. She raised her hand, offering it to Gaia, who depowered and took it without question.

"Wait." Riley said, reaching for her arm, but his hand phased right through. "...Gaia..."

"It's okay." Gaia responded with serenity.

Rayn stood, taking her other hand, and the twins' irises began to glow with a mystical bioluminescence to match their mother's.

"It seems we've followed similar paths after all." She told Jessica with a proud grin, "I am eternally grateful to you for keeping my boy safe, and..."

"*Ahem!*"

"And *you*..." she glared at Connor for the sins of his past.

"I don't think I'll ever be able to forgive you for your role in this whole thing, but it's also because of you that I'm able to hold my children again. So, for that, I'll try."

"Hmph." He grunted indignantly, expecting something a little less frosty.

"Now, we don't have much time. Where is th-"

"*Catalyst*?" Riley chimed in from above. "How'd I guess? Take a number. We'll call you when it's your turn."

"No." she insisted, releasing her kids' hands and levitating herself to meet him, pinning Bas and Fen with a gravity well when they reacted to her advance. Looking him over as if she were giving him a scan of her own, she gave him a frown that grew to an impressed smirk. "You're coming too."

"Where exactly do you think you're taking us? Not that I'd be opposed to getting out of here, mind you."

"We're taking you away from wraiths that've broken through from the antiverse; the dark counterbalance to our universe's light. They tear through into our plane of existence, drawn to outbursts of enhanced biological energy, like a beacon, and hunt down anyone powerful enough to contain them without burning out. They corrupt and infuse their victims with negative energy from the dark dimension, and thin the veil between the two as they expand their power and strengthen the bridge between realities. They take the purest love and twist it into the sickest hate. They're coming *here*, for the catalyst and for *them*." She explained, holding her gaze on the twins, who had gathered around Connor and the Lights. "*We* are part of an intergalactic corps of sentient beings with access to the Source. We've been

charged with using the great power that brings, to maintain cosmic balance, and thereby prevent the annihilation of everything. Basically."

"So, if these…wraiths? get the Catalyst, they'll raise an evil army capable of destroying all of existence…and I thought I was being clever by assimilating it. So now, space patrol is putting me into interstellar witness protection too?"

"Yes, and no." she said, scrunching up her nose, as her crew became restless.

"Oh?"

"You'll all be put through training, and ascension… Then, if all goes well, you'll be inducted into the corps." Emilia revealed. "I haven't spent all these years away from my family in hiding. I've been fighting to protect them and everyone else, so that they'd never have to find out why they *should* be afraid of the dark. But now the darkness is at our doorstep, and we can't afford the luxury of innocence any longer."

"We're gonna be *superheroes*!" Rayn whispered to Gaia, trying to contain his excitement.

"Shhh! Listen…" she scolded him, directing his attention to the dome.

"It's gone quiet. What do ya think he's up to?"

The storm raged on, but the glacial assault ended, and sleet cooled magma inside miles of fissure vents, sending walls of steam up from the bubbling ocean and casting a dense fog around the dissipating cell as the tide crept back in.

"Is he giving up?"

"Not a chance." Connor stated with absolute certainty. "He's charging up for something bigger."

"Like what?" Rayn asked, but Connor just sighed and shook his head at him.

Through the lifting fog, shadows grew like ink stains, as stygian wraiths ripped themselves free from their interdimensional bonds, and descended upon the burning eye of the storm.

"This is bad." Gaia said, looking up at all of the shadows moving by, headed toward Reave.

"No, this is good! Look. They're more interested in him than they are in us. See?" Emilia corrected her, easing some of her concern.

"For now." The Grey said in his high, raspy voice, looking up like everyone else.

The polymorph's colours began to change, and her wild flowing 'hair' pulled in like snail's eye stalks, reflexively camouflaging herself at the first hint of the dark entities. Her comrade-in-arms sprung into the air and hovered in place, allowing his wings to release their pent-up energy with a humming blur as he cracked his joints, and pulled loose the spike weapons growing out of his thickening exoskeleton. The golden tattoos of the Annunaki liquefied and covered his body, waking him from his daze as the sentient tumour encased him and became a wildly hypertrophic organic armour.

"What's happening?" Rayn asked, generally.

"This isn't enough…" Connor mumbled.

"We don't want to dra-" Emilia started.

"You don't understand. We need to make it stronger!" Connor insisted, powering up further, as plasma surged throughout his body, and the Lights showed their first signs of fatigue in handling the workload.

"We need to go, now." The Grey responded, directing his irritation toward the polymorph, who was concentrating with all of her willpower.

The energized barrier swelled with Connor's boosted output, and his confidence with it. Unfortunately, his bullheaded misstep revealed a hint of their presence within the barrier. A single wraith broke file and latched on, drinking his power through it with rabid avarice, and he could feel his own life force being drawn through the conduit to feed its unquenchable thirst.

"It's draining…too fast. I can't stop it." Connor panted, as sweat poured down his gaunting face and stained his now loose fitting bodysuit.

"Disengage!" Emilia ordered.

"I can't!" Connor insisted through clenched teeth, as his body tensed and the Lights began to flicker and strobe in a photonic seizure.

"Where *is* he?!" The Grey shouted.

As the polymorph began to speak, she vanished with a gust of wind in a blur back through the portal. The Grey breathed an exasperated sigh of relief and disappeared just the same. Then Emilia, with Gaia and Rayn. Anxiety had been brewing in Riley since their arrival, and now he knew why. They were taking the people he'd sworn to protect, right under his nose.

"Wait!" Riley screamed, reaching out as he shot himself after them.

"*Wwwaaaiiittt.*" The meaty symbiote exerted, vibrating tendons like they were vocal chords.

Riley tried to deke around, but wasn't expecting it to be telekinetic, and ate dirt before he'd advanced more than a few feet. A roar pierced everyone's ears, and Bas carried through with the charge as he tucked his

wings and torpedoed through the gateway after the twins. Meanwhile, Fen wrestled with the chewiest toy he'd ever found, before being zipped away with them a second later, right ahead of their spiky flier.

"Riley…" Connor wheezed.

"How are you holding up?"

"Shouldn't've done that. I'm dying."

"Don't do that."

"Heh. It's out of our hands now…" Connor resigned, staring up at the wraith as it stared back into him, seething with rapacious intent.

Though the path had been cleared, and all of his instincts told him to go, Riley couldn't bring himself to leave his friend to die. Running a gamut of scans on Connor and the Lights, he was quickly able to isolate their connection to the projected barrier, and through it, identify the negative polarity of their converted life-force within the stream.

"…I've got an idea. I just need you to hold on a little longer." Riley instructed.

"I'll…try." Connor gasped, barely able to summon the energy to speak, and only held upright by the convulsing light-being that lost control of its tool.

The Lights had become trapped in the exchange, tethered to and sustained by the conduit, but being fed upon by the wraith, the same as Connor. They faded and shrank, matching his diminishing physique, which now resembled that of the poor soul Riley found trapped in its ancient body aboard the arkship, so long ago.

Small jets of steam shot out from around Riley's head and neck, dissipating the heat build-up generated from overclocking his own quantum microprocessors to make the calculations necessary to flip the poles on the transfer. As the finalized data compiled into an executable, Riley detected movement from the portal, and Emilia's unseen speedster slowed down as he approached, just enough for Riley to know that his time was up.

"*NOT YET!*" Riley blasted with sonic amplifiers that staggered the runner and gave him the split-second he needed to dodge his gasp and transmit the code to the flow.

"Not cool!…MAWP!" the speedster moaned, stumbling around and gaping his jaw, trying to pop his ears. He was long and lean; built for running, and wore a masked suit, aerodynamically contoured, but otherwise identical to Emilia's.

Riley sent the code again and again, but nothing happened; there was far too much interference for the signal to get through. Spinning out of reach for the second time in under a second, Riley leaned forward, reaching out to Connor, and Connor back to him. Just as the last ounce of strength left him, Riley made contact, throwing the torrent into reverse and causing a feedback that knocked him clear through to the other side of the portal.

"Riley!" Gaia called out as she ran to his side, fanning away the smoke coming off of his charcoal arm and pouring out from cracks in his epidermal layer. Healing hands were laid on his chest, and his techno-organic biology responded as though it was the body that he was born into.

"Gaia?" Riley responded, sitting up and looking around in surreal awe at this new environment.

This hidden world was the nerve centre of their corps, populated by countless powered beings of various alien species from across the galaxy.

"Where's Connor?" they asked each other at the same time.

Bas and Fen had come running when Riley appeared but stopped in their tracks when another man came through the portal, tripping over his own feet as he ran from the explosion that collapsed the gateway behind him.

"Report!" Emilia ordered.

"He-…he did it! He killed one!" the speedster exclaimed.

"What?! How?!" the Grey squawked, as the others gathered to hear.

"What do you mean? Tell me *exactly* what happened." Emilia asked as calmy as she could.

36

FACE-OFF

There was muffled shouting, and movement faster than Connor's blurred vision would let him see. He reached out blindly as the last bit of him was drawn into the flow, being pulled toward the gallows of the antiverse. As his soulless husk began to fall, Riley's hand grazed his, and Connor was slammed back into his own body in the violent reversal. All of the energy that had been drawn from him poured back in an instant, like a shot glass being filled by a fire hose, and he was immediately overloaded by an additional influx of power that was now being stolen from the wraith itself.

Time slowed to a creep, and Connor was dizzied by the echoes of a billion trapped souls as they escaped from it and into him, and the wraith was dragged back to the antiverse. He watched Riley float away, carried by the shockwave of the explosion, as Lichtenberg figures snailed up his forearm, and the light in his pupils briefly flickered before rebooting. Meanwhile, the speedster looked like he was wading through quicksand, trying to outrun the blast, as the hardlight barrier that had been protecting them from Reave and the wraiths was gone.

Though the Lights remained bonded with the conduit, their collective consciousness hadn't returned. They, along with the remnants of the wraith's tainted victims and all of their power that kept it in this dimension had been funnelled in with Connor; a cozy stew of superpowered alien schizophrenia.

As the sphere around him expanded, matter became undone, converted to energy, and flowed into him, compounding the feedback loop and exponentially expanding the destructive surge. The energy blasting out of Connor scrubbed the space around him of anything but him, until it was nullified by the meeting of his counterpoint.

Standing a the edge of the exhumed void, Reave stood ablaze with dark fire. Wraiths clung to him like starving remoras, trying to absorb what excess energy those within him couldn't contain. His eyes burned black and his skin blistered, sizzling under steady regeneration, while his body bulged and contorted as it adapted to the darkness gestating within him. Raising his

arms back, he leaned into an odd runners stance and began charging his energy. The tails of the tattered wraiths wisped away as they blew in the wind of his overflowing power, while their anchors shifted further into this dimension.

A malevolent growl rumbled like thunder.

"...Finally..." Connor said with a shudder.

Channelling his overwhelming power through the conduit, and using his integration with the amplified Lights to focus and condense it, Connor stopped resisting the crushing inundation of power, and let it all flow into the baby neutron star forming between his hands.

The Aegis was pulled in by their gravity, absorbing and storing the energy that had destroyed everything else around them. Steam rose from the glowing hull as it moved through the boiling slurry of crushed glass, cooled lava rock and murky salt water. The reserve core had been overloaded, and the ship was attempting to defuse itself while its central processor was lightyears away.

As Reave launched forward, trailing violet-fringed vantablack lightning from clouds of his own ash, portals tore open around him, shooting shrapnel bullets from the arkstation's point of origin. Teleporting himself within a foot of Connor, and waiting for it all to arrive, the look on his face shifted from manic rage to tranquil adoration. With the banished wraith's stolen power now residing within Connor, Reave's dark throng saw him as one of their own.

The physical world bent and strobed between positive and negative dimensions as their proximity reverberated reality around them, causing space-time to splinter across the planet. The Aegis began to swell, splitting at the seems in the moment before detonation, then blinked back to where it had started, undamaged, and still recharging its main core. A prehistoric whale squealed in distress as it squirmed, beached and cooking in the muck, while a giant limestone nose materialized by the renewed ship. The space junk that Reave had thrown, vanished and reappeared, partially buried and heavily rusted, further inland.

"Yyyeeeessssss..." Reave hissed, opening his arms and waving Connor in for an embrace.

"No." Connor shot back, tearing open the sphere between his hands, and pressing it into Reave's exposed sternum.

Silence and white-hot annihilation.

PRESSURE MAKES DIAMONDS

"We're not just going to abandon the Earth!" Riley shouted, protesting in outrage.

"It's out of our hands now." Emilia said, sympathetically. "But all is not lost."

"What do you mean?" Riley asked.

"The monsters that invaded before I left. Their species was created alongside the catalyst in case its use ever baited the wraiths. They're a trap; a weaponized GMO that was accidentally released. Within a direct line of sight, the wraiths see them as they'd see you or I, but become trapped when they try to possess them. They're not immune, but they are resistant to their decay, and their voracious nature drives them to clear out the undead meat plague caused by possessions of those too weak to be retainable hosts. " She explained as though it were nothing more than a cultural novelty to a tourist.

"That's not what 'all is not lost' means." Riley groaned, "That's pretty much the opposite."

"What I'm saying is that they aren't the real invaders. They're the security system and the cleanup crew."

Bas puffed out his chest but acted like he didn't hear them, while Fen let out an anxious whine, and curled up in a ball, waiting for Connor. Gaia squeezed her eyes shut tight and focused on finding Connor's distant energy, but on a planet of those like them, it was as pointless as stargazing at noon.

"There are still people alive there. Families that have struggled to make it this far…to be fodder?"

"They serve their purpose. We serve ours." The bug injected but was quieted with a backhand from the alien-suited alien. "What?! It's not like *they're* going extinct." He spitefully added, pointing to the sea of lost and confused bystanders that had been carried through first.

"…He's a prick in many ways, but he's not a liar. We found two separate populations living on the island, in addition to the arkworlders. That's why it took so long to get everyone through. We have a viable

population to sustain humanity right *here*, and there are rumours of other arks that actually accomplished what they'd set out to do. Lesson one is letting go."

"He said we got one though!" Rayn insisted, "let's go do *that* to the rest of 'em!"

"You two are staying right where I can see you." she told him sternly.

Emilia nodded to the Grey, who smirked and activated one of the instruments on his gear. Gaia's light faded, and Jessica's mind became a place of unnerving solitude. A firewall with unintelligible encryption restricted Riley's access to his body's new functions and dulled his cognition. He was reintroduced to confusion, frustration, and fatigue, suddenly being brought back to the vulnerability of baseline human. With the push of a button, they'd all been depowered, or comparatively handicapped.

"Umm...what's going on?" Gaia asked with worry as she repeatedly failed to use any of her powers.

"Your powers qualify you for training, but until you've achieved mastery over them, they'll be a crutch at best. At their worst, you'll be a danger to everyone around you. That is *not* tolerated here. In phase two, we'll begin work on honing your given talents. In phase one, you'll earn the skills to build a solid foundation, strong enough to carry the weight of this responsibility...That starts now. Welcome to The Forge."

EPILOGUE

The following afternoon

The Aegis sat dormant atop the jagged monument to their conflict, powder-coated in carbon, and cooling in the ocean breeze. A black pillar stood among the sunken islands that formed it, and held the ceded ship aloft in the clouds as if the Earth itself had reached out and caught it. Inside, dust drifted lazily through beams of light shining in through the empty cockpit and settled in the quiet shade. Riley's severed appendage ran in sleep mode, quietly scanning for his return with the lonesome ping of its emergency distress signal sounding off like a lost fawn.

Waves crashed around the rocky base, and wind whistled through outstretched stalagmites, while a flock of tired seabirds squawked at each other as they came to investigate this new perch. When the first bird tried to land on the arm of one of the stone scarecrows, it was met with a static shock that turned it into a cloud of pink mist and smouldering feathers. The rest of the flock scattered, then retreated back to the mainland, and pebbles began to drop from the anthropomorphic rock formation.

Though it wasn't the lifeform that the Aegis was searching for, and his bioelectric signature wouldn't register on its sensors, the ship recognized genetic markers in the ashy figure shuffling toward it from a pile of gravel. Lights turned on throughout the ship, and the refabricator started printing and filling a crystal tumbler.

The end, for now.

Congratulations, you made it! I hope you've enjoyed my debut effort, because there is more on the way. I've been developing an expanding universe full of the weirdness hinted at here. Please don't forget to rate and review. Thanks.

-   Leon Soma

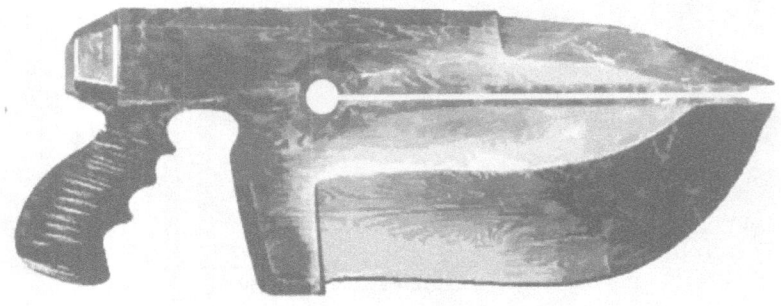